WHITE FLIGHT

WHITE FLIGHT

BILL HILLMANN

TORTOISE BOOKS

CHICAGO

INTRODUCTION

Reading a book, we are told in this incipient moment where Artificial Intelligence threatens, is soon to become passé. Why read a book when AI can read it for you? AI, we are told, is an infinity of PhDs working on a problem forever without cease. A human is a singularity bound by time and place. We live in the moment, and our lives are of our time, and when our lives have run their course, we are dead and buried, but AI never dies and never perishes and never stops; against it we are nothing.

The thing is we are human, and we are time-bound, and we are mortal, which means we die, and because of this we have something that AI doesn't have, and that's the experience of living within our time while also knowing that our time is limited and that we are perishable. This knowledge that we always carry can be called human wisdom, and writers who write from their times and of their times, understanding also that their time is limited and that their place in time is circumscribed by chance, practice in their writing the art of witness. Witness is something that AI cannot do, nor will it ever be able to do.

To say that I was here and this is what I saw, heard, smelled, tasted, and felt, is something only a human can do. The writers most concerned with witness are humanity's truth-tellers. A truth-teller tells it like it is: this is what I felt and this is what I understood to the best of my knowledge to say so, and as a truth-teller I will say so no matter what happens to me, whether that happening is that people ignore my witness, or whether they attack me for my witness. Make no mistake, truth-tellers may be ignored, or shunned in an era of political correctness, but they also win Nobel Prizes, and they are the first to get sent to gulags or shot in autocratic regimes.

All of this is preamble to say that Bill Hillmann is a literary artist and a truth-teller whose coming-of-age novel, *White Flight*, is an artifact of human witness that merits your attention. He is a product of Chicago's working class, a tribe of people whose stories don't always make their way into literary novels. But let's not forget that the Harold Washington Public Library on Ida B. Wells Drive is one of the most beautiful monuments built by Chicago workers and laborers in the last fifty years. It is an artifact of the highest level of craftsmanship. Masons, concrete workers, steelworkers, carpenters, plasterers, electricians, painters, tile-workers, duct-work installers, elevator and escalator craftsmen, and countless other workers all came together and in a moment of inspiration crafted an extraordinary monument to books.

Bill Hillmann's book, *White Flight*, is the work of a craftsman in both senses of the word. In an earlier life, Hillmann was of the tribe and lineage of the same workers who built the Harold Washington Public library. In his case, as he tells it, he was a ditch-digger, a rebar-tier, a fabricator of carpentered forms, and a concrete pourer. He did demolition and cleanup. In short, he was a laborer. And then, somehow, who knows how or why, he transformed himself and became a writer and as a practiced writer, he became a craftsman. He is a maker of sentences, and paragraphs, and because he was both a laborer and now a writer his book gives voice to the workers who sweat in the summer, and shiver in the winter; who start work in the morning ready to go, and who finish at the end of the day exhausted and ready for a cold beer.

Hillmann's book talks of these men, of what they are feeling and dealing with, of the world that they're coming from and of the world that they're trying to escape. His workers swear and sweat, they fight, they talk of getting laid; unchecked passions spool forth into uncensored demotic speech—hilarious, hurtful speech that leads to fighting, fighting that leads to crime, crime that leads to death, and death that leads to long-term intergenerational family dysfunction. He writes their stories in an inimitable idiom and argot that is true Chicago.

—   Joseph G. Peterson, author of *The Perturbation of O*

PART ONE: KNUCKLEHEADS

CHICAGOANS FILLED THE DARK, MUSTY, AND MONSTROUS SAINT ANDREW'S GYMNASIUM TO THE RAFTERS. The ring sat elevated in the center of the room like a brightly lit theatre stage where only the most brutal of truths are revealed. They surrounded it, a shadowy mob thirsting for blood and spectacle, and maybe a few there for the artistry of another time, the old days of The Gloves that only exist now as black and white photos and grainy videos. Their bodies swayed on the floor behind the gray folding chairs, sipping clear plastic cups of Corona that glowed amber from the large square metal frame of lights that hung above the blue-canvassed ring. I shuffled my black thin-soled shoes along the canvas. The purple blood speckles swirled in a wild array at my feet like a new galaxy birthing into existence.

"Mean thoughts, Joe. Mean thoughts," Brother Alex murmured from the apron. Strands of golden hair gleamed atop his enormous bald head. Mean thoughts? *There's only darkness in my soul tonight, Brother. Mean is all I know.* An image flashed in my mind of my fist exploding through my brother Blake's head.

The smokers walked in and out of the smoking room near the side exit; each entry and exit puffed plumes of cigar smoke into the auditorium. A scratchy burn rasped at my lungs. *Fucking bastards. Can't they do that shit outside? I wish I could walk in there and smash all those scumbags.*

The tuxedoed announcer clutched the chrome microphone that dangled down from the rafters as he read from his notes in the center of the ring.

"Ladieeees and Gentle-men! In our next bout, the Chicago Golden Gloves Light-Heavyweight Open Division Championship. Out of the blue corner, representing the Beverly Park District, Terry O'Sullivan!" His voice boomed to the rafters as most of the crowd erupted.

O'Sullivan loomed across the way. His mean face winced jagged and robotic inside the black leather Everlast headgear. His pale muscular shoulders trembled in the bright light. He smacked his gloves together with a hollow thud.

"And in the red corner, representing the Windy City Gym, Joseph Walsh!" The cheering flickered through the crowd, weak and tepid. *It's just the guys from the gym.* A vile snicker rattled in my chest. *They want O'Sullivan? Good. Fuck them. Cheer for him. I'm only here to sacrifice that foolish, naïve, weak child inside me. I'm eighteen now. No more kid shit. You're a fucking thirty-year-old ex-Navy Seal? Good. Fuck you! I want blood and disaster. Takes a man to show them all I'm a man now. A miserable, destroyed child. That's what a man is, isn't it?*

I bounced on my toes. Ref Francis frowned at me in his powder blue uniform; his white mustache quivered as he waved us to the center of the ring for the final instructions. A bunch of corrections officers sat up front; a fat one with stupid face yelled, "Aye Terry, why ya pick'n on a little kid for?" The group chuckled. "How old is he, fifteen, fer Christ's sake?"

I glared at him. "Fuck you, you sack of shit!"

O'Sullivan cracked up as the guys in the front row roared; one poured a quarter of a beer on Stupid Face's bald spot.

"No talking to the crowd or I'll take a point, Joe," the ref scolded.

I nodded as Sal pulled my mouthpiece out of his shiny black-and-gold Windy City cornerman's jacket and shoved it in my mouth.

"Shut it, you," he muttered.

Ref Francis gave us his final instructions. I heard none of it, just saw Terry's angular face grimacing across from me. *Finally we get to see how bad a motherfucker you really are, Terry. Like they all been say'n. I hope you are. I hope you fucking kill me right here in this ring, in Saint Andrew's in front of them all.*

We touched gloves with a nervous thud, then walked back to our corners.

"Box with 'yer brains, Joey, not 'yer balls," Sal ordered before stepping out through the ropes.

The bell rang and I hurried over. *I'm gonna bust his shit early.* 1-2-3, my shots slipped around his blue gloves and slammed into his headgear. *He's easy to find.* I shot a lead right at his chin and he rolled with the shot, taking the snap out of it. *He's slick, though.* I let my hands go in a snappy flurry. He leaned back into the ropes, shelled up like a nervous blue snapping turtle. I unleashed several deep thudding body shots around his elbows, then slipped a right uppercut between his gloves. His head popped out of its blue foam protectors as I looped a left hook, and my red glove smashed into his ear. The crowd stirred in a low uneasy murmur. "Watch out Terry, he's a scrappy little motha-fucker!"

O'Sullivan held, and he woke up after that. As the round progressed, he jabbed to my chest and bounced on the springy canvas fluidly, and followed with a right cross that shot in straight. Blackness exploded in my vision and my ears popped—like a billion memories shot out of them, never to return.

"Move your damn head, Joey!" Sal cried from the corner. I grinned. *Fuck that.* I walked forward and hit him with ten or twelve shots that he mostly blocked, then he slugged me again with the right, this time on the chin, and suddenly I rode on a tilt-a-whirl, the room spinning around me. *Now we go to hell.* I bent deep at the knee, stepped in, looped an overhand with all my might and caught him on the chin. His eyes wobbled in his head a little as he twisted and slung a left hook through my jaw. My mouthpiece shot way out of the ring, spinning like a Frisbee into the fifth row where it clonked a busty blonde who sat snuggled up with a fat cigar-chewing Italian.

I stumbled toward them to ask the blonde for my mouthpiece back. Ref Francis grabbed hold of my arm and looked at me startled, his long pointy nose raised. He pointed to the corner. *Is this the first eight count of my life? Good, 'cause I fucking need one to clear my head.* I looked to my corner. Sal hurried through the ropes into the ring. *Fuck, they stopped it?!* Brother Alex slammed the stool down. *The round's over.* I giggled. *The fucking round's over, Joe! Get your shit together.* I never heard the fucking bell through the roaring of the crowd. As I stumbled over, Sal shot a long narrow hose of cold water in my face from the rubbery white bottle. I gasped as he pushed me down on the stool.

"You ain't doing nothing I told you!"

"I got him, he ain't so bad."

"He is so bad, he's gonna fuckin' stop you. You see this towel?" He squeezed a white towel in front of my face. "I'm gonna throw it in before ref Francis evens got to fuckin' stop it."

"Sal, I know I'm gonna lose. I don't care. Don't throw no towel in." I pleaded.

"I'm gonna do what I gotta do to protect ya, kid."

"Sal!" Fearless materialized ringside and tossed Sal my mouth guard.

"Thanks!" I grinned.

"Joey, box! Please!" He put his hands up in prayer before his leathery face. "Please, kid!"

"I ain't no fucking kid!"

"Fine, you ain't a kid," Sal urged. "You're a man, a big bad man. Now box like a man."

I bet you're sitting there right now reading this thing wondering: "How in the hell did that scrawny little knucklehead, Joey Walsh from the old neighborhood, end up fighting in the finals of the Chicago Golden Gloves?" I picked up boxing in the 'burbs of all places, if you can believe it. You're dying to know how all that went down, I know you are, but first I gotta tell you about the aftermath of that night, the night Angel got shot and Ryan went up there to the North Pole and my sister Rose got caught in the crossfire and Dad took me out on the run to Grand Beach to try and save me from the city...

Chapter 1: Exile

ROSE LIVED.

Despite her heart stopping three times, she made it through the night. That mean little .25-caliber slug tore her insides up as it rattled through her rib cage, lacerating her lung and that big and so vital liver. The diligent hands of the surgeons did miraculous work to get her through to the next morning, but she hadn't escaped the jungle just yet.

Dad and I rocketed like a smoldering comet clear across the northern Indiana night to the old, white house in Grand Beach. Then he launched straight back to the hospital in Evanston to Rose's bedside as if lightened by the release of me and my heavy sins. Rose lay near-comatose on a respirator; she roused on and off in her morphine haze. She would peer across her room where our father sat alone, steadfast and bawling violently, afraid to leave her for a moment, afraid to let her die alone. My father was a stark man, dark and brooding, but he loved each of us with a terrible gravity, a power I was just beginning to understand.

I washed Angel's blood off of me in the downstairs bathroom sink. It made a murky, brownish-red circular pool before the drain slowly drank it down. Called the hospital, they'd transferred him to Weiss Memorial. He was stable. I called his house and it went to voice mail. The cool tan receiver trembled at my ear. *Beep.* "I... I..." *I'm sorry. Why can't I talk?* I entered a vacuum. *I can't breathe.* I just hung the phone up on the hook. I sat down on the fuzzy couch. *What did you want to fucking say?* I held my head in my hands, elbows propped on my knees. *I wanted to tell you I love you, Angel, like a brother. I wanted to tell your mom I'm sorry, that I wish I could have helped you more than to just carry your dying body down the alley to the hospital, I wish I could have been a better friend to you.* I wanted to scream but all the fire and fury sank into my heart, where all the gravity pulled it together, pressing it in on itself like a tiny baby star condensing a monstrous nebulous cloud.

Grandma Walsh got me a blanket as I lay down on the couch and tried to sleep. Suddenly I am in the Lincoln floating in the cab with my best friend Ryan. He squeezes the chalk-white .25 in his stubby freckled hand. They see the group on the corner. Rose is there. "What the fuck is she doing here?!" I am inside Ryan's body, his hand and fingers crinkling with Angel's blood as he takes aim; the shots *pop*, *pop*, and suddenly Rose is in our aim, and *pop*.

I woke up breathing hard, my hands bloody, I rubbed them and only found my own sweat. *No. He didn't. There's no way he shot my sister on purpose. It was a fucking accident.*

◆

I woke in the afternoon on the brown fuzzy couch. The sun leaking in through the hazy front windows.

Uncle Marc's voice came from across the room. "Howdy, sleepin' beauty." He lounged in the pleather recliner. A red Budweiser cap sat on his head and a stubbly grin spread on his mug. "Your dad told me to tell you your sister is alright. Well, she ain't alright, but she's gonna make it."

"Thanks."

"Howya been, kid? You look like ya been to hell and back."

I giggled and sat up.

He went on. "Come on over to my place, your aunt made you a couple sammiches."

I followed him out the back door through the thick woods and into their small red house with white trim. Aunt Jackie made me two big roast beef and Swiss cheese sandwiches with Hellman's mayo on rye bread. I ate them quickly, sipping a can of RC. She rubbed my shoulders as she passed behind me. "Everything will be OK," she whispered.

Everything will never be OK ever again, Aunt Jackie. "Thanks," I told her with a sad grin.

"You want to call home?" she asked with a warm smile.

I stiffened at the thought of talking with Ma. What the hell could I say? The anticipations of her misconceptions of what had happened that night, her questions...what the fuck would I tell her? *Well Ma, let me put it simply, my goddamned best friend shot your daughter.*

"Naw, no, but thanks, Aunt Jackie. The sandwiches were really good."

"Your crazy cousins are gonna be here soon, they can't wait to see you," she said as she took my plate and slipped it into the sink.

◆

A bus pulled up outside and Big Bob, Ace, and Allen jumped out. As soon as they came in they bunched up around, greeting me. Ace's red hair was long and combed down across his face; Allen was compact and athletic. They looked at me wide-eyed like I was a galactic war refuge from another universe. They tried not to ask questions but their eyebrows were all hiked up with unease. It was hard to explain it all to them, but they listened.

◆

That night we sat around the fire pit in Grandma's woodsy backyard. The warm orange fire popped and swirled in the low breeze, throwing an undulating yellowish glow onto our faces. The stench of the burning pine sent my mind into some other time, ancient and primitive, yet natural. *Wonder what it was like to be a caveman...just surviving and dying out in the wild. Imagine all the horrific suffering those motherfuckers would go through in a lifetime.* Uncle Marc sipped a red-and-white can of Budweiser; a Winston sizzled between his knuckles. He sat stooped yet enormous on a gnarly log like a white ape, or some late version of *Homo erectus*. We sat across from him on a few stumps in a shell formation, a small but attentive audience. His scarred face stared into the fire—at once fierce, tender, and amused.

"We were gaggle 'a cretins, my brothers and me. Especially when we were teenagers. We were the wildest bunch 'a knuckleheads you ever seen. Seven boys, the Walshes." His voice flowed in a gravelly singsong. "Your dad" (he nodded toward me) "was the meanest son-buck the whole Northside 'a Chicago. He hit so damned hard, he hit guys and they wouldn't wake up for a week. Ever heard that saying he rearranged his face? Well, your dad, he hit a guy on this side a his head" (he pointed to his right cheek) "and the fella's nose'd be over here and his other eyeball be hanging out!" We giggled as the fire popped and coughed up a tall spike of flame before us. "Everyone 'a us could fight though, you had to growing up in Rogers Park. But when your grandma moved us all out here, we just didn't know how to act. A lot 'a the rich Chicago socialites, they got their summer homes here. The Daleys and all that. Well, we'd be at a party and some politician's kid'd be saying something snobby and *wap*, he'd be on the floor with a broke nose. And then Ma would be over to their house the next day to apologize, and we'd all still be laughing about it on the porch when she got back to yell at us. The rich kids didn't like it though, and after a while they got some big football player, he was playing for Notre Dame, I mean he was a lineman, a defensive end, six-four and all built like a brick shithouse, well he wanted a piece 'a us. He was older than most 'a us and the only one old as him was your daddy." He pointed at me with his big coarse index finger. "So one night your dad was down here and the Notre Dame cat was down here and he wanted to fight. Your dad wasn't shy, said fine, and about a hundred and fifty kids all congregated down at the beach. It was about midnight and we had a big ole bonfire going and Notre Dame Man was there and your dad walked on down to the beach to have a chitchat." Uncle Marc hiked up his eyebrows as the smoke swirled around his head. "It was like a ring entrance for a big TV fight, he come down the long wooden steps to the sand with us brothers, we were like his entourage. So your daddy says 'You got a problem with my brothers?' And Notre Dame Man says 'Your brothers are a buncha white trash assholes.' So your daddy put 'em up and the big ole boy come thrashing and throwing punches, he was half a foot taller than your dad and fifty pounds heavier den him. Your daddy did one of these they call it a triangle defense in martial arts." He held his fists together over his head with his elbows out his arms making like a triangle. "And Notre Dame is whaling away and your daddy stumbled a few times and he didn't throw a single punch, for a second I thought he wasn't gonna, then when Notre Dame let up just a hair on his punch'n, your Daddy crouched down and came up with some kinda super-uppercut like that Streetfighter video game."

"Rayu!" Ace chimed in; his dark freckled face grinned.

"Yeah, like that guy, Rayu, he was like *arrucin*! And I never heard a sound like it. Notre Dame's mouth crunched shut. He floated up in the air a little and then came down like a high-rise building being demolished, hit the sand and the sand burst up around him and I am not shitting you every single person on that beach ran away as fast as they fricken could. I ran too! I thought he was dead! I look back and your dad is out there in the firelight, he rolled ole boy over and kneeled down over him, making sure he was breathing I guess. I just kept running. The police down here didn't like me too much and I think they were looking for me at the time anyways, so I beat it!"

We laughed heartily, soaking it all up like sponges.

A voice shot out of the dark woods. "'Member when Timmy stole the cop car?"

"Hey Uncle Ron! How are ya?" Allen said as Ron's narrow, bald head emerged in the flickering light.

"I'm OK." He walked up beside me, watching the fire. "Hi Joey."

"Hi Ron."

"Sorry about your sister." The firelight painted his pale face and hawk nose orange like the setting sun.

"Thanks, she'll be OK," I said looking over at Allen, who nodded. "Timmy stole a cop car?" I changed the subject.

"Yeah." Uncle Marc grinned and puffed his chest out with pride. "So we were at some house party just down the street here, when the cops showed up. And everybody ran like usual and the cop is chasing us and all the sudden I hear the squad car take off. It starts rolling around to our secret hiding spot under the bridge over here. It stops on top the bridge and on the speaker it says, 'Alright you Walsh boys, we got you surrounded. Now Ron, Marc, and Manny come out with your hands up and your pants down. I wanna see those bleach-white buttocks in the moonlight.' We come running out and sure enough it's Timmy on the loudspeaker. Well he howls like a wolf and peels off. He led them coppers all over the place, he was stopping in front of mean old ladies' houses and giving them a what for on the loudspeaker, 'Missus Evans come on out here, you're under arrest on the charges a being a crab ass, and smelling like cat shit.' The coppers couldn't catch him on account he had the police radio on and could hear everything they said and where they were looking for him."

"How the hell did he get away?" Bob asked.

"He just parked it out in the dunes, got on the radio and said, 'Fuck all you pigs! It was fun but I gotta go!' then cut home through the woods."

We guffawed and looked at each other in wild wonderment. There were so many damn stories about the brothers, the original knuckleheads. Us cousins heard them stories over and over, sneaking into earshot of our uncles and fathers rehashing the "Drinking Days." For you fathers out there: no matter how hard you try to hide your past from your sons, they will learn about you. The harder you try to hide it, the harder they'll try to find you out. And when they hear the stories, they'll listen with a furious intensity that'll mark them for life. We all inherit our father's karma.

My father was the oldest of seven boys. His father left them when my dad was still just a boy. Losing your father out of your life at that age carries unfathomable weight. It is a transformative thing. You can go on to destroy yourself, or go on to build a mountain of yourself. My father had done both. But when you lose your father at that age you come to a deeper understanding of what a father is. What a father's value is. My father understood that value and became a father to more people than just the children he sired and adopted and raised. There were many people out in the world, many who I didn't even know who considered him their father, and not just my siblings, or the younger brothers he practically had to raise. Being a father gave him the deepest pain and joy of his life.

◆

They left me in Grand Beach for a few weeks, informed me I'd have to go to summer school to make up the days I'd missed once the move to the suburbs was final. In total it'd be about two months of being a dropout. It was fun, mostly running around with my crazy Indiana cousins, smoking weed and listening to Wu-Tang Clan and Rage Against the Machine.

◆

Then one day my sister Jan showed up. I was smoking a Winston on the porch waiting for the cousins to get home from school. She rolled up front of the house in her green Tempo; her big curly new wave hair sprang up all around her dark Dominican face. She just cranked down the window and said, "Want to go see Rosie?"

"Sure." I squashed my smoke, hopped in, and we headed toward the city.

As we approached the skyway bridge she turned down the radio. "So, I wanted to tell you." She reached over and took my hand in hers. "I'm pregnant, Joey. DeWayne and me are having a little girl."

"Wow! Really?"

"Yep, we want you to be the godfather."

"OK!"

We soared up the Skyway bridge holding hands and watching the high-rises of the city come into view on the horizon. Our hands so different in tone. Mine a light sandy tone, hers a deep chocolatey brown, but there we were brother and sister. Even though she was adopted from the Dominican Republic, she was my sister before I was even born. She was one of the souls who was waiting for me, listening to Mom's tummy, feeling for my kicks.

"It's crazy how much everything is changing so fast. The move, a baby."

"I saw the new house."

"Yeah, what's it like?"

"It's fricken' huge! There's a cute park across the street, and we got a big backyard. All the houses around are like mansions, it's so nice."

"How the heck can we afford that?"

"Dad! You didn't hear? This company brought him in as a partner, he's making a hundred grand a year!"

"Really?"

"Yeah, we're rich!"

"Holy shit." I'd always just thought of Dad as a worker, a carpenter, maybe a boss of a crew but not an owner or nothing, a boss of a whole company. But he'd been working hard, building his reputation, and had learned to bid projects. He possessed the kind of ground-up experience that makes you a rare commodity. He had the knowledge of how to make a project work and the expertise to lay out an excellent bid. He could handle the math and there was really nothing he couldn't do. And if he had to, he could still throw a tool belt on.

Excitement coursed through me. I couldn't wait to see Rose. As we slowly eased through downtown, thoughts flew through my mind. What could I say to cheer her up and make her laugh? I envisioned her on the hospital bed all bored and wanting to go home. I'd tell her, "Don't worry, Rose, you'll be home soon, then I can whip you in Monopoly like usual." I giggled as the high-rises eased past.

I didn't tell Jan that Dad forbade me from going back to the neighborhood, but she seemed to know. She took a long way, never getting off the highway until we were up in Evanston.

We walked into the trauma unit. Why the hell is Rose still here? She should be in her own room somewhere on her way home by now. She'd been shot over a week ago for Christ sake.

I stepped into the room. She lay asleep on the inclined hospital bed, her blue gown draped over her and open on the side. Her face was paler than I'd ever seen it, so many shades lighter than her biological sister Jan's. Strands of her light brown frizzy hair flowed out and lay on the white sheets. The respirator sucked and pumped air into her lung; clear tubes and colorful electric cords sprang out of her at all different points.

The IV tube ran up to a big bag full of clear fluid hanging above her. Blood collected in another contraption that plugged a hose into her side. The electric cords sent information from sensors monitoring her heartbeat and other vital activity up to a towering series of computer boxes set all around her. *Is she fucking dying? Is this why Jan brought me here? To say goodbye?*

My eyes followed the cords up to her heartbeat dancing across a screen. The gravity of her condition squeezed my throat like a massive vise.

Then her eyes opened.

"Hi Joe!" she said weakly and excitedly.

"Hi Rosie, how are you?"

"I'm doing OK, I missed you."

Warm molecules stirred and threatened to explode in my chest but I held them in with all my might.

"I missed you too, Rosie, I love you."

Rose closed her eyes and slipped back into the medicated daze she'd been floating in when we'd arrived.

I looked at Jan. "Is she OK?"

"She's fine, Joe, just sit down and wait. She'll be back in a minute."

We sat in the soft cushioned chairs with the sunlight cutting through the vertical blinds and splaying black swords of shade across the tile floor. After about three minutes she woke again, looking at me; she picked up the conversation where we'd left off.

"Did you hear we're moving?"

Excitement pattered in my chest.

"Yes, I heard to a big house in the suburbs!"

"They said it's blue."

"Yeah and there's a park across the street and a big backyard."

She fell again, descended into the haze and was gone.

A stern-faced nurse came in and checked the machines. "Your sister needs her rest, guys, she's having a little trouble breathing today."

"OK Joe, let's just go then."

"OK." I stood up and looked longingly back at Rose.

As we got to the door she opened her eyes. "I love you, Joseph."

"I love you too, Rosie."

We walked out into the hallway as it finally came. The hook swung hard and implanted in my heart and set. It unleashed a deep soundless yell from my lungs. *It's your fucking fault!* The wires wrapped around my chest and squeezed just like that seagull that'd grabbed my lure and tangled himself in the line when I was a little boy fishing on the star dock at Montrose harbor, the one that'd turned into a trembling blur of white feathers in Da's hands. Just a natural creature caught up in the confusion of their world, in need of an act of compassion to set it free. I fell to my knees clutching at the wound. *I'm the seagull.* Jan stood over me saying something, then she helped me to my feet and put her arm around me and walked me down the hall to the elevator.

I'm the seagull. You knew that, right? I'm the fucking seagull. I been the seagull all along. Maybe you are too.

Chapter 2: Nebula

ONCE SCHOOL WAS OUT, WE STARTED THE MOVE. Ma came and brought me out to the fancy old suburb of La Grange, Illinois. We cruised through Countryside's strip malls; excitement surged through me. The suburbs was a place I'd only seen in the movies and TV shows. We drove down La Grange Road, past huge mansions. One big brown house had a long sloping roof that came to a peak four stories in the sky. *No way we fucking live here.*

"Ma, we live on this street?!"

"Yes, just up here near the library and movie theatre," Ma said.

We pulled into the driveway of a smaller blue-and-white house with less luxury and style than the others. I hopped out of the van. *It's still big though, way bigger than our house in the city and any house I've ever been in, really.* I ran around and surveyed the empty house. *We got a huge attic and a big ol' backyard with two tall trees, a two-car garage, and a fricken sandbox!* Two luxuriously huge mansions sat on either side of our house. We shared a driveway with a yellow Victorian-style home with a wraparound front porch. A BMW sat on their side of the driveway.

I lay down in a sleeping bag on the floor in the attic that first night by myself. *Fucking feels like I'm in outer space.* I sighed, puffing a smoke, looking out the window in the ceiling at the half-crescent moon. *I'm the man on the moon. Huh, the thug on the moon maybe. The fuckup, the shitbag in exile. The fucking wannabe gangster, the dumbass knucklehead. Maybe I can be somebody else out here.* A star hung beside the moon gleaming bright. *Why do you always got to be such a motherfucker? Even when you was eight, fer Christ sake.*

Da, I remember going on the walks with him on his Sunday walks down Ashland to Foster, then back on Clark Street. Everybody did it, even Pat when he was young, everybody. But everybody had that day when they got too old to go. But there was always a younger one to pick up the slack and I was the last one, the youngest. Jan and Rose, they stopped going one day 'cause they were too old to be seen in public with their

Grampa and they had other cool stuff to do. So I said I wasn't going either so I could be big and mature too. I remember he came walking up in his three-button collared shirt, his black hair slicked back in perfect slices with Sheba trotting beside him and called to us and the girls said no and I was thinking about it and I just said no, like a stupid little prick. And he went walking alone on his walk. I sat on the porch and I didn't have a fucking thing to do, I was just trying to be cool like my big sisters and Ma came out and said, "You know, Da is more than just your Grampa, he's a person too with feeling and he's your friend. He must feel pretty bad. You kind of stood him up, ya know."

"Yeah, I feel bad too."

"Well, think about that," she said and walked inside. "Maybe you should get your ass in gear and catch up to him."

I sat there for a minute as the sparrows chirped happily. *Poor Da has to walk all alone.* My chest ached. I rubbed it. *Alright, alright, I'll go, jeez!* I started walking after him. He walked fast and tugged on Sheba's leash to keep up. I jogged after him. He cut through the arterial alley as I tried to keep up. *My chest hurts so bad!* I couldn't run but I walked fast. When I turned onto Olive, he jogged across Ashland with Sheba trotting behind him. I ran to the corner gripping my chest, it felt like it was all pumped full of helium. I tried to yell to him. Tears wet my face. I finally screamed "Da!!!" He stiffened when he heard it. He didn't look back. I fell to my knees crying. "Da! I'm sorry..." *I know you can hear me, please wait.* But he didn't stop and he didn't look back 'cause I think he was crying too.

You gotta stop being such a piece of shit, Joe. This shit is hurting everybody you love. I flicked my smoke out the attic window. *Shit, what if it starts a fire out there? All you ever do is think about yourself. You're a selfish prick. What about Dad?* I hadn't really seen him since the night Rose got shot. I didn't know but he was at the hospital and working around the clock. He was giving every waking second to us. To be the father his father wasn't. Doing shit he probably didn't even know how to do but finding a way for us every day, and here we were fucking up like idiot little brats. The whole time he's thinking he's doing good and then bam, he almost loses his daughter and his son in one night.

I heard his quivering voice as we rode up the Skyway bridge that night: "I love you." It was like it was the hardest three words he ever said in his life. *You gotta be better for him. You gotta become a man like him.*

Maybe it was so hard to say because he was going through the hardest day of his life, his daughter might be dying, his son was all mixed up in some terrible shit covered in blood. I bet he just wanted to hear his dad say I love you to him right then. *But he ain't never gonna hear his dad say I love you to him ever again and he wasn't there when he needed him anyways. You're so lucky to have your dad, Joe.* Ryan, I saw him locked up in Juvie, a murder charge hanging on his head. Angel with the bullet in his stomach, a junkie. *Maybe they wouldn'ta ended up like that if they had their fathers in their life like you. Can't you see all you have to be grateful for?* Tears beaded in my eyes as I looked up at the stars through the little moon-roof window. *You stupid motherfucker. It's why you're here an don't have a bullet in you or a murder charge on you. He's the only reason. He gave you life and he saved your life.* I saw myself that night covered in Angel's blood from when we carried him to the ER. I was bloody like a newborn, born into a new life.

◆

In the morning, Ma's van pulled into the driveway, packed with boxes and full of all the little ghetto kids she babysat. The doors opened and they all poured out; the five-year-olds looked around, scared.

"Where the fuck we at?!" this girl Briana said.

"This one a dem Freddie Krueger neberhoods," DeMarcus told her. "They gon' kill us!"

"Shut up and stop swearing!" Ma scolded them.

I giggled. *The Northside Hillbillies have arrived in the suburbs.* I grinned and started unloading the boxes and carrying them inside. After we finished, Ma let the kids play in the big backyard for a while before heading back to the city.

I was out there shooting hoops on the basketball rim the second day. The neighbor's little blonde-haired kids came outside. The boy was about four years old and the little girl was maybe three; they wore matching white overalls with yellow dress shirts and white shoes. The two of them came up to the chain-link fence. DeMarcus and Briana walked up to them eating orange popsicles.

"Hi," the little boy said.

"Whats up?" DeMarcus replied. The popsicle dribbled orange dots on his dirty white Nike t-shirt.

"I have a question," the little neighborhood boy said, scratching his chin thoughtfully.

"Shoot, whiteboy," Briana said.

"Mommy!" He turned to his blonde mom, who was sunbathing on a white lawn chair in a white bikini with big black sunglasses on her face. "She called me whiteboy!"

The mom didn't respond. She just sipped a bloody mary as she lay there listening to Jon Bon Jovi on her little CD player.

"Okay," the little boy scrunched up his face. "Why do you have that paint on your face?"

"Whatchutalkinbout? There something on my face?" Briana asked DeMarcus.

"Your face has very dark paint on it."

"My skin black."

I guffawed and looked over.

"He's never seen a black person up close before," I told them.

"You ain't never seen a black person before?" Briana asked. "Not even on the TV?"

"Yes, but I thought they put paint on their faces," he replied.

"Boy, you dumb as dirt," she said.

"What, is you retarded, mothafucka?" DeMarcus asked.

"What's a mothafucka?" he replied.

"You a mothafucka, mothafucka!" DeMarcus answered.

"Mothafucka!" The little girl said real sweet and excitedly.

"Oliver! Matilda! Come here this minute! I'm going to wash your mouths out with soap!" The mom sat up on her lawn chair, her heavy breasts flopping around in her bikini top. They hurried over and she took them inside.

I giggled watching them go in. *Well, you met their first black person, and learned how to swear! You're welcome, you little lily-white babies!*

◆

They left me out there in the big empty house while they drove the van back to the city to continue loading furniture and boxes. I lay around listening to Metallica and smoking squares. I got tired of the music, clicked it off, and just listened lying on the rug in front of the fireplace. *It's so quiet, such a strange fuckin place. I can't even believe we're gonna live out here.* I got up and walked to the window and looked out at the house next door.

The blonde neighbor lady walked up to her kitchen window and looked at me. I waved. She scowled and pulled her drapes shut. *Bitch, in our neighborhood, we all come over and welcome new people when they move in. Over here all you fucking do is scowl out your window. What kind of fucking people are you?*

It felt nice when the van would come back. I'd work real hard to keep all the bad thoughts away, I'd carry stuff that was too heavy, and I'd be sweating and breathing hard when the van pulled away again. Then as my breath slowed I'd fall back into my thoughts. My girlfriend (or ex-girlfriend, I guess) Hyacinth sitting on her blue porch, alone. Rosie, Rose in that horrible bed surrounded by machines. The wires looped around my mind and I'd be laying there tormented as the van drove back to my old life and uprooted it from Hollywood Avenue.

We finished the move. The neighbors we shared a driveway with actually did invite us to dinner at their house, but only my parents. It didn't go over so well. In fact, within fifteen minutes Ma walked out of their front door in her nice cream dress and stepped painfully down their front steps on her bad knee.

Dad followed her out. "Mary! What are you doing?"

"I ain't putting up with that! She didn't even cook that meal! I saw the delivery truck." Ma continued to the sidewalk. "She took it out of the bag and put it on those nice plates!"

"I'm sorry," Dad said to the neighbors then shouted after Ma. "Would you come back here, please?"

"She's a phony! I hate fake people. You know what she is? She's a trophy wife. You stay, I ain't putting up with that crap!"

Dad gave up and followed her back home. *There goes the neighborhood!* I giggled, watching from the TV room.

◆

They enrolled me in Saint Joseph High School in Westchester for several weeks of summer school. St. Joe's was a lot like Gordon, a long one-story brick structure that sat up on a little green hill. It snaked out into different little star-like wings. The big dark brick gymnasium loomed tall above it. Westchester was full of Italians and Greeks with slicked-back hair and gold chains, guys that talked like the characters in *The Bronx Tale*. A lot of Mexican gangbangers with hairnets went to Joe's from Cicero—Kings, Counts, and Two-Six, all with nameplate rings. The black kids from

Maywood, Bellwood, and Austin enrolled there also; a lot of them dressed all thugged out, too, with bandanas hanging out of their back pockets. It miffed me to think that there was dangerous suburbs, but what the hell did I know? Then there was the gigantic basketball kids; some of them were the top Division I recruits in the nation. Saint Joe's was a basketball dynasty. Isiah Thomas had gone there, and they'd just came out with this documentary called *Hoop Dreams* about two recent team members. It was a unique little institution. The Christian Brothers ran it, and a lot of families sent their screwups there, knowing very well that the Brothers would impose serious and sometimes physical discipline into them. Summer school sucked, no AC, but it was better than having to repeat freshman year.

I wandered around the school before lunch break and went down to the dark basement of the gym to take a piss in the locker room. A heavy thud smacked into something in an off-kilter rhythm.

"Come on! Hit that thing!" a beastly old man's voice growled. "The right, the cross, turn into it! Hit that thing hard! What are ya, a sissy?!" Another buzzer blared. "Thirty seconds! Go hard! Everything you got! Don't stop!"

The thuds intensified. Chains jostled. The storage room door creaked open a crack; a hard yet flickering triangle of light flooded out in the dark hallway. I nudged the door open and peered in.

A huge old man loomed behind a strongly built guy bouncing around a heavy bag. A lamp in the far corner of the gray concrete room glowed like a powerful orange sun. It splayed their menacing contorting shadows across the floor toward me. The muscular guy ripped his black-gloved fists into the white heavy bag leaving faded indentations in the cloth. *Am I fucking hallucinating?* His tenacious blows popped and wobbled the bag as it bounced on the metal chains hanging down from the concrete beam that ran across the ceiling. The big old man slapped the boxer's arm hard. The boxer flinched, then fired back into the bag savagely. The bell rang and the sweating boxer fell into a tan metal folding chair, breathless. Droplets of perspiration fell from his curly black hair as his face grimaced in exhaustion.

The old man saw me, stomped over, and shoved the door open. "What do ya want?" he spat in a hurried lisp.

"Nothing." I shrugged.

He slammed the door in my face.

I went up to the lunch room, grabbed a tray, got two hot dogs and some fries, and went to look for a seat. Everything was full; the kids were already eating. Then this clean-cut kid looked up at me. He had a little golden crucifix dangling atop his white dress shirt, and he started waving me over.

"Right here, buddy!" he motioned to the kids sitting across from him at the long table. "Make some room! Whatsdamatter wit you?! It's da new kid!"

The kids squeezed over and I sat down across from him.

"How ya doing? I'm Georgie da Greek." He reached his firm hand across the table to me.

I shook it. "I'm Joe."

"Well welcome to Saint Joseph High School, Joey. These are the Sophomore year general track rejects." He made a big gesture to the kids sitting near him. "Juan..." (He motioned to a fat Mexican kid with thick sideburns.) "...he aint never met a burrito he didn't like."

The guys chuckled.

Georgie nodded to the kid next to me. "And you got bucktooth Paul."

"Aye I ain't buck tooth no more!" Paul complained.

"You gots big-nose Anthony." (He motioned to a tall Italian kid with a big crooked nose.) "And nappy-headed Ronnie." (A light-skinned black kid flicked Georgie off from down the way.)

"So where you from?" Georgie asked.

"Edgewater."

"What the heck is Edgewater?"

"It's a neighborhood on the North Side."

"From the city, okay." Georgie gave me an impressed nod. "But what's da matter wit you, Joey? You look like you seen a ghost or something."

"I seen this big old guy in the basement training a boxer." I told him.

"That's Brother Alex, he's crazy. He trains Golden Glove champions. He's had like three of 'em."

"Boxing champions?"

"Yeah it's a big tournament in the city," Juan said, stuffing a big dripping Italian beef in his mouth.

"Remember when you went down there with Brother Alex, Anthony?" Georgie asked.

"Shut up." Anthony replied.

"Anthony got his big nose busted and never went back," Paul said as Anthony self-consciously rubbed the left nostril of his crooked nose.

"Who busted his nose?" I asked.

"Brother Alex did!" Ronnie informed me. "He's fifty-five, but he'll beat the crap outta ya."

"No shit?" I said. "He is huge."

"Yeah, he weighs 250, of course he busted my nose," Anthony whined.

"Anthony thought he was tough," Georgie informed.

"Shut up, George. Nobody can take that training, Brother is nuts!" Anthony bit his hot dog and chewed aggressively.

"Well, they say if you can take the training Brother Alex puts you through, you're gonna be a champion. He's never entered a guy in the Golden Gloves that didn't win a championship," Georgie said, and hiked up his thick eyebrows.

"Man, I want to train with him," I sighed.

"Well, just go down there! He'll smack you around a little." Juan patted my back. A grin spread on his chubby face.

The bell rang and we put our trays up and headed to class. I walked the halls in a daze as the kids flooded past. Could I really start boxing that easy? Fear swelled my stomach full of helium. *Just the fucking thought of it scares me.* A mean-looking Italian kid with slicked-back hair walked past. *Could I take him? Shit, I really want to try out boxing.* I fought all right in the street with my hands, and I figured that'd help. A big tall black kid from Maywood walked confidently ahead of me, his wide shoulders cutting his tucked-in dress shirt into a V. *Tank whooped my ass but Tank was a freak of nature. He killed a dude. Who knows, maybe I'll get big and strong and swole up like Tank one day.*

I walked into class and sat down amongst the rowdy summer school kids. Spent the rest of the day daydreaming about being a boxer and fighting in the Golden Gloves but I was too much of a chickenshit to go introduce myself and ask Brother Alex if he'd teach me.

◆

I sat on the sloping steps near the front of the school; they led down to where the buses parked in the emptying parking lot. *Ma's always late to pick me up. Well, I guess I'm not that high on the priority list right now with Rose still in the hospital. I miss her. How fucking long are they gonna keep her?* This big black dude with a short fade and a pencil tucked in the crease of his ear stepped out of the school doors behind me and sparked up a menthol; he wore brown Timberland boots and saggy blue dress pants.

"What up?" he said to me as he passed.

"Shit, what's up with you?"

"School out, it time to get high."

I giggled as he took long steps down the concrete steps to the parking lot. A shitty blue station wagon pulled up near him full of black gangbangers wearing sideways ball caps and bandanas. They all looked at him real excited to see him. As the station wagon creaked to a stop, he spun and ran right back toward me and the entrance to the school. All the station wagon doors opened and they poured out with bats and bricks. One skinny cat with a blue pick stuck in his afro wound up and tossed a brick but it missed and cracked on the steps near my feet. A dorky kid with clear spectacles had just walked out, and the door slowly swung closed behind him. I jumped up and grabbed it just before it shut.

"Hold that door, nigga!" the black dude yelled as he sprinted toward me with all the others fanned out chasing him.

I opened it and he ran in.

"You betta come on, fool," he grabbed my arm and pulled me in.

As we pulled the door shut, I looked back at the six dudes running up the sloped steps and grass. A tall skinny guy in a red Pippen jersey jogged up, took his small aluminum bat, and smashed the narrow window. The glass spiderwebbed but the wiring held. *What the fuck did I get into now?*

The first black guy bounced backward in the shady hallway and laughed as they tried to pull the locked door open. "Come on," he nodded to me, and I followed him as he ran through the quiet halls.

We cut into a bathroom way down at the far side of the school. He heaved deep breaths as he paced the open windows that sat across from the line of toilet stalls. The scent of piss and fresh-cut grass mixed as he finally caught his breath.

"Shit, you fucking saved my ass! Thanks."

"Who the hell were they?"

"They Moes."

"They're Stones?"

"Yeah."

"What is you?" I asked.

"I'm a Foe."

"A Moe?"

"Naw, nigga, I'm a Foe, a Four Corner Hustla."

"I never even heard a that shit, you all Folks?"

"We Peoples, we ride with the Five, we just don't get along with Moes is all...I fucked one a they girls and then I knocked ole boy out when he got salty." Sweat made his white button-up T-shirt cling to his wide back as he turned to look out the open door.

"Now they say they gotta break my arm. Fucking dum niggas." We waited a few tense moments watching out the windows and hallway for any sign of them. Nobody came. "Aye kid, I owe ya one, I'm outta here, don't be going back out for a while, OK? They catch you they finna fuck you up."

"All right." I shrugged.

"What's your name?"

"Joe."

"That's my name too but they call me Jay. Aight, Joe." He held his big black fist out to me.

I bumped it with mine. "Awright, Jay."

He flashed a big toothy grin and slipped out of the bathroom, his diamond earring sparkled. *How the hell I meet some motherfucker like this in the burbs?!*

◆

A few days later I was walking down the hall when I got a playful pop to my shoulder.

"What up, Joe?"

"What's up, Jay?" I said as he passed the opposite direction. "They still looking for you?"

"Hell yeah they is!" He twisted around to flash a grin. "They looking for your ass, too!"

All the sudden Brother Alex appeared, barreling down the hall like a loose bull in a black suit coat with his little Christian Brother collared shirt. He punched Jay hard in the chest, and the whole hallway erupted in laughter.

"Language, Jay, language!"

"Damn!" Jay clutched his chest. "I mean, darn, Brother Alex."

"That's right, darn is acceptable."

Brother punched him in the arm.

"Brother, stop, I'm sore from the other day."

"You haven't trained in a week, Jay, ya big wimp. I had a show fight for you but I called O'Brien and told him it's off 'cause you're too much of a dummy to train."

"But I been busy, Brother, I had to work."

"Excuses, you always have excuses, Jay, and excuses don't make champions, they make losers."

"Come on, Brother, I can beat this guy."

"Yeah, yeah…" Brother continued down the hall. The ceiling light reflected off his enormous round combed-over balding head.

"I'll be down after school today, Brother, you got my word."

I thought about it and nudged Jay. "Aye, I wanna learn to box."

"Yeah? Brother Alex don't play, boy, you betta be ready for some torturous-ass shit."

"I am."

"Alright, come on down to the basement after school, I'll introduce you and put a word in for you."

"Thanks, man."

◆

I sat in social studies and as the teacher spoke about ancient Rome, my mind drifted. The next thing you knew I was boxing under the lights at the United Center, a championship bout! The crowd roaring as they announced me: "Joe 'The Warrior' Walsh." Naw, "Joe 'The Killer' Walsh." Naw, "Joe 'The Supernova' Walsh." Yeah, fucking supernova, but nobody'd know what it meant, that's good though, get in their head trying to figure out what the fuck it means. Then I could beat their ass while they're pondering that shit. I looked across the ring; Evander Holyfield stood there looking at me real dark muscular and stern, and I snapped the fuck out of it. *I ain't fighting no Evander Fucking Holyfield!* Well, I guess eventually if you're good, you gotta fight bad motherfuckers like that.

I walked down the dark steps into the basement of the gymnasium after class, no sound of anyone hitting the bag or the buzzer, just voices.

"Naw, Brother, this kid, he smart, he tough, he saved my ass the other day."

"How'd he save your ass?"

"I can't say, Brother, just that he ain't no punk and he finna be good."

I stepped into the doorway.

"There he go! Joe, what up man, come on in."

I stepped into the room nervously. Brother Alex stomped up to me in faded black pants and a loose soccer shirt. He towered over me with a grimace on his pudgy shaved face.

"What's your name?"

"Joe Walsh."

"Take off your shirt, let me get a look at you." I took my shirt off. "Puny arms, OK shoulders, pretty-boy face." He slapped my jaw softly. "Where do ya live?"

"La Grange."

"Oh goodness, a little La Grange prissy boy."

"Haha, I'm from Chicago."

"What side?"

"North Side."

"Nothing but wimps on the North Side. The South Side is where the real hard men are." He patted the image of a soccer ball on his big lumpy chest as I giggled. "Alright, you want to learn to box?"

"Yeah."

"You watch boxing?"

"Yep."

"Who's your favorite fighter?"

"I don't know, I like Tyson and Trinidad and Holyfield. I like Roy Jones a lot. But probably that guy Gatti, his fights are awesome."

"Hmm... alright, you got a mouthpiece?"

"No."

"Jay, show him how to wrap his hands." Brother reached into the big metal boxing locker and tossed me two old blue cloth wraps, then stomped off into the hall.

Jay walked me through wrapping my hands, teaching me part by part.

"Now, Brother he gonna bust you up the first day 'cause he don't wanta waste his time on nobody. If you soft, you won't never come back, but if you come back then boy, he gonna make you a champion." He wrapped my wrist. "You been in fights before?"

"Yeah, a bunch."

"You win 'em?"

"Some of 'em I won and some of 'em I lost."

"That's good, you ain't real unless you lost. You ain't no man 'til you take an ass whoopin'." He sliced the blue wrap between my spread fingers. "I ain't lost no fight in a while, but boy I lost before. It's real losin' that makes you who you are." He attached the Velcro to the wrap around my wrist and grinned at me with his big straight teeth. "You finna' spar, boy, now don't hold back on Brother, he ain't gonna hold back on you."

"He's like 250!"

"Yeah but he slow, so be quick wit it," he said as I guffawed. "But he gonna be teaching you stuff while you spar, so use it on him. Protec yo self."

Brother came back in with a cup of hot water and a mouthpiece in it.

"Now form this in your teeth."

He pulled the mouthpiece out and jabbed it in my mouth. It burned a little, then slowly formed into a mushy bond around my teeth and hardened quickly.

"Get him some headgear and gloves."

Brother opened the tall metal locker; a nice assortment of professional-grade boxing gear hung from the hooks and sat on the top shelf. *This is some fancy shit.* Jay grabbed a black Everlast headgear and fitted it around my head. *Feels like a snug helmet. It's blocking out my peripheral vision.* Chills danced along my neck. *Damn, I got real headgear on like the old-time boxers in the black-and-white photos.*

We headed into the adjacent room, a big musty wrestling room with a red foam mat covering the floor. In the middle was a white image of a helmeted charger, a Roman warrior. Chest-high red rectangular padding covered the walls. Electronic lamps in the ceiling flickered.

"1965 Chicago Park District Heavyweight Champion before I chose the cloth," Brother lisped. "I was knocking out wimps from the North Side every chance I got. The dorks from La Grange didn't even show up at the tournaments."

Brother pulled on a glove. The second one he yanked on with his teeth.

"Put yer hands up. Look, this is your guard." He pulled my fist up. "Now put your left foot out front of ya, your right foot behind you, bend those knees a little. Good, now turn your shoulders, point your left at me. First punch you gotta learn is the jab, now you shoot it out straight." He showed me in slow motion. "And you twist your hand at the end and squeeze your fist. Got it? OK, now jab."

"Huh?"

"Hit me in the chest!" He smacked his chest and stuck it out at me.

What the fuck is he talking about? I jabbed him tentatively in the chest. It felt like hitting a big boulder.

"HIT ME HARD!" Brother's lisp dissolved into a deep roar like it came from the bowels of a cave.

Jeez! I jabbed harder.

He jabbed me; his glove split between my guard and crashed into my nose. My head rocked back. Stars sprouted through my blackened vision. *Did he just punch me in the fucking face?!*

"Hit me!" Brother yelled, glowering at me.

I shot an angry punch back that slammed into his chest.

"Good! Harder!"

I jabbed again and he shot a thudding jab between my gloves again. "Keep your hands up! Look, you gotta block my jab with your right." He showed me. "You just see it coming and you catch it like it's a ball flying at you. Jab me."

I jabbed and he blocked the shot, deflecting it off target with ease using the palm of his glove. He jabbed at me and I tried to block it but it just smashed my own glove into my face. *Shit!* Stars emerged from the darkness.

"You gotta meet it hard! Not like a wimp!"

He jabbed again and smashed the cuff of my glove into it and pushed it down. *OK, I got it.*

"Good, but don't reach out with it or I'll do this."

He jabbed, I blocked it again, and then he shot another jab over my glove that stung me square in the mouth. *Son of a bitch, this is hard!*

I dug a jab back into his chest like a dagger, then another and another, backing Brother up. He stopped and—*Bam!*—smashed another jab into my guard. I tried to block it with both hands. I jabbed him again.

"That's good, you're mad, I can work with that. Pretty boy's got a temper."

Yeah, I want to beat the fuck out of your big Oompa-Loompa ass! Brother shot another couple jabs at me and I blocked them partially, then fired mine back.

"Alright, break," he said at an arbitrary moment.

My arms and back burned as I struggled to breathe. Blood oozed in my mouth from my lip. I giggled happily. *Ain't thought about anything, nothing, not my past, not the city, not Rose, nothing.* My chest heaved and all the emotions swirled around in me alive and healthy like I set them free, like the particles swarmed up from where they'd been weighing me down all the time.

"Pretty good, Joe." Jay shot a string of water into my mouth from a big green plastic bottle. "Hang in there. You having a good time, kid?"

"This is fun, Jay. I love it."

"OK, yo lip bleedin' a little but ain't nothin' to do but let it bleed."

We went another three rounds jabbing the hell out of each other until my arms burned like red iron. Then Brother called Jay to gear up.

Jay took his shirt off, revealing a heavy muscular build. He loomed taller than Brother but Brother outweighed him by fifty pounds with those thick veiny legs. They commenced full sparring; the shots boomed through the wrestling room. Jay threw with power and speed but Brother Alex smothered him, bullying him around the room. In the third round Brother pushed Jay into the padded wall as Jay wilted. Brother's face turned to a vile grimace as he bent at the knees; he seemed to harness some dark force of the universe to deliver these resounding blows to Jay's chest, liver, spleen, kidneys, and ribs. *Damn, how is this old fucker doing it!? He's a fucking sadist!* Jay finally collapsed, completely spent. He lay heaving on the shiny red wrestling mat; sweat droplets rained off his brow.

"You still think you can fight next weekend?" Brother asked, looming over him.

"Nope."

"You been smoking again, haven't you?" Brother undid the Velcro with his teeth and pulled his gloves off, glowering down at Jay.

"Yes, Brother."

"Jay, you coulda had a chance at a Golden Glove title but you can't even stop smoking."

"I know, Brother, but I stopped that Mexican last month, didn't I?"

"You did good then, but he'd kick your black ass now."

Jay looked at me and we all chuckled heartily. We wrapped up and put the boxing gear away, hung to dry with the fan on it.

"Come back when you're ready to get serious, Jay," Brother chided him.

"OK, Brother." Jay grinned exhaustedly.

Brother then looked at me with a sneering grin. "And the La Grange wimp, if you want, you can come down and box again tomorrow."

"Sure," I said excitedly.

Jay and I walked out of the gym into the bright afternoon sunlight together.

"You gonna come back ain'tchu," Jay said, squinting at me as we paused on the loading dock.

"Yeah, hell yeah! I wanna box!"

"Good." He lit up a menthol. "You keep coming back, you gonna get good." He grinned remembering something. "You use this shit on the street, you'll be killing kids." Jay giggled, puffed his smoke, and headed off across the lot to catch his Pace Bus to Maywood.

◆

I came down to box with Brother every damn day for two weeks. I learned how to seriously fucking jab, how to block a jab when one came back, and even to keep my right on guard while jabbing, 'cause you know, if they jab with you, you'll get caught. The burn in my arms slowly faded until holding my arms up felt normal and made me feel safe instead of terrified. Brother Alex taught me to turn the jab over and snap it for power. And how to bend my knees and step in with it and drag my back foot afterward to get my legs into the next jab. Then Brother started showing me the cross, and how you really gotta turn your damn hips and shoulders into it like you're swinging a baseball bat for power. Brother had a way of bringing the beast out of you. He'd get you exhausted then scream in your face, "What are you, a wimp?!" Spittle bursting everywhere like a damn geyser. Then he'd slap the living hell out of your friggin arms and back. His hands were smallish and long but it made them like whips. He'd punish you into an absolute rage where there was no thought, no time, nothing but vicious action, ferocious punches, fierce defenses. You became a machine, with a raging beast at the controls.

And I gotta tell you, I fucking liked it. All the shit that happened back in the city, the rage, it all bottled up inside me. Training hard like that, it gave me a way to express it and communicate it back into the universe.

When the pantywaist summer school kids heard I was boxing they started talking their shit at the lunch table. This curly-haired kid with acne from Berwyn named Paul got real big and bad about it.

"He's fucking boxing, dude," Geogie the Greek guffawed. "He'll pulverize you, Paulie."

"He ain't that tough," Paul said.

"Maybe I ain't." I shrugged. *But I'm down to find out, motherfucker.*

"See," Paul said, then glared at me. "I can take you."

"I'm going down to train today."

"Ohhh shit!" The tabled erupted. *I didn't fucking mean it like that, you assholes.*

Paul said: "I'll come down there and kick your ass."

Really, you fucking suburbanite pussy? I shrugged. *Maybe he is a badass.* "OK." I grinned. "Maybe Brother will let us spar."

"Are we negotiating a sparring match between Paulie the Putz and the young lion Joey Walsh?" Georgie the Greek said with mock excitement. "Tickets are five dollars, fellas, you can prepay now or at the door, it'll be six bucks, no freebies. Juan I know you went back for seconds on the spaghetti today and may be short but if that's the case I will put you on an IOU at fifteen percent interest..."

The whole lunch table agreed they'd come down and watch us spar. The lunch bell rang and we all got up and headed to our classes. *I doubt he'll come. But fuck, what if he does? I can see if this shit Brother's been teaching me is real. Maybe I can take somebody out. Paul's a little taller than me, about my weight...* An image flashed of Paul beating the living shit out of me like Tank did years back in the old neighborhood. A trail of butterflies flickered through my stomach. *Well, maybe I ain't ready. Naw, fuck that shit. I am.* My eyes burned. *I ain't letting this fucker beat my ass.*

◆

Paul, Georgie, and five other kids came down to the wrestling room after summer school let out. Brother called Paul's house and talked with his mom and she agreed to let him spar. Brother made him a mouthpiece and taught him some basics, and the next thing you know, we squared up in the red room. The long rectangular lamps rigged into the white concrete ceiling glowed down on us. The thick black padding of our headgear shrouded our faces in deep shadows. *Holy fuck man, Joe, you're about to spar!* I heaved for breath. *How the hell am I already tired? Just do what Brother taught you.* Juan and the other kids high-fived and grinned eagerly.

"Brother Alex," Georgie asked respectfully, "May I?"

"Go ahead, Georgie," Brother agreed impatiently.

"Ladies and Gentlemen thank you for joining us this afternoon, we have a special attraction sparring session. In this corner..." He motioned to Paul. "...representing Berwyn, Illinois, we have Puny-Armed Paulie!"

The guys giggled and clapped.

"And in this corner, representing the Edgewater neighborhood of our fair city, we have Joey 'The Supernova' Walsh!"

They cheered again.

Georgie clinched his fists closed his eyes and arched his back reeking his face into the light. "Let's get ready to Rumble!!!!" The kids hooted and hollered. *Everybody from Lil Beebee from the Dead End Docks to Georgie the Greek out in Westchester wants to be Michael Fucking Buffer. But Georgie is a bit of a performer...might have a shot at it.*

Brother brought us up close to each other and instructed us, "No hitting below the belt or behind the head. When I say break, break, when I say fight, protect yourselves."

Paul grinned at me confidently. Some kind of wire gleamed in his yellowish teeth as he stepped backward and put his little mouthpiece in. *How could you be so fucking sure of yourself, motherfucker? All's I feel is absolute fucking terror.* The particles of fear swirled in my back into a spiraling storm.

Brother shouted: "FIGHT!"

Paul bounced forward and jabbed at me. I knocked his jab down, then fired one back. It popped his head. He sneered as his friends laughed. He glared at them and he came at me wildly, throwing loopy punches. I stepped back and threw a one-two. Both smashed him in the teeth. He stumbled 'n seethed angrily through his mouth guard. Then he rushed at me lurching back with his chin high. His eyes trembled as he swung for the fences. I took some of the shots on my guard. They knocked me sideways. *Shit, he's strong!* Fear flooded into my chest. These particles ignited in my back as I threw a vicious one-two that caught him clean in the head and discombobulated him. His hands flew up at his sides for balance—his eyes wide and blinking. As he wobbled around I slide-stepped in and caught him with another mean jab on the chin. He spun away and jogged across the red room.

"Don't turn your back!" Brother yelled at him.

He cowered, crouching down and put both his black-gloved fists on the red mat. Did I get him? He spit out his bloody clear mouthguard.

"My retainer! He broke my retainer!"

The other kids moved in to look at the damage. It took a while trying to get the bloody broken retainer out.

"Damn," Georgie said. "He fucking molly-whopped you, Paulie!"

"Language!" Brother sneered at Georgie as he bent down to help Paul. "He had the balls to fight, leave him be."

Well, needless to say that was the end of fucking sparring for the day.

As I rode the Mannheim bus home through the forest preserves I floated in a vague fog of pride. *I'm a boxer, maybe not a good one, or a really real one, but I'm a boxer 'cause I went all out with a kid my own class, even if it's a beginner class.* My Pace bus passed a long trail cut in the woods. About forty yards in, a young buck stood on the trail, his horns just sprouting out of his skull as he trotted forward curiously, nose down. *Now I gotta go find some kids that're serious about this shit, kids that are fighting matches, to see if I can hang with them, and hopefully maybe even become one of them.* The buck disappeared into a blur of woods.

I came down for the next session all pumped up over what I did with Paul.

"You did pretty good against a Berwyn crybaby," Brother said as I geared up.

"It was fun, Brother."

"Well, maybe we'll get you a fight sometime. One of the park districts, or a show fight somewhere."

"OK!"

"You're gonna have to train for months, and you're gonna have to go around to the gyms and spar a lot of different guys, tough kids from tough parts of the city. It takes a lot to get ready for a fight."

"OK, I'll do it, Brother, whatever it takes."

"Alright then." He reached out and shook my hand and the miserable torture started up again.

♦

I know what you're thinking, boxing probably made me real confident and shit. It didn't.

Brother beat the fucking confidence right out of me with all those punches and slaps. He broke me down and humiliated me, but instead of making me embarrassed, it gave me this pure form of humility. I was scared, but once I got hit I lost all the fear. I lost all the insecurity. I just responded with mean hard punches and tightening my defense. I forgot everything that happened, but when the round ended, I was still standing and I knew I'd landed some blows. Even though I beat myself up about my mistakes, I knew I was getting better. I was getting calmer under fire. I could see the punches come slower. I blocked them easier. I landed cleaner with better balance. But it gave me no confidence at all. It made me fear and respect everyone around me more, and anytime I even felt slightly threatened, my body came alive, ready with positrons swirling through my back and neck, ready to ignite into action in a split second with straight hard punches right on the button. I was never at ease, and this dark rage coursed through me underneath everything, threatening to explode at any moment.

I felt in awe of it. Of the strange cosmic power of it. I tried to slowly gain control of it, to harness it like the accelerator at Fermilab.

Chapter 3: Collider

SUMMER SCHOOL ENDED FOR ME but I kept going to work out with Brother. It was around that time that this Fermilab program I'd gotten into was supposed to start. I didn't know if I was still on for it 'cause I'd lost touch with my physics teacher Mr. Dydecky at Gordon Tech High School. He was part of the program and the one who helped get me accepted. Ma called in and figured it out. I was still on and they were fine with me going.

I told Brother about it. He was OK with it but said he'd have to push back my first fight another two weeks to August.

On the first day, Dad drove way out there into DuPage County. At the gate, they checked for my name and let us through, then we drove down the long road through woods and past a little town. A tall concrete building emerged in the distance. Grassy fields lined either side. Near a fence post, a huge furry brown face stretched its mouth; its big purple tongue reached out to snatch a leaf on a small tree on the other side.

"It's a real buffalo!" I yelled.

"Yeah," Dad said. "They got a small herd."

As we drove in deeper, buffalo emerged all over the field. They trotted along and others ate grass. The calves played merrily. The huge concrete structure loomed over the woods. Two concrete sides curved inward and then went straight up ten stories with glass windows between them. It looks kind of like a funky graffiti H. A long pond sat out front.

Dad dropped me off at the main entrance and I went inside. I peered upward as I entered the revolving door. The whole middle of the building was glass, open; you could see way up. Two trees sat inside, and a fountain bubbled nearby. *Fucking nice digs, Joe.*

I noticed Dydecky near the sign-in table. He grinned when he saw me, his thick bushy black eyebrows twisting happily. I walked over; his chest puffed with pride, his white button-up shirt stretched, and his pens jostled in his pocket protector. A big cool-looking poster of the universe surrounded by absolute darkness stood beside him. It read *Fermilab's*

First Illinois High School Seminar. Dark Matter: A Quest To Understand the Most Abundant and Mysterious Questions of the Universe.

"Joe. You made it." Dydecky jumped up and reached across the table and gripped my shoulders, his big grin still plastered across his face. "You are going to have a lot of fun."

"I hope so, Mr. Dydecky, I'm real grateful you helped me get in. I don't know if I belong with these kids, they look pretty smart."

"No, no, no, you earned it, kiddo. You'll fit right in, you'll see."

Skinny little Scott from Gordon Tech saw me from across the way and gave me a grin and a wave. I waved back.

"I'll see you around, Joe. Good luck," Dydecky said, and shook my hand eagerly.

We checked into our little dorms and they brought us down to an auditorium. Young dweebs from all over the state filled the big steep circular room. This beautiful dirty blonde sat on the other side of the auditorium. Her elegant long nose pointed up at the tip as her green eyes beamed excitedly. *Damn, she's a fucking babe.* Her thin athletic body and perky boobs just about gave me a hard-on. I glanced around at all the dorky kids chatting away about *Star Trek* or whatever the fuck. *Well, competition's low.*

But about half the dweebs were staring at the blonde, too. This one tall pompous-looking dork chatted her up from the row behind hers. *He looks kinda like DiCaprio, but if DiCaprio was playing an arrogant, stuck-up piece of shit.*

After the speeches broke we went into the corridor of the main building. The DiCaprio queef held court with the dirty blonde and a few of the dweebs. He loudly boasted in a falsetto bass: "When we won state in lacrosse, I thought to myself: Brad, live it up, it can't get much better than this. Then Yale accepted me and they came back with the offer of a full scholarship. I'm filthy rich, I don't need it, but what the hell, they say it's good for the ol' resume for when I'm looking to get a doctorate down the line, so why not?"

He noticed me listening, trying to hold in my utter hatred of him, then he threw some extra *oomph* on it.

"Hey, hey, what happened? You get beat up for your lunch money?"

"Whatchu say to me?" I asked.

"You have a black eye," a nerdy kid wearing a red bow tie piped in. "He's making an assumption about how it occurred."

"Naw, I'm a boxer, I get black eyes all the time."

Brad shot his chin upward and grinned pompously and started to say something when I cut him off:

"And I give 'em out too. Anytime you want."

"A threat of violence in a federal institution?" his sidekick guffawed.

Brad shook his head. "Wow. Well, I thought this was a top program. How'd a lowlife like you get in?"

"Program? I'm just here to steal some shit."

The blonde lit up and giggled. Brad winced at her.

"Come on, gentlemen," he said. "There's got to be someone more interesting to converse with."

As they walked away, she stayed, grinning at me. Brad looked back at her and sneered.

"Wanna get high?" she asked.

"Uh-huh."

I followed her out the side door. She pulled a little bowl out of her pocket.

"I think Brad likes you," I said as I exhaled a stream of smoke.

"I think Brad likes himself." She made a jerking motion with her fist near her crotch.

"Haha... You're right." I laughed. "He's a jaggoff!"

She toked and exhaled. "I've known so many pricks like him, they're all exactly the same."

"What's a pretty girl like you doing in a dweeb factory like this?"

"Don't you have someone to punch in the face?"

"I do." I coughed on some smoke. "I do, but today's my off day."

She rolled her eyes. "Maybe I should punch you." She made a fist and cocked it, grinning.

"Go ahead, right on the kisser."

She lifted her fist to my mouth and I caught it and gave her knuckles a peck.

Her eyes lit up in the falling sun that slowly sank into the surrounding forest. *I want to kiss you.* She leaned in towards me.

"I'm Joe."

"Faith," she whispered.

The door opened and we popped away from each other. Professor Tompkins, this prick who gave a speech at Gordon one time, walked out in his powder-blue three-button polo. He sniffed the air with his big nose and gave us a stern disgusted glare with his fake n' bake tan face.

"Are you smoking cigarettes out here?"

"Yes, sorry, we won't do it again," she muttered.

"You better not, missy." He wagged his finger at us.

She grinned and he went back in.

"What an idiot," she said, and bugged her eyes out at me then pushed me softly through the door back inside.

◆

The next day we ended up in a big boardroom. Tompkins came in and walked up to the podium. He whisked his sandy-blond feathered-hair to the side as he gripped the podium. A gold Rolex glimmered on his wrist. *I really hate this motherfucker.* He cleared his throat and began:

"We have some time to kill. I want to put you guys through a mathematic problem-solving puzzle, it was recently used at Argonne to assess and weed out candidates. They gave fifty bright applicants a chance to solve and they only gave them a half hour to finish. No one solved." He glanced at his watch. "We have twenty minutes.

"Four people trying to escape a flood come to a roaring river in the night. They have one torch. There is a narrow bridge stretching over the treacherous river below. The bridge can only hold two people at a time. Without the torch, it'd be too dangerous to cross and they'd fall in. The water is rising and they only have fifteen minutes to get across before the bridge is swept away. They are all of varying capabilities. There's a young fit lacrosse player like Brad here, he can run across the bridge in one minute." Brad grinned as his sidekick snorted and patted his back. "Then there's a guy with some athletic ability but not so much brains like Joe, he can do it in two minutes." The dweebs giggled as my face reddened. *You cocksucker.* "Then there's a pretty young lady, but she's not so sure of herself. She's scared, a damsel in distress, like Faith here." Faith scowled at him. "She will take five minutes. There is one more and he is very portly and has two left feet like Ted over there." Ted patted the yellow striped shirt snug against his big belly. "He will take eight minutes to cross the bridge. The question is, can they all get across before the bridge is swept away? Now for our less able minds in the group." He looked at me. "Someone will have to bring the torch back for each trip across."

I started scribbling notes in my spiral-bound notebook. If it's so hard then it's got to be the least intuitive solution. I started working on it in that mindset, bringing the five and eight over first. As I worked two kids stepped to Tompkins excitedly and tried to solve. It felt like a gut punch, all my hopes to solve deflated. *They won already?! Damn, these kids are smart. Who were you kidding, you idiot.* But Tompkins looked at their notes, shook his head, and sent them back with a dismissive wave. It sent a rush through my arms as I picked up my pencil and reworked the equation. *I never competed scholastically before. This is fuckin nerve-racking!* It thrilled and daunted me. Once I thought I had it and started to go up but then looked again. The math was wrong, it took seventeen minutes to cross the bridge. Faith and I swooshed past in the raging waters to our inevitable death. I sat down. Tompkins gave me a pitiful laugh. Brad and his little nerd clan giggled along with him.

Finally I figured it out. I double-checked it. I was fuckin right, it's the least intuitive solution. The first thing you had to do was take the one and two across and then come back with the one and then send the two slowest across together because they canceled each other out. *Send the two back for the one. Or maybe not, maybe just leave fucking Brad over there all by his bitch-ass-self.*

I walked up to Tompkins and handed him my paper. He glanced at his watch and rolled his eyes. Then he looked it over. He jolted stiff staring at the solution. He glared at me, then went through the problem again and grimaced.

He looked up at the room.

"Times up, guys" he said, crumpling my paper up and tossing it in the garbage.

What the fuck?

"Well, none of you would have gotten the job."

"Wait, but I had it." *Motherfucker, I did!*

"No, you didn't, go sit down."

"I had it right!" I pleaded with my hands. *I can't believe this, you fucking prick.*

Dydecky entered the room.

"What's going on fellas, and…" He scratched his chin. "…gal? I guess would be the right phrase." He glanced at Faith. She giggled.

"We're doing the Argonne problem!" the kids yelled urgently. "The problem they used at Argonne."

"Did anyone solve?"

"Naw, nope, almost." The kids answered.

"I solved it," I said, walking back to my seat.

"Joe." He hiked his bushy black eyebrows at me. "You solved it?"

"No, he didn't." Tompkins shook his head in disgust.

Dydecky put his hand up, shushing Tompkins. "How'd you solve?" he asked me as he stepped to the whiteboard and grabbed a green marker.

"First Brad and me go over."

"The one and the two?"

"Yeah. Then Brad brings the torch back."

"OK, then what?"

"Then slowpoke Faith and tubby Ted go over together."

"Hey," Faith said, and blushed; Ted chuckled as his rolls jostled.

"The five and the eight, uh-huh."

"Then there's a problem, I could take the torch back to get Brad, but I'd rather leave his ass over there on the other side."

The room erupted into laughter as Brad looked around surprised by the response. Dydecky scowled at me and put his hands on his hips.

"Finish, Joe."

"I go over, get Brad, bring him across, and he gets to go to Yale and live happily ever after."

Dydecky glared at Tompkins and shook his head, then placed the marker on the tray and turned to the room.

"Everyone," he said, then raised his palm toward me. "Joe has solved correctly."

They clapped and cheered, and some of the nerds got up and patted me on the back. Faith mouthed: "How the fuck did you do that?" and grinned. *I have no fucking idea,* I shrugged.

"Bravo, Joe… Now, are you guys ready to see the accelerator?"

"Yeah!!!" We clamored out of the door.

"Slowpoke!?" Faith ran up to me grimacing real cute-like. She squeezed my hand and gave me a big kiss on the cheek and hopped away with the rest of them.

Scott walked up to me and handed me a scribbled-on piece of paper. The solution appeared at the bottom.

"You got it too, how'd you do it?"

"There were three of us and we just ran through as many possibilities as we could and found it."

"Yeah right, you were sitting by yourself." We walked into the hallway.

"I know, these kids give me the creeps."

"There's some weirdos here, that's for sure."

"So you and blondie, huh?" He hiked his eyebrows.

"Yeah, she's a damn fox, I can't fucking believe my luck."

"Well, Joe, I knew some stuff happened and you had to leave school but I wanted you to know I was always rooting for you."

"Thanks, Scott."

"Pretty crazy we both made it, huh?"

"Yep."

"Let's go see this damn accelerator, I can't fucking believe I'm here!" I said as an old, white-haired physicist walked past and gave me a surprised look. I gave a forced smile and said sorry.

We headed down to catch up with the group and followed them into the Collider Detector area. The enormous intricate detector filled the huge cube of a room. *Fuck, it's so much bigger than I imagined!* The detector sat open in a series of half circles. Big blue magnets lined the inner rim with white contraptions wired in between. The big reddish-orange steel frame encircled the inner ring. An elaborate nest of white, red, and baby-blue wires ran in every direction. Power sources, computers, instruments— my eyes raced around. *It's like the inner workings of a brain. Target the mind and the body shall fall.* I giggled. A physicist in a white hard hat stood at the base with a clipboard. He peered up at the instruments that loomed above like an enormous opened-up spaceship. A young female Asian physicist stood inside the open detector; she cranked a socket wrench on one of the magnets. A tall stepladder sat nearby but she stood on a platform inside the detector itself. *It'd be nuts to actually stand inside that fucking thing.* She seemed microscopic in comparison to the elaborate contraption. *Well, this is it, Joe, one of humanity's greatest creations. Who let you in here, fucker?* I giggled. Faith walked up beside me and slid her soft hand into mine. She looked at me. Her green eyes sparkled as her beautiful face spread into a smile.

"What do you think?" she asked.

"It's incredible."

We followed our group into the concrete accelerator tunnel, holding hands. A blue rectangle-shaped line of magnets lined the tunnel wall. A red row of magnets with square yellow connectors spread across the floor. Above the magnets, two gray ducts with red fasteners ran along the wall near the ceiling. *Positrons and electrons run through these things at damn near the speed of light. How the hell did they figure out how to do this crazy shit?* Every few hundred feet it seemed to change. Metal cooling structures sat along the floor. We let the group get out ahead of us. Then it was just us in the loop—no one in sight before us or behind us. I took her by her hands and started to spin with her slowly.

"What are you doing?"

"We're particles," I told her. "I'm an electron. And you're a positron."

"And what are we going to do?"

"Collide, of course."

I stopped spinning her and pulled her close in my arms and she tilted her head and closed her eyes and I leaned in and *bam* our lips collided and the sparks flew through my mind at light speed.

"Total annihilation," she whispered as she ground herself against me warm and firm.

As we finished our tour of the accelerator Dydecky and a little tubby guy with a big white beard and long curly hair walked up to me.

"This is him? The kid with the black eye?"

"This is him, Dr. Erickson, he's a boxer."

"A boxer?" He looked at me urgently. "Don't you know that'll knock all your brain cells out?"

"Yeah." I shrugged.

"He says you're a bright kid. Why do you want to box?"

"I don't know, I love it."

"Oh well. If you love something there's nothing you can do about it, right? You just have to keep pursuing it."

"Yeah." I grinned.

"Well, come with me. I want to show you something, tough guy."

We walked down the long hall and descended some steps.

"Have you heard of a particle called a neutrino?" he asked.

"I think I read about them," I replied.

"Well, neutrinos are very interesting fundamental particles. They're what make up the parts of an atom, they're what make up electrons and nuclei. CERN's accelerator is beginning to outpace us, and that's fine, but we have a new project we're working on." He walked us into a big room full of cluttered desks. *Fucking physicists are messy motherfuckers.* A huge structural drawing of the accelerator and a launch site spread along the far wall on a big long sheet of paper. *What the fuck is this?* Another architectural drawing showed a tunnel into the ground and a second structure. "We're going to shoot neutrinos from our accelerator all the way to Minnesota. We'll have a target there deep underground." He walked up and tapped the underground structure. "We believe we can find out some things about dark matter."

"Dark matter? On the particle level?"

"It's exciting, I know. It will give us a key to a great mystery of existence."

"Unbelievable."

"I thought you'd like this, Joe," Dydecky piped in.

"So, are you telling me that dark matter is made of neutrinos?"

"Well, it must be, right?" Erickson asked. "It has mass and we can detect its gravity, therefore it must be made of neutrinos. But we need to prove this, and so we will be shooting billions of neutrinos through one thousand miles of bedrock in hopes to hit the target. If we are successful, we will come to better understand dark matter on the particle level."

"This is amazing!" I said. "When does it start?"

"Well, we're still finalizing the proposal." He pointed at the blueprint. "These things take years. But with luck, we'll begin construction in three years." He patted me on the shoulder and glanced at Dydecky. "You were right, I like him." Erickson smacked Dydecky on the back, then looked back at me. "Who knows, maybe you'll be working with us one day."

"Yeah right!" I burst into laughter. "Good one, Doctor Erickson."

"What exactly is funny about that?" Erickson turned sober and cold. He grew closer to me, peering into my eyes. His blue eyes trembled and his long white puffy hair suddenly seemed like a lion's mane. "You solved the Torch and Bridge." A tinge of anger trembled in his voice. "I know some of the most brilliant minds in physics who failed it." He shook his head and his face softened. "I am always looking for unique and unusual minds. I have a collection of them. They are some of my dearest colleagues. I bring in physicists from all over the world into the projects I lead. But what I've found is that even when you bring a Chinese, Indian, or African physicist in, he is often from the same socioeconomic background as most physicists. There is a term called a Subaltern. It is a person who has unique challenges in their society. I understand that you have experienced a great deal of suffering in your young life." He looked at me ponderously and reached out and tenderly squeezed my shoulder with his coarse fingers. "These traumas reshape the mind in surprising ways we are only beginning to understand. You solved the Torch and Bridge in twenty minutes, then one of my team members tried to hide your answer, and you stood up to him and solved it from memory and even made jokes in your solution." He glared at me with a mixture of anger and pride flexing in his brow. "Yours is the type of mind I need in my teams. Because if your teenage mind is strong enough to stand up to the Tompkinses of the world..." (He reached out his index finger and tapped it into my solar plexus.) "...then maybe you would stand up to me when I needed it most." He poked his own flabby chest viciously.

Erickson turned to walk away and continued to speak. "I will be watching your career closely. Do not give up on physics, Joe, don't you dare." He pointed his finger upward and wagged it as he disappeared down the hall.

"Who the hell is Erickson?"

Dydecky motioned for me to sit at one of the cluttered desks with him. It was full of papers, scribbled equations, and a half-drunk cup of black coffee. I looked at the cup: *Man, I want to take a sip*. But the idea of really doing it fucking grossed me out.

"Erickson is a very important physicist. He was one of the physicists named on a group Nobel Prize in 1985. Most people say there should have been far fewer names in the group, and all of them say Erickson's would have been amongst the few at the very top of the list. But he's that way, he wanted everyone to get their due credit. He tried to get the cleaning lady included in the group. They caught him and he explained that they'd make these terrible messes: papers, coffee mugs, plates of half-eaten food, cigarette butts, overflowing ashtrays." (He pointed to an ashtray on an adjacent desk.) "And when they came back in the next day the facility was spotless. He said it was like she knew which papers to throw away and which to keep. He's a character, isn't he?"

"He's cool!" We got up and headed back to join the group. *Joe, what the fuck, you just met a Nobel Prize–winning physicist, un-fucking real. This is like a dream come true.* I glanced back at the messy room with the blueprint at the far wall. *This is the real thing.* Tears welled up in my eyes.

"Dydecky, thanks, man."

"Joe, you wouldn't be here if you didn't belong," he said and grinned at me.

If you fucking say so.

◆

That night Faith snuck into my dorm room and we made out and screwed around and after she lay with her head on my chest.

"Now that was total annihilation," I confirmed.

"Shut up!" She giggled. "So you're really into physics, huh?"

"Yeah, I love this shit," I said excitedly. "It's all I can think about sometimes. You?"

"Not really. My parents want me to go to the University of Chicago, and a lot of the professors do research here. But I don't want to be a physicist."

"What do you want to be?"

"I don't know, a lawyer or a doctor, something like that. You want to be a physicist?"

"Yeah, I'd kill to work out here."

"Well, then maybe one day you will."

"That'd be dope."

I sighed, thinking about Hyacinth back in the old neighborhood and how I fucked it all up. *Well, here we go again.* Faith lived two towns over from La Grange, in Riverside. *You can ride your frickin' bike over to see her.* I was thinking how I didn't even have any friends out there when she squeezed my hand. *I guess you got one now. Ask her, you fucking pussy.*

"Would you be my girl?"

She nodded yes and kissed me on the cheek.

◆

We played around with the accelerator for a few days, saw some awesome presentations on dark matter, and brushed shoulders with some of the top physicists in the world. On the last day they had us write a reflection on dark matter and our own little theory of what we thought it was. I wrote:

Everything in existence is in tension, the universe the galaxies the solar systems the planets right down to the insides of our minds. The fact that the universe exists and has shape, in fact an evolving shape, seems to say that it needs something to be in tension with, a kind of non existence with an equal force that is within the universe. Dark matter could be a manifestation of that force that non existence universe or a Dark Universe which can squeeze existence back into non existence. I believe that dark matter is the answer to the shape of the universe, its origins and its destiny.

We all packed up and headed out front. Dydecky gave me a big hug and his card. "Call or write whenever you need me, Joe. Good work."

"Thanks, Dydecky."

I took a deep breath and stood out in front of the two tall structures leaning in on one another. Faith gave me a peck on the cheek and got in her parents' SUV. She made the phone symbol with her hand and put it to her ear and mouthed: "Call me tonight." I grinned. I glanced over and Brad gave me a dismissive sneer and put the phone up to his ear and wagged his head obnoxiously. I went to put the phone up to my ear, then just flicked him off.

I turned to look up at the tall building. The two curved structures with the glass seeming to web it together. It stood back, lit by the darkening sky fading bluish-black. Sad electrons swirled through my stomach. *Hope I see the inside of this crazy fuckin place again someday. This is the coolest shit I ever been part of. Yeah right, why the hell would they ever let a kid like you in here again? This shit was once in a lifetime.* I sighed as Dad began to roll up the long driveway in his dirty construction truck full of bins and tools and blueprints. *You'll be lucky if you end up a construction worker and not some real fuckup like Pat, locked up in the pen or some shit. Locked in a little cell far away with nobody that loves you around, just a buncha violent nutcases to keep you company.* I sighed. *No, Joe, you ain't going in there, and plus he'll be home soon. Just a few more months.* Dad pulled up with a prideful grin under his white mustache. *Well, at least you made him smile.*

Chapter 4: Rose

MY SISTER ROSE WAS ALL LOVE. She was always a sweet sister to me and she was sweet to all of us, really: siblings, parents, cousins, nieces and nephews, uncles, and aunts, it didn't matter. She was the heart of the family in a lot of ways. When we were little Rosie'd constantly get the giggles and she'd get this delighted squeal that'd fill the room with a warm joy and put me in a playful craze. My sister Jan was different. She was a fireball, moody and at times wicked, but often just witty. Dad loved them a lot but didn't know how to handle them; he only knew how to handle boys, and that to settle down boys you threatened and hit them. With Jan and Rose when they were getting too rowdy and weren't listening, he'd call them over and bonk their heads together. And they'd run off crying, and Ma would scream at Dad, and he'd just laugh. Be careful with your daughters—don't show them a man who loves them can hit them or hurt them physically. It teaches a bad lesson.

Rose got mixed up with some real knuckleheads; they were the black version of Dad, I guess. They were tough and bad boys. Samson, her ex, was a high-ranking GD from the Jungle. He hit her and she hit back and it was a messy passionate relationship, toxic and horrible, full of highs and lows. Rose got sucked into it like a vortex into another dimension. It was terrible; there was nothing any of us could do to save her. I'd stabbed Samson that one time, but even that didn't do much. Rose was so full of love and joy it was hard to see her stuck in that terrible relationship. Samson was literally the exact wrong person for her, like they were positrons and electrons, but opposites do attract; they need each other to know they fully exist. Rose was free now—well almost free. She just had to get out of that hospital bed and off those machines, so she could come home and take her place as the heart of the family again.

As Dad and I rolled past the tall mansions nestled between the pretty green trees on LaGrange Road on the way home from the Fermilab summer program, he looked over at me and grinned.

"We got a surprise for you," Dad said as we pulled into the full driveway.

Everybody's here. What the hell? "Is it somebody's birthday?"

"Close."

I walked into the kitchen. Rose slouched at the dinner table, pale and thin. Her light brown face grinned as everybody chatted around her. *Rose.* The wires fell to my feet. My eyes burned so bad. My breath huffed and puffed as I tried not to cry. *She's home.* I walked up to her.

"Hey Joseph!" she said faintly.

"Rosie." I hugged her real hard. "Welcome home, Rosie."

She hugged me back. "How was your Fermilab thing?"

"It was fun as hell," I said, and sat down beside her. "How do you feel?"

"A lot better…" She held in some tears. "I heard you started boxing."

"Yep."

"Are you gonna have a fight with the lights and the ring card girls and everything?"

"I think so."

"I want to see that! I'm gonna be yelling from the front row, 'Go Joseph!'"

"Alright, I'm gonna fight a real boxing match and I'm gonna win it for you, okay?"

"A boxer and a physicist, what are you, some kinda wannabe Renaissance man?" my brother Rich chided me, his big gnarly reddish-black beard bobbing around as he laughed.

Meanwhile Blake threw his fists up like the Fighting Irish mascot; he was a seasoned cop now in Humboldt Park, and his clean-cut look reminded me of Tom Cruise in that *Far and Away* movie. "E equals MC squared, ya mothafooka!" he said, his pointy nose sticking up.

We laughed as Ma cut up some Bakers Square apple pie. *Everybody's so happy.* I took a big bite of the sweet pie. *Almost a whole family again. Just gotta get Pat home.*

"So Rosie," Rich said. "I hate to be the one to bring this up. You gonna stop hanging out with dirtbags now?"

"Shut the hell up, Rich!" Jan scolded him.

"Seriously, we're out in the suburbs now! Come on, make some friends out here and things might really turn around for all of us." Rich implored.

"It's true, Rosie," I said. "It's better out here, people are nicer. There's less problems."

"Well, that's good."

"No more of the gangbanger crap," Blake piped in.

"Exactly," Rich said.

"Shut your stupid mouths!" Jan yelled, hugging her pregnant belly as she stood behind Rose. "She's been through hell and all you want to do is blame her for hanging out with the wrong people?" She glared at Rich. "Have some common decency, fer Christ's sake! 'Rose, welcome home, I love you.' It's that simple!"

"I love her, that's why I'm bringing this up!" Rich whined.

"Hey, aye!" Dad yelled, and glared at Rich from the end of the table. "This is a celebration. Don't bring up any of that bullshit from the old neighborhood. I don't want to hear none of that crap!" Dad seethed.

Rose blinked back tears as she scooped up some pie with her fork.

I rubbed her back and leaned in. "It's gonna be better out here, Rose," I whispered. "You'll see."

Everything settled down as the nieces and nephews rambled around. Ma got everyone's attention, "A toast," she said, raising her glass under the little chandelier. "To Rosie coming home and Joe graduating from the Fermilab program, and to a new life for the Walshes in the suburbs."

"Here, here..." We all raised our glasses full of sparkling white grape juice and clinked them under the chandelier light. We grinned, looking into each other's eyes as circular flickers of light swirled through our faces and hands. I took a sip of the sweet bubbling juice. *It's like we escaped into onea them fancy movies.*

◆

Later that night I was lying in bed drifting off to sleep when Jan and Rose started arguing in the next room. *You two going at it already?*

Rosie sobbed. "I thought the scar would go away!" she yelled through tears. "No one is ever going to love me like this."

"That's not true, damnit! Stop saying that!" Jan scolded. "Joe! Come in here please."

I got up and went over to their door and looked in her nice little room with the big window above her bed. Rose lay in her bed sniffling, with Jan standing over her. The little brown metal lamp on her bedside table glowed orangish-yellow like the streetlight outside our house in the city. *Be gentle.* What the hell is going on? The essence of Da seemed to permeate the room in a warm glow.

"Come here." Jan reached her hand towards me.

"What's up, Rosie?" I asked.

"You have to help me." Jan took my hand and squeezed it with her small strong fingers. "Show him, Rose."

"Noooo!"

"Damnit, Rosie, show him! He's your flipping brother!" Jan pulled back the covers. Tears slid down Rose's face as her body throbbed and she squirmed as Jan raised the blue plaid pajama shirt, revealing her creamy brown skin.

"No! No, no, no!"

A two-inch-wide dark purple scar ran from the waist of her pajama pants up the center of her stomach past her belly button. The barbed hook scratched and dug through my innards. I closed my eyes. *What'd you do to her?*

"Rosie, I'm so sorry," I told her as tears singed my eyes. I reached out with my other hand and took Rose by her cool hand and stood there still holding Jan's hand.

"Is it, is it ugly?" Rose asked me.

"No, Rosie! Nothing about you is ugly."

"See?" Jan urged.

"It's just a scar, Rosie. It just means you lived. It means you survived this thing."

"Do you think boys will still like me?"

"Rosie," I sighed. "You are beautiful, don't worry about that. But way more important than that, you are a beautiful person inside where it counts."

"You think so?" She grinned, her voice twisting inside the sadness to a little peak of joy. "Would you ever be with someone who looked like this?"

"Rosie... I'd rather be with somebody who lived than somebody who ain't never lived."

"Really?"

"Plus scars are cool." I grinned wickedly. "I wish I had a big ol' scar!"

"You can have it." She giggled. "It's different for boys."

"All that scar means is you made it home." I squeezed her hand. "We still have you, Rosie. I love that stupid scar. It's part of you."

"I don't want it."

"I know but you'll see, you're gonna find a good person that's gonna love you for the rest of your life, scar and all."

"You really think so, Joseph?"

"I know it." I squeezed her hand. "I promise."

She smiled.

"Thank you," Jan whispered and spliced her fingers through mine.

"I love you, all right?" I said.

"I love you too," Rosie replied softly, the tears pooling and absorbing the glow of the lamp light.

◆

Becoming a real boxer ain't easy. There's more to it than just punching a bag or even sparring a few times with beginners. You gotta go to real gyms and spar hard with fighters who are competing. You gotta join the community, the clique, ya know? Like, "Aye my guy needs some work, he's in the finals of this tournament, can you come over and mimic this guy? Or give him movement, or come forward on him and dig to the body?" Then when you need it, they return the favor. You gotta learn the lingo. Like, a slip. A slip can be if your feet slip on the canvas, sure, but when a real boxing guy says, "He slipped my jab," he means the boxer dodged the jab at the last second, so the punch slipped past the boxer's head. Got it?

Becoming a complete fighter is the quest, to complete the atomic structure, to become a whole and defined particle. It's like putting together a hundred-thousand-piece puzzle; it takes many tiny additions, many perspectives. You might see something in somebody else sparring—some feint, some angle on a jab that becomes this important missing piece in your arsenal, your defense, and maybe even your understanding of how to combine the two to unify them into that whole atomic structure. Back then, I was a nearly clean slate other than the solid jab, high guard, and ferocity Brother Alex equipped me with. I was a brand-new firm sponge trying to soak up every drop. That's how you gotta be if you're ever gonna make it as a fighter, 'cause if you come to fight in this ring with a bunch of holes in your puzzle, real fighters will annihilate you in a few seconds, and you'll deserve it. Matter of fact they'd be doing you a disservice if they didn't discombobulate you. Because you're disrespecting the art. Don't come into this ring unless you're ready, motherfucker. This ain't no game. It's gonna get hard in there, harder than anything you ever felt before. So you better have something worth fighting for way deep down inside you, 'cause these fighters will eviscerate you if you don't. 'Cause they all got something they're fighting for that's bigger than them and bigger than you.

A lover and a fighter, right? That's what all us guys believe we are anyway. I was putting in work on both fronts. I started dating Faith pretty damn seriously. She was hot, she was smart, and she liked me. We did a lot of shit together. We went to the movies, bowled, went for walks, rented movies, smoked weed and drank, screwed around, banged, made about as close to love as two teenagers can muster, and spent all our free time together.

I went straight back to boxing too. Thundered right back into shape. In early August, Brother said it was time that I got some real sparring. So he took me to a show fight at the Carlisle just to watch and ask around for guys my weight to spar with. Rose'd been a little sad and worn down. I asked her if she wanted to come with and she perked up. Brother picked us up and we headed over.

They'd set the ring up in the center of the big banquet hall. A huge bright glass chandelier hung above the center of the red-roped black canvas ring. They made us stay out in the entrance hall. The black and Latino fighters warmed up in the hallway as the mostly white banquet attendees sat at round tables covered by white tablecloths, eating and drinking.

We stood near the doorway chatting. A slick black fighter in shiny red trunks, red knee-high socks, and black shoes with red tassels cracked mitts and stepped in circles with his thin old black trainer, who called for lead rights in a deep raspy voice.

"Come on now, Bean! Let it go!" Bean shot the right in like an arrow, then lurched backward trying to evade his trainer's slaps with the mitts. His eyes gleamed, framed by his shiny red headgear. His jersey read *Simons Park* across the back.

"Joseph, this is great! Are you really gonna fight with kids like this guy?" Rose asked.

I nervously shrugged.

"Well, Rose," Brother said. "Some of these kids are very experienced. Joe has to start with beginners like him. But we need him to spar with better fighters so he can learn."

"You're gonna spar with that guy?" She pointed at Bean.

"Maybe." I shrugged nervously. *Bean'd kick my ass!*

The lights fell, and the room grew tense. A real announcer in a tuxedo stood with a cordless mic in the center of the ring to emcee the introduction.

"You really gonna fight in a ring like this?" Rose asked, wide-eyed.

"Yeah!" I shrugged. "I don't know!"

"I want to fight like that!" She put up her dukes as I giggled.

"Oh no, I remember when you slapped Samson, you got power!" I said as she muffed my head sideways.

We giggled as the bell rang and they came out hands high and feinting at each other. I smiled watching Rose watch the fight. *First time she's looked happy in week.*

I imagined myself in the ring as Bean struggled with a short stubby Mexican who glued himself to Bean's chest. Bean stabbed a lead right into the Mexican's forehead. The Mexican thudded a left hook to his chest. *Fuck, could I take those shots? Can I hang with these badass fucking kids from the West and South Side? Both those kids'd beat my ass.*

"Tough kids, huh?" Brother asked. "You sure you want this, pretty boy? You aren't in La Grange anymore Joey-boy..."

My eyes singed with embarrassment. *You asked for it.*

"Yeah, Brother, I do..." I whined.

Rose nudged me. "Come on, Joe. You can do it!" she said and pantomimed a boxer. "You're gonna be like Rocky in there."

"Yo Adrian!!!" I yelled.

The Simons Park District in Humboldt Park swept all their first three fights. Then this short, compact bantamweight in the white Simons jersey took on a kid they announced as the reigning national champion of Canada. He wore an official-looking red uniform with a red-and-white Canadian flag across the chest and another one on his headgear. The first minute, the Canadian kid shot almost mechanical five-punch combinations that sprang the Simons kid's head back.

"*Vamos*, José!" one of the Simons Park kids screamed from the back of the room.

José awoke and surged forward, bobbing under the Canadian's shots and springing up with his own. The crowd roared as he battered the Canadian to the ropes. Then he dipped low and swung a tremendous overhand right like he was pitching a baseball. It cracked downward into the Canadian's jaw and sent him tumbling forward jelly-legged. *Holy shit! Who is this fucking kid!?* The suits went nuts as the ref counted in the Canadian kid's face. José ran to a neutral corner.

"Why's he counting for him?" I asked Brother.

"It's a standing eight count they use when a kid is dazed to see if he can continue," Brother replied.

The ref finished the count and asked the Canadian to walk to him. He tried to step forward but wobbled sideways. The referee waved his hand over the Canadian's head and hugged him.

"He knocked him out!" Rose yelled.

"What the hell is that?"

"They stopped the fight," Brother said. "That little Puerto Rican kid is good."

"So, it's a knockout?"

"Yeah, he's done, fight's over. RSC, Referee Stops Contest."

After they announced José as the winner, José and his team came barreling through the hallway.

"They thought they was gonna come down here and fuck us up? Hahaha..." The pudgy bald-headed coach from Simons boasted in a thick Puerto Rican accent as he walked past us.

"Good fight!" I said.

"Nice one!" Brother called after them.

"Good fight?" The Simons coach stopped and looked at me like I was crazy. "That wasn't no fight! That was a fuckin asswhoopin!" he guffawed. "*Hijo de puta!*"

As they de-geared José in the little office in the corner, Brother and I walked in.

"This kid needs some sparring, can he come over to your gym for some work?" Brother asked.

"This kid? The whiteboy? He wants to spar?"

Brother nudged me.

"Yeah, I really want to spar with you guys."

"OK but aye, we spar hard, OK," he said, unwinding the tape on José's hand. "You see what my kids can do."

"He's a beginner," Brother said, "but he wants the work. We're looking to get him his first fight soon."

"OK, we spar Tuesday and Thursday, 5 PM." He reached his hand out. "I'm Chupi."

"I'm Brother Alex, this is Joe." We shook his hand. And that was it. I was in.

As we headed out Rosie messed with me. "I want to see you fight but just don't go get RSC'd, Joe!"

"Come on, Rosie, I can take a punch," I said trying to assure myself. *Fucking hope I can, anyways.*

◆

I sat down the next morning sipping some coffee with Rosie on the enclosed back porch. The big, grassy yard splayed out before us. Sparrows chirped in the tree branches. The neighbors' fluffy gray cat tiptoed daintily along the top bar of the chain-link fence between our back yards as Kelly, our white-and-brown English Setter, barked and nipped at her.

"My baby brother the boxer. So, you really gonna spar with those Simons Park guys, Joseph?" Rose asked.

"Yeah."

"You nervous?" Rose admonished me. "Don't be, you're good! You'll do fine."

"If you say so, Rosie," I said and took a sip. "How are you?"

"I'm so happy! I'm so happy to be out of that godforsaken hospital."

"Was it really bad in there?"

"It was so hard, Joseph, I hate hospitals. I never want to go back. I kept getting new roommates, people that got shot too. It was nice because we had someone to talk with. But they kept going home. I was happy for them but I kept wondering when am I coming home? Why can't I go home?"

"It was the .25. It bounced around."

"Yes, a girl got shot in the chest with a .45. She got out in a week! I cried so bad that day. The whole day. I couldn't stop crying."

"They said you died in the hospital, is that true?"

"Yes," she said and took a sip of her coffee.

"Do you remember it?"

"Yeah, it was just nothing. Death is nothing, Joseph. It's just a big nothing."

I sighed and took a sip. *Fuck. I thought she would have seen Da or something.*

"There's nothing poetic, there's no light, there's just nothing."

"Rosie, I wanted to tell you, I'm sorry for everything that happened with Samson and Mickey and Ryan."

"What, wait. Ryan? I know Mickey shot us, but Ryan?"

"Ryan got in the car that night."

"Really?"

"I almost did too. Dad grabbed me before I could."

She hyperventilated. "'Cause they shot Angel."

"I'm sorry, Rose."

"They just shot so many times, Joe. It was so horrible, the pain. The pain of that, my god. It burns. I wanted to die."

"I'm sorry for all of it."

"Did Samson really shoot Angel?"

"Yeah, well, he, he was one of like three dudes that shot, it might not 'a been him."

"He shot at you?"

"Yeah, he looked me right in the eyes and smiled."

"How could you, Samson?" She closed her eyes and gripped her temple. "My little brother?!"

I reached out and held her shoulder.

"I'm just, I'm sorry for everything that happened that night, I wish, I wish I could take it all back."

"It's not your fault, Joseph, I shouldn'ta been over there that night," she said, sniffling. "I was looking for a gun to shoot Samson."

"Really?"

"'Cause he hit me. I just hated him and loved him so much." She started to cry. "He killed someone. He's in county fighting a murder case."

"I'm sorry, Rose."

"It's OK, he was gonna get himself killed or go to prison sooner or later." She got up, holding her stomach. "I'm not feeling good, Joe. I'm gonna lay down."

"OK, I didn't mean to upset you."

"It's alright, I'm fine," she said as she headed up to her room.

The next day Ma took Rose to LaGrange Memorial because of the fatigue. They sent her home. She came into the house woozy and went upstairs to the bathroom. When she got up to flush, she glanced at the toilet bowl. All the water'd turned dark red.

Ma called a nurse friend of hers and she told her to bring her to Loyola. They rushed her to the emergency room. The doctors found massive internal bleeding. She was bleeding to death right in front of us and none of us could see it.

They did emergency surgery. When Rose came to after surgery and found out she was stuck in the hospital again with no release date in sight, it devastated her. She wanted to die. She slit her wrists with the knife from her dinner tray and they put her on suicide watch. We tried to cheer her up but she didn't want to see any of us. She just wanted to be alone.

◆

Early the next week Brother picked me up in his messy Chevy and drove me to Simons Park in Humboldt Park on the West Side. We cruised through Independence Boulevard. *Back in the hood, huh?* We passed a brick corner store with a dozen black teenagers standing outside in droopy pants and big white T-shirts. *Looks like the North Pole, except ten times bigger.* Nerves coursed through my shoulders. *This is gonna be some tough-ass shit.* We crossed over into Humboldt Park. The corners flipped like a switch to Latinos. The Simons Park field house stood long and dark-bricked on a quiet side street. A few pops rang out in the distance as we walked into the front doors.

"Those are just fireworks," Brother assured me.

Fireworks my ass, Brother, I'd say a .22. I giggled. *Real funny, Joe. Them bullets might a taken someone's life. Put 'em in the hospital for months. Maybe it was a .25.* The wires squeezed in my chest. My energy dropped through my feet like a cannonball of dark matter. *What the fuck are you doing here?* I didn't even want to spar. We took the stairwell down and found the gym in the musty, dark basement.

We entered a small, low-ceilinged room. It smelled like sweat with a little hint of sewer. Chupi greeted us from a wooden bench. The blue floor ring filled the whole room except for a narrow aisle near the lockers. A skinny old dark-skinned black man named Johnny Carter welcomed us with his deep, raspy voice; he was the one that was working with Bean the other night. Later I'd learn Johnny'd fought a long legendary pro career. They'd sent him all over the world. He pulled off some huge upsets before he hung 'em up. He'd spent most of his prime in prison, otherwise he would have become a name you heard of. Now he ran the boxing program at the park and sketched for a local design company. He wore thick eyeglasses and was slowly going blind.

Three of the kids from the show fight wrapped their hands and chatted. Bean, the welterweight, stood about my height with light skin and a little afro. As I spliced my wraps through my fingers, he mumbled with a thick Puerto Rican accent that he won the Chicago Park District Open Division that year. *He looks like he could be Rose and Jan's biological brother. Imagine what Rose's biological brother would think of you. He'd probably want to beat your ass for doing a shitty job.*

José, the kid that'd stopped the Canadian, said he was ranked fifth in the nation for his age. His older cousin Pedro jumped rope in the ring, his potbelly bouncing.

We went to warm up in the mirrors in the adjacent room. José bobbed around swiftly, shadowboxing beside me. His gold chain jangled below his short, buzzed head.

"How old are you?" I asked.

"Thirteen."

"That guy you beat, he was really a national champion of Canada?"

He winked; two diagonal lines appeared carved into his right eyebrow.

"Yeah," Pedro chimed in, sweat beading in his box cut. "He was twenty years old, too."

"Damn!"

We finished warming up and geared up. Brother pulled my headgear on and fastened it. *You don't want to spar these tuff fucking kids. They're gonna fuck you up!* I sighed. *Do it for Rose, you fucking pussy.*

"You ready?"

I nodded.

"Come on in," Bean said as he stood there in a gray sweatsuit, leaning his back against the corner with both his gloves resting along the top ropes.

Shit, you never got in a ring before. How the hell do you do it? I stepped one foot through the middle ropes. Then I tried to bend and slip my head through. My head conked the vertical rope divider and kept me out. *Fuck!* The room burst into chuckles.

"What's dis? This kid! You gonna get knocked out trying to get in the fucking ring?" Chupi quipped as I giggled. I scooted backward with my one leg through the ropes. Then I ducked under and through. As I stood my headgear nicked the rope. It bounced merrily as I stumbled onto the foamy canvas for the first time.

"All right!" Chupi clapped, watching me with his light hazel eyes. "I knew yous could do it!"

What the fuck you doing? You don't even know how to get in a boxing ring, now you're gonna spar hard with these real fighters? Fucking this is stupid. Don't do it. Just get out of the ring. The nerves made the canvas spongier as I teetered around. *It's like a damn trampoline, but soft.*

"OK." Chupi looked at me. "Ready?" He clicked on the bell.

"No!" I shouted.

"OK... OK..." He clicked it off.

"What's the matter?" Brother asked, playing with my headgear.

"I don't want to do it, Brother," I whispered. "I'm scared."

"Joe..." Brother whined, embarrassed. "We came all the way over here for nothing?" He hiked up his eyebrows. "OK." He started to unfasten my headgear.

Why are you doing this? I closed my eyes and saw Rosie crying on her hospital bed, all alone.

"OK, OK." I pushed Brother's hand off my headgear. *If Rosie can get through that, you can do this.*

I looked over at Chupi crouched over the timer. He watched me with his eyes wide, a peculiar grin on his lips.

I nodded to him.

"Alright!" He flipped the switch, then raised his fist triumphantly as the guys laughed. "*Hijo de puta...*"

The electronic bell rang. Bean reached his glove out. We touched gloves. Then he backed up slickly, then bounced on his toes circling me. I followed him clunkily. Bean stopped and barked angrily as he jabbed at me; I partially deflected it. I jabbed back; he parried my punch and moved sideways. Moving forward, I threw a right that caught only air. I stumbled off balance.

Bean moved and feinted. Then he unleashed a six-punch combination on me—angrily barking with each shot. The light punches came from surprising angles. They dazzled me. I fired back. He slipped my jab and popped me again. I dug a body shot and a jab to the chest hard. He came back with a good right cross that sent stars through my vision. I clinched him. *I'm sorry I wasn't a better brother to her, alright?* We broke and reset. *I'm gonna be better.* Hopeful excitement sent me walking into a three-punch combo. *That didn't hurt.* I jabbed him hard. It rocked his head back. *Fuck! I landed a punch!* Bean hit me with three jabs as he boxed me around to my left. It didn't affect my joy. *I landed. Rose'd be cheering her ass off right now!*

The bell rang and we switched out with José and Pedro. *Twenty punches to one. You lost the round but hey maybe next go around you can make fifteen to five. Fuck it, he's got like thirty-something fights under his belt, you're just trying to get to one.*

"Not bad," Brother said. "But throw more punches."

"OK," I replied as I observed the sparring. They sparred intensely. The cousins thumped each other as I waited, still geared up. José ripped quick mean and deadly punches on his older cousin as he turned swift circles around him. Pedro didn't give a damn about the blows raining in on him. He loaded up and cracked his little cousin when he could. *These kids are way meaner in sparring than Bean. They spar like it's a fucking fight.*

They put me in with Pedro. *This kid's so little it feels like cheating.* I jabbed the hell out of him as his jabs came up four inches short. He tried to slip his way closer but I picked him off with ease. *Shit, I'm kicking his ass!* He reached with long overhand rights that missed. I pelted him with one-two-ones. He started to land to the body and that brought me back to reality a little.

"Don't forget you the bigger guy, Joe," Johnny rasped.

I nodded and let my punches go a little softer until the bell rang. The ease of it gave me confidence. *Rosie, I just kinda sorta beat a real boxer's ass! He's six inches shorter and twenty pounds lighter, but still.*

José got in next. I grinned, drunk on success. *He's too short for me, too.* The bell rang. I worked the same stuff on him with my jab but he ducked them and caught me with some good body shots. Every moment, he closed the distance more like he was sucking me into a black hole. The confidence decompressed in my chest. Then it happened. I threw a hard jab. He slipped under it and came over the top of it with an overhand right. My chin slapped against my throat and I forgot everything. I plunged into the black hole. *Where am I?* I floated somewhere behind my shoulder watching as he bounced backward. My perception slowly flowed back into my body. I clinched him desperately. *I'm in a boxing ring in Simons Park on the West Side.* He tried to work in the clinch. *This little Puerto Rican kid is trying to blast me into another fucking dimension. I should just quit. This kid is really hurting me. Naw. Fuck that.* I released him and started moving and jabbing sharper. As he ducked another jab I hit him with a hard right cross and he stuttered back a little. He lunged out and hit me with three hard punches but nothing like that overhand. I clinched him. Fear and anxiety bubbled up all over my body. It swelled in my throat. *I can hardly breathe.* The bell rang and I almost jumped for joy. *I survived! If he'd a hit a guy his own size with that punch, he'd of knocked him cold!*

"What, you surprise you make it out alive?" Chupi asked.

I shrugged. *Maybe...*

"You did fine," Brother said.

Chupi and Brother undid my gloves and headgear. Dad'd showed up and grinned at me from the doorway. I de-geared, dazed with my successes and failures. Seeing these guys fight the other night, shit, they were dynamite. I guess I couldn't tell if Brother was carrying me or not. I stuffed my gloves into my bag. *Those kids from Saint Joe's who came down to spar with me, they're nothing like real boxers.* I looked over at Bean stepping smoothly through the ropes into the ring; he trotted around with the padding of his headgear framing his grinning face. *These kids are real boxers, from a real gym and I held my own with 'em.* Rose was right. The bell rang and the terrible dance spun back into action.

As Dad and I cruised down Kedzie the kids and the gangbangers flooded the streets.

"You did pretty good in there. Those kids are tough," Dad said.

"That little one, the young one, I think he could be famous one day the way he punches," I said, rubbing my achy head.

"He'll do good, but these Puerto Rican kids and the black kids, they hit their prime earlier. You'll see when you get to be about eighteen, you'll start to feel it. Everything will just get easier. You'll be stronger, faster, you'll start to catch up and maybe scoot past them."

"Think so?"

"Yeah. Just hang in there, you'll see."

A series of gunshots sounded off in the distance. *Rose...*

"When you think Rose is coming home?"

"A week maybe, maybe two. The doctors don't know."

"I miss her."

Dad coughed and covered his mouth and looked away out his window.

"I want her home too," he said in a strained voice, like he needed a drink of water. "She's so smart. We were playing that memory card game the other day and she beat me every game."

"Yeah, she's tricky, she always gets me in Monopoly."

"I feel like it's my damn fault. If I would have just given her more attention. I didn't know she hung out up there in the Jungle. My God!" He screeched the work truck to a halt at a red light and grimaced at me. "Did you know she hung out up there?" His jagged chin trembled.

"No," I lied.

"I guess I was working too much, but I was trying to get you damn kids out of that godforsaken neighborhood!"

"Well, you did good, Dad. Just look at our new house! We're frickin' rich!"

"We're not rich. We can barely afford the damn mortgage."

"Well, it's still pretty good, Dad."

"I guess. I just want a better life for you kids."

"Well, I think we got it now," I said. We got on 290 headed west in the thick traffic with Blue Line trains barreling down the center past us. We passed under the bridges Dad'd helped build and repair in the decades he'd been trying to escape the city.

◆

José had given me a little mouse under my right eye. I rubbed it looking in the visor mirror as we pulled up to the driveway. Jan's green Tempo was moving in reverse in the driveway and as she pulled away, her side panel dug into the neighbor's black BMW.

"Jesus Christ, Janet!" Dad's eyes bugged out as he stopped the truck at the mouth of the driveway.

Jan paused, twisting her head around frantically. Then she hit the gas and tore the BMW's rear bumper loose.

"What the hell is she doing!" Dad roared, laying on the horn.

The neighbor lady ran out her door and down her wraparound pouch screaming and pulling at her hair.

Ma opened the window in the TV room. "Jan, you idiot!" she yelled.

"What the flippin hell!? They parked too close to our side!" Jan continued pulling backwards, scraping a big green streak on the rear quarter panel of the BMW.

"Stop! Stop now! You're making it worse!" the neighbor lady screamed.

"Janet put it in park right now!" Dad hopped out and stormed up to her car.

"Is she crazy?!" the neighbor lady said, dialing her cordless phone. "I'm calling the cops! Who is she, the maid?!"

Jan got out; she was wearing her purple and gold WIU shirt with the bulldog with the studded collar on the front.

"That's my daughter, you stuck-up bitch!" Ma responded.

"Oh, from another marriage?"

"She's adopted from the Dominican Republic! Janet, get your ass inside!"

I giggled as I slipped past the carnage.

"Joe, all you're gonna do is flippin' laugh!?" she said, throwing her pudgy hands up. "What a great brother you are!"

"What do you want me to do, Jan?" I laughed. "You suck at driving!"

I giggled watching as the neighbor lady tried to push the bumper back into place. *Look at that snobby bitch! That's probably the first time she ever got her hands dirty in her whole pristine life.*

◆

I headed over to Faith's house. She freaked out about my black eye and got me some ice. We sat in the carpeted TV room on her little blue couch and put the leg rests up.

"Baby," she said as she reached in and touched the frigid plastic bag of ice to my eye. "Does it hurt?"

"Naw, I didn't even notice it 'til you said something."

Her pretty face frowned with concern.

"It's fine," I said. "Just give it a little kiss."

She leaned in and kissed it tenderly with her nice smooth firm lips.

We headed out for a walk, holding hands in the warm summer air. We went to a nearby park; the Des Plaines River trickled slowly past. The brownish orange sun began to dip below the blackened tree line.

"Are you sure you want to keep doing this boxing stuff?"

"Yeah! To be honest, I didn't think I could do it."

"Those kids were real good. You're just learning."

"I was gonna quit. Just tell Brother no, I didn't want to."

"Why didn't you?"

"I just started thinking about Rose."

"Your sister? How's she doing?"

"She's fighting, I guess. In her own way. She hurt herself the other day."

"I'm sorry, Joe."

"I figured if she can get through all that, I can fight these guys. I can survive too. And I tried, and I did," I said as we walked the long metal pedestrian bridge. It jostled and creaked and hummed rhythmically. We stopped with the slow-flowing river easing past below the brown planks. I leaned my back on the cool metal railing. She grinned and kissed me with her glossed lips.

I said: "I think I'm falling in love with you."

She popped back. Looked at me frightened with her deep green eyes, then she grinned. A breeze flowed through her dirty blonde ponytail, splaying the hairs in long strands.

"I think I am too," she said, and kissed me again, then cuddled her face into my neck as I held her there. *You a lucky motherfucker, Joe. How the hell did all this shit turn out right? Don't fuck it up like last time. Be good to this girl.* I kissed the soft hair of on the side of her head. She smelled like conditioner and peaches. *She deserves it.*

◆

After a few sessions at Simons Park, Brother decided I was ready to make the pilgrimage to one of those mythical boxing meccas, the Windy City Gym over on Ogden and Kostner in K-Town on the West Side. You probably heard about Windy City, haven't you? A former world champion named Johnny Coulon opened it way back in the 1920s. Back then it was at 63rd Street on the South Side. Tony Zale, Sugar Ray Robinson, Ezzard Charles, and Sonny Liston all trained there for parts of their careers. Muhammad Ali boxed at Windy City when he wasn't at 5th Street in Miami or camp. If you had to make a list of the five greatest gyms in history, it'd be on it. The gym'd changed hands two times due to deaths, and a few years back, two of its fighters, Andrew Golota and Angel Manfredy, landed on the cover of *Ring* magazine together. The head trainer, Sal Calderone, was an old-time keeper of the true secrets in the art of boxing. He knew the tricks and the craft. He could complete a fighter and'd done it several times, and if he blessed you and blew the power of his wisdom into your flame, there was no end to what your fire could engulf. I didn't know half that shit back then. I was just some fifteen-year-old knucklehead with a tiny little smoldering flame wavering in the breeze. It coulda burnt out just as easy, and yet...

The gym sat on the second story of a wide red-brick factory at the corner. The entrance opened onto Ogden. A long line of cars sat parked on the street in front of the old wooden door. A small simple sign rigged into the bricks above read *The Windy City Gym*. We pulled up out front. *That's it?* I thought it'd be a big flashy sign like in that movie *Gladiator*.

"Ya nervous, pretty boy?" Brother muffed my head.

"Naw." I giggled as my hands trembled. *I ain't nervous! I'm about to train in the same gym as world-ranked professional boxers but naw, Brother, just another day in the office.* We got out and walked along the sidewalk toward the entrance. *I'm sure I'll whip 'em all.* I giggled.

A lump of antimatter slammed into my stomach. *A frickin' thirteen-year-old has been kicking your ass for the past two weeks. Jesus, what the hell are you doing coming here?*

We climbed the big dark industrial spiral staircase. *Fuck, you forgot your wraps!*

"Brother, I forgot something in the car."

"OK, here, take the keys. Hurry up! Sal's waiting on you."

I jogged out, grabbed them, and came back. I climbed the twisted staircase. At the top, a white door sat cracked open. A sliver of bright golden sunlight poured out of the door into the dark stairwell. The sounds of incredible motion throbbed through the tattered white door: the mechanical thunder of the speed bag, the whirring whip of the jump rope, deep thuds, the jostle of chains, grunts, shouts.

I stood frozen in fear at the door, my mind painting images of an outlandish boxing circus. *This is where real fighters train. It's one of the greatest boxing gyms in the world. You don't belong here. They're gonna laugh when they see you.* Rage flashed in my shoulders as I paced before the door. *Fuck it, I'm going in. If they laugh, I'll tell 'em, "Fuck you!" and try to fuck 'em up sparring. I can prove myself anyplace. I can earn my right to be here!* A deep thud cracked into a heavy bag. *No way, pros train here! They'll fucking kill you! Shit. Well, do it for Rosie. She'd go in.* Some dark gravitational force sucked me back into the shadows of the staircase. *I'm sorry. I can't.* I turned and stepped a few steps down. Suddenly the door burst open. The bright light and sound exploded into the stairwell.

Brother's monstrous silhouette grimaced down at me. Long heavenly rays of light shot over his shoulder and stabbed at me. "Joe, what the heck are ya doing out here?!" Brother shouted. "Come on!" He waved me in. "They're waiting for you."

I stepped into the huge room, squinting in the bright light pouring in from the big steel-framed skylight. Beneath it, two fighters slugged one another inside an elevated blue ring. A thick collage of boxing photographs covered the walls near the entrance: fighters—some pros, others amateurs—spanning decades. Their eyes peered out, questioning, "Who's this white boy?" as I passed them into the gym.

"Joe Motherfucken Walsh," I muttered.

Twenty fighters worked feverishly throughout the floor in a rhythmical agonized symphony. No one so much as glanced my way. The boxers in the ring cracked each other with symmetrical punches. *I've only seen punches like that on TV! Is this a fucking movie?* The sweat burst off their headgears into misty sprays lit golden by the sunlight pouring down from above. *This's the most beautiful damn place I ever seen.*

Heavy bags hung all over the gym. Vicious, hard-faced men, Polish and Mexican and black, dug thudding punches into them. They all moved in idiosyncratic styles and rhythms but they all possessed a certain class in my eyes, because this was the place you came to learn class as a fighter. This was the real thing, as real a thing as there ever was.

I followed Brother past a giant muscular Polish guy with a box cut who bounced around a tall, green heavy bag hung on a chain and industrial spring. He fired shots into the bag that rang like cannon blasts.

"That guy looks like Andrew Golota."

"It is," Brother replied.

"Holy shit!" I glanced back as Andrew sneered and ripped a left hook low into the bag.

Brother walked me up to a short Italian guy with a big serious presence. His thin black hair was slicked back along his scalp; he wore a well-kempt mustache and a neatly trimmed beard.

"This is the head trainer, Sal."

He looked me over and asked, "This kid got any fights?"

"Not yet, we're getting him one next weekend."

"You spar much before?" Sal asked, peering at me sternly with his chin tucked into his throat.

"I sparred a few times."

"Well, you see these guys here sparring?" He motioned to the ring as the men dug shots into each other. "We spar hard here. We don't have time to wear kid gloves with ya."

"OK." I shrugged angrily.

"Alright, we got a couple guys to give you work. How many rounds you can go?"

"I been three before."

"OK, we'll watch you and see if we need to pull you out."

I self-consciously shadowboxed a little, watching the fighters in the huge mirror. *Hope they don't laugh.* I shot sharp jabs at their reflections. *Like that? How 'bout you, Golota?* I popped a jab at him. He felt my stare and shot a monstrous glare at me. *Shit!* I stiffened. *Pretend you don't see him!*

I geared up. Sal came over and smeared Vaseline on my headgear, nose, brow, and cheeks.

Two guys sparred in the blue ring. Their classy moves and style seemed choreographed like a deadly ballet. Their small frames launched punches in volume. *How the hell can they punch so much in one round? I'd be dead tired.*

The bell timer fastened in the wall rang, and the red bulb flashed as the symphony paused.

"Aye, Rico," Sal shouted. "Stay in, I want you to work with this kid. He ain't got no fights yet."

Rico nodded as the other fighter exited and flopped down on the bench—globs of sweat dripping off his nose and headgear.

I climbed up the blue apron of the ring. It felt like ascending a glorious mountain. I stepped through the ropes into the warm, hazy sunlight blazing through the skylight. Rico stood about three inches shorter than me. Tattoos littered his thin arms and face. *They look like the kinda gang tattoos kids get in juvie.* An image flashed through my mind of Ryan getting tattooed at the facility over on Roosevelt.

I bounced around the ring with the heavens glowing down on us. Then I leaned my back into the ropes. *I seen guys do that. Fucking try and make it look like I ain't scared out of my fucking mind.* I slumped my shoulders and looked around in awe. *Fuck it, I'm scared. What if he knocks me out?* Rosie's voice whispered in my ear: *Just try, Joseph.*

The bell rang. I looked around. *I ain't ready, though!*

"Time out!" I muttered through my mouth guard.

"Huh?" Rico said and looked at Sal.

"Did he just say time out?!" Sal said from the apron as Brother and a few guys laughed.

"Joe!" Brother yelled from the floor. "There's no time outs in boxing!"

But I can't fucking breathe! Rico shook his head, then reached his glove out and touched up with me. I put 'em up. *Fuck, here we go!* Rico dug a jab to my sternum. I jabbed back and Rico, with his feet planted, slipped my jab and hit me with an uppercut left hook. I bounced back. *His punches are snappy enough to jolt me but he ain't trying to hurt me.* I feinted a jab. *How the fuck did he stand right in front of me, make me miss, and hit me without ever moving his feet?*

"That's it, stay right in the pocket, Rico," Sal said from the floor.

What the fuck's the pocket?! I jabbed. He slipped the shot, letting it slide past his head while he countered with a left hook. I froze and ate it. *How the hell is he doing this?* His head floated right in front of me, within reach. I swung and his head disappeared, then—*bam!*—another shot popped me in the mouth.

"Jab to his chest, kid." Sal's smooth voice rose above the rhythmic cacophony of the gym.

I dug a jab that he deflected with his shoulder, then I doubled up and hit him in the chest; the shot moved him. *I outweigh him a bunch.* He put me back in my place and walked me into the corner and dug some mean hooks and uppercuts to the body that felt like a bee stinging me in my organs. I spent the rest of the round paying for mistakes I didn't even know I was making before the bell mercifully rang.

"You know how to block body shots?" Rico asked.

"No, not really."

Rico walked me through picking body shots off with my elbows. He had a polite and easygoing personality, basically the opposite of his tattoos. "Look, your elbows and arms are like your shields. But you got to move them 'cause I'm trying to get around 'em with my punches." Patience and kindness oozed through Rico's guidance. "It don't feel good when I get around them, do it?"

"Nope."

"See 'em, block 'em," he said, twisting and shielding his organs with his arms as I mimicked him.

"How many fights you got?" I asked.

"Man, when you as experienced as me you lose count." He raised his eyebrows. "I'm getting ready for the Pan American Games next month. Leaving for Team USA camp in Boulder, Colorado, on Thursday. I just wanted to come into camp ready, so thank you for the work, because you're helping me get ready to represent the country."

"Wow!"

"So come at me hard this round. I want to work on my slips and my defense. You got a good jab, so throw it a bunch. Double it, triple it, let your hands go, don't hold back. If you hit me, it's my fault I got hit, OK?"

Holy shit! I'm helping a guy get ready to represent the country in an international competition! This shit is nuts. Don't he know I'm just some goofy knucklehead? Some wannabe gangbanger? Can't he see that? I gotta tell Rosie about this!

I threw everything I had at Rico, even an uppercut with poor technique 'cause nobody had even taught me how to throw one. Rico countered to the body. I blocked a few with my elbows, but not all of them. *The way he slips my jab and cross is a thing of beauty. It's like sparring with Pernell Fucking Whitaker, he stands right there in front of me but he's like a ghost when I swing. He disappears, then reappears and fucking clocks me.* I threw more punches with little success. I got him in his shell along the ropes. I ripped a wide shot. He vanished, bounded across the ring and lined me up with his jab, then dug body shots. *This shit is like trying to figure out a Rubik's Cube.*

The bell rang, and Sal called me over to him. He doused my head with cold water as I watched Rico chatting with some guys across the way. His graceful attitude made me feel like there was nothing to prove, nothing to do but just hone my craft. His concentration was ferocious but he wasn't trying to dominate me; he was trying to extract the best from me so he could undermine it with his tricks and tactics. I remembered the shots that landed, how he rocked back and hit me. *He's manipulating me but at the same time he's teaching me. It's like he's displaying what's possible in the art of boxing.* The path to his level seemed pretty fucking insurmountable but Rico's charm and wit pried the door open before me.

The ten-second warning clicked. I smashed my gloves together. *Maybe I can do the things he does one day.*

The bell rang. I thundered out and threw seven punches. He rolled my hook and caught me with his left hook. I threw a jab and it landed. *Wow!* He grinned and nodded, then let six punches go on me as I shelled up and tried to pick the body shots off with my elbows. I unleashed seven of my own shots as he slipped and rolled them. *How does he do it?* He popped me with an uppercut left hook. I unloaded again; he dug a body shot. He shot a hook at my head and I rocked back and Rico missed; his red glove sailed over my shoulder. *I slipped a punch! Fucking A!* The round flew. The bell rang with me missing with five punches as Rico bobbed and weaved right in front of me. I stepped out through the ropes. *Well, Joe, you landed about one out of every ten fucking punches you threw. But fuck it, it still feels like a great accomplishment!* And it was.

Rico and I sat down to de-gear together on the apron of the ring with our feet on the long blue bench. Sal and Brother unfastened our headgear. Huge beads of sweat drizzled from our faces.

"I like this kid. He's real good for a guy with no fights," Rico said.

"That's big compliment coming from Rico." Sal raised his eyebrows as he pulled off one of Rico's gloves. "He's an Olympian."

"Thanks!"

"He might go an' win the Pan Ams."

"Hope you're right, Sal, I hope you are." Rico looked at Brother Alex. "Excuse me, sir, are you a priest?"

"I'm a Christian Brother."

"Yeah! Brother Alex, right?"

"Oh, I remember you. You're friends with Dennis, aren't you?"

"Yeah, Denny. Wow that guy had power! Oh, man."

"I remember you won the Golden Gloves that year. Same year Dennis did, didn't you?"

"You got a good memory, Brother Alex. So this is your new future Golden Gloves champ here?" He nudged me.

"Well, if he has the commitment and focus he might have a chance in a couple years." Brother muffed my head.

Sal came up and grinned at me. "Ya know, I always ask every kid that comes through these doors this one question." His face turned dark and stern. "Ready?"

"Yeah." I shrugged.

"What are you fighting for?"

I looked at them as they grinned at me waiting my reply.

"I don't know. I done some bad stuff when I was younger. I was a messed-up kid..." I looked around at their faces. "I think I'm fighting to prove I ain't bad deep down, ya know? Maybe prove it to myself. I don't know."

"Welcome home, kid." Rico patted my back.

"My sister...she's in the hospital. She got shot. She almost died, then she got out, and then she had to go back. She's going through a real bad thing. I think I'm fighting for her, too."

Sal put his hand on my shoulder.

"I got shot too. That's why there's a hitch in my step. Bullet in my spine. I remember being in the hospital a long time. It was a big fight. Woulda meant a lot to me if I had someone fighting for me out there." He peered deep into my eyes as if he'd spotted something way down inside them. Then he turned to Brother. "Well, you can bring the kid back anytime for work."

Brother shook Sal's hand.

"Thanks a lot, Sal," I said, beaming.

Sal let me work the floor a little with the pros all around. I tried to mimic them, digging body shots and slipping imaginary punches.

As Brother and I walked out of the ancient wooden door and into the afternoon sunlight, I grinned. *Science ain't never tasted as sweet as this.*

"Sal said I could come back anytime!"

"Good, Joe." Brother patted me on the back. "You did great, ya big wimp."

◆

Brother got me a Park District fight set up for the next weekend against a Mexican kid from Back of the Yards who'd had one fight, 1-0.

Inside Faith's cool basement, I pondered it all. The lamp glowed orange at the little table beside the couch as we snuggled under the fuzzy brown blanket. Her firm leg wrapped around my blue-jeaned thigh, and the heel of her little foot snug in the nook of my knee. Her head buried in my chest as her soft face lay atop my beating heart. My fingers damp with her, and that electric scent that always ignited me endlessly.

"You nervous, baby?"

"Yeah, it's so damn confusing. I'm excited but it's like I'm torn in two."

"How?"

"One minute I don't want to fight. I just want to chill here with you and relax and be a normal kid, ya know?"

"You can," she said, batting her green eyes at me. "You don't have to fight."

"I know, I know, it's like, why am I bringing this on myself? What if he knocks me out? Or breaks my nose?"

"I don't want to see you get hurt. Your black eye is barely healed." She touched my eye softly with her creamy smooth fingertips.

"But then the next minute I want to knock this motherfucker out! You know? I know I'm gonna win. I'm going to destroy this fucking guy, I hate him!" I said, looking at the panel ceiling.

She giggled, looking at me naughtily; her elegant upturned nose twitched.

"Then it's like, I don't even know him, why the hell do I want to hurt him?" I said as she brushed her fingers through my hair. "It's confusing as hell."

"Baby, just know, I won't think any less of you if you don't fight. I think you're tough already. And cute too," she said, and kissed me with her berry-scented lips.

"But then I think about Rosie. She's going through so much. She's in there suffering every day. She hates the hospital. Maybe, maybe if I go out there and win, maybe it could help her somehow."

"You're so sweet, Joe," she said. "You're gonna dedicate your fight to your sister?"

I nodded and held her close.

◆

After we finished our last training session before the fight, I sat exhausted in a folding chair with Brother sitting beside me. He leaned forward in his chair like he was looking for some words that were just out of reach.

"How you feeling?" Brother asked.

"OK..."

"You ain't gonna wimp out on me, are ya, pretty boy?"

"Naw, Brother, I can't."

"I know," he said sadly. "I wanted to tell you, Joe. I've been praying for your sister all along."

Really? I gasped. The thought of him praying for Rose opened up the wires that'd been constricting my chest. "Thanks, Brother." I grimaced back some tears.

I packed up and headed out. I was sitting on the Cermak bus and about to transfer at Mannheim when something whispered: *Why don't you go see Rosie?* I stayed on the Cermak bus and took it to First Avenue and walked over to Loyola.

I headed up. Rosie's room was real dark. She lay on the white bed in a loose blue hospital gown with a bunch of machines hooked up to her.

"Rose?"

She opened her eyes and stared vaguely ahead with an unamused gaze. I walked in.

"Joseph..." She looked so sad and weak. The wires dug into my chest as I tried as hard as I could not to cry.

"How are you?"

"Tired..."

"I love you, Rosie."

She looked at me but her eyes were vacant. This thick white bandage covered her wrist.

"I love you too... How's boxing going?"

"It's been hard, Rose. I been sparring against real tough guys. They kinda beat me up sometimes. I get scared. It's real tough. But then I think about you, Rosie. You've been going through hell all this time. You're the toughest Walsh out of all of us. The bravest too. You inspire me, Rosie..."

She looked at me startled as I sat down in the chair beside her.

I went on: "I keep going for you."

"Thanks," she whispered.

"I got my first fight this weekend. I'm gonna win it for you." I looked her in her eyes.

"I wanted to go…" Her bloodshot eyes trembled as I took her hand in mine. *You're with me everywhere I go, Rosie.* I knew if I said it I'd cry, and I didn't come there to cry. We just stayed there like that for a while holding hands as the machines sounded. She slowly drifted to sleep. I fell into the shadowy room: the cold, the chemical smell of cleaning product, the monotonous electronic rhythms, the nurses flashing slowly past in the hall. *This ain't no place for a person to die.* I stood, and looked down at her pained and wilted face.

Please God, protect my sister. I bowed my head, kissed her cool hand, and left quietly.

◆

Like everyfuckingbody, I couldn't sleep the night before that first fight. Nervous particles ran through my veins—positrons cycling through me at nearly the speed of light until, *bam*, awake again. *I don't even want to fucking fight. Do I really have to?* I dozed. I am in a droopy roped ring, in a big smoky green room. A muscular boxer bounces around me. His face is cast in the shadows of the headgear. Then the light catches his face. Tank grins at me wickedly. I panic. I run to the ropes and try to climb through when the barrel of the chalk-white .25 materializes from the darkness outside the ring. Ryan's pale chubby hand grips it. I see his snarling brow, the freckles trembling all over it. His eyes glow like smoldering green lanterns.

Naw, Joey, you gotta fight. I spark awake. *Fucking Ryan. You motherfucker.* I gripped my head, remembering the time Tank whooped my ass and the way Ryan looked at me afterward. His voice played in my head. "You didn't even try." *Fuck you. Fuck you and your hard-ass shit. Always had to be the realest motherfucker, huh, Rye? Look where it landed you. In a fucking cage like the animal you are. You shot my fucking sister, motherfucker! Get the fuck outa my head!* I seethed. My body flexed as I lay on my back in bed. *I wish I was fighting you, motherfucker. Let's see how bad you are now. I'm a motherfucking fighter now.* Some heavy ball of dark matter fell through me downward into the bed and deep down into the pits of hell. *Who are you fucking kidding? You ain't no fighter. You couldn't even beat up half the kids in your own little neighborhood.* I got nothing after that, not even a blink of sleep.

I didn't want anybody to go except Dad. In case I got my ass whooped, it'd be less embarrassing. Brother and I pulled up in front of the

Armour Square Park District field house, a big old tan building with arched doorways and wide concrete steps out front. The gigantic new Comiskey Park loomed behind it.

"I'm from the Irish side of Bridgeport," Brother said. "We used to come over here and beat up these dagos all the time. First we'd beat 'em in softball, then we'd beat 'em up in the bar across the street. You got a little dago in you, don't you, pretty boy?"

"Yeah, Sicilian."

"You'll fit right in with these Armour Square wimps, with your little slicked-back hair."

He muffed his hand through my gelled hair. I pushed his hand away and tried to fix it. *Come on, Brother! I gotta look good, this is my first damn fight.*

We parked near the tennis courts. Workers had erected the ring in the middle of the court. A couple metal bleachers stood beside it. Brother had made a deal with the pudgy Italian head coach for me to represent Armour Square, and I joined the gym with a handshake. They gave me a nice white-and-black Armour Square jersey and trunks.

As the sun set, the tennis court lights high above the fences clicked on, illuminating the ring in a white glow. Spectators milled the bleachers and chairs surrounding the ring. The fighters were mostly kids my age. A pudgy-faced kid with reddish-brown hair and freckles showed up with a Mexican coach. *Motherfucker looks just like Ryan. Well, that can't be him.*

He walked up to the official's table. "Manny Flores," he said to the official.

"That's your opponent there," the official said, aiming his pen at me. Flores gave me a glare. *Motherfucker must be half Irish or something.* He grinned with crooked teeth.

I walked off. *Fuck, my first fight I gotta fight a guy that looks like my best friend that's in juvie for shooting my sister? This is some creepy shit right here.* I closed my eyes. *It isn't Ryan. He doesn't even look like him that much. It's just the freckles. Well, the teeth too. What if he really fucks me up? Motherfucker's from Back of the Yards, that's a tough-ass hood.*

I took a walk around the park to ease my nerves as the sun disappeared over the tracks in a faded orange haze. *You're just a wannabe gangster, a punk-ass piece of shit.* I gripped the chain-link fence of the baseball diamond, watching the tennis courts fill with people. *Well, we gonna see if you really is what you think you is now, Joey-boy. All you gotta do is go out there and beat Mexican Ryan's ass.* I closed my eyes and thought of Rose. *What if she kills herself? Please don't do it Rose. Please. Please don't. We need you. What the fuck am I even doing here?* It was so dumb. I just wanted to go home and play stupid Monopoly with my sister.

"Yo Joe!"

I turned to see Jay walking up with his big wide toothy grin.

"You came?!"

"I told you I would. I'm man 'a my word, cuz," he said, squinting in the twilight. "What the hell you doing over here?"

"Hiding."

"What?"

"I don't want to fight, man! I'm scared. I want to quit."

"What the hell you talking 'bout? You done lost too much to quit now." His dark hands gripped the fence beside mine. "What you put yourself through all this torture and sparring for?"

"I don't know, man. I just don't have nothing inside me to fight with...but then I think of my sister."

"What's up with her?"

"She got shot, man. She's been in the hospital for months. She got out, then she went right back."

"Damn..." A silence bubbled around us as we watched the tennis courts fill. "I know how it is... sometime it take a long time to come home. What's her name?"

"Rose."

"Rose, well, you already know you gotta do it for her."

"Yeah...I know."

"Do it, Joe, it's fun."

"Yeah, I am, I'm just afraid, man!"

"Good. Be nervous, be scared, and handle your business anyways."

I nodded. "Thanks for coming." I said as we walked over to the ring.

Dad showed up and found a seat in the bleachers. They'd scheduled us for the third bout. I anxiously watched the first two as the crowd wildly cheered the neighborhood kids. One of the local kids got stopped. The crowd booed the stoppage. The abrupt end caught us off guard. Brother and I hurried to warm up and break a sweat. The announcer called my name. We approached the ring. Brother rubbed my shoulders as he followed me.

"Mean thoughts, Joe...mean thoughts..."

Fuck it. He's shorter than me. I got the reach. I stepped up the stairs to the ring. *He don't have the skill of the guys I been sparring with, and I scored on them! Fuck him. I can beat him!* As I stepped through the ropes, doubt socked me in the stomach. *Well, I got a chance anyway.* He stood across the ring with his white trunks pulled up high at the waist and a Mexican-flag headgear. They announced him as El Rojito and his family and team cheered; a chubby blonde lady I figured was his mom stood in the bleachers.

"Let's go Rojito!" she yelled in a whiney Chicago accent.

"In the blue corner," the tuxedoed announcer said, "with an unblemished record of zero and zero. Representing Armour Square... Joe Walsh!" The crowd erupted, giving me a standing ovation.

"Nice having some fake home-park advantage, huh, Brother?"

"Milk it up, kid, you might need it," Brother said.

Woulda been funny if I was like, naw, I'm from the fuckin North Side. Fuck Bridgeport! The thought gave me the giggles. *Naw, it's cool, Bridgeport is a tough hood. Get serious and stare this fucker down.* He talked with his trainer across the ring. I looked up above him as a seagull swooped through the dark sky and landed on top of a streetlight. *Da? What, you came over to watch the fight? I know you been watching over Rosie, Da. Thank you. I'm gonna win it for her.* I saw Rosie in her hospital bed trapped so sad and pale. *If I win it, she'll come home.*

The ref called us to the center of the ring. I stepped toward him. The soft canvas padding squished under my feet. We faced off. His face grinned pompously between his headgear, like he knew something I didn't. The eagle killing the serpent hovered on his foamy forehead. *I guess he does know something. He's been here before. I ain't, and he knows it.*

The ref didn't like the high trunks. "You're good down to here," he said, drawing a line a few inches below the top of his white trunks. "Protect yourself at all times, and at the bell, come out boxing."

We touched gloves. He turned away and jogged back to his corner. *He thinks he's gonna come over here and fuck me up.* I lingered by the ref. The ropes trapped me in the ring. An image flashed in my mind of him thundering punches on me as I slumped along the ropes.

"Can I call a time out?" I asked the ref.

"What?" he said, grinning at me.

"Time out!"

He laughed and shook his head no.

"There's no time outs in boxing, kid."

"Fuck," I said as I walked back to my corner.

I can't breathe. The fear swelled in my stomach like a ball of helium. It rose up into my chest, until I flexed all my muscles and it twisted into a popping rage. I glared at him across the ring. He smiled snidely at me like Ryan used to. *He's trying to take your heart. With all the shit you been through motherfucker, there ain't no way to take this heart.*

Brother slapped my arm and pointed in my face.

"Smash him!"

I nodded as he climbed down the stairs.

All alone now, Joey-boy... I looked across from me and saw Ryan's face inside the headgear. *I always wondered if I could whoop your ass, Rye. Now's my chance.*

"Time in!" the ref shouted, watching me with a curious grin.

The bell rang. He shot across the ring in a low crouch—bobbing and weaving. *It's off, it's fake. Not like the kids at Simons or Rico.*

He pantomimed a jab a few times from too far away. I parried them and glided to the side. Then he jabbed and landed. I stuck a stiff jab in his mouth that stymied him. The crowd erupted. I came back with a straight right. He jabbed and we tangled. He worked his free hand in the clinch, hitting my ribs. I stuck him hard in the ear. The ref broke us and he warned me. I shook my head, acknowledging him. *Fucking guy's making it ugly.* My heart pumped hard now as the rage broke into particles and started accelerating around my arms and legs like the big loop at Fermilab. I rattled off one-two's. He fired back. I danced out of reach as he fell off balance. I stabbed a jab into his forehead. *He don't have shit. I know it. Now I'm gonna make him know it, too.* I walked him down, stepping steadily forward. He reeled a little and ran. My height and reach advantage made it target practice. I won every exchange. He faltered some toward the end of the round. I knocked his headgear loose. He angrily played with it. The bell sort of saved him. I sat on my stool as he complained about the loose gear to his coach.

I'm fine, I'm in control, but what if I get tired? I never had this type of energy rushing through me, only in fistfights, and fistfights are short, quick. *There's four more minutes of fighting to do.*

Brother climbed in the ring. "You're doing good, pretty boy," he said, leaning over me. "Kick his Mexican ass. When he starts running, stay on him. These Bridgeport girls are all falling in love with you." Brother rinsed my mouthpiece.

"I didn't come here for no girlfriend, Brother."

"Good, now go smash him!" Brother shoved my mouthpiece back in.

Everything's going my way. My whole stomach and chest gasped empty and hungry. *Why do I feel so weak and scared? Well, at least I won one round!* As I stood up from the stool something spoke to me. *This is the last round you'll ever box. If he knocks you out, that's it. It's over. No point to keep going.* The dark matter in my soul swelled around me like two huge shadows of who I was and who I wanted to be. *Whatchu gonna tell Rosie? You tried? Fuck that.*

I came out slow again. He lunged in and looped a big overhand right that surprised my jaw. Time froze. *I'm falling. I'm unconscious. This is the end.* I saw Ryan glaring at me. I planted my feet and twisted with all my might. The best one-two Brother taught me, the one he drilled into my heart, mind, and body, fired out of me like two particles soaring at the speed of light. The jab popped Flores's head up. His chin floated right in front of me as the right cross crashed into it. His knees popped. He stumbled sideways. The referee grabbed my arm and pointed to the neutral corner. The crowd's roar deafened me.

Did I do something wrong? Is his headgear loose again? The referee counted in the kid's face. *It's a standing eight count!*

"That's it, Joe!" Brother screamed. "The one-two! Keep throwing it!"

The referee finished the count. Flores bounced on his toes angrily. The ref signaled for us to fight. Flores rushed in and threw a wild flurry. Some landed, others whiffed. His wild aggression overwhelmed me. I tied him up. He flurried again. I ducked a hook and he hit me with two more punches. Then I tied him up again. The ref looked at me curiously as he broke us. *I'm fine! Fuck this motherfucker.* I fired one-two's down the pipe. He lunged in and compacted the collision. I boxed, moved, and lined him up. He desperately grabbed me. It descended into sloppiness as the round ended. *We look like we can't box! Fucking guy's making me look bad.*

I slumped into the corner. *Why'd you do it, Rye? Fuck, it could have just as easily been me in the car. What if I woulda just shot into the crowd like that?* I looked out and saw Dad in the stands. He grinned proudly. *He fuckin' saved me.*

"Good work but stay on him!" Brother shot a line of cool water in my mouth.

The energy in my body drained. No more positrons and electrons. The dark matter lay on my shoulders and chest like a heavy blanket.

"I can't breathe!"

"Take deep breaths! Deep breaths!"

I did and it got better by the end of the minute break. I got up off the stool and he got up. Our eyes met from across the ring. We nodded at each other. We'd taken each other's best punches.

The referee had us touch up. We grinned. *Guess we know each other pretty good by now. We grew up together, for Christ sake. Might be an even fight.*

I utilized my jab early to control him. He pressured me and pinned me against the ropes in the middle of the round—pelting me with body shots. The crowd went crazy, urging me off the ropes. I finally got off them and hit him with a perfect one-two. We went toe-to-toe, with a lot of clinching. The bell rang and we collapsed into each other's arms exhausted and held each other up.

"Good fight," we said in unison, and laughed.

It happened but it's over. I forgive you, Rye. You crazy fucker. I love you.

We went over and congratulated each other's corner. His corner guy doused my head in cold water and my exhaustion cleared for a startled moment. *Did I win? I can't remember anything. Of course I lost.*

"Did I win?" I asked Brother.

"Of course you did!" Brother replied.

"Don't lie to me!" I shouted and walked to the center of the ring.

The announcer, an Italian in a tux, read the cards. "And the winner by unanimous decision, out of the blue corner, representing Armour Square, Joe Walsh!" *I can't frickin believe it!* They raised my hand as the crowd cheered.

The ref let go of my hand and a chubby, bald, Italian guy handed us our trophies. I put my arm around Flores's shoulder.

"I thought you won," I told him.

"It was close," he replied as we went to the corner and climbed out of the ring. The doctor checked us out and I looked at my shiny blue trophy. It had a little golden boxer throwing a jab at the top.

Jay walked up and patted me on the back.

"Did I really win?" I asked him.

"Joe, I'm always gonna keep it real with you. It was close, damn close. But then you caught him the second with the one-two and I had you up. But then the third was close, too, but you finished strong and I said, 'Aye, who did the better work?'" He scratched his chin. "'My guy. My guy put the best work in.' You won."

"Thanks, Jay." We bumped fists.

Brother grabbed me by the face.

"You did great!" Brother said, and rubbed his thumb under my eye. "You got a mouse, put some ice on it when ya get home."

On the ride home I kept thinking about the fight and trying to remember it. I asked Dad a half-dozen times, "Did I really win?" and finally he said, "It was close, but you had more panache and you caught him with some good shots and gave him the standing knockdown. He got you a couple good ones too, though." He chuckled. "You were tough."

We soared along I-55 with the rooftops of Bridgeport easing past us, the tall cathedrals spiking up, and Comiskey Park towering over it all like a spaceship. *Alls I can remember is a few of the times he hit me.* I looked at my blue trophy. *Fucking feels like I lost.* I touched the shiny glove of the boxer. *But if they said I won, OK, I'll take it.* I asked Dad to take me to Loyola.

Dad waited out front while I hurried to Rosie's room with my trophy. I knocked.

"Come in," Rosie said faintly.

I opened the door; she lay in bed sleepily.

"Sorry I woke you up, Rosie."

"It's OK."

I walked up and handed her the blue trophy with the golden boxer.

"This is for you, Rosie."

"You won?!"

"Yeah, I won it for you."

She looked at it.

"Thanks, Joseph," she said and laid it next to her in bed.

"I wanted to quit before the fight."

"Why?"

"I don't know. I was sad, I was thinking about you." I sighed. "Rosie, we can't quit. You and me, we gotta keep trying."

She closed her eyes. "I'm so tired, Joseph."

"But look at this, Rosie." I touched the trophy. "You know what this means?"

"What?"

"We can be different people out here. We're free, Rosie. You're gonna get out of here, and you're gonna start a whole new life."

"OK..."

"Go back to sleep. I love you."

"I love you too."

I left her as she drifted back to sleep with the little golden boxing figure jabbing at their air gleaming beside her in bed like some mythical guardian.

And not too long after that, Rose came home for good.

PART TWO: THE BROTHERS WALSH

Chapter 5: Brother

MY FIRST CLASS WITH BROTHER ALEX was a total fucking trip. None of the kids cared about general track Sophomore History, but that only seemed to challenge and incite Brother. His room sat next to the library. A wall of windows cut across it on a diagonal facing out to a green field. Knuckleheads filled the straight rows of desks. He got up to the podium in his black button-up clergy shirt with its white square-collar thingy. Beads of sweat glistened on his huge bald head as he gripped the podium aggressively like a gorilla preparing to do a circus trick.

"You know why we're all sitting in this room today? Why Europeans first came to this continent? Columbus set out to find a direct path to India and the Far East because he wanted to secure a faster trade route for these."

He reached into the podium and pulled several little plastic containers with red lids. He popped the lids off; a few of them tumbled to the podium and bounced on the floor around him. Brother Alex gathered four of them in his hands, brought them to his pummeled nose, and took a deep sniff. He glared out at us over the open containers.

"SPICES!" Brother said, like a possessed man; his lisp shot spittle out at us. "You want a smell?" he asked Georgie the Greek in the third row, who nodded. Brother rushed out from behind the podium and shoved the containers under his nose. Georgie leaned his nose over the lids and smelled deeply. He fell back into his seat and gave a playful sigh that broke most of the classroom up.

"Spices!" Brother said eagerly as he walked the rows of desks, giving other kids a chance to sniff. "It's the motivating factor! It changed history, it brought Columbus to the New World."

A fat kid sitting beside me tried to sneak a Starburst and midsentence Brother smashed him in the chest of his powder-blue button-up shirt. Everybody giggled as he coughed the orange Starburst onto his open spiral-bound notebook.

"Queen Isabella didn't know there was a whole new continent waiting to be discovered. European scientists had long theorized that the world was round. But it took our desire for spices to prove it."

I didn't give a crap about history. Some of the war stuff interested me but I sure as hell didn't care about Columbus's raping ass. But Brother Alex's raw energy made history fun. I leaned on the edge of my seat as he bounced from facts to crude jokes about spices and how they shaped Columbus's voyage to the Americas.

Brother held a PhD in history. He obsessed over all the little nuances and absurdities and read every book on the Civil War ever published by a respectable press. He could have taught at a university but chose to stay at Saint Joe's because it was his calling to work with young men; he was the one of the winningest coaches in Illinois high school soccer history. Helping to form boys into young men and send them out into the world made him incredibly proud. Boxing was just his side project, really.

◆

A couple weeks into the school year I flopped onto a folding chair down in the boxing room, unwrapping my hands after another grueling Brother Alex training session.

"You ready for the test?"

"I think so."

"'I think so' is bullshit!" Brother loomed over me; his monstrous shadow swallowed mine on the cold concrete floor. "Did you study?"

"Kind of."

"If you study for this test you'll get an A," Brother said angrily as he hung my bag gloves in the equipment locker.

"Brother, I'm not a great student, OK? The only stuff that sticks in my head is stuff about stars and molecules."

"That's nonsense! If you study for this test Friday, you'll get an A. I dare you," he said. "I dare you to try and study for this test!"

"A dare?!"

"Yeah, one knucklehead to another. I dare you to study."

"I don't know..."

"Oh is the La Grange Wussy afraid?! Afraid of a measly little test?!"

"Come on, Brother..."

"Let me get this straight, you want to fight in the Chicago Golden Gloves but you're afraid of a couple pieces of paper and a Scantron? Oh no! The test is coming for you, Joey! Run!" He frowned and hiked his brow way up.

I couldn't help but giggle. "Okay, fine! I'll study."

We shook on it.

I went over to Faith's house. She sat on the couch studying, and I said fuck it, I might as well study too. I turned off the TV and pulled out my history notes and started going over them. I studied for two nights in a row, and when the day of the test came, it was easy. I breezed through it giggling 'cause I knew all the answers.

After school I came down to box. I warmed up by hitting the bag softly—shaking my arms loose. Brother barreled into the equipment room with my test in his hand.

"Ninety percent. You studied, didn't you?"

"Yeah."

"Well, study harder!" He swatted my head with the papers. "Three more percentage points and you'd have gotten an A minus."

I snapped a one-two-three that jostled the bag.

"Don't study like a wimp. Study like a man! Organize! Note cards! Drill the facts into your head. When I was studying for my PhD, I had to read the same material five or six times to understand it."

"OK." I stabbed a jab into the bag.

"You think you're not good at school, right? Your whole life you got bad grades. People told you you were a dummy."

I dropped my fists, sighed, and glared at him. "Yeah."

"Well, you're not. The only difference between you and the Honors kids is they care. They care, and try and work hard, and study hard. They're excited about learning!"

I grimaced, jabbed, and dug two hooks to the body.

"Smarts are relative, the mind is a muscle. You can make yourself smart. You can improve your IQ."

"Come on, Brother. That's not true." I threw a mean five-punch combination.

"There are studies on it, Joe. It's a fact. You're not a dummy. You're just a lazy-ass when it comes to school. There's kids in Honors that have real learning disabilities, but they work harder than the other kids. They overcome their problems and they succeed. There's no challenge in life that can't be overcome with hard work, discipline, and focus." The bell rang and I stood in front of the swaying bag looking down as Brother glowered over me. The shadow of the bag swung back and forth between our shadows.

Electrons and positrons collided in my brain. Tears welled in my eyes. I wanted to punch Brother right in the chest. Images flashed through my mind of the faces of teachers and other students, the humiliations in classrooms at Saint Greg's—a lifetime of failure in school, and nights at home watching television or playing Nintendo when I should have been doing homework. *He's fucking right. I never tried.*

"Don't ever listen to anyone who tells you you're dumb. You're not. You're smart. You got a ninety, a B plus. Good work." He held the papers up in my plane of view, then he slapped them with his free hand. "Now study HARDER!"

◆

So I did. Brother motivated people. He bullied them in the best possible way. He bullied the best out of you and made you lift yourself up to your highest potential. My life turned into a perpetual motion machine. School, then boxing, then over to Faith's house at night. Her parents worked as researchers. They owned a big beautiful house down the street from Oprah. Her mom made us tea and always tried to help us. Faith took AP classes and held a 5.0 GPA.

There was no competition. I could never catch up with her, but her studying inspired me to work harder and get stuff done. And it didn't hurt that after we were done, we could fool around on the couch in the basement.

The silence in their house shocked me. At my house the TV constantly blared, kids ran around yelling, people argued, and nobody ever checked that I did my homework. If I asked for help with homework and didn't understand something, Dad just smacked me upside the head and said "Think!" I wondered if I was raised in a family like Faith's, could I have been successful in school like her? Maybe not, but just being there every day rubbed off on me. My grades all shot up to A's and B's, and I started thinking maybe I could go to college.

◆

Mid-semester I came across Brother and this wiseguy named Ted Waiss arguing in the hall. Waiss was a big strong kid with slicked-back hair. He was a real smart Honors kid and a witty arguer. He built a rep for luring teachers into debates and then getting in their heads and ripping them apart in class.

If Waiss fucks with Brother, I'm gonna knock the shit out of him. I listened as I closed in on them.

"Taxing the rich isn't going to hurt anyone except multi-millionaires!" Waiss whined.

"Higher taxes for the rich is never the solution. Higher taxes are going to raise the price in goods. That's called inflation. The money your family has in the bank will be worth less, while simultaneously their taxes will rise. All of this will hurt the average American household."

Waiss halted mid-step. "Brother, they're approving the tax plan in Congress today."

"I just watched the vote at lunch on C-SPAN. Republicans voted it down unanimously."

Waiss's face turned the same beet red he'd been making teachers turn in front of their classes for the past month.

That's when I realized Brother dumbed down his lectures for the low track. Brother went deep into things for the Honors kids. He was pragmatic enough to hide his monstrous intellect and complexity when it wasn't needed.

He could crack crude jokes to help motivate you one minute, then jump to the highest-level debate on current political issues the next. He took *National Geographic*–level photographs and controlled and designed the whole landscaping at Saint Joe's, which won damn awards. He shredded my perceptions of what a person could be. He instilled in me a work ethic and a refusal to hold myself back or limit my own potential by saying "Oh, I can't do that." He taught me to think, "I want to do that, and now how can I figure out how to do that and then push myself until I achieve it." Brother was an institution at Saint Joe's, and he helped me redirect my life in so many ways.

I ended up winning the Chicago Park District Championship at the welterweight novice division. It wasn't that stiff of a competition. In the semifinal I fought a chunky black kid, and in the finals I beat Flores again. I got a good look at the open-division welterweights. Their fast, snappy hands and combinations made me realize I needed a lot of experience before I could fight in the open class. If you fought Open, it meant you could end up fighting anyone in the country in your age bracket, from an average fighter to an Olympian. Still, being a champion of something made me feel good and proud.

I ended the school year with a 3.5 GPA, and I moved up one level to college prep in all my classes, even math.

◆

I kept fighting and I kept winning.

It didn't matter where they were from—the South Side, the West Side, or what. I started finding them with all my punches. I even edged an Open kid at a park district show. My one-two-threes rattled off on them with ease. My record climbed to 7-1, and I even avenged my one loss.

One night at the Carlisle they matched me with a thirty-five-year-old man and I slugged toe-to-toe with him for three straight rounds. I busted his nose real bad and hurt him, but he caught me with a bunch of big shots, too. But at the end of the fight they raised my hand, and later we found out he'd fought more than twenty fights and fought Open once in the Gloves.

When I got home and tried to go to sleep, I dozed shallowly. I woke up and sat on the toilet and my hands wouldn't stop shaking. I watched them trembling in the moonlight coming in from the window; they morphed into resonating molecules. *Did he hurt me? I don't know. I don't fucking care.* I took a deep breath and tried to stop them from trembling. *I ain't telling nobody. I don't want nobody to ever tell me I gotta stop boxing 'cause boxing's everything to me.*

The year flew past in a blaze of wonder, like a circular storm, like a twisting black hole; the gravitational winds ripped away my conceptions of who I was. Like all the electrons in my being were suddenly flipped and held a positive charge. *You are not a bad guy, Joe. You are good. You can do it. You can win. Win fights, win in school, win in love. You can do anything you want. You could be a physicist working at Fermilab, you could be a world champion. Everything is possible and open to you. And you deserve it. All of it. The universe is in the palm of your hand. And it is an open, limitless universe.*

Seems like some real crazy shit for a knucklehead like me to think, right? Well, it turns out the world don't work like that. Gravity fucks everything up. The world is mean. The world is ugly. And the world will eventually catch up to you.

◆

It was around this time that my oldest brother Pat came home from prison.

I got home from school one day and climbed the stairs into the kitchen. He sat on a wooden stool at the counter in a white dago tee, skinnier than I'd ever seen him. He wore a trimmed mustache and goatee. It was crazy to see him free.

"Pat?!"

"Aye, kiddo." A tired grin lit up his face, and crow's feet shot out into his temples.

Fuckin' Pistol Pat. I walked up and hugged him; he felt strong.

"How are ya?" He patted my back with his huge paw.

"Welcome home, Pat, it's great to see ya."

"It's great to be home, kid." We looked each other in our same blue eyes.

Jan saw me greet him from the back porch. She'd had her baby by then, a little brown baby girl named Melinda, but rather than making introductions Jan picked her up and huffed off furiously. I sighed. *She still hates Pat's guts, huh.* I couldn't blame her because whenever he used to get mad at her, he'd say she and Rose weren't really a part of the family 'cause they were adopted. *Fucking asshole.* Pat noticed her go and took a deep breath. *Probably just insecure 'cause of all the shit he put us through.*

I squeezed his shoulder. He gave me a sad grin. "She'll come around," I said.

He sighed. "I need a square."

We went out on the small side porch for a smoke.

"This is a weird place out here." Pat stuck his round chin out. A string of misunderstanding marks dented his brow like dings on an old front bumper.

"Yeah, it's quiet but it's alright." Traffic sifted past on LaGrange Road. A nicely manicured green park full of flower gardens sat across the street.

"Yeah, I guess I was expecting the sounds 'a the old neighborhood."

"The gunshots and shit?"

"Haha. Yeah, maybe." He smiled. "So you're the Chicago Park District champ now, huh? You wouldn't believe how the guys went crazy in the joint when they heard that. My kid brother, a Chicago Park District champion."

"Thanks, I got lucky I guess." I looked out across the street as the sky fell to an orangish-blue twilight.

"Aye," he said, remembering something. He dug into his shirt neck and came out with this golden crucifix the TJOs had stolen in a jewelry store heist way back when I was a little boy. "I can't believe they gave it back to me after all those years."

I pulled the matching crucifix he'd given me way back then. "I been wearing mine all that time."

A little tear sparkled in his eye as he ran his fingertips along the golden surface. "They transferred me a half-dozen times, but I guess it just kept getting shipped around with me. Then bam, like *Back to the Future*, there it was."

"So how was it in there, Pat?"

"Kid, it's been a rough ride." He let the cross dangle from his neck. He pulled on his Marlboro and looked out along the horizon. "I ain't never going back there. It's a bad place full of bad people. Nasty little cowards with big ol' muscles. I'm gonna start a new life out here."

"Good, Pat." I put my arm around his shoulder. "I'm glad."

"It's gonna be great, kid." Smoke sifted up from his nostrils as he peered out to the darkening horizon.

I puffed my smoke and let my exhale trail over my shoulder. *He's got a chance, anyways.*

I closed my eyes. Da's dark face and slicked-back black hair swirled into my mind. He looked me in the eyes, sad and worried. Da's voice, his real voice whispered in my ear: *You have to help him, Joe.*

I opened my eyes as Pat let out a plume of smoke.

"You alright, kiddo?" he asked.

I tried to speak but nothing came out.

"Yeah," I finally said, blinking back a few tears.

I will, Da. I promise.

◆

It was no small miracle that Pistol Pat was coming home from prison ready to try and make a go of it as a normal part of society.

Pat'd seen the kind of hell in prison that would keep any normal person trapped in a cycle of violence for eternity. He'd embraced the darkness and became a general for the TJOs in there. He used to sit at the table with King Kong and various other leaders of the Peoples Nation: calling shots, managing shanks, smokes, commissaries, policing of the nation, and organizing hits on their rival nation, the Folks. He survived riots, shanked a lot of Folks and knocked out a bunch of them too, and he'd been stabbed, beaten brutally unconscious, and even choked to near death by a corrections officer. There was plenty of dope in the prison system and he'd gotten high often.

But Pat had gotten clean in the end. All the terrible violence he'd been through hadn't erased his tender heart. There was still plenty of goodness in him and even a whiney, wimpy little child, too. Pat was a house of shattered mirrors. Everything he did and said was a lie, the good and the bad; it was all an illusion. Now was his chance to try to pick up the pieces of himself at thirtysomething years old. Make a go at the good life.

Pat was the oldest and I was the youngest. I was never a rival to him, so I'd never felt his nasty side; our relationship was more like an uncle and nephew. Blake, the second-oldest and Rich, the third-oldest had a radically different experience with Pat, and they hated him with a special kind of malice I couldn't fathom then.

Putting the pieces of a broken mirror back together ain't easy, but it's doable. During summer break, Pat and I started working construction together. I'd been lifting weights down in the musty basement of the YMCA with Georgie the Greek. Georgie and I had been in a months-long competition to try and max out 225 on the bench press; we were both about 5'10" and 160 lbs, just high school kids. Pat said he could bench 315, and my brother Rich cried there was no way. So Pat came down for a workout with Georgie and I.

We walked down into the basement of the huge old YMCA on Ogden, and through the low-ceiling white hallway that wound around into the musty back racquetball courts with the thirty-foot ceilings. They'd converted two of the courts into an old-school iron pit for bodybuilders and power lifters. Huge mirrors lined each wall of the two rooms; the images reflected off of each other at bizarre angles that made for constant motion in each direction; the reflected images rose above and compounded and shrank into infinity, telling your future.

We warmed up a little with just the bar, repping it out. Pat stood beside the bench in his white wife-beater with his big ol' gray Celtic Cross tattoo on his shoulder, stretching his triceps. His face winced; his trim mustache and goatee twisted up in an O. Pat stood 6'1" and 220, and was in pretty good shape from lifting weights all day in prison. Georgie and I tried to max out with 225, our arms trembling as we tried to get our elbows to lock out. We both failed.

Pat threw 275 on the bench and pulled it off the rack. Some strange grunts started rumbling in his chest as he lifted his butt way up off the bench. I stood above Pat, poised to spot him. As he brought the weight down to his chest, he let out a little trumpet of a fart. I burst out laughing as Georgie chortled and jumped back away from us. Then Pat pushed, and the metal plates trembled and moved slowly and steadily up. He put it up four times and racked it.

"Well, your butt was two foot off the bench and you ripped ass, but you sure as hell can probably bench 315." I told him.

"It's Ma's chicken cacciatore, always give me the shits!" Pat said, sitting up on the bench. "It ain't pretty but I get it up there don't I, kid?"

"Alright youse got us on the bench but tomorrow we squat." Georgie told Pat.

"I can't squat, my knees are shot."

"Typical," I told him.

Pat stood and looked himself in the mirror behind the bench, flexing his big pale arms. Pride and hope trembled in his brow as it hiked up, surprised by his success with the bench but knowing that he'd earned it benching out on the yard. His golden crucifix sat nestled on his chest hair. Then he peered up higher into the cacophony of reflections and his face drooped into a long gaze.

"Pat," Georgie broke the silence; he grinned as he placed his foot up on the bench and propped his hands on his knee. "Can I give you some completely unsolicited advice?"

Pat shrugged yes, still looking into the reflections.

Georgie continued. "I think you got a real future as an extra in House of Pain music videos."

I cracked up.

Georgie kept at it. "I could manage you, put youse in touch with the right people."

"Oh, shut yer trap, who is this guy," Pat asked me. Then he addressed Georgie. "You're having an identity crisis. Look, you're Georgie the Greek, not Georgie the Guido."

"Damn!" I burst out laughing.

"Okay, Pat, okay," Georgie said. "So you can rep out 275, but you'd never catch me in a foot race."

The banter rambled on endlessly as we lifted that summer. We hit the gym four times a week. The time just flowed; Pat and I felt like two parallel rivers joined together in a flood. He unleashed corny, good-hearted jokes that kept us laughing all the way. It felt like I'd pulled him into this other dimension in the suburbs, a place of fun and rebuilding and goodness. Every day we felt further away from the darkness of the old neighborhood.

◆

Towards the end of summer, I finally saved up enough money to go half on a Jeep Wrangler TJ with Dad. He'd been wanting to buy me some ugly-ass Ford but I made a deal with him, and Ma helped, and then there it was, a beat-up used red Wrangler TJ with a tan cloth top.

I took Pat on a drive out into the big expanse of woods south of the Des Plaines River on LaGrange Road. We rode with the top off, just the metal structure around us with the tan padding over the red bars. The sun blazed down on us, as the wind breezed through our short hair. Pat wore his dago tee and I had on a dirty T-shirt with the sleeves cut off. Tool thundered through my speakers. The greenery surrounded us as we climbed a long slope and wound around a little pond full of bass and bluegill. A tall white crane stood in the waters, his head bowed, his long beak poised to stab at a fish.

"Kid, you're really growing up," Pat told me, pulling on a cigarette.

"Trying to," I giggled as I drove.

"Man, when I heard you stabbed that bitchass GD that was beating up Rosie, I was like 'Dat's my little bro!'"

"Shit man, what else could I do?"

"Do whatever you gotta do is what you do, Joey," he said, as we drove past another pond. "Sometimes I think about Mickey and Ryan, ya know."

"Me too."

We rolled along the river, and the thick woods hung over the road and cast us in a dark shadow like a curtain of cool dark matter.

"Mickey's fighting the murder charges," Pat said. "He's still in County. Ryan's over in juvie on Roosevelt, he'll be coming home when he turns eighteen. If he stops fighting and shanking motherfuckers in there."

I sighed, imagining the hell Ryan lived in every day. The wires constricted around my chest.

"He's turning into a big soldier for us," Pat went on. "The Kings are giving him tall props. They call him 'Ryan the Red.'"

"I don't want to hear about him," I sneered.

"Why not?!" Pat recoiled. "Ryan loves you."

"He fucking shot Rose!"

"No he didn't!" Pat shot up in his seat, peering down at me.

"She got hit with a .25! Come on, do the math, that was our gun."

"They can't tell the difference between a .22 and a .25."

"They didn't find no .22 on them after they crashed."

"Maybe they tossed it out the window."

"The doctors said it was a .25."

"You're speculating, kid."

"You're in fucking denial. Look, I'm done with that shit, Pat. I want no part of it. I don't even want to hear about it!"

"Okay, okay, it's just what I know. Mickey, Ryan, all of 'em. I love 'em. I miss 'em."

"I know, me too. I'd give anything to go back and keep Ryan from getting in that car that night."

"Just be grateful Dad pulled you outta that."

"I am, every fucking day. Now it's your turn, big bro. Time to get you out for good, get you that American Dream."

"White picket fence and 2.5 kids, a dog, and a wife with a big ol' ass."

"That's it."

"You're on your way too. How'd you land a little dime piece like Faith?"

"I'm lucky, what can I say? But really, Pat there's a new life out here if you want it. But you gotta leave all that shit back there in the old neighborhood. Don't never go back."

"You're right, kiddo. You're so right."

We coasted up to the long Lemont bridge. First we passed over the shipping canal, then the Des Plaines River. The two waterways flowed parallel—one natural, and one that society had interrupted with its mighty machinery. I cranked the volume full blast and floored it. Tool exploded into the air as we soared across the bridge north towards home.

◆

There was a lot of push and pull with Pat in the family.

It was easy for me to forgive him, but his addiction and his violence had created a lot of wounds over the years. My brother Rich, the third-oldest, had grown into a hairy, gnarly, redneck-ish, gun-toting heavy metal guy. He was a married father of two now, with a home out in Brookfield, not too far from the zoo. He fucking hated that Pat was back out on the construction sites. Rich was running crews, and Pat and him rubbed each other the wrong fucking way. When Pat went away, he was a full carpenter, and Rich was just working summers like me. Now Rich was a full journeyman carpenter, and was having some success running work as a foreman.

Rich warred a lot with guys. He wasn't too good at dealing with a boss. The problem was he was too smart. Which is ironic, because they'd diagnosed him with learning disabilities as a kid. He had a hatred of school that dated back to this creepy third-grade teacher at Saint Greg's who would humiliate him in class. She was some kind of sadistic pedophile. She pinched him and stuff like that. Ma came to school one day and stood outside the room and listened to her picking away at him as the other kids laughed. Ma stormed in and screamed at the bitch and got her fired, but the damage was done. After that, all Rich wanted was to be a carpenter like Dad. He obsessed about projects and read plans when he couldn't sleep at night, which was often. All those blue lines just made sense to him, and when a foreman told him to do something a certain way, if Rich didn't like it, saw it was wrong, or knew a better way, he'd finally get fed up, argue with them, and throw a fit. Rich's interpersonal work site problems forced Dad to make him foreman to keep him working and keep peace on the jobs. Pat, the oldest, couldn't handle Rich telling him to do stuff. Pat had more experience on big jobs. But he'd lost a lot to those years in prison. He'd get frustrated and spaz out on everybody.

I tried to keep the peace, but it wasn't pretty. Rich didn't like that I got along so good with Pat. He started riding me hard. Trying to get me to quit or refuse to do something. He'd tell me to go dig a huge hole with a shovel by myself. I'd shrug and just dig it. I love hard labor, going home exhausted and dirty. There's something spiritual about it. I'd be in there with my shirt off, digging all covered in dirt and sweat, cracking jokes with the Mexicans nearby. Rich'd come to check on me, see how much I'd gotten done. His eyes'd bug out at how quick I worked. My jolliness infuriated him. Rich didn't like hard labor; he felt it was below him because he was so skilled as a carpenter. I didn't give a flying fuck. Rich also never worked out or liked sports. For him, digging a big hole by himself would have been utter misery; he'd be heaving for breath with his potbelly jostling, his weak arms burning, dying in the hot sun. But I was in incredible shape. I'd be down there, my muscles catching a pump, my six-pack rippling as I twisted to throw the dirt, getting high on the exertion, images of sparring partners I owed a beating flashing in my mind, muttering 'I'm gonna fuck you up, motherfucker,' and giggling at the thought. We was just opposites, I guess.

Pat took my side every time with Rich. He warned Rich that I could probably already beat his ass in a fistfight. And I knew I probably could; Rich was never any good with his fists. But things were different when Rich had a weapon. He'd avenged his best friend Simon's murder back in the old neighborhood; he'd snuck up on Spider with a baseball bat and split his head and made him all but a vegetable. Now Rich was a hunter, and a good one, an incredible shot with his compound bow or shotgun. He'd killed five trophy whitetail in his first seven years hunting, and made one impossible shot on a twenty-three-point nontypical who was leaping a fence at seventy yards going away. Dad saw the shot, saw the bullet burst through his furry chest and spew a gallon of blood out of his heart. The buck died right there, hung up on the metal fence, his legs still kicking as the nerves sparked their last.

I started taking Pat's side. No matter how hard Rich tried to split us, he couldn't. I could see Pat struggling, trying to get back in the groove, but his ego was getting the better of him. Rich was often right, and that depleted Pat, made him want to give up and give in, especially when Dad showed up and screamed at him for doing something wrong. Pat wanted to be the good guy, the hero of the job site, but those shattered pieces of him were keeping him from being that, and we all kind of knew it.

Soon there was another tumultuous morning on the job site. Pat went berserk on Rich about some minor technicality on a crash wall we were rebuilding on a bridge out on the South Side, about how the rebar was an inch out and how we should have to re-drill everything and re-tie the iron, and he called Dad and Dad started screaming at Rich, but the one measly inch didn't matter because we would fudge it in. All the screaming was for nothing again, the damn third time this week.

Rich and I were taking our lunch break together in his white company pickup truck while Pat was pouting and complaining to Juan over on the grassy embankment.

"Look at this motherfucker, he's such a fucking idiot!" Rich sighed, his dark tan arms gleaming in the sunlight. "An inch is nothing! And then he wants to fistfight me over it?!"

"Just chill out man, he ain't gonna do shit." I told him, taking a bite of my peanut-butter-and-jelly sandwich.

"You know what that motherfucker needs? He needs a baby."

"Pat?!"

"Once you have kids everything changes, man. You only care about them, and you just stop with the petty shit, ya know?"

I thought about little Simon and Anna, their cute little faces, and how Rich had changed, he'd stopped smoking weed and drinking so hard.

Rich went on. "And now I got this motherfucker on the site. He's a real threat, to me and to my kids. You know, he used to threaten to kidnap you when you were little, if Ma got between him and grandma's money. Do you even remember that shit?"

The memory of that twisted into my mind. Seeing Pat calling to me from down the dark alley, all strung out and sick-looking. Did that shit really happen? Would he really have kidnapped me? An image of Pat grabbing little Simon and throwing him in the old Lincoln flashed in my mind.

"Look man it was all just strung-out junkie talk."

"Yeah? What if he talked about Simon like that? I just want to fucking put a bullet in that motherfucker."

"Stop that shit, man."

"Blake says no cop in this city would pursue charges once they saw Pat's fucking rap sheet. No jury'd convict me in a million years. A father of two, clean record."

I winced. *Well, if they knew what I knew about you, they'd reconsider.*

Rich opened his little red lunchbox and picked up a ham sandwich in a plastic bag. Underneath it was his glossy black .38 semiautomatic.

"Oh come on," I sighed. "What's that shit?"

"What do you think? He's fucking threatening me! We got a homicidal maniac on our crew."

"He's not homicidal, he's just stressed. He's doing fine."

"Like hell he is. He's driving me nuts, and he threatened me the other day. You don't know how it is, you think of him as some cool older brother. Well, he killed at least seven people that I know of."

"I know about all that shit. But he deserves a fucking second chance!" I took my lunchbox and got out of the truck. "If you wanna fucking shoot him, you better be ready to shoot me, too! Because I'll testify against your ass. Trust me."

"Little bro, what the fuck?"

"I'm fucking serious." I slammed the door and headed over by Pat and listened to him bitch and moan.

The next morning, they went at it again. I was on the other side of the bridge prepping some material. They were standing the wooden forms around the green rebar structure when it erupted.

"You little pussy!" Pat yelled. "I'll knock the fucking shit out of you!"

Pat's big muscular body loomed over Rich's smaller pudgier frame. Rich scampered back as Pat's thick arms flexed and his Celtic Cross tattoo trembled. Rich pulled out his wooden-stemmed hammer from his tool belt and cocked it back. Pat pulled his metal hammer with the blue rubber grip. I sprinted over and opened Rich's truck door and found the lunchbox. I opened it and pulled up Rich's sandwich and there it was.

I took the glossy pistol and slipped it deep into my nail pouch. As I hurried towards them, I took the pouch off and hid it behind the rumbling generator. As I got close they postured. Rich took a tentative swing at Pat's midsection, and Pat hopped back and swung down at Rich's extended arm, but both only caught air. The other workers pleaded with them to stop; their neon-orange and -yellow vests made 'em look like a bunch of bees swarming around a hive.

"Pat! Quit it, all right?" I squeezed between them and pushed Pat back.

Once I was between them Rich swelled up and got real tough. "I'll fucking split your head!" he roared. The other workers pushed in, and several of us tripped and toppled to the hard concrete bridge deck. Pat came at Rich pawing with his big blue-gloved right and cocking back with his big metal hammer. Rich took off running for the truck. Pat chased him, laughing wickedly. Rich jumped in and slammed the white door as Pat reached in the open window, grabbing at Rich. Rich dug into his lunchbox and then his eyes bugged out. He started the truck and peeled out of there as Pat grabbed at his shirt. The truck shot off down the bridge, smashed through a big orange barrel, and tore out of sight, kicking up a trail of dust that hung in the air.

Pat turned around triumphantly.

"All right, now I'm the foreman! Let's go, get that string line up," he yelled at Juan and the rest of the guys. They all looked at him uneasy and headed back to the wall.

Dad showed up and screamed at Pat, and Pat finally just went back to work. I pulled Dad aside and we got in his truck.

"What the fuck is happening out here?!"

I pulled the .38 out of my nail pouch and gave it to him.

"What's this shit?!"

"Rich was gonna shoot him, but I took the gun before he could get to it."

"Jesus." He looked at the gun in his lap.

"Don't ever put them together again."

"Richard is a father. He'd never do anything to jeopardize that."

"He was gonna kill him. Blake convinced him he'd get off if he did it."

"Richard was not going to kill Pat." Dad pawed at his mouth with his pale muscular hand. "Why the hell would he do that?"

"Look, you don't know how bad it was when they were kids. Pat was a fucking monster to them."

"That shit was a decade ago! I don't know why they can't just get along now!"

"Could you imagine if the worst monster of your childhood showed up to work with you?"

Dad winced and scowled, his big hawk nose twitching.

"Why can't they just let that shit go? Can't they see I'm trying to help them both?"

"I can see it, but it don't matter what you and I can see. They got bad blood, and it ain't never going away."

"We all got the same fucking blood!" Dad dialed Rich's number on his cell phone. "Where the fuck are you? Stay right fucking there." Then he glared at me. "Get out."

Dad peeled out of the construction site in his big white Suburban.

I walked up to Pat, who was nailing 2x4 kickers onto a form.

"Be careful with Richard, all right?" I told him. "He ain't right in the head."

"What's he gonna do, shoot me?" Pat said, pounding a nail through the kicker into the hole he'd drilled into the concrete slab. "I'll take that gun off him and jam it up that little bitch's ass."

Some of the guys laughed, uneasy. *You woulda had to, big bro.*

Dad finally gave in and moved Pat out to work with Uncle Marc on the Ford Heights crew.

◆

School started back up.

Pat came down to watch me spar, and boxed a little with Brother Alex. Pat caught Brother with a sneaky southpaw left that surprised him, but Brother still kinda bullied him, got him tired, and Pat couldn't answer the bell for the third round.

"I told ya he'd kick your ass," I said, grinning at Pat exhaustedly sitting with his back against the red mat wall.

"I smoke two packs a day, for Christ's sake."

"No, no, he does have a little bit of a left hook," Brother said.

"See!" Pat whined and gave me a goofy grin.

"Well, what do ya think, Joe?" Brother asked. "Want to try for the Gloves?"

"Think I'm ready?"

"Well, you got nine fights, you're going to graduate to Open soon. This'll be your last chance at a novice title."

"Okay, okay, I'm in," I said.

"Can I be part 'a this? Joe, Brother Alex, can I be part of the team, like hold a spit bucket or something?"

"It's up to Joe," Brother said and shrugged.

"Whatduya say, kiddo?" Pat asked.

"Well, I can't think of a better corner, my brother and Brother."

"All right!" Pat grinned. "I think I'm good on the sparring though. Maybe ten years ago I coulda made a run."

"You like them Marlboros too much!" I chided him.

"Damn straight," Pat said. "But really. Brother, Joe, it's real good for me to be around this, ya know? You inspire me, Joey." He looked me in my eyes; his trembled a little. "Ya really do, kiddo."

◆

There's a boxing tournament in Chicago that is the secret heart of this city. The souls who come to witness it understand something about what this city is. What makes this city. When they venture to the ring in the center of the Saint Andrew's auditorium, they are surveilling the new generation of Chicago, inspecting its deepest, most ferocious core. These fighters will go out into the world in many different directions; some will continue to fight and go to the Olympics and turn professional, others will become moguls in business, some may become powerful politicians, and others will commit terrible crimes and die in pools of blood on these Chicago streets but you can trust me when I say that this tournament is where you must go if you want to see the heart of your fair city in all its glorious and horrific wonder. You will see Chicago bleeding and fighting on. You will see Chicago knocked down hard and watch it rise. When you witness this tournament, this terrible and glorious monstrous beating heart, you will know your city and its territory more than you ever could have before because they come from every corner: Austin to Cabrini, Beverly to Rogers Park, and every outstretched suburb and town and even from the depths of Gary, Indiana, because Gary is Chicagoland too, just like Maywood and Schaumburg and Moline. Chicago has swallowed up the land and crossed borders and drawn the young warriors on this singular quest to become a Chicago Golden Gloves champion. When you watch the Gloves you are peering into a century of Chicago, systematically refined into ten minutes of galactic fury. If you dare to see the Gloves, you will see all that Chicago was, is, and will be. And most importantly you will see the darkest and brightest aspects of yourself as a Chicagoan.

We were down in the storage room at school when Brother broached the subject.

"Joe, you sure you're ready for this? We have to step things up if you are."

"Yeah?"

"There's no promises. You might draw a really tough kid, maybe even a twenty-year-old man."

"I know."

"If you're sure you want this, if you're willing to train harder than ever, and really go for it, I'm with you, Joe."

"I am, Brother."

We shook hands and the horrible torture began again. My mind drifted as I hit the bag. *Am I really ready for this? I want it real bad. I can hold my own sparring with the pros and open fighters at Windy City. I'm giving out eight counts in show fights. A lot of guys say I got a good shot at winning the Novice.* Brother slapped my back viciously. *I gotta cut weight to make welterweight.*

"Harder!!!!" Brother roared behind me.

I can't fucking believe I'm really gonna fight in the Gloves. My thoughts morphed into emotions: fear, joy, rage. My body fell into a shocked tension; the punches flowed as my mind clicked off. Free. Listening to Brother's directions—a budding medium of destruction.

On the opening night of the preliminaries Brother and I headed over to Saint Andrew's Gym on Addison, just a few blocks down the street from Wrigley Field. It was a squat red-brick building with just a little white sign above the wooden doors.

"What is it?" I asked Brother as we walked in.

"It's the gym for the grammar school."

"Weird."

"They've held the Golden Gloves here for almost eighty years."

Inside, the floor shined in a strange wooden pattern. Folding chairs filled the ground level, with the blue ring in the center. Bleachers stood on either side, then on the second floor, larger bleachers climbed to the ceiling.

"How many people can fit in here?"

"A few thousand," Brother said. "You make it to the finals it'll be full to the rafters."

I looked up at the wooden bleachers that sat atop the elevated level that reached up to the arched ceiling. *Fuck, this is gonna be epic.*

They matched me with a black kid from Whiting, Indiana. Pat showed up and was so nervous it actually calmed me down, having to explain how everything works.

"Be careful," Pat told me before the bell. "Hit 'im in the balls if you gotta, Joey."

"No! No, don't tell him that!" Brother said as they climbed down the steps. It actually cracked me up.

I felt real good and smooth in there. I lit him up pretty nice. Rosie was screaming the loudest out of anybody. The kid from Whiting couldn't punch, but he caught me with a right hook to the eye. It triggered swelling instantly. I busted him up for it and in the last round he tried to go all crazy on me, clinching and pushing and hitting on the clinch. It infuriated me, so I threw him clear across the ring. He almost flew out through the ropes.

"Hell yeah!" Pat jumped up and shouted. "Attaboy Joey! Bodyslam that motherfucker!"

Brother had to wrestle Pat back into his seat. The ref warned me as the crowd laughed. I dominated with the jab the rest of the round and advanced to the semifinals.

That's the first time I got a look at Andy Velez. They matched him up with Flores. Velez came into the ring with his cornermen waving a big old Puerto Rican flag behind him. He stood tall with insane eyes and a pointy nose with big flaring nostrils.

"I fought this guy," I told Pat as we sat in the bleachers.

"Which one, the Puerto Rican?"

"Naw, the Mexican redhead. Flores."

Andy Velez rushed out and threw combinations so vicious his flying arms looked like a series of lightning bolts. Flores wobbled and the ref gave him an eight count.

"Damn! You gotta fight this guy?" Pat asked.

The ref waved it on and Velez dropped him right away. Flores got up but staggered badly to the corner. The ref waved it off. A first-round knockout, thirty seconds into the fight.

He got out of the ring and him and his corner walked past me and stopped. Velez glared at me; two little ink teardrops hung under his right eye.

"You next?" his big dark-skinned cornerman said, and looked me up and down. Velez gave me a real bitchy nod.

Pat jumped up. "We ain't scared!"

They glared at each other. A glint of recognition flickered in the cornerman's beady eyes.

"*Vamos*, Capone," Velez pleaded to his cornerman. Capone gave us a dismissive wave. A little gang tattoo sat in the web between his thumb and index finger.

"Capone, huh? Well call me Hymie Weiss, motherfucker. See you soon," Pat said and threw up the J.

"Pistol..." Capone said real ominously as they turned and walked toward the dressing room. Capone threw up the pitchforks gang sign over his shoulder so we could see it.

"I knew it, they're fucking MLDs. I was locked up in county with that little weaselly bitch."

"Pat, we gotta behave, they'll kick us out of the tournament," Brother demanded.

"Sorry, Brother Alex," Pat said with a sigh.

Chupi from Windy City walked over to us, along with José.

"Aye, I gotta tell you something," Chupi said. "I'm Puerto Rican. I love to see Puerto Ricans win. But this guy, he got way more fights than ten. He real good, I mean, he real good! Brother, if I had a novice that had to fight this guy, I'd pull him out the tournament."

"OK," Brother said, flustered. "We'll consider it."

"'Cause he too good for Novice. You a nice kid, I don't want to see you in with this guy, he a *tramposo*."

"A cheater," José explained.

"I knew these bitches were cheaters," Pat snarled to himself.

"Thanks," I told them, my head swirling with the thought of getting knocked unconscious by Velez.

We drove home in Ma's van. The rainy city flowing past the window in dreary neon. *So it's me and Velez next week. Fuck, he looks all of twenty years old.* He looked like a top nationally ranked fighter let loose on a novice. *But I beat Flores's ass three times already, too. But I didn't drop him or stop him.* A big semi truck blew its horn as it soared through the rain water beside us. *I knew I could draw a real tough guy but damn, Velez is bad.*

"Don't worry, Joey." Pat squeezed my knee. "You're gonna fuck him up, and I'm gonna drop his bitchass coach, too."

I burst out laughing. "Hell yeah!"

"Do not cause any trouble!" Ma scolded Pat from the front seat.

◆

Brother burst into the equipment room as I was wrapping my hands.

"Well, I called around, Velez's book says he's got three fights."

"That's all?" *Three fights my ass! That guy is rattling off eight-punch combinations with power.*

"He stopped all three guys in the first round," Brother said, yanking some gloves out of the cabinet.

Shit. My hands shook as I imagined getting stopped bad in front of Faith and my whole family at Saint Andrew's.

"He's twenty years old, from Puerto Rico. He moved here six months ago; he's a Teamster, truck driver. Look, pretty boy, something's up with this guy, I know. If you want to pull out of the tournament I'm not gonna think any less of you."

"Thanks, Brother."

"But if you want to take a chance and go for it, I'm with you."

Fuck...Pat, he says I inspire him then I go and quit? What kinda inspiration'd that be? I made a promise to Da, I'd help him. I held my head in my hands. *Fuck it, when it gets tough, Pat, just go right ahead and shoot up again.* I sat up and looked into the cinderblock wall across the way. *I'm a better fighter than Flores. But I never stopped anybody. I'm just a fucking kid, barely seventeen. Shit.* I stood up. *Fuck these fuckin MLDs, I ain't quittin'.*

"I'm fighting, Brother. We'll go out in a blaze a glory if we have to."

"Naw, naw, naw, we have to find a way to win, Joe."

He clicked the bell on, and we went back to work.

◆

Something about seeing that MLD really fucked Pat up. It triggered this nastiness in him. He'd been working construction and had saved up enough to buy a car. But as soon as Pat got the car, shit went south. He started acting funny. That hopeful glint in his eyes faded. He started showing up late for work and missed days. Then one day he didn't show up to lift weights at the YMCA.

I bumped into him in the driveway and asked him why.

He just shook his head. "I'm not feeling good." Two deep shadows swallowed his eyes.

"Pat, man, you can talk to me."

"I know, Joe." He glared at me. "Stop it, you sound like Ma."

"I love ya, Pat. I can help you try, I..." The words escaped my grasp as Pat angrily cut me off.

"I don't need no help, I'm just sick, OK? I got strep throat." He held up a white paper bag from Walgreens. "Here's my antibiotics, alright?"

"Alright, alright... You coming to the fight to help in the corner still, right?"

"I wouldn't miss it for the world, kid." He grinned sadly as he headed up the driveway towards the side door.

The neighbor, a muscular blond lawyer-looking guy, glared at Pat from his backyard.

"What the fuck are you looking at?" Pat shouted at him.

The neighbor just grimaced at Pat, then turned and got in his Beamer.

◆

The night of the semifinals Pat showed up looking real sick and crazy. We sat in the bleachers as Velez and Capone waited on the steps near the glove table for it to be our turn to glove up. Pat kept staring at Capone.

"These motherfucking cheating-ass bitches," Pat sneered at them. "I bet they fucking put some shit in the glove, that's why he hits so hard."

"Naw, Pat, come on."

"That's how these bitches are, Joe, I know them! I had to survive in the pen with them for years."

Our time came and we stood around the big glove table. Dozens of gloves lay atop the table, blue and red with white at the knuckles. The old black glove manager wore a black skully with a Golden Gloves insignia on it. He thoughtfully selected the gloves, double-checking his clipboard. Pat hovered around Velez, inspecting his every move.

"Aye what's that?!" Pat said and grabbed Velez's hand. Velez pulled it away fiercely. Capone stepped between them.

"Let me see them hand wraps!" Pat implored.

"You think we need to cheat to whip this bitch-ass whiteboy?" Capone said, grimacing into Pat's face.

Velez held up his white-taped fists. Pat felt them as the glove table manager came around and inspected them too.

"Somethin' ain't right with them wraps, they're hard as rock!" Pat whined.

"All right, all right. Enough already!" Brother Alex nudged Pat as we headed over to warm up. The glove manager approved them making marks on the tape with a felt-tip marker and went back behind the table.

Nerves coursed through my stomach as I slipped through the ropes into the ring. Velez entered the ring with two full Puerto Rican flags draped over his front and back, clipped to each other at the shoulders. He danced around the ring fluidly with the flags fluttering around him, glowing in the bright lights. I tried to touch up with him and he wouldn't. He glared at me with his long narrow muscular face. His beady crazed eyes said 'I'm gonna fucking kill you!' I glared back. *Alright then, fuck you.*

"Now don't let him unload on you like he did on that last guy," Brother said. "Move, move your head, punch."

"OK," I nodded.

"Fuck that motherfucker up for the old neighborhood, Joey!" Pat shouted at me. "Show 'em where we from!"

The bell rang and Velez stormed across the ring and threw an eight-punch combo. The shots stunned me; flashes of white blinded me. I managed to slip and roll and counter with a straight right. I danced out of the corner as Velez reset and grimaced at me, frustrated. Then he thundered in again. The shots zapped in, relentless, like the rapid-fire lasers from a Star Wars TIE Fighter; they sent bright electronic flashes through my vision. *Fuck, he's gonna stop me!* The crowd simmered, uneasy.

I danced away. As he thundered in, I slipped under his jab like José in the basement of Simons Park, and threw a desperate overhand right that crashed into his temple. I'd closed my eyes and when I looked up Velez was stumbling backward on his heels. His shocked eyes wobbled in their sockets. *Fuck, I caught him!* The crowd exploded in a shocked roar.

"Fuckin-a right! MLD killa motherfuckers!" Pat roared from my corner.

The ref stepped in and gave Velez an eight count. He furiously put his arms out and shook his head no. My mind throbbed as my stomach stirred woozily.

"Knock this bitch the fuck out!" Pat screamed at me from the corner.

The ref waved him on. Velez stormed back over and hit me with another five punches. They flung in like antimatter obliterating my brain matter. I swung an overhand and missed. He hit me with an uppercut that lifted both my feet off the ground. My body went rigid. *I'm outgunned. How the fuck can I beat this motherfucker?*

I lunged in and landed another overhand right and clinched him. He fought furiously to break the clinch. *I ain't letting go till the ref fuckin' breaks it.* The referee broke the clinch and looked at me closely in the eyes. I moved and boxed but Velez swiftly cut the ring off on me and landed at will. A precise right cross surprised me. *Damn!* The room went on a tilt. *TIME OUT motherfucker! I gotta take a knee. Clear my head.* I started to kneel. The bell mercifully sounded. I plopped down on the stool as Brother climbed into the ring.

"Are you OK, Joe?" Brother asked, uneasy.

"I don't know."

"Fuck 'em, Joey, just dip under and explode on this spic," Pat urged.

An old bald guy in a white button-up shirt started screaming at the judges' table ringside. He threw a fit and grabbed an official by the collar, waving a fistful of papers. Other officials got up and tried to calm him down.

"Fuck you, if you won't stop it, I will!" He climbed up the steps and keenly slid through the ropes beside me. An anchor tattooed on his forearm read *US NAVY*. He grabbed the ref by the collar.

"This fight's over! That man is disqualified!" He pointed at Velez. "A park district coach put a call in to Puerto Rico. He was a finalist in their national championships last year, in the Open!"

He walked up to Velez and Capone and pointed in Velez's face.

"You will never box in this city again!"

"I knew they was fucking cheating!" Pat climbed through the ropes, tripped and fell as Brother tried to grab him. Pat slipped through Brother's hands.

Capone spun around and puffed his round chest out. Pat hopped up and threw down the pitchforks gang sign at him. "Fuck you, bitch-ass MLDs!"

Capone's eyes lit up; he rushed at Pat and reeled back to swing on him. Pat looped a left hook that smacked into the MLD's temple; the shot sent his legs stiff and wobbly like a newborn fawn. Pat clipped him again behind the ear and dropped him face-first. His pudgy belly boomed on the springy canvas. The crowd erupted as the melee spread through the ring: security, fighters, trainers, and spectators dove through the ropes from all sides. Velez zoomed at Pat, I rushed between them. Velez swung a sharp cross at me. I dove under the shot and tackled him into the corner, he was light and almost dainty in my grasp. He tried to punch at my head but couldn't get anything on the shots from his back. Security and fighters finally pried me off of him and wrestled us all apart. Two enormous black security guards in gray shirts escorted Pat out of the gymnasium, gripping each of his arms as he wined and shouted. Dad screamed viciously at Pat, following them out.

The ref called us to the center of the ring. Velez stormed off and climbed out. I stood there alone with the ref, with the crowd on their feet—distressed, murmuring, still discussing and arguing about what exactly had occurred. Then finally they *shhh*-ed each other to hear the exact words of official announcement.

"On disqualification, the winner in the blue corner, Joe Walsh!"

The faces in the big dark room started to show a stunned kind of reverence.

"I told you!" Sal shouted, scolding several of his fighters who had their own theories about why the bout was stopped.

"Nearly forty bouts, if you want to fucking see em!" the old bald official who'd blown the whistle yelled to the crowd. He slammed the papers down at the ringside table as several trainers and fighters hurried over and pushed in and got on their tippy toes to see the paperwork. It was records they'd faxed over from Puerto Rico. Sal popped out of the mound of guys with his hands gripping the top of his head; his eyes bugged out.

"That guy stopped a lotta open fighters!" Sal said as I climbed out of the ring and down the steps. *Well, that was a fucking mess.* I pushed through the confused faces plopped down on the bleachers near one of the locker rooms. My family and Faith came over as I held my throbbing head in my wrapped hands.

"Well, congrats!" Faith said half-heartedly. "How do you feel?"

"A little woozy." She kissed me on my forehead.

"He's a cheater, baby," she said. "They did the right thing."

Rich came up, with little Simon hugging his leg.

"See how Pat is now? What if he got you kicked out of the tournament?" Rich asked. "All that work for nothing…"

"Stop it, he was just trying to protect me."

"Protect you? That was just some of his old gangbanger shit came back to haunt him. That dude's an SD or something."

"An MLD," I corrected him.

"Lose that fucking loser," Rich urged.

"He's our brother, ya know? And he's trying to do good."

Rich picked up Simon; his long curly blondish-brown hair bounced around as he grinned at me. "Well, he did real good tonight."

"You won!" Simon said. I gave him a high five. "Uncle Pat is stupid!"

"See? Even he knows." Rich said.

They all took off. I stayed with Brother Alex to watch the rest of the fights. The old official guy ended up being Larry Richards, the head Illinois boxing commissioner for the pros. He was also active in USA Boxing. He came up to me later as I watched the bouts in the bleachers.

"Kid, you were fighting your heart out, but that guy is a cheater. He has thirty-seven fights." A half-dozen lines spread across his forehead. "He's too good to be boxing a novice." He squeezed my shoulder. "You're only seventeen, I wasn't gonna let him stop you and hurt you. You got stones, kid. I like that. Good luck in the finals." He looked up to the stands at Chupi and winked, then he walked off.

I looked over. Chupi grinned and held his hand like a phone to his ear. I burst out laughing. *Thanks*, I mouthed.

So that's how I advanced to the finals of the '97 Chicago Golden Gloves. It made me really grateful they'd stopped it when they did. Looking back, that was one of the most important moments in my career. I couldn't defend myself against him—just too much skill, speed, and power. A month later he beat the number-three ranked boxer in the nation in a clean decision at a show fight in the burbs.

It felt kind of anticlimactic as I sat there in Saint Andrew's watching the fights, but guys from all the gyms kept coming up to me and patting me on the back and saying, "You was doing great!"

They invited me to their gyms for sparring, and everybody felt bad about it and was glad they'd stopped it and was glad they DQd Velez. They all were laughing that I gave him an eight count, and said I must have a good punch.

Sal was laughing so hard. He came up and gave me a kiss on the forehead and said, "This kid has got something. You know that guy, he's way too experienced, he's real good, he could turn pro right now probably. How many fights you got?"

"Eleven."

"You'll see when you got twenty, thirty fights under your belt. You'll see why they stopped it, because it's dangerous to let a guy like him in there with a novice. He knocked that kid out last week, just disgusting." He headed on in to the ring in his black cornerman's jacket with the gold trim and the golden Windy City Gym letters across the back shining in the bright lights.

"That's terrible, letting that guy in Novice," Fearless Martinez, a top pro with a mean scowl, said to Sal as he walked past.

"I know!" Sal stopped halfway up the ring steps. "And he gave Velez an eight count, I can't believe it!"

McGary's kid won a close decision against the muscular guy from Pug's Gym, but his nose bled all over the ring.

"So it's McGary and me in the finals," I said as Brother and I headed out of Saint Andrew's.

"Now we gotta get you in even better shape! More sparring, more running, if you really want to win this thing."

◆

At home, I sat bewildered on my bed. *I wonder what my face looks like.* We had a two-week break before the finals to train, so it would have time to heal up. I got up, looked in the mirror. A faded mouse hung under my right eye. *That kid from Whiting did worse damage. Velez knew exactly where to hit you to hurt your brain, to get it to want to turn off and put you down. He hit you in the chin, the temple, the jaw. All those spots make your body betray itself. You gotta learn to do that shit, be more accurate. Maybe use that with McGary. He showed strong skills. Good feet, but not much pop.* I shadowboxed in the mirror in my bedroom. *His dad trains fighters out of their garage in Beverly on the Southside, he's got two Open guys in the finals. McGary's sixteen.* I double-jabbed and shot a right cross. *That's good. It's just two high school kids going at it.*

Pat came home. Dad gave him some shit as he went up to the attic. *Fucking Pat dropped that MLD. That shit was nuts. Well, he got a KO in Saint Andrew's at the Gloves anyways. Inside the ring and all! Fucking looney toon, can't let that old gang shit go.* I could still practically hear Pat pistol-whipping that Assyrian King to death in that pharmacy all those years ago. *I guess you can't just flip a switch and change. Fucking guy's been at war with the world for a decade, now he's just expected to snap out of it?* My stomach turned at the thought of him all strung out, those big bags under his eyes. All the shit he did. *Did he really stick a gun under a pregnant lady's dress? Is that same dude my brother? Am I fooling myself thinking he'll straighten out?* I sighed and closed my eyes in the dark room. *Joe, he's your fucking brother, you gotta help him.*

Ma and Dad started arguing. Dad called Pat down from the attic.

"What's this shit?"

"Oh come on," Pat whined. "It's painkillers, I hurt my hand the other day. I got a prescription!"

"Pat, we can't go through this again," Dad said.

"We want to help you, honey, but you're doing heroin again," Ma pleaded.

"No, I'm NOT!" Pat screamed. "OK, fine. I can't take this shit anymore. I'm out of here."

The weight of it hung on me like a cloud of dark matter pinning me to the bed. My brother's new life was disintegrating, out there in the hall just outside my door. I gasped. *I believe him. He ain't on fuckin drugs, he's just fuckin sick!* I punched my pillow.

Pat went back up to the attic and gathered his things.

"Thanks a lot, Ma and Dad," he said obnoxiously as his feet thundered down the steps and out the door.

◆

With all that shit dancing through my mind, I dug in and trained harder than ever. To be fighting in the finals thrilled me. They always drew a capacity crowd.

I showed up at Windy City and the guys treated me like I was famous for what I did to Velez. Fearless hugged me, put his arm around my shoulder, and walked me over to meet some of the pros that'd just finished sparring. He introduced me to a pale Mexican guy with sweat dripping off his chin and thick scars all across his brow.

"Meet Rocky Lopez. He's fighting for a world title next month."

"Nice to meet you, Rocky."

Rocky bumped fists with mine.

"This is the kid I was talking about that knocked the crap outa that Open fighter last weekend."

"They're always trying to sneak Open fighters into Novice," Rocky sighed.

"Remember when they caught that guy from Saint Louis loading his gloves before he fought you?" an Assyrian guy with black mustache and beard chimed in as he packed up his headgear. I recognized him as Anwar Oshana, an Assyrian guy I'd seen on an ESPN Tuesday night fights card.

"He stopped him in the second round." Fearless nudged me.

"The amateurs are the worst for cheaters," Anwar said, and winked at me. "Good job."

"Are you kidding me?" Fearless guffawed. "The pros are ten times worse!"

"A hundred times worse," Rocky said.

"Everybody's cheating in the pros, kid," Fearless told me. "Don't go pro unless you aware of that shit."

"If it ain't the commission not piss-testing properly, it's a judge getting a check. Or the ref is in somebody's pocket letting the other fighter cheat."

"The cards are always stacked."

"And it's usually the scorecards."

"There's too much money in it for them not to cheat."

I listened and soaked it up. *Damn, these guys are top pros and they know who I am? This is crazy. Shit, they're pros and here I am barely made it to the finals of the novice division off a DQ.* I giggled. *I guess a fight's a fight.*

A squat little Asian featherweight sparred aggressively with a series of boxers cycling in for him. His drenched Korean flag shirt clung to his chest. Sal observed closely. I watched as I shadowboxed in the mirror. Sal glanced at me.

"Joe, can you give this guy two, three rounds? He's getting ready for a title shot."

"Sure," I said as excitement swirled in my stomach.

"We're trying to build his endurance, OK, he's going fifteen and you're his last three. Throw a lot of punches, move-move pop-pop. We need to push him here at the end when he's tired."

I geared up as the Asian fighter banged away. Sal motioned me in at the break. I climbed in. He huffed and puffed, leaning on the ropes as Sal doused him with water. *He looks real tired.* The bell rang and the Asian threw quick combos on me through the first two rounds. *Move-move pop-pop, just like Sal said.* He shot a jab but took a long time bringing it back to his guard as he tried to smother me. *Just counter that jab.* I clinched, Sal shouted to break. I feinted my jab and he reached in with his jab as I drop-stepped. I knocked his jab down with my left, twisted and loaded for the right, planted my feet into the blue canvas, and fired my cross over the top of it. It felt like a particle slammed straight through its collider target. His chin snapped and twisted. He thudded straight to the canvas on his knees, then fell back on his backside. The damp red-and-blue yin and yang symbol glowed in the sunlight flowing down on us through the skylight. Sal shouted and climbed up on the apron as the guy rolled over and got right up. He shook his head, laughed really hard, and touched up with me.

"Sorry," I said as Sal sighed.

"Don't forget, you're ten pounds heavier than him!"

I nodded and took a lot off my punches and let him work. He caught me with some shots, then collapsed exhausted at the bell.

Sal climbed in the ring grinning over him. "Well, it wasn't pretty but you did it, fifteen rounds. Now twelve is gonna feel like nothing." He showered water over the fighter's head from a green bottle.

"Good work, kid," Sal muttered to me as I climbed down from the ring.

Fearless and Rocky stalked the floor between rounds with their bag gloves on.

"Did you see that shit?" Fearless guffawed.

"Who the fuck is this kid?" Rocky replied.

I looked up as they pretended they weren't talking about me and walked around. Then Fearless flopped down next to me. "Well, um, kid, I'd like to be your manager."

Everybody in earshot burst into laughter.

"What?" He glared at them. "All I want is twenty-five percent. Deal?"

I chuckled and pulled my gloves off.

The Asian guy flopped down beside me giggling exhaustedly.

"I never saw the punch coming, it was just there, bam." He laughed. "Thanks for the work, you're real good for a kid."

"Thanks," I said. *Is this guy really that good? Fuck, if I dropped him, what's a world champ gonna do?*

Boxing is such a situational sport. You can do something to a really good fighter one day in sparring and then be blown out by a guy who sucks the next day. The next week the Asian fighter won the vacant IBO world title down in Florida. It's a lesser belt but still a meaningful one.

Meanwhile I came into the gym that next Monday and Sal still couldn't believe I caught him. I ripped combinations into the bag near the guys that lounged on the apron of the blue ring.

"Fucking this kid reads him, he's not bringing his jab back home and wha-wop! Counters him. Puts him down!" Sal beamed. "He was bringing his jab home in the fight though! That was one of the final pieces we needed, kid." He winked at me.

Sal's starting to like me. 1-2-3 roll, the bag jostled. *But I'm Brother's fighter. But maybe somewhere down the line if I make a name for myself, I could be one of Sal's fighters and turn pro.* Jab-jab-jab, feint the cross, circle. *I gotta keep Brother with me though. That'd be a good fuckin' corner, Sal and Brother. Art and Fury.* 1-2-3 roll, I squatted and right hooked to the body, and then nailed a left hook to the liver that popped the bag into a wobbly spin.

Fearless glared at me pridefully.

"You dropped that dude, Joe," he said as I danced around a big brown heavy bag. "Don't ever forget that. You dropped a champ."

"Naw. He just walked into it." I shot three jabs into the bag.

They all looked at each other like they'd heard some final piece to a cosmic puzzle they'd been contemplating.

◆

Saturday night of the finals came. Brother and I got to Saint Andrew's early. Budweiser had decked the whole ring out with Budweiser foam ring posts and canvas. A heavy gray cloud hung inside the ring like a glob of dark matter holding the invisible destiny of the boxers about to enter it. A weak queasiness came over me. I got in the ring to work out the nerves. I jabbed and moved. *I ain't afraid. McGary can't stop me, but he could beat me on points.* I threw my 1-2-3 into the air, trying to snap each shot in the shadowy room. *He knows how to let his hands go like an open fighter. He's more savvy than me but I still think I could best him and bust him up a little.* I dug body shots into the air. *Brother's got me in such good shape I can't imagine anyone going harder than me. They say you win the fight well before you step in the ring. Well, I feel like I won it already.*

I danced to my right and shot a right jab like Ali, imagining the roaring crowd that'd be there in a few hours. I plopped down on the wooden stool. *I just can't let him outbox me. They been giving me great work over at Windy City. They taught me all kinds of tricks.* I looked out at the blue canvas littered with thousands of purplish blood splatters. I got up and danced over the splatters on my toes, sticking one-twos into the darkness. *Thank God I ain't a bleeder.* I pivoted and threw an uppercut.

Brother and I waited on the bleachers near the dressing room as the crowd filtered in. All the sudden Jay walked up in a blue Adidas track suit.

"Jay!"

"I heard you made the finals, boy, I couldn't miss this!"

"Thanks for coming, Jay."

"Bust his nose for me."

"We plan to, Jay," Brother said. "He's a bleeder."

"Good luck."

"Thanks for coming, man."

We bumped fists and Jay headed off to get a seat as fight fans filled Saint Andrew's to capacity. The dark room turned electric. Big bright ring lights hung from the roof. The announcers wore tuxedos. The card girls looked amazing in their skin-tight red-and-white Budweiser dresses, high heels, big hair, and huge asses.

Sal came up and greeted us.

"Kid, I know you're unattached, but do you guys want to represent Windy City for this fight, for when they announce you?"

"Sure," I said excitedly.

Brother thanked him.

"Thanks to you, Mr. Brother," Sal said. "He's been giving us great work."

Pat showed up with a bunch of hoods from the old neighborhood. They came up to me looking crazy and mean, their brows flexing like a gang of Cro-Magnons. This murderous motherfucker named Rickey gave me a snide grin, scratching his leathery neck.

"Remember me, Joey?" Rickey asked. "From the old neighborhood?"

I looked at him. A big scar ran down his cheek, and another on his flexing throat. *Yeah, you burned that Royal's eyes out with the hot pokers, always talked about it like it was the greatest thing you ever did in your whole miserable life.* Then I glared at Pat.

"Can I talk with you, Pat?"

"Yeah, what's going on?"

We stepped to the side.

"Whatchu doing hanging with these guys?"

"Aye." Pat recoiled. "What if them MLDs come back? You'd be happy they was here."

"Pat, what about starting a new life and all that?"

"Look, I'm trying to protect you, can't you see that?"

"Whatever, man. Can you just make sure they don't start no stupid shit up in here?"

"I got 'em under control." He turned to them. "Aye knuckleheads, let's grab a beer. Let the kid focus."

They went over to the beer table and started drinking. They found a spot in the bleachers across from me, all of 'em edgy and sniffling like they caught the same cold. *Motherfuckers are on blow in here? Fucking Pat, man, what the fuck are you doing?* A vision flashed from when I was just a helpless little boy: Pat all strung out, holding a gun to Ma's head. My body tensed violently. *I ain't a little boy no more, motherfucker. I can't fucking go through this shit again. Doing lines to get amped up, then when he needs to come down he'll be back to smack.* I closed my eyes and sighed. *Stop it, he's not snorting coke. He just brought the guys in case some shit pops off.*

McGary brought out a couple hundred Irish Southsiders. They all congregated near the beer tables—a big sea of green and old-timey caps. My whole family came, a bunch of the guys from Saint Joe's too.

We got in the ring, and they announced McGary. His crowd went absolutely nuts over by the beer table.

"And in the blue corner representing the Windy City Gym, Joe Walsh!" My cheering section roared. A lot of the Windy City guys and the fighters who knew about Velez cheered for me in little patches sprinkled throughout the crowd. The TJOs went nuts as Pat waved them to their feet.

"Let's go, Joseph!" Rosie yelled loud and obnoxious for me. It made me giggle and relax. *I got Rosie Walsh with me, motherfucker, better watch out. Toughest person in the whole room.*

McGary looked slick in his red finals uniform as he kicked his red high-top boxing shoes out in front of him.

The bell rang. McGary bounded forward and tried to put his jab—right cross—left hook on me, 1-2-3, and use his feet to escape my shots. I caught air with my three and he came back with his combination. *Just throw with him.* I exchanged with him and put power on my two. The two caught him and snapped his head back. The crowd reeled, and I dug a hard hook into his heart. He flinched, then grabbed hold of me. *I'm stronger than him.* I twisted him in the clinch and worked my free hand until the ref broke us. McGary volume-punched me from the outside. I threw with him. We connected a lot. He rocked my head back. I stuck my hook through his guard. Then he came over my hook with a cross and we tangled up again. At the bell I shook my head walking back to my stool. *I ain't never threw more punches in a round and I still think he outpunched me by a few.*

"Close round, Joe! You gotta put some power on this kid! Hurt him! Bust that long nose 'a his!" Brother said as he filled my mouth with cool water. "Come on, prettyboy, everybody's watching! Your girlie's out there in the crowd." He pointed out toward Faith and my family. "You gonna let him kick your wussy La Grange ass in fronta her?"

"Hell no!"

He popped my mouthpiece in. I stood up and looked out at Faith, who watched in the second row, worried. Her green eyes glistened. I winked at her and she smiled.

The bell rang.

"Don't forget! You're from Edgewater, Joey!" Pat roared drunkenly from my corner. The guys from the hood all roared, throwing up the J hand sign.

I smashed my gloves together and shot out to meet McGary. St Andrew's rocked and rolled as we lit each other up with combos. Two battles unfolded, the battle in the ring and the battle of the cheering outside it. *His crowd outnumbers mine two to one but mine got more pep. If it's close, I ain't getting the decision. I gotta get an eight count on him.* I caught him with a hard jab. A bright string of blood ripped out of his nostril. I kept dinging him. His nose fattened and bled. It dribbled over the white Budweiser letters on his chest. As we clinched it mixed with our sweat, and slathered us in a slimy red goo on my neck and collar bone.

He heaved through his mouth. *He can't breathe through his nose!* The round ended as the warring factions in the crowd exploded in unison.

"That's it, Joseph!" Rosie shouted. I glanced over. Jay stood by her and my family, cheering me on.

"Keep working on that nose!" Brother shouted. "If he bleeds too much, they'll stop it! Break it open like a fire hydrant, Joe!"

Pat climbed up on the apron.

"Joe! What are ya doing?! You gotta break this kid's fucking nose!" Pat tried to get in the ring. Brother pushed him out.

"Only one second allowed in the ring," the ref yelled at us.

Pat turned around to his guys and did a wacky dance on the apron as they roared.

"I'm one-and-oh in the Gloves!" he shouted, then stumbled down the steps and fell onto a guy in the front row. *Fuckin shoulda never let him in my corner.*

"I'm sorry, Brother."

"It doesn't matter, Joe. Just stay focused on that nose!" Brother urged.

I kept my jab on the nose. He bled. The ref kept stopping the action to look at the nose; it grew big, fat and broken. The doc checked it and let it go. My cheering section shouted, "The nose! The nose, Joey!" McGary glanced in the stands scared and held his gloves high over his face. *Trick him.* I feinted my jab at him and gathered all my strength and dug straight right at his solar plexus. It careened in like a meteor. As it collided, I felt the wind shoot out of him. His elbows came down to guard his body as I aimed all my focus on a stiff power jab that smooshed dead center into the bridge of his nose. He clinched desperately. His face lay on my shoulder as the blood streamed down like a hose and flowed right down my back. *They're gonna stop it!* The ref broke us. The crowd recoiled at the blood—a lot of low grossed-out *Ewwwws*. The ref grimaced at the blood pouring down. It covered his mouth and dripped from his chin. The ref shook his head sadly, hugged him, then waved his hand over McGary's head. The crowd erupted, sending their energy into me; I leapt up in the air and my arms shot up triumphantly.

Holy fucking shit! I'm a Golden Gloves champ! I ran over to Brother, who'd climbed up on the apron. I hugged his big round torso as he slapped my bloody back.

"The La Grange Wimp did it after all!"

"Damn right! I owe it all to you, Brother!"

"You're a Golden Gloves champ now, Joe!"

"You taught me how to win... I love you."

Pat ran up behind him. "I told you!" he yelled drunkenly.

"Oh yeah," I sneered at him. "I couldn't a done it without you, big bro."

Pat grabbed me around the shoulders and turned to the guys all cheering near my corner. One of 'em had a camera and Pat threw up the J gang sign with his free hand as the guy snapped a few shots.

I wrestled free out his grasp. "I don't want no part of that shit," I said.

They announced me the winner and raised my blue-wrapped fist. The Southsiders booed and threw a fit as my family and fighters all over the gymnasium cheered.

"Quiet, ya crybaby micks!" Rickey yelled from near my corner.

They handed me my blue-and-gold trophy. I closed my eyes. Da's smiling face popped in my mind. I looked up into the lights and said, "It's for you," and it felt like the roof opened up and the message soared up to him.

I climbed out of the ring into a pandemonium of hugs and high-fives. Faith rushed up and grabbed my shoulders and gave me a big kiss. Her hands slathered and stuck to my bloody skin. "You're gross!" she said, with a big sexy smile.

I took pictures with everybody and my trophy. As it died down, we headed toward the exit, Jay pulled me aside.

"Joe, I like your sister, but you my guy, so I gotta ask permission. Can I ask your sister out?"

"You fucker." I punched him in the shoulder. "Yeah, I don't care, as long as you treat her nice."

"Thanks! Joe, you know I will, man. On everything. You got my word!"

I strolled toward the exit of Saint Andrew's with Faith and my family. Little Simon held my trophy up like I'd won the Olympics. Strangers congratulated me and patted me on the back. I feel like the fuckin' king of Chicago.

Pat and the guys lingered near the door. Pat walked up and gave me a hug.

"I'm proud of ya, Joey."

"Thanks Pat, but come on." I nodded toward the guys. "They're no good, Pat."

"Come on, Joey," Pat whined. "I ain't seen 'em in years." He muffed my hair as I walked away. "You're a Golden Gloves champ now but don't forget, you're still just a snot-nosed kid to me." He looked at me with the same blue eyes as mine, but the bright ring lights were caught in his and seemed to shatter them into a million tiny pieces. I just walked past him.

As I got to the door I looked back at Pat as he sniffled. Big shadows swallowed his eyes in that old nasty look he got when he was high. *The only snot-noses here are you and those clowns.* I turned and walked out the door into the roaring and merciless cold of the Chicago night. *What the fuck, Pat? I thought you were gonna change.*

Chapter 6: Enabled

BY THEN THE NEIGHBORS WERE MAKING OUR LIVES SO MISERABLE that living there on LaGrange Road just wasn't an option anymore. Ma had already brought those ghetto babysitting kids out there, where they'd taught all those trust-fund kids next door how to swear through the fence. And Jan, who they thought was the maid, had ripped the bumper off their Beamer. Then Dad started using the backyard as his own second construction yard. He parked a Bobcat back there, and a few gnarly pickup trucks full of generators, tools, and material. The crew'd show up looking like bigfoots in Carhartt every morning, trying not to bump the neighbor's BMW as they pulled out of the shared driveway at 6 a.m. Plus I was always walking around with black eyes and shadowboxing in the backyard. And on top of all that, my folks had moved their gang-leader junkie son straight from fucking Pontiac prison into one of the most pristine suburbs in Chicagoland. These soccer moms, lawyers, and doctors weren't having it. They started calling town hall, the cops, and DCFS on us.

The last straw was the day I came home from school with a cop car in the driveway and some of the babysitting kids' parents walking their little rugrats out of the house. I hopped off the bus and walked up to the neighbor lady as she talked with the cop.

"We caught her other son behind our garage last month. I think he was trying to burglarize it. And that's their youngest there!" she said bitterly, pointing at me.

"You fucking with my family? Fuck you, you stupid bitch!" I yelled.

"Hey! You can't talk to her like that!" The pudgy officer spun around and glared at me.

"Fuck you too, pig!" I told him. As he started towards me, fidgeting with his radio, I jogged into the house.

Dad was in the kitchen on the phone.

"Your mother's been arrested," he told me. He was talking with the lawyer.

They released her after a few hours. That weekend Ma made the cover of *La Grange Suburban Life*. They had a picture of our house under the headline *Illegal Daycare On LaGrange Road Shut Down*.

I came downstairs and the paper sat at the long glossy table between my parents. I picked it up and read it. The article explained the illegal twelve-kid babysitting operation. She was only allowed five on her license.

"Twelve kids? Big wup! I had thirty-three in Chicago!"

"Mary, this shit's gotta stop," Dad said, gripping his short white hair. "You're gonna end up in prison!"

"What am I supposed to do for money? Go work at Jewels?" she said, smacking the table. "I can barely walk, fer Christ's sake!"

The paper had interviewed the parents as they left our place with their kids, but all the parents said they liked the way Ma took care of their kids and that she was a good babysitter.

I closed the paper. There it was, my parents' dream, their suburban escape, the big blue house on LaGrange Road. *Suburban Life. Well I guess the Walshes were never meant for the suburban life after all. Big surprise. What the hell were we thinking, moving to a white-collar suburb? We were blue-collar to the bone.*

◆

Ma and Dad bought the lot beside Rich's house in the working-class side of Brookfield next to the quarry and the GE plant, and we started building a new house ourselves. The house in La Grange sold, but we stayed nearby, moving into an apartment above Gram in the three-flat she'd bought when she followed us out to the suburbs. We'd just stay there while we finished building the house, and probably to keep an eye on Pat and her.

Gram'd asked me over around the time Pat moved in with her. She sat in her wheelchair in a big blue flower-pattern housedress beside her bed, big and obese like Ma, with thin blackish-gray hair. She held a spiral notepad and ticked off items from lists she'd made of her jewelry, dolls, antiques, and paperwork. It was all organized in piles on her comforter; she told me to put the important things in the big gray metal safe in her closet.

"Why you doing this, Gram?" I asked, holding a small Chinese doll. Its eyes rolled around, opening and closing like an insane person.

"'Cause Pat's moving in! He might steal it!" she said, ticking her doll off the list.

"He wouldn't steal from you, Gram."

"Oh, he's a little devil, Joey." She handed me a fancy golden necklace with a big green stone pendant. I put it on a shelf in the safe. "Oh, he's so charming though..." She picked up a short blonde wig, put it on, and adjusted it. "He's gonna do good but I gotta be careful."

"Whatever you say, Gram."

My suspicions sprouted roots as I listened to Gram yelling at Pat below my feet as I tried to sleep in my room in the apartment above them. This dark cloud engulfed him; soon he was avoiding me. Then his old girlfriend Marie showed up, skinny like a twig and high, and I knew it was over.

I bumped into Pat in the stairwell.

"Aye kiddo!" He headed down the stairs as I lingered at the door.

"Pat?"

He stopped on the steps.

I sighed. "What are you doing hanging around with her, Pat? I thought you were done with that life."

"Yeah, Joe, but I love her. I'm gonna marry her. And I want you to be the best man. How 'bout that?"

The dark matter cloud swooped into my chest and annihilated all my hope for my big brother. "Pat, she's..." I swallowed back the emotion. "She's a hooker."

"No she ain't, goddamnit!" He recoiled like I'd stabbed him in the heart. "Why would you say that about her!?"

"Pat, she's a junkie!"

"Leave me alone, Joe." He turned down the steps.

"Pat, I can't watch you do this shit to yourself again."

He opened the door to the basement apartment and stepped inside. "Whaddaya you know about it?!" He glared back at me. "Leave me the fuck alone!" He slammed the white door between us.

Pat, Gram, and Marie started the same old crap. Gram'd be screaming at them. He'd steal Gram's credit cards and run scams at the gas station across the street, conning people into helping him get cash by using the card to fill up their cars. He'd take their cash and give them an extra five bucks in gas, then run down to the hood and score heroin. He'd tell Gram he was driving around all day using the car to look for work when he was really sitting in the car, parked in Austin, high as a motherfucker with Marie.

◆

Ma stole Gram's credit card and bank statements out of the mailbox and figured out how bad it was. She went down there and threw the statements down on her coffee table.

"Ma, he's running through your retirement! You are going to lose the building."

"Oh my god!" Gram looked at the proof, astonished.

Gram screamed at Pat and Marie when they showed up that night. They left. Didn't move out, just stopped living in the basement. Gone to wherever.

Then Pat started with the calls. He left messages on our machine. One night I came home from school exhausted from training. Ma was at the store and the apartment was dark and quiet. I saw the light on the answering machine and hit the button while I looked in the fridge.

"Ma..." Pat's voice filled the room: grave, tired, and angry. "You keep giving me problems with Gram, you better be careful... Ya know, you got a lot of little kids around in the family. You can't keep them safe all the time... They gotta walk home from school, ya know?"

My crucifix tingled at my chest and started to burn. *I've gotta kill that motherfucker.* My hands trembled as the wires dug into my mind. I imagined him grabbing Rich's kid Simon as he walked home from school, just snagging him by his little arm and throwing him in the Lumina. Simon's little terrified face as he clung to the door, trying to escape. A hook planted in my heart. I crouched in the dark kitchen gripping my chest. The wires squeezed around my lungs. *Jesus Christ, don't you hurt those kids.* I stood. *It can't be real, he couldn't have really said that.* I sat down at the kitchen table and pressed Play. I played the message over and over again. I talked to his voice on the machine. "Pat, I can't let you do this to my family. No more. I'm sorry. I gotta protect the kids from you. They're innocent. I'm gonna kill you, Pat. 'They gotta walk home from school, ya know?' I'm gonna motherFUCKING KILL YOU MOTHERFUCKER!" I dropped my head in my fists on the old wooden kitchen table Dad'd made with his hands thirty years ago, back before Pat's first shot of heroin. Tears poured down on my knuckles. *You shoulda let Rich kill him that day on the job site.* Then: *Naw Joe, Rich has kids to raise. The only one who could go away right now for manslaughter is you. You gotta be the one to do it.*

I felt a breeze and someone behind me. I turned and the door slowly opened in silence. Marie stood in the darkness in the hall. Her thin, withered, wrinkled face twitched. Her frizzy shoulder-length hair moved like dead leaves—her whole body trembling like that night years ago when she came up to the sills and Ryan pissed in her mouth, except worse. She couldn't even talk. She stared at me completely possessed by that hunger in her soulless gray eyes. She just trembled there trying to say something, stammering, "I...I'm si...si...sick..." in the blackness of the stairwell.

I just reached out, caught the door, and swung it closed slowly in her face as she let out a slow screech on the other side and disappeared.

◆

They still ended up back in the basement. Gram couldn't stop them. She hated Ma in a lot of ways. They just never got along. She was always saving Pat from Ma when Pat was little, back when Ma was a fifteen-year-old mom who didn't really want to be mom some days. Now Gram tried to save Pat from his hunger for junk. She gave and gave and gave. She looked at him and saw the little boy she loved so much. The one her daughter had at fourteen with the fifteen-year-old boy that drank and beat them. She remembered the time Dad'd broken Pat's arm throwing him down the stairs. She was always trying to fix the broken places in Pat. The ones that never healed, deep down inside him.

We all knew this shit had to stop. Just...fucking how to stop it?

Then one day, Pat told Gram the cops'd towed her car. Gram called Ma. Ma didn't buy it. She and Rosie drove around the block and found Gram's green Lumina parked a street over. Meanwhile Pat picked Gram up in a cab like they needed to go to the bank and get money so Pat could go to the pound and pay to get Gram's car out. Pat was helping Gram out of the cab when Ma pulled up behind them.

"Ma, he's lying! Your car is right around the corner!"

"Fuck!" Pat shrieked.

Gram grabbed his arm and tried to slap him with her purse. He shoved her and she fell on her plump backside. Pat cut through a gangway and ran to the car. Rosie got out to help Gram while Ma swerved around them and chased Pat for a few blocks. Then he shot out of sight. We all knew where he was headed, though: back to the city.

Gram had finally had enough. She wanted him out, and wanted her car back. She reported it stolen. Even though she knew who had it, she wanted it on record. Plus Pat still had the keys.

So she called Blake. He was on duty, plainclothes. She screamed at him: "I want my car back! Go get my car!"

"You finally kicked him out?!"

"Yeah, I'm never letting him back in."

"Alright, Gram," Blake said, and him and his partner left Humboldt Park and headed up to the old neighborhood.

Blake asked around and found out that Pat'd been hanging at some bar on Clark Street known for heroin, a place that supposedly had a secret shooting den. So Blake went in there in his gray hoodie, his badge hanging on a string in the center of his wide barrel chest, his handsome resting bitch-face scowling at everybody. He started busting up the place, with his partner at the door to keep anybody from running out. Blake cracked a few patrons over the head with his nightstick and busted a few guys in the chops and they started singing, telling him there was a shooting den down in the basement. He went down there, into the scent of ammonia and burnt fingertips, puke and scorched spoons, and sure enough there were twenty miserable dope-sick junkies waiting for a fix, calling out weakly for "Pistol."

Blake wisely figured Pat would end up there at some point in the night. So he went back upstairs and sat on one of the side streets where he could see the front door of the bar. Sure enough, within an hour Pat barreled up in Gram's green Lumina. Blake peeled out towards him. The door to the bar opened and one of the junkies screamed, "Go! Get the fuck outa here!" and Pat jumped back in the car and floored it.

Blake swerved onto Clark behind him in his gray unmarked Caprice. Cop brother and crook brother shot off on a high-speed chase through their old neighborhood. Pat flew north and cut west on Bryn Mawr. He blew through a red light and cut right on the arterial alley where we used to play stickball as boys. He floored it over the crown of Olive Avenue and Gram's Lumina bottomed out. Sparks flew and the front bumper came loose. Blake was on his tail. Pat tried to cut a hard left into our alley on Hollywood and crashed into the McPhersons' garage. He threw it in reverse as Blake screeched to a stop behind him. Then Pat put it in drive and shot down our old alley, zigging and zagging past every pothole he ever made with an M80. As he shot past our old garage, Blake closed on him. Pat floored it as he got to the mouth of the alley. An old lady dragging a laundry cart stopped on a dime on the sidewalk next to Mike Thompson's garage and Pat's driver-side mirror popped her wrist as he soared past.

Blake hit the brakes and pulled up on her.

"You OK?" he asked.

"I think so," she said, rubbing her wrist. "What the hell was that asshole doing?"

"Running from the cops."

"Well, I'm OK. I hope you catch the SOB."

"Naw, we're letting him go. 'Cause he ain't worth getting somebody like you hurt."

"That's nice of you, but I say lock him up and throw away the key!"

"We'll try," Blake said with a grin.

Meanwhile Pat was on Ravenswood, headed past the Denopolises' old house, which was where he'd shot up for the very first time fifteen years back.

◆

When I got word of it, I said to myself, I'm gonna kill this motherfucker. I saw Pat's face in everything I hit: the bag, Brother Alex's chest, his big head.

After our training session Brother rubbed his sore shoulder and asked, "Joe, are you mad at me?"

"Naw, Brother, sorry. I got some stuff going on at home."

"Wanta talk about it?"

"Naw."

"How's your brother Pat?

I winced. *Bad? I don't know. I ain't my brother's keeper.*

"I've been praying for him, Joe." Brother put his hand on my back, and the crucifix that clung to the skin of my chest fell away. "Sometimes that's all we can do."

That's not all we can do, Brother. I can kill him. I can put an end to this shit.

"Thanks Brother. Maybe you're right." I stuffed my gear in my bag and walked out into the dark hallway, away from the light bleeding out of the equipment room and glowing on the shiny smooth floor. *Please God, let that motherfucker overdose and die so this can be over.* I stepped deeper into the dark hallway. *If you don't take him, I will.*

◆

The iron forty-five-pound plates rattled on the dark rusty bar as I exploded upward before the mirror in the musty YMCA basement. Big veins popped out of my swollen neck; my shoulders strained as I locked my hips, finishing the deadlift. Pat walked swiftly into the room in the mirror behind me. I released the bar and it bounced on the heavy rubber mat as I spun around. "I'm gonna kill you motherfucker," I muttered to the empty room. My reflection rippled off in every direction to infinity as uncountable copies of my muscular compact body flexed. *Gotta protect my family. He's evil. He ain't human. A human being wouldn't threaten children.* I turned, crouched down, and gripped the bar. I exploded up and held it at the top and looked into my own trembling blue eyes. *You'll kill that motherfucker. Next time you see him. It's the only choice.* A trembling power coursed through my legs, back, and arms like a legion of positrons. I dipped, slammed the weight down. *You're the only guy in the family who doesn't have kids. What's the worst they could do? Put you away for manslaughter? A couple years maybe? It's worth it.* I exploded up. The mirrors in front and behind me echoed my image like a long string of terrible possibilities.

◆

The Walsh men falling into homicidal thoughts wasn't anything new. We came from a long line of fighting men and killers. The first Walsh to set foot in the United States was Lenny Walsh; he came as a peasant in search of land in the West. He walked across the continent, became a cowboy and an outlaw, shot four men down, and had his arm nearly torn off by a rifle round. He should have had it amputated but instead he kept it hanging limply by his side. The land he acquired out West slipped through his fingers. He never had children. His brother Harry was the one who continued the blood line, after settling in Chicago to work in a slaughterhouse. Harry's youngest son Peter Walsh joined the North Side Gang in Chicago and shot down two of Capone's henchmen before being killed outside a flower shop on Broadway near the Mill. Throughout the decades many men fell at the hands of Walshes or with their assistance, but Pistol Pat took the most lives of all.

No Walsh ever stood trial for the killings they committed.

◆

It was a godforsaken sunny day, beautiful and defiant of the harsh realities of the world. Georgie the Greek was dropping me off from school in his dad's black Audi.

"What's up with your brother Pat, Joey? I ain't seen him in a while."

"Nothing..." *Except he's been threatening to hurt my nieces and nephews, and I'm gonna kill him the next time I see him.*

"Aye there he goes right there," Georgie said as he rolled to a stop behind Gram's three-flat.

"What?!" I blurted out.

I looked up as Pat eased down the alley in the green Lumina. The front bumper was duct-taped on.

"Fuck! That's my brother!" Fear and rage twisted in my chest. *Now's your chance. You really gonna do it? I got to.*

"Yeah." Georgie rolled down the window. "Aye Pat, howya been? You land a gig in a House of Pain video yet?"

Pat gave George a wave. A big cheesy grin spread across his stubbly face. He started to pull into the garage as I hopped out and rushed at his door.

"Whatsdamatter witchu kid?" he said with a bemused smile.

I grabbed hold of the door.

"This fucking car is stolen!" I yelled in his face.

"Wha?" he sighed. "You gettin' crazy?"

I cocked back to punch him through the open window. *Naw, don't, it's a cheap shot, he's your brother.* Pat threw it in park as a crazy sneer twisted into his face.

"You want some?" He flinched away and lay in the passenger-side seat. "I got something for you, motha fucka." He reached into the back seat. *Fuck, he got a gun in there?*

"What the hell's going on, Joe?" Georgie chuckled.

"George! Go inside and call the cops!"

"OK, OK!" Georgie ran inside.

Pat pulled out a metal hammer with a blue rubber grip. He slammed the hammer at my hands as I gripped the car door. I pulled 'em back as he jiggled the door handle, trying to open it.

"I'ma hitchu wit this hammer, Joe! Get off the fuckin' car door!"

George reappeared.

"George! Get him off the car door!" Pat roared.

"If I get him off are you gonna leave?" Georgie pleaded.

"Yeah, just get him off!"

George grabbed me around the chest and tore me off.

"No! George, what the fuck!"

Pat opened the door and got out, gripping the hammer.

"You said you were gonna leave!" Georgie pleaded.

"I know what I said! Get the fuck back, you little bitch."

Pat came at me. He swung the hammer at my head. I dodged it. He swung again as I slipped back. *Damn, gotta get him to drop that thing.*

"What, you need a hammer to whoop your baby brother?"

Pat looked at me, looked at the hammer, and tossed it back through the open door of the Lumina. He towered over me and put his massive hairy fists up.

"Let's see whatchu got, ya little shit."

Motherfucker outweighs me by fifty pounds. He swung his right, I slipped it and swung with my own right. We both missed but he looped his southpaw left hook and it bashed into my temple and sent me tottering sideways. I stayed up as he bounded backward.

"Dat's what I thought! You learn your motherfuckin lesson?!"

I heard his voice on the voice mail machine: Ma...you better be careful... *I'm gonna kill you. You're gonna have to kill me to stop me.*

I rushed at him in a low crouch. He swung his left hook again as I dipped under it and threw my overhand right, which narrowly missed. My weight loaded onto my left foot. I rocked and twisted and all my body weight shot into a left hook. I felt the slightest nick as the weight of my whole body flowed through his chin.

His knees buckled as he staggered backward into the shadowy garage. Blood spurted from his lips and drizzled on his dirty white shirt. *This really Pistol Pat?* His eyes wobbled around in their sockets. *All them years robbing drug dealers, surviving in prison?* He stood before me stiff-legged, tottering sideways holding his mouth. *Looks like a bust-out junkie to me.*

"You got me...you got me, little brother."

"I'ma getchu again."

I pressed forward, hands high. He panicked and smashed a metal gallon of paint off the shelving unit at me. I parried it. He picked up a can of Raid and threw it. It bounced off my head as I tried to duck it. Then he stood his ground, reached out, and tried to bear-hug me. I twisted on a short right cross that dug his chin into his throat and he fell forward on me, unconscious. I nearly fell under his limp weight. I bent my knees, bulled forward as he flopped on the hood of Grama's green Lumina. He lay there on his back, blinking. I straddled him and pulled my face close to his.

"I'm gonna kill you now," I whispered.

Ma appeared at the garage door with my baby niece Melinda on her hip.

"Georgie, break it up!" she yelled.

Pat's eyes cleared for a second and he looked up at me.

"Wha?" Pat said, confused.

I swung my head upward and head-butted him as hard as I could. His face was soft and warm. Georgie grabbed at my shirt, trying to pull me off. I head-butted him three more times; it felt like I was burrowing my head deep into sun-baked sand.

Georgie pried me off him. A big wound gaped under Pat's eye.

I was trying to wrestle out of Georgie's grasp when Pat sprang awake. His arms shot out in front of him and he stood up like Frankenstein's monster. Pat screamed like a banshee and barreled at us. Georgie let go of me and stumbled backward with his hands up, like: Get him, not me!

Pat tried to grab me as I dipped under him, grabbed him around the waist, and exploded upward like a deadlift. He floated up weightless for a second as I twisted and slammed him to the concrete floor. His arm flung out and smashed into a tall mirror leaning against the wall near the side door. One side of the mirror shattered into long vertical pieces and clattered atop the gray concrete floor. The rest stayed whole, reflecting me looming over Pat in the shady garage like a black demon with my crucifix dangling over my heart, the golden surface aglow in the blackness. Pat curled up like a giant fetus at my feet. Gram's wheelchair sat against the wall next to him. I grabbed it by the tire and frame, raised it over my head, and slammed it down on his cowering body. The metal frame broke on his head and arm. He lay back twitching on the ground as a big dark circle of piss radiated from the crotch of his blue jeans. Sirens blared in the alley and resounded inside the garage. *You're running out of time!* A big triangular-shaped piece of the broken mirror lay on the concrete beside him reflecting out into infinity. *Stab him in the fucking throat with it!* I scooped up the long dagger of mirror. It was cool and smooth in my hands. *Hurry.* I straddled Pat and lifted the sharp hunk of mirror over my head, aiming to stab him in the jugular.

The side garage door swung open. Gram stood there in her purple house dress hunched over her walker in the big rectangle of sunlight. She looked at us shocked, and grabbed at her hair.

"NO!!!" she screamed.

I have to! I came down with the jagged mirror just as Georgie the Greek made a diving tackle and smashed into my back. We collapsed into the cinder block wall, smashing the rest of the tall mirror. It fell in dozens of pieces atop Pat's body and clinked to the concrete around us.

"Let me kill him, Georgie!"

"No, Joey, you gotta stop, man!"

We wrestled as my hands bled all over the mirror and it grew slippery. A squad car screeched to a stop behind the Lumina as Ma flagged them down. Georgie and I wrestled and got to our feet again as he pulled me away from Pat. Gram hovered over Pat and bent down over him, covering her mouth and weeping. In the reflected pieces of mirror on top of Pat, her face was not old, it was timeless—the sweet roundness that Da adored, the beauty she was at nineteen that sparked the life that gave both him and I life. It was all there, deep in those shattered reflections atop his bloody mass crumpled on the floor of that shadowy garage as he moaned and writhed, clutching his head.

"Oh Patty, it's going to be okay, baby. Gram is here."

The cops grabbed me and cuffed my hands behind my back and led me down the bright sunny alley towards a cop car. Pat stumbled out of the garage bleeding all over the place, with his whole crotch soaked with piss. An officer asked him what happened.

"I don't know! My brother just went nuts and attacked me."

I stopped and struggled with the officers and spun to face him.

"You ain't my motherfuckin' brother! You're just a piece 'a shit junkie. You see that baby girl?" I nodded at Ma holding Jan's plump one-year-old daughter Melinda. "She's a million times more part of this family than you'll ever fuckin be!"

"He knocked out my tooth!" Pat cried to the officer, then glared at me. "I'm pressing charges. You're going to county, and those savages are gonna fuck you in the ass in there!" He spit a glob of dark blood on the gray pavement at his feet.

They threw me in the squad car but Ma talked to them and they ended up releasing me. Pat left in Gram's Lumina after Gram explained that the car was never stolen in the first place.

I ended up back at Faith's. She burst into tears when she saw my face.

"My god! What happened!"

"I got in a fight with my brother Pat."

She touched my temple tenderly. I recoiled.

"Come into the bathroom." She took me by the hand.

In the mirror it looked like somebody'd taken a belt sander to my temple and buzzed off a patch of flesh. The abrasion glowed like a smoldering red giant star.

"Are you OK?"

"I'm fine. He was bleeding out a buncha spots. I knocked his tooth out." I giggled. "I hit him over the head with my grandma's wheelchair, too."

She hugged me and her body throbbed beside me. I held her as she cried. I kissed her mouth. She wet a cotton ball with peroxide and softly dabbed it along the abrasion. She tried not to cry as she cleaned the nicks on my knuckles and the cuts on my palms from the broken mirror. I kissed the warm tears rolling down her face.

Her parents offered to let me sleep over in the TV room, and Faith and I cuddled up on the couch and I fell asleep and woke up in the morning with a soft blanket snug around me. Faith leaned over me. Her strands of straight dirty blonde hair dangled over my face. She kissed my forehead.

"Good morning," she whispered. Her emerald-green eyes peered into mine. "I love you."

"I love you," I replied as she headed out to school.

I went home where I found out Pat was gone. But, of course, not for long.

◆

Pat ran almost all the way through Gram's retirement. He even got a second mortgage on the building. Gram's equity disappeared.

Pat's habit grew until it pushed the limits of human capability. We braced for the news he'd OD'd or someone'd killed him or he'd smoked somebody. Everything he did was felonious; I wouldn't have been surprised if he passed out at the wheel and crashed into some little kids crossing the street. Going back to prison was probably the only thing that could save his life and save Gram from being totally destitute.

But we all knew Ma was capable of just about anything when she put her mind to it.

Ma got together with her brother John and they made a plan. They got Rich to buy a street gun. They removed the firing pin and went over to our apartment and finalized the plans. They sat at the kitchen table with the nickel-plated revolver between them, sipping coffee and whispering like mischievous children. They giggled and grinned at each other like they had a million times as kids over on Olive in the old neighborhood.

"Now you know, Mary, when the police get you in the questioning room, they're gonna tell you that I told them we planted the gun. Now there's something you need to understand. I will not under any circumstances ever admit we planted the gun." He slid his hand through his thinning black hair.

Ma giggled. "They'd have to kill me before they get me to rat on myself, Johnny."

They both laughed and John asked, "You ready, sis?"

"Ready as I'll ever be, baby brother." They stood up and started downstairs.

"Whaddaya think Dad would think of this?"

"Ya know, I had a dream last night that I was just a little girl, and Da was standing over me looking down at me. He was waving his finger in my face and he said, 'No.' Then he stopped and he looked at me and he grinned. He giggled and said I was 'a naughty girl.'"

Uncle John cracked up.

"I had a dream like that, too."

They opened the door. Grama was watching a soap opera and eating a TV dinner way in the front of the apartment. Her tiny little white lapdog ran over and peed on the kitchen floor when they walked in. Pat slept in the side room.

"John, the silverware drawer," Ma whispered.

John looked at Ma. He hiked up his eyebrows. He grabbed the gun with a rag, slid the drawer open, slipped the pistol in it, and pushed it shut.

"Alright, motherfucker!" John yelled at the top of his lungs. "This is it! I want you outta my mother's house RIGHT NOW!!!"

Gram started, grabbed the big controller and turned the TV volume down. John stomped down the hallway, pulled his knee up to his chest, and kicked the door open to Pat's room. Ma picked up Gram's old peach rotary phone and called 911. The operator answered.

"I need help! My son is acting crazy, and he's got a gun!"

Pat jumped up in a daze.

"John, shut up, I'm trying to sleep!" he whined in that nasally shriek that somehow made Gram feel sorry for him.

"You dirty motherfucker, you have stolen your last dime from my mother! You are outta here today! This is the last day you torment my family!"

"John, shut up, you nitwit!" Gram yelled, getting up from the sofa. "I want him here, he can stay, he has nowhere to go!" She waddled over to John using her walker. "Where's he gonna go, go live in a cardboard box under a bridge, fer Christ's sake?! He just got a job! He's starting on a high-rise tomorrow morning!"

"Yeah, I just got a job. Now get the fuck outta here!" Pat whined and slammed the door shut. John booted it and it broke off the hinge.

"If you don't stop, I swear, I'm gonna pop ya one!" Pat said, cocking his fist back.

"Go ahead, ya son of a bitch!" John put his chin up, thought about it, and said, "Sorry, Mary, I didn't mean it like that."

Ma spoke into the phone with the police operator. "We need your help right away, 927 South LaGrange Road! Come to the alley! They're fighting, my son is a drug addict and he's got a gun!"

"Get the fuck outa here, ya whiny little bitch!" Pat towered over John.

John put 'em up and Pat just closed the broken door again and lay down on his mattress on the floor.

"Johnny, you stop it, he's trying to do better! I forgave him, OK! He's doing fine now!"

"Ma, you are crazy if you think this bastard will ever straighten out, he's a full-blown heroin addict!"

"No, I'm not!" Pat fake cried.

The sirens were picking up, and Ma went out into the alley to flag them down.

The officers parked and hopped out and Ma yelled, "My son was pointing a gun at us! He's a drug addict!"

The officers pulled their firearms and jogged downstairs. John and Pat wrestled around in the kitchen as Gram tried to hit John with the broom while holding on to her walker. The little white dog nibbled on Pat's white tube sock as Pat tried to shake him off. The officers burst in and shouted, "Freeze!"

And they did, and put their hands up.

Ma told the officers to arrest Pat, and they cuffed him.

Pat shouted, "Why you arrestin' me for!" He put up a fight, and the officers slammed him into the refrigerator. Pat started crying out like a little girl as Grama wept and begged.

"Don't arrest my grandson, officer!" she pleaded as she pulled at her hair. "I love him so much, please, I want him here with me! I'm lonely!"

More officers arrived. They asked where the firearm was.

"I don't have any gun!" Pat roared.

"He did! He grabbed it out of one of the drawers!" John said and motioned for the silverware drawer. The officers opened the drawers until they found it.

"They framed me!" Pat screamed. "They planted that here! Let me go, you dirty motherfuckers!"

Grama cried and shouted for the police to leave, and the cops asked Ma and John to come into the station to make their statement.

They questioned them for a couple hours. John said what he was supposed to, but he wasn't the greatest liar, and the officers could tell something fishy was up. Ma, on the other hand, stuck to the story beautifully. Then she started to work the officers over.

"Would you question your mother like this? Let's give your mom a call and see what she thinks of your behavior." The bald sergeant blushed and giggled as he sat across from her in the blue interrogation room. "Let me tell you, officer, my son is a heroin addict, full blown, he's going to overdose. His friend just died a few weeks ago in my mother's car, overdose. Pat was with him when he died, he pushed him out and drove away. Why don't you ask him about that?"

"But Mrs. Walsh, your mother says there was no firearm in her house, and there's no fingerprints on the gun!" Officer Bob pleaded.

Ma folded her arms over her pudgy chest. "So he wiped it with a rag before he put it back in the drawer. Look, my mother is what you call an enabler. She believes all the crap he tells her. She can't say no to him. He's run through nearly all of her retirement. That means she'll become a ward of the state, or I'll have to take the money I'm using to raise the last of my kids, and my own savings for retirement, to pay for her to be in a home until she dies." Ma raised her hands, fingers extended like exclamation marks. "You have kids? Your mom's still alive, isn't she? Imagine if you were in this situation. You'd be desperate, right? You'd want to do something, wouldn't you?" She leaned in, somehow looking down at the officer, who was much taller than her. "You'd do anything to protect your child and your mother from destroying each other's lives, wouldn't you?"

Officer Bob seemed to shrink down in his seat. He dropped his chin into his throat and peered up at her bashfully.

"Well, Bob, I leave it in your hands. You can charge a mother of six and a father of four with planting a gun on their heroin addict son and nephew, to try and save their mother's retirement and all she owns and save him from OD'ing. Or you can call his parole officer and tell him to come pick the asshole up."

Bob took a deep breath. He looked at Ma like he would have looked at his own daughter, if she'd been caught with her hand in the cookie jar. He left the questioning room and returned about twenty minutes later.

"Now Missus Walsh, I have never had a more interesting conversation in all my career here at the La Grange Police Department and I've never had a person be so damn honest with me as you have been today. I want to tell you I have a lot of respect for you and your brother over there, though he thinks he's a better talker than he really is. Either way, I've charged your son with possession of a firearm and assault while using a firearm. I've just got off the phone with his parole officer. They're coming out to get him. The judge will likely order a temporary revocation of parole and then there'll be a hearing. They're probably going to drug test him too, so if you're right about the heroin, there'll be a lot of evidence against him. He will likely serve the rest of his sentence, and whether or not you and your brother over there want to drop the charges or testify in court it won't matter, his parole will be violated soon."

They both got up.

"Have a nice day Missus Walsh, you've earned it."

"You're a real nice boy, Bob. Your mother would be very proud of you. Tell your mom she raised a good son for me, would you?"

"Thank you, Missus Walsh, I think she'll like to hear that."

Uncle John and Ma walked out to their cars in front of the station. They smirked at each other mischievously. Ma leaned in and gave him a big kiss on the cheek.

"Thank you, little brother."

"Thank you, big sis."

They hugged and got into their cars and drove away from the station and back to their lives, back to everything they'd worked so damn hard for.

◆

Things settled down after that, but it all still nagged at me like a goddamned big ol' barbed metal hook set in the center of my chest. I took a long drive out south through the woods. I soared through a big bog as the sun began to fall through the trees. *I ain't proud of what I did. Had no choice in the matter.* I lit a square. *If I had the chance, I woulda killed him. Fucking Georgie the Greek saved his life. It was the right thing to do, or the only thing to do. He was a danger to my family and my family is innocent and the children are innocent and he was a threat to them.*

The bog gave way to a wood and the road shot into it like it was falling into a thorny tunnel. *I hate him. He ain't my brother no more.* I puffed my smoke. *How could I love something like that? A crazy piece 'a shit junkie. Somebody who threatens children.* I cruised alongside a big pond Da took me and the grandkids fishing at once. *Pat ain't worthy of love or mercy.* The darkness seemed to ooze out of the passing forest as the temperature fell. *The sad thing is, he's still alive and still could come out of prison and hurt my family again. I wish he would just fucking die in there and that'd be the end of it.* As the twilight faded my eyes adjusted to the darkness and I couldn't tell if the shadows were beasts or just my imagination, but I didn't fear either. *If he comes out there and tries to hurt us, I'll kill him. Or die trying.*

A deep grief swirled in my whole body as I mourned him, a vortex of dark matter. *It ain't fair that the world could make me love him.* A memory flashed of when I was a little boy, riding down to Montrose Harbor with Pat and Marie, all of us laughing as he sliced through traffic going eighty. *What would they have been without heroin?* I shook the image from my head. My brother's love for me pulsed all around me in the whirling wind in the cab of the Jeep. My hatred and love for him crashed into each other in my heart like mounds of positrons and electrons obliterating each other until there was nothing left but a hollow emptiness. I accelerated through a curve with bare tree branches hanging overhead like dark claws reaching for me. *That guy that used to be my brother...he's fuckin' dead.* I coasted past a pond, the surface just a flickering purple beneath the blackened trees. *I'm sorry, Da, I tried.*

By the time I got to Lemont Bridge, the darkness had swallowed it all. I soared over the canal and the Des Plaines River and grabbed my golden crucifix in my fist and broke the chain off my neck. As the crucifix left my chest it felt like I'd plucked a barbed hook out of my heart. The cool wind rippled through my trimmed hair. I cocked back and threw it out off the bridge into the blackness.

Chapter 7: Isolated

WHEN I WAS EIGHTEEN, all I wanted was to prove I belonged in the men's division of the Chicago Golden Gloves, then go to college and marry my high school sweetheart like two of my older brothers married theirs. I wanted to start a good and simple life. In fact, I wanted to be like my brother Blake. The only problem was I didn't really know him yet.

Life got back to normal with Pat back in prison. Blake seemed to like that I beat the piss out of Pat. He'd always wanted to get him back for all the crap Pat put him through in his youth. Pat'd been a horrifyingly vicious older brother to him. But now Blake seemed threatened by me. Blake and Pat were about the same size, much bigger than Rich and me. We took after Da's body frame: huge leg bones, smaller upper body. Blake and Pat took more after Dad's dad, about six-foot tall and big.

We watched Blake's job as a Chicago cop disturb him more and more. Blake had been an obvious narcissist even from a young age—adoring his own looks, manipulating women, and inflating his achievement in sports and school. But the psychological pressures of his police work seemed to be unveiling sociopathy or even psychopathy. He was using excessive force on guys. Maybe they were bad guys, or maybe just kinda bad guys: it all depended on his mood that day. If you gave Blake lip, he'd get you in a room alone, still cuffed, and find a way to shut you up.

A thirteen-year-old kid who'd shot at Blake years before got out of juvie and was running around Humboldt Park again. He was almost eighteen and still a Spanish Cobra. Blake caught him out behind some factories by the train tracks graffitiing the walls with all that gang shit. It took Blake a minute to recognize him 'cause he'd grown his hair out into a big shaggy ponytail. Then Blake figured it out. And he realized a little construction site with a thirty-foot-deep shaft sat just down the tracks.

Blake told a few of us about it one day during lunch break on this construction site on the Dan Ryan when he was getting some part-time hours in with us. He grinned his big pompous smirk as he and I sat beside each other in the deep shade on the bumper of the open box truck, with the rest of the crew spread out around us in the sunlight listening, eating tacos and drinking Gatorade and ice water out of their big cooler jugs.

"So my partner and I brought him over to the shaft, we told him he was gonna have a fall. He didn't like that, he was scared as hell. We got to the shaft and I took him by his ankles and dangled him over the shaft." Blake dangled the imaginary kid, his eyes wide, grinning like a madman. "And he's screaming and crying. He flipped out and pissed his pants. The piss ran down his stomach and neck and all over his face until his hair soaked it all up like a big black frizzy mop of piss dripping down into the hole."

The crew laughed uneasily.

Blake said they played with that kid for an hour. "The site was real secluded," he said. "Nobody could hear him crying for help. Nobody could hear his screams."

But I heard elsewhere that the kid was actually trying to get away from the gang. He was doing graffiti and street art. Some corrections officer lady who actually gave a crap about the kids had found a way to reach him. She'd mothered him and pushed him to pursue his creative side. He was trying his best and this was one of the only things the gang understood. They liked his art, but they wanted him to do a big ol' mural of a cobra over by the Kings' side, and he'd agreed to do it as a release from his duties as a Cobra. Then he ran into Blakey. When the kid came out of that hole it was like he'd been baptized back into the Cobras. He came out of that hole ready for war: broken, disturbed, ferocious, and dead-set on killing somebody. He went to the Cobras and said, "Fuck it, let's roll on some flakes tonight." He didn't stop shooting for a month straight. Who knows how many Peoples dropped, how many innocent children dropped—normal people caught up in his furious revenge on this world.

The Peoples finally got him in a car fleeing a drive-by. One of those Puerto Rican Kings knew the secret, to shoot the seat backs in a car speeding away. There is no escape. The kid squirmed low in the passenger seat, trying as hard as he could, but a bullet found him clean in the spine and severed his spinal cord. So by the time Blake told us the story, the kid was just sitting out on his porch in his wheelchair with the Cobras day after day, hoping a King would come and put him out of his misery. But did Blake feel bad? No. Every time he rolled past the porch he sang out "Piss Mop... Piss Mop... Piss Mop..." as his partner giggled.

I heard later that Piss Mop started smoking crack as an escape from the torment, and all his teeth fell out. Then one day he hit the rock so hard that they never called him Piss Mop again.

I gotta be honest, I didn't give a shit about that poor kid. His world was so abstracted from mine, so far removed from me way out in the 'burbs that I couldn't care less, even though I did still want to kill a Cobra over what Spider did to Sy all those years ago. But mostly that life existed as a distant memory, a past life. Something that only came back in sudden nightmares, but I'd always wake to the nice quiet of Brookfield. The sounds of my family safely going about their days.

I worried about Blake though, his heart. It was like with my old best friend Ryan back in the old neighborhood, the way his soul hardened and darkened before my very eyes. The goodness still survived inside Blake, especially with his children; he fathered them playfully, but this other side of him startled me. A viciousness. He was still a good guy, but a good guy with a dark side. And that war between his dark side and his clean side perpetually raged, and he didn't seem to always win it, and I wondered when the dark side would flash into our relationship. And I didn't want it to, because I'd already lost one brother.

◆

When Blake talked with me and asked me things about my life, it seemed more like an interrogation than a conversation. Each time I told him something good I accomplished, he winced. He didn't like my success in sports, success in school, success with girls. He started saying little things around Faith, things I'd only hear in passing.

"Joe's really punching over his weight with you, huh? You could do better, but he sure couldn't."

Faith would just blush. Blake's wife Karen was always nagging him to stop. I couldn't believe my own brother'd say something like that to the girl I loved. I'd glare at him, ready to hit him, and he'd just chuckle and stop. But it'd come back here and there. "The age of consent is seventeen..." he'd say. Faith'd just turned seventeen. I was about to turn eighteen. Psychopaths, they test the water before they dive in. Looking for weakness, bending your reality to their sick view.

How the hell could an eighteen-year-old kid know what was coming? I had thought he was a good father and faithful husband, a decent person, somebody I'd want to be like. I figured he was just kidding around.

But I'd started to put it together that Blake and Karen were in an open relationship and were into swinging. In fact, they were a little notorious in the community. They'd sometimes lure other couples into the lifestyle; there was a string of divorces that could be traced back to double dates with them.

Karen was pretty and a sweet woman, but Blake'd had a real beauty when he was out at Drake before little Johnny came along. She was a gorgeous blonde who was at Drake, too. She was extremely rich. Her dad owned half of Des Moines. She was a lot like Faith. She had that same upward-tilted nose, those same beautiful light green eyes. There was an alternative life in Blake's mind. A life where he married that girl. Finished his degree and never left Des Moines. They gained tremendous wealth together, traveled in luxury. He'd become the new king of Des Moines. He'd donate the money for a building at Drake they'd name in his honor.

But fate didn't allow for that and now he was in the pits of hell— Humboldt Park, the heart of gangbanging in America. The place where the *Gangland* TV series would return year after year, episode after episode, and Blake knew all those cases, all those brutal murders, all those infamous bastards who tormented the neighborhood where he had to show up for work every day.

Meanwhile here I was growing up in the 'burbs, free from all the nonsense, driving around in a Jeep with the top off and a beautiful young girl who loved me. On top of the world. Why did I get it so easy? Why did I catch all the breaks? Well, maybe I wouldn't have it so easy. Blake was gonna see to that.

◆

Things with Faith and I cruised along great. We were best friends, positive influences on each other, and the sex was incredible. We were in love, about as in love as two high school kids could get. Spent all our time together. She had little nicknames for me. She called me Beyba after the way Blakey's baby daughter Sarah said baby when she was three. It was the sweetest little thing. I started calling her Beyba, too. Our love created this little language of our own. We bought each other little gifts and wrote each other love letters. I hardly spent time with the guys. She didn't have any girlfriends, really. She was so beautiful. How hard must it be to be an object of desire from every guy you ever meet? How must that stroke your ego and at the same time make you feel in danger from the way they look at you? She was just a kid, seventeen. All the girls in her school hated her 'cause she was the hottest girl in the school, and all their boyfriends wanted her. The power and isolation that has to bring to you. She wasn't just a beauty though—she was classy, smart, one of the top students in her school; she'd already gotten accepted into Wellesley, this prestigious all-women's college, part of the Seven Sisters to the Ivy League. They'd offered her a full scholarship. It was a big dream come true for her. She loved the idea of these empowered women working together to change the world. It hurt that she was leaving, but I knew our love would withstand it. We'd visit every chance we had, and have summer and winter break.

She wasn't just book smart though—she was street smart. Witty and funny, too. She did impressions and made hilarious voices. She liked to party, smoked weed and drank with me. We went back and forth between real sweet and soft lovemaking and nasty sex, kind of violent, but in a safe way with rules and boundaries. We were always holding hands, touching. People would actually stop us on the street and tell us what a beautiful couple we were. We'd just laugh and thank them.

Faith volunteered at this soup kitchen in Cicero pretty regularly. She even got me to go with her. It was nice to help feed hungry people. It made us both feel so good. We went a couple times a month, serving the needy people soup and bread, and cleaning up the tables and washing dishes, and just sitting and talking with them. This one little old lady with purplish red curly hair named Susie came in every time we were there. She didn't have anyone, and we made a little friendship with her. Susie'd always sneak her little black Chihuahua Frank in, in her purse. She'd feed him little bits of meat while she talked with us. We mostly just listened. She'd tell us all about how her family passed away slowly until she was just there all alone, and it broke our hearts and made me think about Gram. It even made me forgive Gram for all the enabling she did with Pat and his heroin addiction. Loneliness is a terrible thing, and Pat preyed on it. Susie'd always slip us a five-dollar bill and tell me as she left, "This is fer you twos. Now, take her out for a nice hot dog or a taco or something," and we'd laugh and tell her no and just give it to the pastor as a donation to the soup kitchen. It felt like God's work or something. I never would have gone and done something like that if it wasn't for Faith. She made me a better person. Brother Alex loved her too. Damn near every person we ever got to know just loved her.

It wasn't only that she was perfect in so many ways, though. She was also there for me through every up and down. When I lost a boxing match for the first time she cried and hugged me and took me home and put a cold steak on my eye to keep the swelling down. She told me: "Don't worry, you'll kick his ass next time." And I did. When I was winning a fight, she was yelling and cheering me, and when it was a close fight, real close, and the crowd was going crazy, she was the only voice I could hear screaming, "Go Joe! Get him! Kick his ass!" When I had been exhausted from training and having problems at home because Pat was putting us all through fucking hell, and I just wanted to quit, she'd taken time out from her own studying to get me back on track.

One night after I got a C in my Honors trigonometry class I sat at her desk as she was sitting Indian-style on her four-post bed doing flashcards in the low-lit room. Sarah McLachlan's "In The Arms of The Angels" played softly in the background. I was checking my answers for the practice test and realized I was wrong on three questions in a row. My mind just spun like that crazy circle they always had us drawing with the triangles inside it. I slammed my book shut and gripped my head.

"I just want to quit, Faith. I'm not smart enough. Going to fucking college was a stupid idea."

She hopped up, danced over softly, and sat on my lap. She touched my face, cooing to me. Her dirty-blonde hair dangled between us.

"Joe... You are smart. Look at how far you've come. You are in Honors classes now, all Honors classes. So you got a C on your math test. So what? It's Honors, it's harder than all the other classes the other kids are taking." She softly kissed my forehead with her damp lips. "You are so damn determined, Beyba, that's one of the things I really love about you."

I leaned my head back and looked at the ceiling in agony.

"I'm sick of this shiiiiit!" I whined.

She laughed and touched my neck with her smooth fingertips.

"If you study for the next three hours, I'll give you a blow job, OK?" she said and smiled.

"Haha..." I laughed. "Alright! I fucking love trigonometry." I raised my fists triumphantly.

She laughed.

"But you don't have to give me a BJ unless you want to," I told her.

"I do." She grinned wickedly, her green eyes sparkling in the yellowish desk lamp light.

And I did, and she did, and I got a B on the next test, and I brought it to her. I climbed her front steps after school as she waited for me on the porch wearing her blue sweater with WELLESLEY in white letters across the chest, and her short shorts. I proudly brandished the test with the big red B at the top.

"What? B for better?" She scrutinized it.

I took my blue pen and wrote a J next to the red B. "B for Blow Job, more like it." I grinned, took her in my arms, and kissed her sweet lips. "What would an A be for?" I whispered, and nibbled her ear.

"No! No way!" She twisted in my arms, repulsed. "I am not putting that thing in there! It hurts!"

"Well, I had to ask, Beyba!"

◆

You could imagine a guy like me was a little overprotective of her.

This new Italian restaurant opened up in La Grange Park. I went with my parents. It was really fucking good. I wanted to take Faith, and asked her while we were down in her basement nestled up on the couch. She said no 'cause she knew the kid of the owner.

"Tony DiStefano. He's such an asshole. He came on to me at a party one time right before I met you. He got real aggressive. He cornered me in the laundry room and pinned me to the wall and just, like, whipped his dick out. I tried to stop him, and he came all over my shirt."

"Jesus." I held her softly in my arms. "What did you do?"

"My friend came over and she had a soda, and I just took it and poured it all over my shirt and left."

"I'm gonna kill that motherfucker!"

"No!" She tensed, her eyes bugging out. "No, no, you can't do anything!"

I just shook my head in disbelief. I held her as she cried in my arms under the warm fuzzy blanket.

It turned out Tony DiStefano worked as a busboy at the restaurant. A few days later I went over there and ordered a meal. He was a big Italian kid with slicked-back hair walking back and forth busing the tables in a white apron. As he passed me, I looked at him.

"Aye, are you Tony DiStefano?"

"Yeah, how'dju know?"

"Just checking. I heard your dad owns the place. Good food."

"Thanks. We really appreciate that," he said. He cleared some dishes on the table next to mine and headed to the back room.

I grinned and finished eating. I left my money on the table with a nice tip. I waited until he was alone back there. I picked up my steak knife and followed him into the back room. I burst through the swinging door behind him. He spun around.

"Aye the bathroom's over there!" He pointed.

"You know Faith Harvey?"

"Yeah I do, she's a real..." He giggled. "She's a real nice girl."

I slapped the shit out of him. He grabbed hold of me and we wrestled in the small room. I pinned him against the cabinet and brought the knife to his throat.

"Woh!" he yelled. "Don't! Shit!"

"Shut the fuck up," I told him. "You ever come near her again, I'll fucking kill you, you understand that?"

"Yeah. OK!"

"Do you, motherfucker?" I pressed the knife into his throat. A line of blood slid from his Adam's apple down the blade as he squeezed his hands around my wrist.

"Yes! Please! Just chill."

"Let go of me, motherfucker."

He let go. I walked out as he quivered against the cabinet, gripping his throat as a string of blood dribbled down onto his white apron.

All hell broke loose at Faith's school. People started blaming her, calling her a liar. She brought me down to her basement and sat me down on the couch. She sat rigidly beside me.

"I have to break up with you, Joe," she said, quivering, holding a pink tissue to her nose.

"Why?"

"You don't understand. Now everyone knows!"

"Yeah, they should fucking know, that fucking piece of shit."

She burst into shivering tears. "You made it all a million times worse. I'm going to have to transfer out of RB."

She folded over, held her face in her hands, and wept.

"I'm sorry." I stroked her back softly. "I just can't stand the idea of someone hurting you."

"I will never tell you anything ever again."

We broke up for a few weeks, then I started calling and begging her for forgiveness. She stayed in school, but shit was bad for her. It seemed like every time I stood up for her, I made things worse. I didn't know what to do. I just wanted to protect her. We all want to protect the people we love. She finally took me back, and we went for a drive and found a nice spot out in the forest preserves to talk. We parked by a big pond as the sun was starting to set over the glistening waters. She cuddled up in my arms in the back bench seat of the Jeep.

"I'm sorry," I said. "I just wanted to protect you."

"Look, it didn't happen," she said with this flat dead tone in her voice. "He never did it. I made it up."

"Fuck. I put a knife to that kid's throat and he didn't even deserve it?"

"Just don't ever bring this up again. Let's just start over again like it never happened," she said, staring off at the orange sun rays dancing atop the trembling surface of the waters. *Is she just saying that so I'll let it go? Or did she lie to me?* I watched her green eyes peering out into the distance as the deep shadows of the treeline slowly stretched out and engulfed the pond. My chest ached as the wires tightened on it. *I love this girl so goddamn much. Maybe too much...*

◆

Nearly losing her made me realize how much I loved her. Made me realize I wanted to marry this girl. In my family almost every relationship started in high school or sooner. For me, marrying your high school sweetheart wasn't out of the ordinary, it was the norm. So I went out and bought a promise ring. I was going to ask her to marry me, and we'd wait till after college. Figured if we made it through the long-distance thing, we'd make it through anything. But still I was just a fucking kid, and was unsure.

I was eating lunch on break one day with Blake. We were both picking up some hours working construction on the weekends. I had the ring in my pocket. I was carrying it around with me, maybe to give it some mojo, I don't know. I rolled the ring in my pocket, feeling the smooth gold. *I still feel like a kid. Am I just being a clueless, gullible idiot? A romantic idealist? I need some fucking advice.* I glanced at Blake chomping on a Maxwell Street Polish beside me in the dusty cab of the box truck. He'd married his high school sweetheart...

"Fuck, man... I think I'm going to ask Faith to marry me."

Blake looked ahead, kind of shocked.

"What do you think? Is it too early?"

"What do I think? Pshh..." He sighed and fought back a grin. "When I was your age, I didn't want to get married. That's the last thing I wanted..."

"Didn't Rich ask Nancy to marry him at eighteen?"

"I think he did, yeah."

"I love her, man. I love her so much. I want to be with her forever."

"You gotta decide that on your own, kid."

"I mean it worked out for Rich and Nancy."

"Yeah, it did." He sighed. "It's up to you, man. Pop the question if you feel it," he said, and nudged me with his elbow.

"Yeah, I think I'm gonna. What about you, what's up at work? Any crazy stories?"

"Pshh, I'm working this stupid rape case. Fucking rape is such a weird thing. A lot of people don't know, but when it comes to serial rapists, they almost never ejaculate, but the woman usually orgasms. It's about dominance," he said. "And that the woman orgasms, doesn't that say something to you? For me, I say rape doesn't exist, not like people say it does. If she orgasms, doesn't she want it? Look at soap operas, there's a rape every episode. Millions of women watch those things every day. You know what I mean? I always wanted to have my own soap opera," Blake nudged his elbow into mine. "Cavemen, they just whacked 'em over the head with their club, dragged 'em into a cave, and banged 'em," he said, as a wicked grin spread across his face. "What are you going to do, charge a caveman with rape? It's natural. Most rapes you hear about, all those statistics, they're false. The only real rapes are the serial rapists, the sex fiends grabbing women off the street, pulling 'em into alleys. The rest, pshh, damn hard to prove." Blake crumbled up the Polish sausage wrapper and put it in the brown paper bag.

He popped the door open. I got out too, pulling on my work gloves. "When I was in the frat at Drake, we had some of these little sluts accuse us of that shit." He swung his head back and puffed his chest out. "Fuck, like I need to rape anybody! I'm a damn stud! We'd tell 'em, 'It wasn't no rape, it was a quickie...' Seriously, if a girl goes into a room with me alone, I'm going to have my way..." He laughed wickedly as he rolled a little neon-green foam ear plug in his fingertips and stuffed it in his ear. I followed him to where we were working, a concrete pier with large patches cut and half broken-out, revealing the rusted rebar underneath the surface.

Well, thanks for the advice, big bro... I popped my ear plugs in, and the roaring sounds faded. *Why the fuck did he tell me all that?* I watched him pull his dust mask on and fit his clear plastic work glasses. *Fuck, this is the guy who's enforcing the law against rape, and he doesn't even believe it's real?!* He put the rivet buster on his hip and angled it upward into the concrete pier. He pulled the trigger and the jackhammer came alive like a machine gun. A white cloud slowly engulfed him. I popped my hard hat on, flipped the big plastic visor down over my face, and grabbed my gun beside him. *Fucking sounds like a rapist his damn self. You know what I do to rapists, you fucking asshole? Just ask Tony DiStefano.* I smashed my tip into the concrete wall beside him and pulled the trigger; a big hunk of concrete exploded off the wall and pelted my chest.

◆

Back then I was so young and idealistic. I was in love with the idea of being in love. I had a vision of marrying Faith, having kids, and making a career as a physicist—the American Dream. I was so happy for my brothers Blake and Rich; they were doing it. I never would have imagined that they didn't want me to have those things, or that they could be jealous of me. I loved them and respected them. I wanted the best for them and expected the same in return, but adults have demons, and in my family those demons were bigger and more vicious than in most normal families. Being blue-collar in Chicago came with a certain kind of darkness. And you couldn't become a full adult in that world until you knew that darkness deeply. And once you knew it, there was no going back.

◆

Thanksgiving came around. Faith was over, looking hot as hell with her short flower-pattern dress and classy heels. Karen was drinking hard. Blake kept filling her glass with white wine. At some point, Karen got me down to the basement to look at something while Faith went upstairs where the kids were having a pillow fight. I stepped down the stairs behind Karen to the carpeted floor of the basement.

Karen spun around and threw her arms around me, her bangs and blonde perm bounced around her face.

"Joe, you've grown up so fast, you're so big and strong now."

I chuckled at her drunken antics. She leaned in and tried to kiss me, pecking the air between us.

"What the hell are you doing?" I pulled back, out of her arms. "Karen, are you crazy?"

"What?" She grinned. "Come on..."

"You're my fucking brother's wife, is what!"

"Come on, it's just a little fun, Joe."

Karen reached out and slid her fingers on my abs and chest. I pushed her hand away. I staggered away from her. I glanced back at her in her mauve blouse and bleached jeans. *Jesus, is she for real?* I climbed back upstairs to the living room and sat on the couch. *What in the flying fuck just happened? Did she really want to make out with me or something?!*

Springs bounced upstairs. *Kids are jumping on my bed?* I grinned and headed up there to see. As I got to the top of the stairs, Blake came barreling toward me in a hurry from down the hallway. His four-year-old daughter Sarah chased after him, holding a pillow raised over her head. I locked eyes with her and raised my eyebrows. Blake recoiled as he neared me, and tensed his big torso; he wore a Drake sweater with a cartoon bulldog with flexed fists, and it seemed to come alive, like it was about to swing at me. Fear streaked across his angular face. I gave him a puzzled look. He peered into my eyes questioningly.

"Did you?" he muttered.

"What?!" I said disgusted.

Then Blake's eyes lit up. He giggled and thundered down the steps past me.

"Daddy! Daddy! Pillow fight!" Sarah tossed the blue pillow after him. I caught it and laughed. Then I chased her around the corner with the pillow.

All six of the nieces and nephews ran around in the spare room jumping on the bed, crazy, hitting each other with pillows. I jumped in the room and roared like a monster. They squealed. I smashed Cody with the blue pillow. Symon nailed me with one in the head. I pretended it knocked me out and fell on the floor. They squealed and smashed me, and little Bobby jumped on me and smothered me with his pillow until I died. I lay there dead.

"You killed Uncle Joe, Bobby!" Sarah said, real worried. Everyone got quiet. Two-year-old Bobby really believed I was dead. He hovered over me.

"Oh no!" He put his ear to my chest listening to my heart. Then he smacked me on the forehead and I sprang alive. I roared, scooped him up, and body-slammed him onto the bed. All the kids rejoiced. *Faith would've loved that, where the hell is she?*

"Is Faith up here?"

"How the hell would I know?" Johnny said and flung a pillow that whizzed past my ear.

"She's in your room," Sarah said, real sweet.

"Thanks, Beyba." I leaned down and kissed her blonde head.

I walked into my room next door. I saw Faith lying on her back on my blue bed. She saw me and sat up and pulled down on the ends of her dress. Her body trembled. I sat down beside her.

"What's up, Beyba? Are you OK?"

"I'm not feeling good."

I got up and closed the thin wooden door and lay down with her on the bed. I put my arms around her.

She recoiled at my touch.

"Just don't touch me, please." She rolled on her side and sniffled.

"What's wrong?" I pleaded. "What the hell's going on?"

"I'm sick, I just don't feel good. I want to go home."

"OK, I'll take you."

We got up and left. She quietly held her stomach as I drove us along the tracks toward Faith's house. *Fuck, that was some weird-ass shit with Karen.* Faith looked out the window, sad. *How the hell could I explain that to her? She'd flip out. Karen was just fucking drunk. Whatever.* I pulled up in front of her house.

"Please don't come in. I'm fine," she said hurriedly, and hopped out.

"Alright, I hope you feel better, Beyba," I called after her.

What the fuck is going on? I watched her enter her house. *She didn't look back and wave, or nothing. Fucking goofy-ass drunken Karen, and Blake rushing past me like that.* I threw it in gear. *Was he up there playing with the kids? Those two were acting so fucking weird today.* My tires screeched as I sped off. *I swear to God, that motherfucker keeps acting shitty, and I'ma drop him.*

◆

Denial is a funny thing. We all live our lives in some form of denial, when death could come for us any second. But it's more than just that. You ever read a story about some pillar of the community who ends up getting charged with raping twenty or thirty women over a few decades? Shit like that pops up in the news every so often. How the fuck does someone get away with that over and over again, for so many years? Do you really want to know? Or do you just want to read about it, get appalled, find your safe space, and move on with your daily life thinking, 'That could never happen to me.' Well, it does happen. It happens to people like you and me every damn day. How do these sick fucks do it, is the question. It's like they use this cloak. The cloak has many folds and layers to it, but the fabric of the cloak is shame. Not just the shame of being a victim, or being stained because of it, but the shame of the people who love you and who failed to protect you. The fear of hurting them by telling them the truth. And maybe even the horror that they might not believe you.

I called Faith up the next day. We were supposed to go to the mall together for some Christmas shopping.

"Hello," she answered in this dead flat tone.

"How are you?"

"I'm not feeling good."

"What happened yesterday?"

"Nothing, I just started feeling sick."

"Are you sure nothing else is going on?"

"I have to go." She started to cry.

"I love you."

She hung up.

I sighed, holding the smooth receiver to my forehead. *Guess I ain't the easiest guy to fucking talk to.*

Fear wound wires around my chest. Fear that I'd lose her again. *I'm gonna just ask her. Just ask her to marry me. Fuck it. Stop being a pussy and do it.*

I went to see Faith a few days later. Her mom told me she was in the basement, and I headed down with the ring in my hand. *I'll take her for a walk to the woods and find some quiet place, and just get down on my knee and ask her.*

She sat on the couch in her pajamas. She did look sick. She was super thin. Her face was kind of sunken-in, like she hadn't been eating. That relieved me a little. *That answers that, she was just sick.* I sat down beside her and hugged her. *I can put my big stupid conspiracy theory about Blake and Karen to bed, and things can get back to normal.*

She curled up in my arms on the sofa as we watched MTV. Kurt Cobain's voice swirled through the room: "My girl, my girl, don't lie to me, tell me where did you sleep last night."

I felt the ring in my pocket.

"We've been together for three years. What if we ended up getting married?" I told her.

She pulled away from me and sat up.

"Joe. We have to talk."

"What's up?" I sat up with her.

"This isn't working out."

"What do ya mean?"

"I want to try..." She paused, looking away from me. "I think we should start seeing other people."

"What?!" It felt like she'd sunk a big old rusty hook dead center in my heart. I almost cried out. Then I spun into a rage. "Are you fucking serious? You want to break up?"

"No," she said, touching her fingers to her lips and reaching out and touching my knee. "I just think we're being too serious, and I'm going away for school. I just feel like we've got to be realistic."

"Fuck you," I said, and stood up. "I been telling chicks no left and right, just for you, and now you drop this shit on me?"

"Stop it, Joe." Tears beaded in her eyes. "You're hurting me."

"You want to break up, fine." I stared walking towards the steps. "We're broke up then."

"No, I don't want to break up." She pleaded. "I never said that!"

"Well, I said it." I hurried up the stairs.

She called that night and cried and told me she didn't want to break up.

"Well, I don't want to see other fucking people. I want you, all or nothing."

She sniffled.

"Please, please, don't break up with me right now, I need you," she begged.

"If you got some big secret, you can tell me. And if you don't know what you want, then call me when you do. Otherwise leave me the fuck alone!"

She called again a few days later, and we made up, and things started going good again. Then they went bad. She wasn't doing her homework, and her mom was having to help her. Then she started lying to me, saying she was busy.

I was driving around one night when she was "busy." And sure enough, I saw her silver Sebring convertible, with the top up for the cold. Some hippie dude in the passenger seat with his arm around her. His curly blonde hair was longer than hers; the strands dangled over her shoulder as they flowed under the cool electric light.

I rolled up behind them at a stoplight and popped the door open. The frigid cold spilled in. *I'm gonna fuck this motherfucker up.* Then: *Naw, you know what? It ain't even his fault. It's hers.* I closed the door. *He didn't fucking lie to me, she did.*

I pulled up beside them and rolled my window down. The brisk air hit my face. "So you're busy, huh?" I glared at her. She recoiled out of his arms. "Real fuckin nice." I floored it through the red light. A gray minivan screeched to a stop as I shot through the intersection.

I called up this silly cheerleader chick named Meg that'd been following me around for a few months. I picked her up; she was cute, a redhead. She had a nice ass and a cute smile, but I didn't give a shit about her, and she didn't even know me. We pulled in to a quiet side street in Berwyn. I pounded her in the back seat and she came twice and I finally stopped and both of us were covered in sweat. Her scent was foreign, and disgusted me. I drove her home, and she leaned in to kiss, and I just pulled away.

"Have a good one," I told her.

"Want to get together this weekend?" she asked pitifully as she got out.

I snickered, looking away out the window.

"See ya around," I told her, and she slammed the door shut.

This little satisfaction of the revenge on Faith vanished quickly. I hated having sex with some meaningless person who I didn't give a flying fuck about. She just liked me because I was popular or some stupid-ass shit.

Faith called and begged me to take her back. I lay on my bed and listened for a while, rolling the golden promise ring in my fingers, watching it throw slivers of light around my dark room.

"Well, I should let you know, I fucked somebody." I told her.

She gasped.

"See... honesty. Nice, ain't it?"

"Do you...did you like it?"

"No, I fucking hated it!"

"I didn't like it either. It's good though, 'cause now I know. I know I only want you."

"Why the fuck did you go with that fucking guy?"

"We just talk, Joe."

"You can't just talk to me?"

"I can, but no, some things, some things I can't talk with you about."

"Like what?!" I threw the ring across my room; it dinged against the wall.

"I just can never tell you about some things."

The ring rolled along the hardwood floor, then rang quietly as it wobbled to a stop.

"This sounds like fucking crazy talk to me, Faith." I sighed.

"You love me. You really, really love me. I know you do. You're just... It's just, it's dangerous to tell you things, Joe. I don't want to hurt you."

"Faith, I'ma letchu in on a little secret...lying to me fucking hurts me. The truth ain't never hurt me."

"Just please, please, forgive me, OK?" she said. "I love you and I'm ready now. I just needed some time."

"Alright." I sighed. *What the fuck can you do?* "Alright..."

◆

Faith was always kind of flirting with an eating disorder. She made jokes about it to lighten things up. A lot of pretty girls force themselves to vomit after meals. They starve themselves, over-exercise. She started to get really skinny, painfully skinny. She said her doctor diagnosed her with an ulcer. She didn't want to go out to eat with me anymore, because I'd always ask her why she didn't finish her food. People stopped telling us we were a beautiful couple. They just watched us with these worried looks on their faces.

Susie at the soup kitchen pulled me aside one Saturday afternoon.

"What's the matter with Faith?" she asked, fixing her purple hair with her thin old hands.

"I don't know, Susie. She says she's sick."

"She's as skinny as a blade 'a grass. Get her to eat, ya big oaf!"

"I try."

"Don't lose her, Joey. There's something really wrong with her. You two are my favorite couple, kid. But if you don't help her, poof, she'll be gone like that."

"I know."

Susie riffled through her purse as Frank squeezed out and sat in my lap. His little black nose twitched worriedly as I petted him.

"Buy her a taco, Joey, buy her ten," she said, and handed me a twenty. "You have to help her!"

"I don't know how."

"Talk to her!"

I took the twenty and bought us ten tacos on the way home. I ate mine as I drove. Faith picked at hers. I watched her elegant fingers with the turquoise nail polish dip in to the open tinfoil wrapper and pluck out little hunks of asada. She didn't even finish the meat.

"You gotta fucking EAT, FAITH! Take that fucking taco and bite it!"

"Nooo!" She crumpled the tinfoil in a ball.

"Why?"

"I'm sick. My ulcer hurts."

"Bullshit."

She just went silent and held her stomach. I took her home.

She started struggling in school, too. She ended up getting the first B she'd ever gotten in her whole life. She wanted to drink all the time, and she drank hard on the weekends with me. We'd listen to CDs and fool around in the backseat, but she didn't want to go all the way anymore. I stayed patient about it.

Then it finally started, inevitable as the earth swallowing you at the end of your life. We were making out in my room one cold night under the heavy cloth covers in my bed. It was dark, but our eyes had adjusted and there was just enough light from the moon and the light on the electric pole in the alley outside my window. I started fingering her softly. She was real wet, but not hot like she used to be; she was cool inside. Then she stopped me.

"Let's just take a break," she said.

I lay on my back. The frustration finally got the better of me.

"Would you just FUCKING tell me what's wrong?!"

"No, no, I won't tell you! I can't tell you! You will do something crazy, I know you. I know it. I can't tell you anything, Joe. You're fucking nuts! My god, you put a fucking knife to someone's throat!"

"He fucking tried to rape you!"

"No, he didn't!" She hyperventilated looking up at the ceiling. "Stop saying that, stop fucking saying that, don't ever say that word to me again!"

"So you were lying."

"Yeah. Is that what you want to hear? Yeah, I lied to you. I always lie to you about everything."

"And I fucking almost killed somebody over it! Real nice."

She started to cry. I took her in my arms softly and held her. "Look, is this what you want? Us?"

"Yes, I only ever wanted to be with you. It's just so hard to talk with you anymore...can we just go back to the way it was?"

"Yeah, we can. Just don't fucking lie to me. If you don't want me, you don't want me. Fine, I'll go find somebody else."

"But, Joe, I love you. I only ever wanted you."

"Alright, let's do it, let's keep trying."

We started to make out again. The cloth of the sheets clung to us snugly, creating more heat like we were under a heavy cloak. We got naked and after some play, I slid inside her. It was different. Her face winced. She closed her eyes and gripped the bedsheets. The cloth seemed to stretch up around us. This coolness surprised me, like the Chicago winter had seeped inside her. Then she stopped me. I hopped off her, frustrated, trying to untangle my legs from the cloth sheets that strangled them.

"Why?" I asked as she trembled.

"Just tell him..." she muttered softly to herself. "Just tell him..." she whispered. "Joe, your brother did something to me," she said, holding her stomach.

"What?" I said, disgusted. "Which one?"

"Blake, he did something very terrible last Thanksgiving..."

Her words stabbed me. I kicked at the sheets that still clung to me. I rolled away from her and peered into the mound of covers that'd grouped up on my side of the bed. In the dark, the folds seemed to open up into crevasses as I peered into them; I saw Blake's face as I approached him that day, fearful, the way he flexed at me, the relieved look; I heard his snicker in my mind. Then I saw baby Sarah throwing the pillow. *It was just a game. He was playing with them. He's a father and a good man!* I knocked the pile of covers off the bed. *What if he isn't? What if he's a monster?* The sheets were suddenly full of wires that tangled my legs and sucked me into the mattress. *He raped her on this bed?!* I closed my eyes and fell downward toward the core of the dark energy deep inside my bed. *No!* I opened my eyes and sprang back into the room.

"What the fuck are you talking about?! There's no fucking way. Stop fucking lying to me!" I jumped up and pulled my Levi's on. "You want to break up, fine, but don't you fucking lie to me about my own brother!" She trembled, looking up at the ceiling of my room as she seemed to sink deep into the bedsheets in the dark.

"He doesn't believe me…" she muttered to herself, hyperventilating. She twisted under the sheets, wrestling with this dark energy in them.

"Blake is a good man. He'd never do something like that! Get the fuck out of here, you fucking lying bitch!"

She took a deep breath, then flung herself out of the deep hole she'd been sucked into. The sheets clung to her sweaty belly as she rose, and she clawed at them, prying them off of her. They followed her to her feet. She finally tore free from the last of them.

She dressed in a rush and left. And that was it, the end of us.

But it didn't end it in my mind. Faith had planted a seed in there. It grew terrible roots. No one wants to believe someone they love is a monster. But I started to riffle through my memories. And even though every foundation of my life, every understanding I had of society and family screamed 'No fucking way!' I started to believe her.

◆

Remember playing cops and robbers as a little kid? The simple joy of the good guys and the bad guys. You know, it'd have been so easy to just lie and make Blake a fake good guy and simply just a piece-of-shit cop. But shit ain't simple in this godforsaken world. Human beings are fucking complicated, and if you can't handle that, get your ass back to the kid's division. This here is for adults.

It was right around then that Blake heard a call on the radio in Humboldt Park—fire, mom and child trapped on the third floor. He and his partner flew over there. Flames shot out of the windows of the second floor of the red brick building on California near Division. The mother screamed for help out of the window, holding her two-year-old in her hands—naked except for the white diaper. The local fire truck was busy fighting a big five-alarm blaze in a factory in North Lawndale. It would be a few minutes before a ladder truck could get there, and the flames weren't waiting on nobody. The woman held the dark-skinned Puerto Rican baby in her arms as smoke billowed up in angry typhoons around them.

"Please catch my baby!" she screamed.

Blake stood under the window with his partner and a few good Samaritans trying to help. They prepared to catch the baby in a bedsheet. A WGN TV van showed up. The cameraman jumped out with the camera on his shoulder and started rolling. The mother finally kissed the baby on the forehead then she reached him out of the window, his bare little feet peddling in the smoky air. Blake and the guys peered up and braced for him, their arms locked under the sheet. She let go. The baby began to fall slowly. He was coming down perfectly as they held tight below. But as the baby fell past a cable he grabbed at it and his body swung violently and as his grip broke his little body angled past them and into the street. Blake sprang into action; he cut through two parked cars and as the baby fell like a Hail Mary pass headfirst toward the blacktop Blake dove and stretched out completely and caught him just a foot above the blacktop and certain death, and Blake slid belly-down on the pavement and rolled over and held the baby on his chest. The baby gasped wide-eyed, then looked at Blake and gave a big toothless giggle. Blake burst into laughter. The cameraman was right on it and caught it all.

"My god, is he OK?!" the woman screamed.

Blake held him up with a laugh. "He's laughing his ass off! I guess he's fine."

"Thank you! My god, thank you!" She wept from the window.

Stuff like that happens to cops. They get into more sticky situations than you may think. The CPD was in a little trouble over a police racketeering thing, and something with gambling machines in bars. They needed some good PR, so they told Blake to go ahead and ham it up with the *Tribune* about his days as a wide receiver at Drake. The WGN TV video got picked up in multiple markets, and the *Tribune* put him on the top half of the cover of the Saturday paper. The headline read, "The Cop With the Softest Hands."

They delivered the paper to our house in Brookfield. Ma beamed at her seat at the dinner table. She handed the paper to me.

"Well, it's gonna be hard to top that," she said.

I didn't look at it. I stuck it under my arm and headed to the kitchen.

Mom went on. "Everybody was so shocked that the baby was strong enough to grab the cable like that. I wasn't. I've been taking care of kids that age for thirty years. I seen babies that age do scary things, Joe. They're like little orangutans."

I sighed and flopped the paper down next to the coffee machine. I saw him there in his cop uniform holding the baby on his hip, chin up with his pompous grin like some kinda cop superhero. *Well, I guess they don't know he has a thing for raping teenage girls and torturing gangbangers.* I sighed. *Fuck, he saved that little baby boy's life.* I couldn't help feeling a little pride. Is he a good guy or a bad guy? *Good and bad and fucked up, and sometimes fucking awesome, and sometimes a miserable piece of shit. A rapist, a torturer, an abuser of power, a hard worker, a decent guy, a fucking hero on the damn cover of the Trib.* I poured a cup of coffee and took the paper to the couch with me. *What the fuck can you do? People are fucking messy.*

I sat on the couch and sipped the steaming cup of coffee, looking out onto the snowy side porch full of birds and squirrels feeding on the seeds and peanuts Ma put out. I remembered one of the times I saw Pat take a shit on Blake. I was about five years old. We were up in Lac Vieux Desert in the U.P. walking to a shack to clean some fish we'd caught that day. Blake was still small; his growth spurt'd just started. He said something smart. (Blake always had a lousy big mouth.) Pat grabbed him by his throat and slammed him down on the grass.

"I'm gonna tell Mom!" Blake said, struggling underneath him.

"Yeah, and she's gonna tell Dad, and he's gonna kick my ass, and I don't give a shit," Pat replied. He squatted over Blake's small quivering body and pulled the leg of his cutoff black sweat pants aside so his hairy asshole hovered over Blake's chest, and he squeezed out a little light-brown turd that dangled over Blake's squirming body.

"Hold still!" Pat told him.

It finally detached from Pat's ass and landed on Blake's chest. *Yuck!* I grabbed my stomach and swallowed back some puke. *Why would he do that?*

Pat laughed and picked up the string of fish and headed toward the cleaning shack.

"Aren't you gonna even wipe?" Rich asked disgustedly.

Pat kind of scratched his ass. "Naw... I'll let it air out," he muttered.

Blake flicked the shit off his chest with the back of his hand and looked at me.

"Joey, he didn't just shit on me," Blake said, his eyes trembling.

Yeah, he did. I saw it. It was gross!

Pat looked back at me excitedly, the string of fish dangling over his shoulder. "Let's go, Joey!" he said, with so much joy and warmth, like he hadn't just literally defecated on a person at all and it was just a normal day at Lac Vieux Desert.

A fat squirrel jumped from the nearby pine tree and smacked a sparrow off the railing. *Maybe he deserved to get shit on.* The squirrel picked up a big peanut and chewed it angrily. *People are so fucking disgusting. I wish I never had to care about anyone ever again. I wish I could just look into the stars and collider data and never have to touch or be touched by another fucking human being.* I sighed, gripping my chest as these wires seemed to wrap around it. *He didn't fucking rape her.* I gripped my heart as the wires squeezed it. *If he did, I'll fucking kill him.*

◆

The depths of Chicago's winter settled in on us. The clouds moved in and stacked up over the lake, and the sun disappeared. We were doing a concrete rehab job in that wild shadowy web of circular on and off ramps where the Dan Ryan and Eisenhower intersect just before the high rises sprout up tall in the heart of Chicago. The subzero temperatures were going to shut everything down, and we were racing against the cold to finish breaking out patches, framing, and pouring them before it was too late.

I was on Christmas vacation, up in the basket lift breaking out patches high on the concrete pier with Blake right next to me. The thick white cloud floated in the space between us as we dug the rivet busters into the concrete, sweating in our Carhartts. Blake morphed into this monstrous shadow moving in the cloud. *Is this motherfucker my brother? Or some fucking demon? I want to put the tip of this rivet buster to his head and pull the fucking trigger.* I saw his brains flying out of his collapsed skull.

At the end of the day we came down out of the lift and unhooked our harnesses from the metal basket. Blake took his harness off and started to gather his shit to leave. *Fucking confront this motherfucker already.*

"Aye Blake." I followed him.

"Yeah?" He turned around real ominously.

"Something happen between you and Faith?"

He puffed his chest out beneath his black Carhartt coat and grinned.

"What are you trying to say?"

I stepped up close to him. "She said you did something to her."

"Like what are we talking about here?" He grinned down at me with his chin up. "You accusing me of something? What? An insult? An assault? A rape? What are we talking about here?"

"You tell me, motherfucker."

He slowly reached out and grabbed hold of my harness at the chest straps.

"Listen here," he whispered.

I swung a right hook and it smashed into the side of his head. His legs wobbled and he gripped my harness and almost pulled me down with him. His knee hit the ground, but he held tight to my harness and pulled himself back to his feet. We wrestled awkwardly as the guys yelled and jumped up to break it up. I tried to hit him with a left hook but he was too close, and we tottered and fell to the gravel. He ended up on top and I hit him but I couldn't get anything on it. He cocked his fist and punched down on me and it felt like he hit me with a pillow. *Are you fucking serious?* I laughed.

He reached out and covered my mouth and nose with his hand.

"Hold still!" he growled.

I broke his grip and rolled him. They pulled us apart. Blake stormed off to his truck.

"That bitch has got you on a leash!" Blake yelled. "She's playing with your head, kid! You want some relationship advice?" He opened the door to the truck. "Dump the bitch!"

"I already did," I yelled back.

"Attaboy." He grinned back at me wickedly, got in, and floored it off the site.

"Why the fuck you fighting with him?!" Rich yelled at me as I walked away.

"He did something to Faith."

"No way in fucking hell!" Rich yelled, following me. "He would never do that!"

I sat down on a dirty upside-down bucket. *He's right. I'm going fucking crazy. I gotta apologize to him.*

"He's your fucking brother Joe! Stop it! That's fucking crazy talk!" Rich pleaded, hovering over me. "If you guys broke up, it ain't his fault!"

"Maybe you're right." I looked off at the traffic whizzing by on the Dan Ryan. "That motherfucker punches like a girl."

"He's a fucking hero, man. He's a fucking hero, he saved that baby on TV. He's a decorated Chicago cop, he's a good guy. He didn't fucking rape anybody, or whatever you think."

"Yeah, yeah, he didn't do nothing," I replied.

What kind of weird motherfucker grabs somebody by their mouth and nose. Real fucking rapey shit right there. I shook my head. *Joe. Listen to yourself! He did not rape your girlfriend.*

◆

At home Ma called me into the kitchen. She sat at the end of the long oak table wearing a big yellow collared shirt and gray sweatpants. Her pudgy face fell stern as she hung up the phone. A few babysitting kids played with toys on the living room floor in front of the big TV. The big purple dinosaur Barney bounced around and got the kids to talk about their feelings on the screen. On Ma's TV in the kitchen, Maury Povich amped up the DNA reveal for a woman on stage with three men sitting across from her.

"Why on earth did you punch Blake?" she asked as I walked in.

"He did something to Faith." I told her and opened the fridge.

"What?!" she spun around to look at me. "That's crazy nonsense."

"She told me he did something to her."

"Listen honey. Blake is a very handsome man. He's successful! He doesn't have to rape anybody!"

"Rapist don't rape people because they're ugly losers, Ma! They rape people because they're RAPISTS!"

"Do you really think they'd let a rapist into the Chicago Police Department?! Look at that cover of the newspaper over on the fridge."

I looked at the *Chicago Tribune* clipping stuck to the fridge with a big magnet. Blake's pompous grin, the way he held the baby on his hip like only a longtime father could, his big chest all puffed out.

"That is who Blake is, a hero."

"You can be a hero and a rapist, Ma." I snapped open the tab on a cold Pepsi. "He also brags about torturing people at work." I took a sip; it was sweet and frizzly. "He's in charge of investigating rapes, and he doesn't even believe rape is a real thing." I sat on a tall stool beside the garbage can; it smelled of pee and poo from the dirty Huggies diapers.

"Look, he's a very charismatic man. A lot of women throw themselves at him. You just don't know how it is for men like him."

"What are you trying to say?" I told her, wincing. *What, you think he's hot and I'm not? That's some twisted shit for a mother to say to their son.* "Do you know that Karen threw herself at me that day? She tried to kiss me."

"Karen?! Now you're going after Karen, too? A mother of four? Listen, it's not their fault you and Faith broke up. Why don't you go talk with her, bring her some flowers and make up, and see if you can get back together and stop punching people who had nothing to do with it."

"Phssh. You don't get it, Ma." I said and headed upstairs to shower.

I disrobed and got under the hot sprinkling water. It coated my dirty stinking skin. *Maybe she's right. Am I just going crazy? Blaming them? I wanted us to be like them.* I felt Karen's hands touching my chest and her fingers tips gliding slowly down my tense abs. My cock sprang erect. *Maybe I shoulda kissed her. Fucked her right there in the basement.* I imagined bending her over the ping pong table, smacking her nice pale ass. *Maybe we both would have loved it.* Then an image of the cheerleader I fucked and the way she came, and how I didn't come, and how I felt grossed out by the whole thing. *I want something sweet and pure, not some nasty cheating sex, living my life like some kinda soap opera, lying to the woman I love. Bouncing from one chick to the next. Having sex with someone else's wife ain't hot! It's nasty, selfish, destructive shit, it's narcissistic. My desire is more important than someone else's relationship? Their love, their future together? I ain't no fucking narcissist. I pretty much fucking hate myself.* I closed my eyes and let the hot water pepper my face and pour down my body. *Maybe I deserved this shit.*

◆

I fell into a dark, deep isolation. After another sleepless night thinking of her, I jumped in the old red Jeep Wrangler TJ and tore off toward I-55 with the windows open and the brutal wind sailing through my ears blunting the thoughts of her that'd been flying through my mind like neutrinos through bedrock. As I soared down 47th, the monstrous General Electric factory sat beside me, dark and empty like a tomb of lost dreams. I slipped the ring from my pocket and rubbed my thumb along the loop in steady circles like a positron gaining velocity for a terrible collision.

Driving fast, I almost missed my turn; I squealed a right and floored it up the ramp to 1st Avenue. I passed under the Harlem Avenue bridge where I'd gotten into it with Blake over dropping a ladder. I stood up to him even then, as a scrawny fifteen-year-old. Screamed right back in his smug face. I squeezed the steering wheel in my fist as prickles ran up my arm and percolated in my shoulder and upper back. *I ain't never been afraid of that piece 'a shit.*

I shot downtown and headed north on Lake Shore toward the old neighborhood, toward home. The lake hovered dark blue, with turbulent waves peaking against the black horizon. I exited at Montrose and pulled up to the harbor and parked.

I walked down to the concrete ledge, my breath twisting into steam around me. The boats were all gone for winter; just the empty star docks sat out there. I remembered going to work on Da's boat in the boat yard during the cold months. What he'd say if I could ask him. *I just wanted something pure in my life, something good.* A small pack of seagulls floated on the ice-cold trembling water. I looked at the ring one last time. Thoughts flipped through my mind—the weird shit with Blake, the way she changed. *Maybe he did do something to her. No. It's impossible, he'd never do something like that to me, to her.* I took a deep breath. *You're a fool. She never fucking loved you.* I gripped the ring and threw it to the seagulls, hoping they'd fly up in the air and show themselves to me. The ring plopped in the center of them and sunk to the bottom. All they did was ruffle their feathers, squawk, and swim away.

Chapter 8: Men's Division

AT LEAST I STILL HAD THE RING. The other ring, that is.

"Is you figh'n in de glovesss????" Anwar asked with a crooked grin, mocking what the old-timer black trainers would always ask around the time of the Golden Gloves.

"Yeah." I giggled as I climbed up and sat down next to him on the apron of the blue ring with our feet up on the long wooden bench lining it. The noontime sun flooded in from the large skylight above the ring and lit the clean blue canvas and cast shadows from the ropes across our backs. Toro Fernandez thundered the speed bag in the far corner of the big, high-ceilinged room as Jermaine Woods whipped the hard-plastic cord of his jump rope into a whirling blur in front of the big mirrors. A fat heavyweight thudded his fists into the big brown leather heavy bag by the office. Willie Williams twisted the dial on the black-and-white TV as smoke lifted off his Winston, snug in the fingers of a green ashtray. The scent of midday training at the Windy City Gym warmed with the bodies and permeated the air with tension and agony.

"Whatchu at, seventy-eight?" Anwar said, splicing his yellow wraps between his fingers.

"Yeah." I pinched the Velcro on my rolled wrap and threw it. It unwound as it arced out ahead of me.

"Aye ain't dat one badass Irish dude at 178?" he asked Fearless, who was on his minute break from shadowboxing.

"Terry O'Sullivan. Yeah, damn, you got a full plate with that motherfucker," Fearless said.

"But just box, you can beat him," Anwar said, his big black goatee bobbing under his mouth. "You're too slick for him."

"Who's Terry O'Sullivan?" I asked as I stretched my blue wraps around my wrist.

"Kid, listen, I ain't gonna bullshit you," Fearless said, putting his Everlast-booted foot up on the bench. "The guy's a badass. He was real good like seven, eight years back, when I was still figh'n in de Gloves, he was stopping guys."

"You was figh'n de gloves?!" Anwar interrupted with mock surprise, reaching his hand out.

Fearless slapped it and continued.

"He went to the marines, then became a Navy SEAL," Fearless said, gliding his hand through his spiky black hair. As it shot back up it whisked sweat into a mist above his head. "Now he's cracking heads at County, part of the riot crew."

"How old's the guy?"

"He's thirty-three. But he knocked a guy out cold last weekend at the racetrack show. He's got a great right hand."

"And the left hook's good too," Anwar chimed in.

"If he hurts you wit the left, just lay down and stay there."

"Pretend you asleep!" Anwar guffawed, his mouth smirking inside his trimmed mustache and beard.

"I ain't scared 'a him." The electronic bell's startling ring blared showing a green light beginning the new round as Fearless bobbed on his toes.

"We ain't saying you scared, kid, we know you ain't," he said as he shot a crisp jab out into the dank air before him.

"We just lookin out for you," Anwar chimed in.

"You come back next year, he won't be around, you'll win it all easy." Fearless shot a right hand and rolled under an imaginary left hook as I flicked him off.

"Hahah, I like the kid," Fearless said to Anwar. "He's a fighter."

"Tough guy over here," Anwar said, nudging me.

Sal appeared, sliding his hand through this thinning black slicked-back hair, holding the *Chicago Trib* with Blake on the cover. "Aye Joe, isn't this hero cop guy related to you?"

"Naw, Walsh is a common name," I muttered.

"He caught that baby!" Anwar guffawed. "Did you see that video?!"

"Fucking crazy bastard caught that baby boy like a goddamn football!" Fearless reenacted the catch, arms stretched. "Touchdown!!!"

"I told myself, I seen this guy before," Sal said. "He's your brother, ain't he, he was at a few of your fights."

"He ain't my brother, alright!" I roared. "He ain't my fucking brother!"

They all looked at me befuddled.

"Woh, OK... OK, kid, he ain't." Sal scratched his head. "Well, can you give these guys some work today?"

"Yeah."

"OK, well, get warmed up, we don't got all day." Sal picked up an old soggy headgear off the apron by the spit bucket. He muttered, "I told them not to put this here!" Then he shook his head and disappeared with it.

I hurried off to get loose and gear up. I pulled my black leather Ringside headgear on. *I like sparring with pros, sometimes I get the better of them but they'd always teach me something. Fucking Fearless though, fuck him for saying that shit.* I hopped in the ring and sparred two brisk rounds with Anwar, just boxing and moving and trying to counter him as he worked his combinations on me. Our bodies flowing in and out of the golden trapezoid of light pouring through the ceiling made distinct by the dusty haze in the air. Sal stalked around, watching the sparring in both rings like a modern art critic, analyzing the artistry of line and philosophical implications of our work while sporadically inserting commentary and commands.

"Ya telegraphing the jab, Anwar, come on! We been working on dat. If this kid can counter you, what the heck's Left Hook Tracey gonna do to ya?"

We swapped sparring partners, and I went to the shadowy red ring with Fearless. Anger swirled in my mind from Fearless's talk about O'Sullivan, his certainty of my limitations as a fighter. *I better box careful with O'Sullivan, huh? What if I just throw caution to the wind and go toe-to-toe with him, how'd you like that? I hate this fucking red ring, this dark energy in it. You like that catch Blake made, huh?* The darkness fell all over Fearless's face: shadows from the headgear, shadows upon shadows masking his frowning face in darkness like a cloak of dark matter. *What if I told you that pig is a rapist?* The bell rang and I thundered across the ring, ripping mean combinations with very bad intentions. Fearless moved and I cut him off and unloaded again. He grimaced at me, shrugged, and put a lot on a jab and dazed me a little, but I came back with three shots and we clinched and wrestled. Sal shouted "Aye! Break!" He stepped upon the apron and glared at me. "Get outa here with dat." He grabbed the ropes and split them open with his knee for me to step through.

"Yeah, get him outa here, I don't want to have to hurt him, Sal."

"I think he might 'a was the one hurt'n you," Sal muttered as he pointed to Jermaine to step in.

Sal unfastened my head gear. "What's dat all about?"

"Nothin'..."

"You an amateur, these guys are pros." His potbelly bumped against my tense abs. "I don't want them feeling like they gotta put you in your place, kid. Work the floor" Sal said, walking away with the headgear. "You better shake his hand before you leave."

We shook on it later, and I headed down the dark steps. *I ain't mad at Fearless. I just don't like people trying to define me with words.* I rounded the stairwell. *A fight is a live and wild thing, any fucking thing can happen. When you disrespect the sanctity of a fight like that, it makes me want to annihilate you.* I burst through the door into the bright daylight of Ogden Avenue.

◆

I couldn't sleep. I lay on my back wide awake every night. When I did drift, nightmares tortured me. I dreamt of Faith, beautiful, pure Faith, my love, her lips so perfect and upturned, so elegant. Strands of her light dirty-blonde hair flipping in the wind. "We're going to be together forever, Joey. I want to marry you." Her walking to me smiling...then dark hands grab her. Drag her screaming to a room, I rush to her but I'm sinking in sand, suddenly I'm floating above her in my room, Blake grabs her by her throat, throws her on the bed. He covers her mouth. "Hold still!" he angrily yells. She tries to fight him. Her body contorts. He yanks her panties to the side and jams himself inside of her. Her body contracts in orgasm, she screams. He shushes her. "This is what you wanted." Then he hears something coming. "Isn't it?!" He jumps up and hurries out. She lies there trembling. She calls out my name. It falls to darkness. Silence, then Bake's pompous snicker.

After that dream I would fear sleep and just lay staring at the ceiling. I wanted to kill myself sometimes. Just go and get my father's shotgun, chamber a slug in it, put the barrel in my mouth, use my toe, and *bang!* My body didn't seem to be mine anymore. Weird tensions coursed through my back and shoulders, a warm rage floating through my arms. Other times I dreamt of fighting. Three guys coming for me, laughing. I hit the closest one with all my might, he barely flinches. And then they're on me, all over me, smashing me, laughing. *I can't breathe! I can't fucking breathe, you motherfuckers!* Awake, I climb out of the cloak of bedsheets and shadowbox in my bedroom mirror with savage ferocity, my muscularity starting to fill in, starting to make me look like a man. *I'm more powerful than ever. I want to kill someone.* Hook-cross. *I want my fist to crash straight through someone's skull.* Dip and dig uppercut, left hook, roll, drop hands, stare into my own reflection, hardening brow, fierce blue eyes. *Better yet, I want someone to fucking kill me.*

◆

Luckily they put O'Sullivan and me in opposite brackets. We both had to win twice to make the finals. My first fight was a lanky Arabian southpaw with a stupid mustache that curled up at the corners of his lips. He was tricky and awkward but I lit him up down the stretch and edged a majority decision.

I sat in the dressing room unraveling my wraps when these metallic booms resounded in the main room. The crowd erupted and I walked back out and there was Terry O'Sullivan blasting a guy. They gave the guy a standing eight count as O'Sullivan heaved, waiting for the count. His pale arms and chest swelled like they'd been pumped full of helium. The ref waved them on to continue. O'Sullivan walked in calmly and slugged a one-two that knocked the guy out; he collapsed so bad his head reached back and touched his ankle. The crowd exploded. Terry looked down at him, winced, and turned away. The ref waved it off with no count as the doctor jumped in the ring.

The room throbbed with the roars. I heard nothing, just watched the unconscious fighter in the stale stark light and imagined myself as him. *That'd be nice. The ecstasy of sleep: no thoughts of her, no regrets, no rage, just nothing.* O'Sullivan jogged to the corner, leapt up on the ropes, arms raised, his shaved head glowing and his wrinkled muscular face grinning. I grinned. *That's my ticket.*

Sal put his hand on my shoulder. "It's a tall order, kid. But if you box, you can win. You try an' slug with him and it ain't gonna go so good."

◆

That shit Sal said infuriated me. But I didn't tell him, just started training more with Brother Alex. Brother had a savage way of training. Windy City is where you go to fine-tune your craft, learn tricks, become classy. I wasn't in need of fine-tuning. I needed brutal preparations for war. Brother gave me that. Running suicide sprints in the wrestling room.

Brother on me endlessly, counting reps, pushing me to break my own record, timing my breaks, cutting seconds off the break without telling me, miscounting reps for the pure torture of it. When I complained, he just screamed in my face, "PUSH!!!" Endless rounds on the bag down in the dirty, dank, old equipment room, Brother slapping my arms and back with his whiplike hands, screaming in my face "HARDER!!! MORE!!! O'SULLIVAN'S GONNA SMASH YOU IF YOU HIT HIM LIKE THAT!!!! HARDER!!!!!"

After another brutal session, I sat down there in the equipment room. The white bag swayed slowly from my last round on it.

"Joe, what's this crap, you punching your brother?" Brother Alex asked.

"Who told you about that?"

"Your mom called."

"He raped Faith." I said it dead and flat, without looking at Brother.

"What?! The cop?" He sat behind me in a chair against the cinder-block wall.

"Yeah, he raped her last Thanksgiving on my bed."

"Joe, that is impossible!"

"Faith told me."

"Joe..." He shook his enormous head, then held it in his small hands. "Did she really say that to you?"

"Yeah, well, not in so many words."

"I have to ask you, Joe. Are you jealous of him? Of him catching the baby?"

"No. I'm so fucking proud of him for that. It was one of the greatest things I've ever seen."

"I'm going to pray for you, Joe. For all three of you."

I sat there staring at the gray concrete floor. With the shadow of the bag sweeping across it, mechanical like a metronome. *What the fuck would you do that for, Brother? God's the motherfucker that let this happen.*

◆

My semifinal was against a black kid from the West Side I'd fought a couple times before and beat. He was about my size, and he'd always made it close. I wanted to make a statement. *I ain't a kid no more. I'm a man, in the men's division.* I dominated through the second round and Sal said, "Take it easy, you got the win."

I glared at Sal. Then looked down at my blue gloves. *This is the moment. You have to stop him now, knock him out.* It was like Sal's words inserted a pack of positrons into my chest. My heart thumped in a fast squeezing motion; the vibrations surged across my chest into my shoulders and down my arms like the magnets in the ring of the accelerator in Fermilab. My heart accelerated the positrons through my arms into my fists. I squeezed my gloves together. *The only way for the positrons to escape is collisions.* I jumped up off the stool, squeezing my gloves together and pacing back and forth. *He can't survive this.* The energy cycled through my arms. *He's gonna have to stop me, he knows that!* Faster and faster I glared at him heaving on his stool. *I'll kill you, motherfucker. I will take your fucking life.*

"That's it," Brother said, sitting on my stool ringside. "Take him out, Joe!"

The bell rang and I lit my man up with a six-punch combination that forced the ref to step in and give him an eight count. The crowd's roars built. I kept the pressure on him as he held and tried to survive. Then I lit him up with a nasty hook to the liver midway through the round and he squealed in my ear and I knew I had him. I caught him with a left hook and straight right. The ref gave him an eight count and Brother Alex yelled urgently, "Thirty seconds! Finish him!" *Brother Alex understands! He wants me to stop him! See, Sal? You understand now? Why the fuck I'm here?*

The crowd stirred and swarmed in the darkness like turbulent waters on the lake. *They want it. They want war. They want total annihilation. He should have never come in this ring if he wasn't fucking ready to die. Of course I have the win, this isn't about winning, Sal. This is a message to O'Sullivan! You have war ahead of you, boy!* The circular energy cycled through my chest and arms, fast like surging electricity. A girl's voice shot through the roaring crowd. "Get him, Joe!" *Faith?* I rushed in, unloaded on him as he exhaustedly covered up. I blasted through his gloves, aiming to punch through his guard and all the way through his head, to knock his fucking head all the way off and into the fifth row. His gloves began to flop all over as mine flowed through them into his head, through his head, and as the ten-second warning dinged he slumped down against the ropes and flopped on his ass, his eyes closed and mouth open, with blood oozing around his black mouth guard. The ref dove between us and waved it off.

O'Sullivan was up next. He stalked back and forth near the entrance to the dressing room, his shaved head glimmering and his big brow blotting out the ceiling light, making his eyes look like empty black caverns. I just stood there staring at him, perfectly framed by the open dressing room door with the big stands full of people still cheering what I'd just done. *I don't give a fuck about them. My only audience is you, O'Sullivan. Did you like it?* He glanced at me, shrugged, and looked away with a painful grimace. Then he threw a sharp uppercut and started bouncing on his toes as his trainer walked up. His trainer waved his hand toward me dismissively and slid the headgear over O'Sullivan's scalp and fastened it. O'Sullivan turned to face me; he grimaced at me and bit down on his mouthpiece. The headgear made his face robotic as he smashed his gloves together at chest height; they collided with a hollow thud.

O'Sullivan looked gigantic compared to his opponent. He stormed out and landed intelligent combinations, though the snap on his punch still elicited that metallic crunch.

And then it was over. I saw him start to throw the right cross and I knew it would crash into his man's jaw and O'Sullivan would follow through and there was no way the man could take it. I turned away before it landed and I stepped toward the dressing room as the crack bloomed into the rafters. His opponent's body smacked against the canvas and the springy cords of the ring ached as the crowd rejoiced. I stopped at the door and closed my eyes; the gravity of it all compressed in my heart like a dwarf star ready to explode.

As the crowd died down O'Sullivan came into the dressing room and his corner cut his wraps off, and after a minute his trainer left and it was just us in the dingy stinking room.

I grabbed my bag and stood up.

"Good fight," Terry said over his shoulder.

"Thanks. Good cross," I replied without looking at him.

"Thanks," Terry said. "I know your brother. He's a good cop."

"Naw, that ain't my brother." I started for the door of the dressing room.

"Aye kid."

I paused, not turning to see him.

"Whatever happens in there, is what it is. I just want you to know, I like you, kid."

"I ain't no kid," I said and went out into the smoky chaos of Saturday night semifinals at Saint Andrew's.

We were set for the Friday night of the finals. I told my family my fight was on Saturday 'cause I didn't want them coming. *If I go out, I don't want them seeing it, telling me I should quit boxing, worrying about me.*

◆

I drove around in the Jeep a few nights after the semifinal, thinking about Faith.

I wanted to tell her I made the finals of the Open. I went to the flower shop, bought a rose, and started driving around near her house. I'd bought her a lot of roses over the years to surprise her, to ask her to forgive me for fights we'd gotten in, anniversaries. *All the lies, all the hurt, her going away for school, we'll never make it, it's over.* I drove toward the gym. My Jeep climbed the old rickety Ogden bridge over Cicero Avenue. As I soared up the beautiful old steel bridge, the whole of the city skyline emerged on the horizon, glimmering burnt orange. *The 1998 Light-Heavyweight Open Division Champion Representing the Windy City Gym, Joey Walsh! What a joke. You'll never win the Open.* Wires cut into my mind and squeezed with the ache of all I ever thought I was and would never be. I ripped the head off the rose and threw it out the window and off the bridge; it sailed into the cold windy black oblivion. *I believe you, Faith.* I squeezed the thorny stem, wrapped it around my right fist, let go of the wheel, and started slamming my fist into my palm over and over. *I'm sorry.* Blood streamed down off my hand and knuckles and the car weaved back and forth across the bridge. *I'm so sorry.* I descended on Ogden into the city and the skyline disappeared again and all I could see was the old lonely factories. I cruised past Windy City and saw Willie in the window of the back rooms. He waved as he puffed his cigarette. *Maybe one day I'll move into the gym with Willie, live in one of the back rooms and just fight—everyone, the whole fucking world.*

◆

The morning of the finals she showed up at my door.

I came down drowsy. She looked horrible. So thin, and with big bags under her eyes. Two inches of her dark roots showed in her hair pulled up in a ponytail. It was chilly but the long winter'd broken for the most part.

"I heard you made the finals. I read it in the paper. I just wanted to say congrats," she said.

"Thanks." I sat on the porch steps. "What's going on with Wellesley?"

"I'm not going." She sat beside me. "It's a long story. I'm going to Butler in Indianapolis instead..." Her face contorted as she fought back a frown.

"Are you OK?"

"Yeah, uh-huh."

"You look thin, Faith."

"No, it's not like that, I've been a little sick."

"Faith, you gotta take care of yourself." I touched her face.

She took my hand in hers. Her hand was so warm and smooth.

"I'm sorry for that day when I screamed at you about Blake. I've been thinking about it a lot..." I looked her in the eyes. "I believe you."

She whimpered and squeezed my hand with all her might.

"Joe, I wanted to talk with you about that...I've been feeling really weird, I've been crazy. They put me on antidepressants..." Tears fell down her face. "Joe, your brother didn't rape me, OK? You have to know that. I'm sorry I said it. Your brother... He's a good person."

Her words fucking eviscerated me. I gasped and clutched my chest where the wires came undone.

"I was just going crazy. I know that now. It never happened." She looked away at the sun rising above the houses across the street into the red sky. "Nothing happened."

"OK."

"I miss you," she said and looked me in the eyes, her creamy green irises surrounded by the bulging blood vessels. "I'm going to miss you forever and ever. Your family." She cried and caught herself. "They're so beautiful. Give the kids a big hug for me, OK?"

"I will. I'm going to miss you too, Faith. I wanted to marry you...I love you."

"I know." She started to cry and I held her and her body shook so violently in my arms, like something horrible was trying to leap out. "I love you so much."

Through tears she said bye and walked away through the little wooden arch in our front yard, like she was walking away down an aisle in a massive red church.

I sat on my porch steps. *What the fuck was that? Did that shit even really just happen? It wasn't true all along? He didn't do it?* Then the darkness returned like a massive cloud of dark matter. *It is true, you stupid motherfucker. She's just trying to protect you and your family. 'Cause she loves you that much.* I bowed my head. Tears dripped down the tip of my nose. *What a fucking angel.*

I stood with all the rage and shame and pain convulsing in my heart. *Men's division, huh?* I peered into the big red sun. *You know what the fucking men's division is? It's where everyone you love is tortured every day and you can't fucking protect 'em, no matter how hard you try. And the worst torture of all may be the one that unfolds inside you. And you face that shit alone.*

◆

Chicagoans filled the dark, musty, and monstrous Saint Andrew's Gymnasium to the rafters. The ring sat elevated in the center of the room like a brightly lit sacrificial altar; they surrounded it, a shadowy mob thirsting for blood and spectacle, and maybe a few there for the artistry of another time, the old days of The Gloves. Their bodies swayed on the floor behind the gray folding chairs, sipping clear plastic cups of Corona that glowed amber from the large square metal frame of lights that hung above the blue-canvassed ring. I shuffled my black thin-soled shoes along the canvas. The purple blood speckles swirled in a wild array at my feet like a violent Pollock painting.

"Mean thoughts, Joe. Mean thoughts," Brother Alex murmured from the apron. Strands of golden hair gleamed atop his enormous bald head. *Am I gonna paint this canvas tonight? Who's blood? His or mine? It don't fucking matter.*

The smokers walked in and out of the smoking room near the side exit; each entry and exit exuded plumes of cigar smoke into the auditorium. A scratchy burn rasped at my lungs. *Fucking pricks. Can't they do that shit outside?*

The tuxedoed announcer clutched the chrome microphone that dangled down from the rafters as he read from his notes in the center of the ring.

"Ladieeees and Gentle-men! In our next bout, the Chicago Golden Gloves Light-Heavyweight Open Division Championship. Out of the blue corner, representing the Beverly Park District, Terry O'Sullivan!" His voice boomed to the rafters as most of the crowd erupted.

O'Sullivan loomed across the way. His mean face winced jagged and robotic inside the black leather Everlast headgear. His pale muscular shoulders trembled in the bright light. He smacked his gloves together with a hollow thud.

"And in the red corner, representing the Windy City Gym, Joseph Walsh!" The cheering flickered through the crowd, weak and tepid. It's just the guys from the gym. A vile snicker rattled in my chest. *They want O'Sullivan? Good. Fuck them. I don't want to be favored and cheered for. I ain't here for that. I'm purging something dark inside me. I want blood and disaster.*

I bounced on my toes. Ref Francis frowned at me in his powder blue uniform; his white mustache quivered as he waved us to the center of the ring for the final instructions. A bunch of corrections officers sat up front, a fat one with stupid face yelled, "Aye Terry, why ya pick'n on a little kid for?" The group chuckled. "How old is he, fifteen, fer Christ's sake?"

I glared at him. "Go fuck yourself."

O'Sullivan cracked up as the guys in the front row roared; one poured a quarter of a beer on Stupid Face's bald spot.

"No talking to the crowd or I'll take a point, Joe," the ref scolded.

I nodded as Sal pulled my mouthpiece out of his shiny black-and-gold Windy City cornerman's jacket and shoved it in my mouth.

"Shut it, you," he muttered.

Ref Francis gave us his final instructions. I heard none of it, just saw Terry's angular face grimacing across from me. *Finally we get to see how bad a motherfucker you really are, Terry. Like they all been say'n. I hope you are.*

We touched gloves with a nervous thud and walked back to our corners.

"Box with 'yer brains, Joey, not 'yer balls," Sal ordered before stepping out through the ropes.

The bell rang and I hurried over. I'm gonna bust his shit early. 1-2-3, my shots slipped around his blue gloves and slammed into his headgear. *He's easy to find.* I shot a lead right at his chin and he rolled with the shot, taking the snap out of it. *He's slick though.* I let my hands go in a snappy flurry. He leaned back into the ropes, shelled up like a nervous blue tortoise. I unleashed several deep thudding body shots around his elbows, then slipped a right uppercut between his gloves. His head popped out of its blue foam protectors as I looped a left hook and my red glove smashed into his ear. The crowd stirred in a low uneasy murmur. "Watch out Terry, he's a scrappy little fucker!"

O'Sullivan held, and he woke up after that. As the round progressed, he jabbed to my chest and bounced on the springy canvas fluidly, and followed with a right cross that shot in straight. Blackness exploded in my vision and my ears popped—like a million thoughts shot out of them, never to return.

"Move your damn head, Joey!" Sal cried from the corner. I grinned. Fuck that. I walked forward and hit him with ten or twelve shots that he mostly blocked, then he slugged me again with the right, this time on the chin, and suddenly I rode on a tilt-a-whirl, the room spinning around me. *Now we go to hell.* I bent deep at the knee, stepped in, looped an overhand with all my might and caught him on the chin. His eyes wobbled in his head a little as he twisted and slung a left hook through my jaw. My mouthpiece shot way out of the ring, spinning like a Frisbee into the fifth row where it clonked a busty blonde who sat snuggled up with a fat cigar-chewing Italian in a black suit.

I stumbled toward them to ask the blonde for my mouthpiece back. Ref Francis grabbed hold of my arm and looked at me startled, his long pointy nose raised. He pointed to the corner. *Is this the first eight count of my life? Good, 'cause I fucking need one to clear my head.* I looked to my corner. Sal hurried through the ropes into the ring. *Fuck, they stopped it?!* Brother Alex slammed the stool down. The round's over. I giggled. *The fucking round's over, Joe! Get your shit together.* I never heard the fucking bell through the roaring of the crowd. As I stumbled over, Sal shot a long narrow hose of cold water in my face from the rubbery white bottle. I gasped as he pushed me down in the stool.

"You ain't doing nothing I told you!"

"I got him, he ain't so bad."

"He is so bad, he's gonna fuckin' stop you. You see this towel?" He squeezed a blood-smeared white towel in front of my face. "I'm gonna throw it in before ref Francis evens got to fuckin stop it."

"Sal, I know I'm gonna lose. I don't care. Don't throw no towel in." I pleaded.

"I'm gonna do what I gotta do to protect ya, kid."

"Sal!" Fearless materialized ringside and tossed Sal my mouth guard.

"Thanks!" I grinned.

"Joey, box! Please!" He put his hands up in prayer before his leathery face. "Please, kid!"

"I ain't no fucking kid!"

"Fine, you ain't a kid," Sal urged. "You're a man, a big bad man. Now box like a man."

I settled in and boxed better early in round two, for Fearless's sake as a thank you, and 'cause it made me feel good, Sal calling me a man. I moved and feinted. I welted O'Sullivan's face with my jab, doubling and tripling it up. He swung and I slipped and countered and he swung and I rolled again and moved. *I'm too fast for him. I can coast to an easy win with my speed.*

"He's running, Terry, the kid's scared!" A voice, pompous and authoritative, whined through the swirling crowd. "Hold still, ya pussy!"

Blake? You think I'm scared, brother? You don't want to see me win, do you? Well, I ain't come here for no fuckin' win. I bounced before O'Sullivan on my toes. *Came here for destruction.* O'Sullivan stepped in and hit me with a right and I nodded at him and laughed. I swung back with my left hook and we traded hooks. He wobbled me as I gathered and launched an overhand right-left hook combo and he fired back with a missile of a cross and we stood toe-to-toe in the center of the ring unloading on each other like old-time gladiators, sweat bursting off our wet headgear into bright sprays lit golden by the loud lights hanging from the rafters. Our energy flowed back and forth like lake swells; at times it was as if we were one chaotic being. The roaring crowd around us echoed and amplified it, sending the energy through the red brick walls and out into the universe.

The timekeeper stood ringside banging the bell with all his might as the pandemonium rumbled through the big room. You'd think that shit'd make me tired, but it fed me like a swelling red giant star swallowing its solar system.

The round came to an end with the crowd on its feet. Sal looked me in the eyes, shocked.

"Beautiful, Joe!" Brother Alex said through the ropes.

"How did you do dat?!" Sal asked.

"I don' know?" I shrugged and flopped down on the stool. *You know how I did it, Sal? It's called the fucking conservation of energy.* I giggled and looked across at O'Sullivan breathing hard on his stool. *Just three minutes left, O'Sullivan, ain't that a shame? Shame it ain't an eternity...*

"You're fighting great, Joe, keep pushing," Brother Alex said through the ropes.

I glared at Sal as he rinsed my mouth guard. I shoulda had Brother as chief second, he knows.

Fuck it. I received the mouth guard into my mouth like the Eucharist. *He can't hurt you. Or maybe he can, maybe he can kill you.* The idea thrilled me. *Come on, O'Sullivan, hit me hard. Hard enough to take all the pain away.* A vision flashed in my mind of the engagement ring slid onto a finger of slimy green muck at the bottom of Montrose Harbor. *Why the fuck was I so stupid? Terry O'Sullivan, come punch the stupid out of me! Knock me into eternal silence, so I can finally be at peace.*

He didn't. He tried though. He hit me with punches that felt like they were going to send me flying up over the ropes and out into the crowd, just like my mouthpiece had gone. But I stayed. I landed on my feet. I unloaded punches back. And the crowd started to cheer both our punches. They stopped cheering for either of us to win, they cheered for the splendid chaos of the war, the fight, the destruction, the spectacle unfolding before them. Blood dripped down from my nose in a steady bead. *I don't care about no fucking crowd. I hate you motherfuckers. You hit like a bitch, O'Sullivan! Why can't you hit harder? Why can't you fucking annihilate me?* We clinched, wrestling wildly. *Maybe if I fall into one of his punches, just walk into it.*

I couldn't do it. The positron was back cycling through my chest and arms as the ref broke us and O'Sullivan took a deep breath. *If you can't get it done I'll knock you out instead, motherfucker.* I surged in and threw a furious twelve-punch combination at the end of the round and he teed off too and the crowd emitted one last elated roar and the timekeeper enthusiastically rang the bell over and over. *Stop ringing that bell.* I stumbled toward my corner. *I can't breathe.* I gasped and collapsed to my knees on the canvas exhausted, and lay down on my back as the crowd oohed. *It ain't just my body, you fuckers. You ever been exhausted in your mind? Your spirit?* As I lay there on the blue canvas I felt her laying her head on my chest. *Maybe she wanted it. NO! She tried to tell you and you screamed at her! She broke up with you. Maybe she was two-timing you the whole time. So what if she was? Nobody's perfect.* I stared up into the bright lights hanging down from the ceiling like a nearing galaxy. *You loved her with all your stupid heart. And you fucking lost it all. You lost everything.*

Terry came over and picked me up and raised my hand. Everyone cheered again. I still couldn't breathe. Our corners greeted each of us and shook hands. And Brother Alex had to help me stand while Sal undid my gear. Brother Alex said, "You were beautiful, Joey, just perfect." He hugged me, holding me up.

Then the announcer stood in the center in his tuxedo holding the mic. Ref Frances held both our hands as we awaited our judgment. The crowd stirred and murmured uneasily. Stupidface even fell silent in reverence. *It's so fuckin' tense... I know I lost. I don't care.* Silence descended on the dark room as sporadic camera flashes burst in the blackness. *I hope they don't give me any bullshit decision over this guy 'cause O'Sullivan's a real fighter and he'll win nationals and I'll just screw around and try to walk myself into a punch so I can feel what it feels like to be nothing for a moment, for a long, extended moment where I can be nothing at all and not a fuckup disaster. Please don't let me win. I didn't come here to win.* I closed my eyes and looked up to the ceiling. *Did you love her to win something? Win some stupid game? Loving someone is a gift, it ain't a transaction. And when you give it to them, you're giving it to yourself as well.*

"And the winner..." *Please, you motherfuckers. I lost, I know it.* "Out of the blue corner! Terry O'Sullivan!!!!" *Thank fucking god.*

I clapped and raised his other hand and thanked the ref for not stopping it, and thanked Sal for not stopping it, and we got out of the ring and strangers kept coming up and saying it was the best fight they'd ever seen, and I kept shrugging and saying disgustedly, "But nothing happened!"

◆

I left the Gloves early and got a fifth of Jack Daniel's at Thousand Liquors with my fake ID and went out driving around the city in my Jeep. I pulled down into the dark tunnel of Lower Wacker, soaring past the cardboard boxes of the homeless camps. *You really got it so bad? At least that ain't your house.* I shot past a decrepit tent. I took a deep slug. *Just drive this fucking thing into one of these cement columns. Or off a bridge into that fucking nasty green river. A Green River float, I could use one of those right now. Just walking down Clark Street with Da. I wish I was a kid again, not some shitty half-adult in a ugly mixed-up fucking world. How the hell did you live in this shithole, Da? You were a good person. How's a good person navigate all this fucking horrible crap? Maybe I ain't a good person. Maybe I deserve this shit too.* I drove around and onto Lake Shore as a fleet of seagulls soared along the cement coast. *Maybe Da wasn't perfect either. Maybe nobody is.* I sipped the bottle as the tissue around my eye swelled up. I hadn't put anything on it, and my nose was swelled to hell, too. I'd bled all over myself, and I stunk of sweat from the fight. *I don't give a fuck. Life is a war and you have to fight it with all your might just to stay human.* The scabs on my hands from the thorns had opened and the wind feathering over them stung and made me think about her. *Fuck it, you loved her and you lost her. We all lose, we all lose every goddamn thing we ever love.*

I sat down at Standee's, this all-night diner in the old neighborhood, and I ate eggs and bacon and hash browns. I inhaled it. *What the fuck would I be if we never left the city?* Some assholes started roughing up a bum outside on Granville. I dropped a dime on my table and walked out.

"Real nice…" I said, approaching them.

"Who the fuck is you?" A tall Puerto Rican in a red hoodie stepped to me, and I loaded up with the ugliest widest overhand right and knocked his ass out. And this pudgy black guy in a black bomber jacket rushed up, and I leapt into a bomb of a hook and dropped him, and his head cracked on the pavement.

The bum stood up gripping his brown fuzzy skull-cap and stuttered, "Ya motherfuckers, you ain't shit." He spit on them both. Then he looked at me and stumbled toward me as I walked away.

I spun on him and yelled. "What do ya want?"

"Brother, that's a nice thing you done, those mothafuckers ain't shit."

"You're welcome," I replied, and started walking away.

He followed. "An' you gots good technique. You a boxer?"

"Yeah."

"Yeah, I know a boxer when I see one. I used to box as a kid, and I fought in the park district for three years."

"Want a drink?" I asked.

We went down to the Sovereign and I bought him a drink and he told me about Lee Roy Murphy, and how he used to spar with Murphy before he got big and went pro and won the world cruiserweight title, and I said I wanted to win the cruiserweight title one day.

And he said, "You could, but you gotta put the work in, and you got'sta believe in God."

"I don't believe in God no more."

"You gots to son, that's all."

I sighed and sipped my whiskey. *How the hell did a God create this hellhole of a world? More like a fucking devil made it. It's full of fuckin demons. They crawl all over me, fucking sinking hooks in me every fucking day.*

"You lost tonight, huh?"

"How'd you guess?" I grinned at my bloody busted face in the mirror across from me in the bar.

"I been there. I lost a lot in my life. You know what I do when I'm losing, losing it all?"

I looked over at him.

"I goes down to the beach an' feeds the seagulls."

"You like seagulls?"

"Purdy birdies."

"They are."

"They call me Birdman." He reached out and I shook his brittle crusty hand.

"Joe Walsh."

We shook and I left him there with his glass of whiskey and went down to the beach to watch the sun rise and it was dull and cold and gray and the black waves crashed viciously on the shore and it was everything that I felt in my heart. *Is this depression, Da? Is this what it feels like?* I saw him lying down on the floor in the kitchen as Gram and Ma urged him to take his medicine. *Do I got it too? Manic depression? Fuck, that's a great life to look forward to. But Da, maybe that's what made him such a great grandpa. All the suffering he went through just to stay with us. His joy. His grandkids. If I have to feel this all the time, I'll never make it to be an old man. He must a had some brass balls and determination not to kill himself. What a great man you were.* I sighed and took another sip of my bottle. *But they say he was a poon-dog when he was manic, though.* I giggled. *We all got our dark side. Even the fucking best of us.*

The sun began to peek over the black horizon, splaying itself on the underside of the mountainous clouds that hung above the waters. Seagulls floated high in the hard cold wind, fighting the gale with a steady calm glide. *I should have brought some bread for you seagulls.* I sat in the sand; my head hurt real bad, like something'd set big barbed hooks into my brain. It pulsed and bled inside my skull. Images came back of the tremendous punches O'Sullivan hit me with. *How the hell'd you stay up through that? You got a chin but maybe O'Sullivan put a dent in it. Put a dent in your abilities, a dent in who you are.* A seagull gliding before the purple rising sun cried as the wind splintered its feathers and he faltered before he regained his glide. *Maybe I destroyed myself after all.*

The crowd seemed to like it. *It's fun to fight but I wasn't trying to have fun. I was trying to destroy myself and it just didn't work. It was like an experiment at Fermilab, trying to annihilate myself, trying to find that perfect collision.* One gull cowered in the wind way out on the long cement pier lined with the dark rusty sheet piling, his yellow beak tucked into his white chest. *I really wish I had something to feed you seagulls. Next time.*

I went home and slept well into the next morning. I dreamt. *I am the seagull again. No. Again? Motherfuckers. Can't I have a new dream?* I lay on my back, humongous in the center of the red ring, my silky white feathered wingspread filling it completely. *I'm tired of this fucking seagull shit!* I try to get up. This black fog above me pins me down. *No, not again.* The hooks swing down from the darkness above; they pierce my heart and my face. I squirm and scream out, it morphs into the scream of the seagull that I caught with my lure by accident when I was a little boy on the star dock at Montrose Harbor with Da. A massive crowd appears, looking down at me from the bleachers, tightly circled like in a surgery observation auditorium. They laugh and point at my wounds. A hook implants in my temple, sending a stream of memories shooting out into the darkness like a ray of photons. They roar sadistic approval. A voice I know from a very long time ago whispers, "Hold still...This is what you wanted?"

I woke on my back in my bed in Brookfield with the birds chirping on the railing of the porch downstairs, sad, devastated. I felt Faith and everything I'd lost hovering above me, just out of reach. I stretched my hand up. *I want it all back.* It faded from me. *It will never come back, Joe. Fuck.* I clutched my aching head. *Who woulda thought growing up would be this shitty? This is a nasty world we live in, with nasty hate-filled people who want to hurt everyone around themselves and can't never be happy for anything.* I saw my fist crushing Blake's pointy devilish nose. *I want to be a decent person, go experience nice things, I want to have love in my life and a marriage and children and a family and it's just a stupid idea because in this world all there fucking is, is war.*

I got meaner after that. Darker, and nearly silent. I'd go days only saying a few words. Something heavy descended on me, some invisible weight, some body of dark matter that followed me always turning my thoughts to negativity, making me see the potential for danger in any situation and readying myself to meet it with full force, all my power and rage in one clean decisive blow. It was a terrible weight, a weight that added to my punching power and my potential for destruction in the ring.

I started to destroy guys in sparring, and in fights. If they couldn't handle me, I floored it. I didn't revel in their fear. I extinguished their desire to box. I wasn't trying to win. I was trying to obliterate them, annihilate them, and if I was annihilated in the process, good. It's a wonderful way to perish. They caught me with their best shots and I'd grin, not because I took the punch, but because they'd almost put me down. I savored the day someone would put me down and down hard and for good. I kept searching for the one to do it but the heads kept rolling, they kept dropping, they kept unraveling under my pressure. They say having a troubled childhood can make you a great artist...well, this was my art and I wanted to prove myself a prodigy. The less I spoke, the more they spoke of me. I could hear them talking, hear them saying things. Things like: he's not that good. I never replied or made it known I heard them. Their words slashed at my heart with razor-sharp hooks, not because it hurt my pride but because they were right. I wasn't that good. I didn't hit that hard. I could be outboxed. I couldn't win at Nationals. I hadn't even won the Open. I loved the pain it caused my heart and I remembered each one of the things they said and who said it and the next time I had the chance in the ring, I smashed that boxer in the mouth with all my might. I boxed furiously to show them I could completely outbox them from bell to bell. I beat up their friends in sparring then looked at them and stared. They began to hate me and revere me and some of them even loved me but in a con-man kind of love, the kind of love that sucks you in, their jokes exaggerating who I was, saying I was going to be a million-dollar fighter one day. I knew I wouldn't and I didn't care. I wasn't here for money or glory. I was here for destruction of myself and others, and for the ecstasy of nonexistence. I didn't want to feel anymore. I didn't want to feel anything ever again. Boxing was my hope for that.

PART THREE: THE BURBS

Chapter 9: Cyclical

THE THING ABOUT DARK DAYS AND DEPRESSION IS, THEY PASS. Life is a series of cycles, peaks and valleys. The more you struggle against that natural state of life, the more you suffer.

Even with all the work at Saint Joe's, the struggle, the A's I'd been getting lately, the honors classes, and the letters of recommendation from Brother Alex, Dydecky, and Erickson, my overall GPA and test scores weren't high enough to get into a good four-year school. It felt as if I'd grappled with the monstrous forces of the universe for months on end, spent myself completely and had nothing to show for it. Eventually they agreed to let me into Elmhurst College if I went to a junior college called College of DuPage for the summer quarter and held a 3.0 GPA.

COD was pretty easy; I got straight A's and started up at Elmhurst.

Erickson taught at Elmhurst College, too. He owned a big white mansion nearby with pillars and a plush green lawn, and he walked to campus. He had a small early version of a collider he'd brought over from U of C. It was his own little lab in the dark basement of the Schaible Science Center where he could play around with peripheral ideas on weekends. He let me help a little. It was fun. I spent a couple months working on the weekends with him; I put pretty much all my free time into it. He even let me present to one of his classes about dark matter.

I made a bunch of mistakes. I stood up there in front of the small class in a white button-up shirt shaking like a leaf, mumbling as Erickson grinned widely in the back of the room.

"No." He shook his head.

I looked down at my notes. *Dark matter is not antimatter. Shit!* I finished my slides and Erickson walked up to the podium beside me.

"Good job overall, Joe, but there were a few slips. Although I love the idea, there is no proven link between Antimatter and Dark Matter. Antimatter is just matter with opposite charge; dark matter is matter that doesn't interact electromagnetically, which causes it to be dark or invisible in our understanding of detection." He reached out and patted my notes. "Other than that, it is a strong introduction to dark matter."

They clapped as I sat down, my heart still pattering in my chest. Erickson gripped the wooden podium with his small pudgy hands, his long mane of white curly hair billowing around him and melding with his long scraggly beard. "But the fact is that around seventy percent of the universe is made of dark energy and dark matter. We think we know so much about the universe and we do know much more today. But in the grandest of schemes, we know next to nothing. All the discoveries from Aristotle to Einstein, we are still just chimpanzees on a rock scratching our heads and looking up with wild wonderment."

We went down to the little lab after class. Sitting on a metal stool next to the wooden work table, I deconstructed one of the control boxes with a yellow handled Philips-head screwdriver. Erickson walked up and sat on the stool beside me.

"Joe, are you OK?"

"Yeah, why?"

"I enjoy your help, but you are a freshman in college. Don't you want to go out and have fun?" Erickson pleaded with his pudgy hands.

"What, get drunk and laid and all that?"

"Well, yes."

"It's just not fun for me, Dr. Erickson."

"Joe, there's more to life than these particles and the stars."

"I know, there's dark matter and dark energy!"

"No, Joe, I mean there's real human contact." He put his hand on my shoulder. The energy flowed from his warm hand into my torso and sickened my stomach. *Damn, that's the first time someone's touched me in months that wasn't Brother slapping my arms or some guy punching me in the head or ribs.*

"You need friends, Joe! Go out and have some fun. Maybe meet a girl. See a concert, dance, play a game, something." Dr. Erickson pulled his blue coat on and started toward the door.

I sighed and dropped the screwdriver. "Alright, Dr. Erickson..."

◆

Even though all of me wanted nothing to do with it, this real loud, charismatic goofball from my dorm, Mike Painter, dragged me out to some stupid sorority party at a bar they'd rented out for the night. I sat at the bar with Painter, drinking and watching the full dark dance floor with the DJ booth at the far wall with the strobe lights spinning sending beams of light through the smoky, packed room. Painter got up to dance with some girls, his wacky long spiked hair bobbing around in the darkness. I sat lonely and quiet as ever; the illusion of their joy swirled around me as darkness and agony twisted in my stomach. I sipped my cold bottle of Heineken. Their darkened bodies melded into one another, twisting and grinding on the dancefloor like a demonic orgy. *Look at them out there, like Sodom and Gomorrah. Fucking each other, lying, cheating, betraying. Meaningless sex. No beauty in that, nothing pure. It's fucking disgusting.* Rage pulsed in my heart as I took another sip of the cold beer. *Hope somebody says something stupid and starts a fight so I can crush some prick's face. Painter and the guys'd get a bang outta that.* I smirked. *Or maybe even better, some big fucker'll hit me clean, or bust a full bottle over my head, or a chair. It don't really matter just as long as it puts me in outer space for a while and sets me free.* I closed my eyes and saw nothing but trembling chaos.

I opened them. A girl caught my eye as she danced wildly with some girls and tall black dudes from the basketball team. The spinning lights from the DJ stands splashed across her small fine face. The light brightened her huge brown eyes. Small dark beauty marks sprinkled her face like an elegant galaxy. Her huge voluptuous lips spread in a big flashy smile. Strands of her wild hair sprang up like curled brown-blonde flames. She swayed her curvy hips bodaciously in her cut-up tan T-shirt and shredded blue jeans. *What is she?* Her ethnicity escaped all deciphering. Black, French, Native American? Our eyes met. She shot from the far reaches of the universe and collided with my shattered mind and my broken insides. *Love at first sight is a silly myth, Joe, for silly mystics.* Then the neutrinos swirled and spun inside me with an unmistakable fury. *Love isn't real, goddamnit. NO! Not again.* For a moment, I didn't want to annihilate anything.

The light moved; her eyes closed and she spun away and disappeared into the dancing bodies. *My brown-eyed girl, where'd you go? How could you leave me like that? You're not real, you're another fake. A phony, like the rest of 'em.*

I finished my beer, got a whiskey neat and sipped it, but my brown-eyed girl drew me out to the edge of the dance floor. We locked eyes again as she paused in mid-sway. She vanished. My heart pulsed. *You don't want anybody to ever touch you again, huh? Well, maybe her.* I giggled. I saw her thick luscious lips reach out and kiss mine. I looked up and closed my eyes. *Do not fall in love with this girl.*

Suddenly she materialized next to me.

"What are you doing here?" she said in a smoky, rich voice.

"I dunno." I shrugged. *What do you mean, like in this fucking solar system?*

Her blonde friend took her by the hand and she slipped back out onto the floor, glancing back over her shoulder, dancing with girls and guys, her sweet eyes singing out to me. She pulled at me like gravitational waves. I stepped into the moving bodies and started to dance. A skinny black girl started grinding her booty against me as I tried to dance with her. My clunky movements couldn't follow her fluid rhythmic gyrations. *You dance like a fucking whiteboy.* I tried to move my hips and find her rhythm. The Ying Yang Twins' "Get Low" flowed through the room. My brown-eyed girl watched me, grinning; she covered her mouth. "Get low, get low!" The black girl dipped way down into a low squat and I tried to get low with her, but my legs were sore from deadlifting and I winced in pain. Then suddenly my brown-eyed girl reached her cool hand towards me and I took it and we moved together close. She showed me how to move; our legs spliced as we melded together. It was as if we were one being. She smelled of weed and lavender. Her skin was smooth and damp with sweat and oils. A tension of wires that'd been taught and trembling released throughout my chest and my limbs and I was fluid with her, flowing to the music. I closed my eyes and I was in the stars floating free.

As the night came to a close, she disintegrated like a sculpture made of caramel, and I didn't see her again for days.

She invades my dreams. A dance floor full of blonde girls dances badly in one terrible synced-up bob. She streaks through the mechanical bodies, flowing, exotic, brown, an orb of fire-like energy swirling around her. The blondes melt as she passes through them. She looks me in the eyes, hers glowing liquid alive, and she holds her elegant long-fingered hand out to me. I wake hard as a rock.

With her on my mind, I went for a coffee at the coffee window in the Frick Center, the main building on campus, I walked past the huge fireplace into the big room with cushioned chairs and tables sprinkled throughout it and the huge windows that looked out onto the long green field that stretched to the white chapel facing back like god watching over the greenery. A blond-haired kid threw an orange Frisbee in a long smooth arc across the field towards a girl in a blue shirt and white shorts. I walked over and got in line at the little coffee shop window; the small window was empty, just a lot of banging and the sound of the steam frother and some clanging dishes. Then my brown-eyed girl rose into view in the window slowly, like she was coming up an elevator, carefully balancing an extra-large latte in her hands. She smiled and handed it to an elderly professor lady.

"Now you have a nice day, ya heard!" she sang.

Her elegantly shaped brown face glowed, and the beauty marks seemed orchestrated by some composer. Her brown hair with blonde streaks curled around her jawline and sprang outwards and swayed as she moved. *Damn, she's way more beautiful in the daylight.* Her smooth brown skin glowed as she smiled; she took orders and disappeared inside the little shop and re-emerged with little paper cups with white plastic lids, full of lattes and coffees. My turn came and I stepped up.

"Hi," she said looking at me bashfully, her big brown eyes sucking me into her universe. The wires constricted around my throat and I couldn't talk. I looked away and ordered a coffee and handed her my student card; she scrutinized it before she swiped it at the register. She disappeared and pumped the coffee into a cup and handed the cup to me. I took it in my hands. "Thanks," I said. *I am completely obsessed with you.* The white plastic lid came loose and toppled to the counter.

"Sorry, honey!" she said.

We both reached for it and our fingers touched, and the sensation of us grinding on the dance floor soared through my body. She looked up at me with a glint of recognition and batted her eyes. I trembled. *Do you really remember me?* She looked behind me as the next person ordered over my shoulder.

I walked away grateful. *At least I know a place I can find her. Maybe even talk with her again.* I glanced back over my shoulder as she laughed her big excited laugh, her long straight teeth gleaming. I sat at the big fireplace to listen to her. *Shit, maybe we can talk. I want to tell her about my crazy fucking ideas.* The fire crackled at my feet as I listened to her sweet sing-songy voice charming everybody with her southern accent.

Some professor asked her where she was from and she said, "Nawlins, baby!"

New Orleans? I always wanted to go there and learn about jazz and blues and gumbo. Her voice danced over syllables. *I wanna chase ghosts down Bourbon Street with you.* I sipped my coffee. *You fucking don't even know her name, you pussy. You're too fucking fucked up and scared to ever talk to her.*

◆

I went back every day to sit at the fireplace and listen. I didn't go back to the window to order. I just sat there every afternoon listening to her talk, like a fucking weirdo stalker or something. I just needed to be near her. Two long weeks passed: dreams of her, imagined conversations, looking up the things she mentioned, enjoying the music she played in the coffee booth, listening to her smooth voice as she sang along.

The obsession built until finally I lay in bed in my dorm room wide awake staring into the dark haze above me. *Look, you crazy Nawlins chick. I'm in love with you.* I saw her recoil in my mind. *Yeah? Well, fuck you then. I don't even believe in love.* Waves of electrified particles washed through my body. *Look, Joe, you're going to love her and you're going to lose her and that's life. Either live, or blow your stupid brains out already. This halfway shit is fucking killing you.* My body tensed and flexed on the bed. I trembled with fear. *If you don't go and talk to this girl you are going to go completely insane. Just get it over with, you dipshit. If she shuts you down at least you know.* The tension simmered and I finally slept.

I went over to see her on a Friday night. The scent of a storm hung in the air as the big trees that lined the walkway swayed and twisted. The growing winds feathered through the thick leaves as I stepped inside the clean Frick Center. *Imagine meeting someone like you in a place like this.* I walked up to the booth of the café. *Just about closing time.* The whole place sat empty. *Well, you got her all to yourself now.*

I stepped up and she sat reading a small book in the little window. Her crazy strands of light-brown hair fell over her face as she nibbled her thick lips. She didn't notice me.

"Whatcha reading?"

"*Junkie.* It's my fave," she said, showing me the cover before she looked up with her bashful big brown eyes.

"My brother's a junkie."

"Well, everybody's gotta be something. Don't they?"

"Yeah, but he's a piece of shit."

"He's your brother, he can't be all bad."

"Last time I saw him, I almost killed him." A vision of the drenched crotch of his jeans flashed in my mind as I giggled.

"There's always a better way than violence."

"Yeah, but there's good reasons for violence."

"There's never a good reason for violence."

"There is. There's good reasons for violence, there's good reasons to kill, and there's even good reasons for war."

"Just like there's bad reasons for kissing someone, bad reasons for loving someone, bad reasons for making love to someone."

"Bad reasons to give birth?"

"Maybe." She rolled her eyes. "Look, what do you want?!"

"I don't know, ever since I saw you the other night, you're all I can think of."

She took her hand off the book and its old dog-eared pages spread slowly open between us.

"Who are you?"

"Who's anybody?"

"Ha...you're such a creep." Then she smiled; her long straight teeth emerged between her thick red lips and she covered them with her palm.

"Don't cover your face when you smile."

"Why?"

"Because you're beautiful."

Her face flushed and she grinned wickedly. "Are you gonna order something?"

"Yeah, a redeye."

"A redeye? You got big plans tonight?"

"I don't have any plans except the Illinois state tournament next month."

"What tournament?"

"Boxing tournament."

"You're a boxer? Yeah, right..."

"I'm gonna be a world champ one day." I giggled after I said it.

"You got a gap in your teeth. It's so cute. What's this?" She touched my forehead where the laces of a glove had peeled a layer of skin off when I'd slipped a punch but didn't have any Vaseline on.

Her soft cool fingertips smelled like cocoa butter. *I just want to grab her hand and kiss it. No! Are you nuts?!*

"You like to hang out with creeps?" I asked.

"Sometimes, if they're not too creepy."

I laughed, and she laughed.

"When do you get outa here?"

"Whenever the hell I want. Let's go!" She shut the shop door in my face. The espresso machine hissed, cups clinked. I stood listening. A few seconds later she rounded the corner carrying a cup, smiling. Her long, smooth strides made her bound up and down like she was walking on a trampoline in high heels. Her tight jeans hugged her curvy, elegant legs. I felt myself step inside one of those dreams I'd been having of her as if nothing in that moment, in her presence, really existed at all. I entered another realm, a place where only the highest focus could exist.

She handed me the hot cup and said, "Here's your redeye, cowboy." A faint trail of smoke sifted from the corner of her mouth.

"Thanks," I replied as she looked me in the eyes and hypnotized me, pulling the conversation out of me with her scent and lips.

"You smoke?" She smiled, and her eyes were wet and dreamy.

"I don't like it. Makes me paranoid."

"I got a jug of Boone's Farm in my dorm room."

"Boone's Farm, really? That's high-end stuff."

She laughed. "Come on." She took my hand and led me down the hallway toward the exit.

I followed her bouncy butt; she felt my eyes and looked back with a sultry glare. She smiled; her big juicy lips gleamed. And I thought for a second. *This is a trick. She's trying to get me somewhere so she can publicly shut me down.* I kept waiting for it. She opened the door. Torrential rain roared down. The blacktop seemed to vibrate; the water splashed like sizzling grease. I stopped as she walked right out into it, smiled, and looked up. She turned and looked back at me as the raindrops saturated her body. Her T-shirt clung to her curves. She swayed her hips and nodded. *Don't be a pussy, get out there.* I stepped out into the cold rain and up to her, and I took her wet hands in mine. I leaned in and kissed her incredible thick red lips. She kissed back slowly and softly and sensually and I met her sensuality and she melted into me like she was made of brown sugar and the water was dissolving her slowly. *Her lips are even better than I imagined: tender and firm like two fresh peeled tangerine wedges.* We kissed for a long time, an endless time—a time so ridiculous with the rain that by the time we stopped and opened our eyes the rain had soaked us to our underwear.

"Okay, cowboy…" She danced away toward her dorm.

Well, here we go, Joeyboy.

She smacked her key fob on the black key reader of her metal dorm building door; she yanked it open and I went in behind her. The water dribbled off of us, leaving a long trail on the blue-carpeted hall. She spun around, her body glistening in the bright hall light. I kissed her hard this time and she pulled back, hurt. I softened my kiss and she ran her hands over my tense sopping wet torso as I hugged my arms around her lower back and she pecked me and pulled back, her drenched hair stuck to her face and neck. I hugged her too tight and she squealed and smiled at me and broke my grip and passed into the stairwell and jogged up the steps with droplets sprinkling off of her. She unlocked her wooden dorm room door and lifted her foot up and kicked it open.

The old stench of hash, incense and perfume hung in the air. She stormed in and went to the computer and moved the mouse and clicked play, and the smoky melody of Portishead's "Roads" flowed into the room. "Can't anybody see we got a war to fight here…" Besides the computer the only light was a little yellow lamp with a dark brown shade over it. The long wall between the computer and her bunk bed was a collage of printed up quotes, poems and philosophy, paintings, photos, advertisements, drawings, fabrics. Above the bookshelf full of books hung quotes I'd never heard of. *Be careful, lest in casting out your demon you exorcise the best thing in you. — Nietzsche.* I stepped into the collage, mystified. Near the bunk bed was a full sheet of a poem, "Morning Song" by Sylvia Plath: *Love set you going like a fat gold watch…* High in the collage was a big colorful painting of New Orleans-style homes, orange with red trim and purple with white trim, cobblestoned streets and the old French street lamps…

She giggled watching me, and pulled her sopping-wet shirt off and flopped it on the fuzzy brown rug. Her unbelievable body heaved like a voluptuous runway model: an hourglass shape, her skin glowing dark in the low lamp light. She stood taller than the girls I liked but not taller than me. She kicked off her heels and yanked her blue jeans off and dropped them on the tile floor near the doorway; they landed with splashy slap. Her purple lace panties hugged her wet hips sloppily.

"Get outta them wet clothes, boy," she said, pulling my shirt up. "You wanna catch pneumonia?"

I pulled my shirt off and unbuckled my pants; they clinged to my hairy legs as I pulled them down. She pushed me into the wooden chair near the desk and fell to her knees at my feet. She roughly yanked my cowboy boots off.

"And these big strong hairy legs! I love 'em!" She ran her fingers in them and clawed at the wet hair and my cock rose in my gray boxer briefs.

She gave it a slap. "Down, boy! Control yourself!" she said, and it sprung up harder than ever as I winced.

"He likes you."

"Well, how could he like me? We haven't even been properly introduced." Her large tits pressed against my thighs and hovered near my balls and straining cock and she made a fist and rapped her knuckles on it through the boxers like she was knocking on the door.

"Hello in there, want to come out and introduce yourself?"

It was pressing at the opening in my boxer briefs already, and I pulled at the cloth a little and the head peeked out of the slit and she cooed and pinched the cloth and pulled it aside and the full head popped out.

"Wow, that is the biggest dickhead I've ever seen." She pushed down on what was left of my pitched tent and the rest of it slid free into view and she made measurements. She gripped the base, she put her palm to the side.

"Nope, it is big, it's a huge dickhead." She grabbed it and put her face close to it. "Hello, Mr. Dickhead! Ohh you're drooling, does that mean you like me?"

I flexed my cock and said, "Yes it does," in a dick voice.

"Well, Mr. Dickhead, I think you're cute, you're so nice and big." She gripped the base of my cock and came close to putting her lips over it. "I think I want a kiss," she said. "Can I kiss you?"

I flexed my cock again and the head strained bigger. "Yes," I said in my dick voice.

"Oh, that's cute." She glanced up at me and she made her lips into a big pucker. Her full big lips made my dick head look normal-sized and she kissed Mr. Dickhead deeply, slid her whole lips around him, and pulled back with a big smack.

"You jealous I'm kissing him?"

"Naw, not at all. Feel free."

"Well, I know his name, but I don't even know your name yet."

"Joseph Walsh."

"I'm Lauren Dupré, nice to meet you."

She reached her free hand out and shook mine.

"It's a pleasure," I said as she giggled and squeezed it harder and I sighed.

"Do you want me to suck your dick, Joseph Walsh?"

"Please."

"Say pretty please."

"Pretty please."

"Pretty please with sugar on top."

"Pretty please with brown sugar all over the top."

She smiled and slid those lips back down and after a few intense strokes a thunder built in my legs and flowed up my spine. I threw my head back as a lightning bolt seemed to shoot out of me into her. I howled like some dark monstrous beast as she looked up at me, sweetly batting her brown eyes, taking it all inside. She swallowed, giggling.

"Damn, boy, you are loud!"

I chuckled.

She got up and took a swig of Boone's Farm straight from the jug. She took my hand and pulled me into the lower bunk and curled up in my arms under the dirty blue comforter. She lay her sweet wet face on my neck.

"I'm scared," she whispered.

"Me too."

"Do you feel that?"

"Yeah."

"That's something. It's really something."

"I know."

We smoked and drank and talked for a while and she fell asleep with her head on my chest. *Well, you was right about falling in love with her the very first time you looked into her eyes. What the hell are you gonna do now?* My eyes wandered near the window. A full ashtray sat on the ledge; below it tacked to the wall was a sketch of a voodoo queen on a tall elaborate throne, her dark afro curling up straight above her head as she sucked on a smoldering blunt spliced in her long elegant fingers. *What'd you do Joeyboy go and fall in love with a voodoo princess? No, you don't believe in love no more.* I touched her cool naked back as her lungs slowly inflated and deflated and a little trickle of a snore rattled out. *You ain't never getting in no relationship again. But she's not the relationship type anyway.* I felt the warm gravity of her atop me. *She's the love type, the crazy fucking love type that soars you into the cosmos and then sinks you deep into her waters until you drown in her forever and ever.*

◆

She asked me into the city. The city for me then was just construction work and boxing. Deeper there were bad memories, and a few good ones too, but I wouldn't have gone to the city for a night out then if it wasn't for her. In some ways she knew more of the city than me, and nothing at all. For her Chicago was a mysterious adventure. For me it was the shattered foundations of myself, a ghost of who I was and the potential nightmares of who I might have been—and wars, old street wars that never ended, only simmered. Still, I went with her because there was no other choice but to go wherever she took me. She said her friend Fred Burkhart was having an open mic that Sunday night called the Burkhart Underground and she was gonna sing a little tune for me.

I pulled up to the side exit of the big red brick Schick Hall. She burst through the brown metal door and her glossy brown eyes stabbed into my chest like two comets. Her shoulder-length brown-blonde hair flowed wildly backward like a torch flame in the wind. She'd made her shirt herself by slicing up materials and pinning the fabric together with safety pins at the shoulders. She'd patched blue jeans into a short skirt. Slices ripped through her nylon stockings revealing her creamy dark skin. She clicked through the drizzle in her vintage heels and jumped in my Jeep. She leaned over and gave me a big kiss on my cheek; it left dark red lipstick lips on my stubbly skin. The scent of herbs and rosemary filled the cab.

We rode into the city, our hands and fingers intermingling. She popped in her *Songs: Ohia* tape. "On the Bridge out of Hammond" came on and sent images of my escape from my past life in the city. We shot downtown on 290 and rode Halsted all the way up.

Burkhart's house sat on Halsted just past Diversey. A big front porch hung over a front door that was set down at garden level. Strange characters milled around out front. A tall Goth guy in all black with long black hair. An old lady in a raggy hippie dress. A pretty teenaged girl with a blonde mohawk. Music thrummed through the downstairs windows.

"Now Burkhart's a big flirt, so don't get jealous!"

"OK."

"He's like my granddaddy. But he's a tart."

Through the front windows upstairs we could see dozens of people milling about. Black-and-white photos on the wood panel walls. The people flipped through big milk crates of photos.

We ducked under the porch and stepped down into the Burkhart Underground. Music poured out as we entered the smoky darkness. Beside us some sort of experimental band chanted and banged loud on several different kinds of drums. Their long dready hair hung down over their bobbing faces. Loud purple and red lights and lit candles lined the walls. A dozen tables spread out in front of the stage area, which was only a cleared space beside the entrance. I followed her as she led me straight down a hall. We passed through black and gray bedsheets that hung from clotheslines; behind them was a small photography space, with a couple enlargers on tables, and washtubs full of beakers. Photos dried on wire lines, pinned with wooden clothespins. A naked vixen upside down, electrical tape X's over her nipples. A homeless man with Coke-bottle glasses and a Cubs cap tilted sideways, smiling with pure joy.

A dreary brown sheet blocked our path. I twisted my head to look closer at the wet prints, and the sheet whipped open. A tall man popped his head in; he had a big white beard twisted into dreadlocks that stretched down to his belly. His fiery blue eyes glowed wildly like some kinda beatnik wizard.

"Is that my Lou?!"

"Burkhart!" Lauren leapt onto him and he caught her in his muscular arms. She hugged him and kissed him on the cheek.

"Hey, baby," he sang like a blues musician; he hiked his eyebrows at me and smiled. "How are ya?"

"Great!" she said sweetly. "How 'bout you?"

"Who's this knucklehead?" he said; she was on his arm now.

She put her toes down on the cracked basement slab and looked back at me. "This is Joe Walsh, my boxer."

I grinned. "Nice to meet you, Fred. I've heard a lot about you."

Fred shook my hand and said, "I ain't no boxer but I punched a few fools in my day. Now I ain't gonna have to punch you one day, am I?"

"I hope not, old-timer."

"I might be old but I'm strong." He flexed his muscle-y arm. "Grip that."

I reached out and gripped his stiff muscles. Lauren gripped it too.

"Fred. you're a fucking strongman!"

Fred grinned smugly, leaned back tall, and said, "I'm sixty-five years old but I don't feel sixty-five. I'm a young man in here"—he rubbed his chest—"and down here." He grabbed his balls, and we both burst out laughing.

"Alright, boxer, you're OK. Now she gets her fee waived for being a bodacious beauty, but you gotta pay. Five doller donation."

I grinned and felt for my wallet. Lauren pulled a ten out of her bra and slid it in Burkhart's hand and said, "That's for both of us, Fred. Now don't you go and spend it all in one place, suga."

"You know where I'm gonna spend it, them chemicals ain't free."

We headed out to the back area of the stage room. "When are you gonna shoot me, Fred?"

"I've invited you, now you just have to show up."

She spun into a pose for Fred. He grabbed the camera that was draped around his back. His camera flashed as she switched sexy poses. She crawled on a nearby love seat and got on all fours and put her butt up in the air. He put the camera under her skirt and flashed a shot. She squealed, fell on her back, and covered up.

"Fred, you devil!"

He giggled and cranked his camera. "Well, now, what did you expect, Lauren? You expect me to be a good boy?"

"A decent man, Fred! I expected you to be a decent fatherly man!"

"I'm old enough to be her granddad." He grinned at me as I giggled. The music came to an end as the thin crowd cheered. They started to break down. Fred jumped up on the mic and made some announcements about who was next and the list being open. I sat down with Lauren on this love seat all the way in the back, and she kissed me.

"Can you believe he took a picture of my tushy?"

"I've got to ask him later if I can buy it."

"You don't need a picture, baby, you can see it anytime."

"Yeah."

"Anytime. You can see the real thing right up close in your face if you want." She stood up in front of me. "Want to see it now?"

She flipped up the front of her skirt. Her shaven light brown pussy flashed in my vision and sent sparks through my mind like somebody'd popped me with a good jab.

"I could put it all over your face sometime, would you like that?"

"Mmmmm," I hummed as my cock rose in my pants. "I want to taste it."

She bent down, kissed me, and laughed and fell into my arms. A poet got up and started reading and I tried to listen as his dark words flowed into a philosophical riddle. A chick got up next with spiky purple hair. Her words sprang into angry rants on women's rights and rape. People kept coming in and out, and everybody knew Lauren, and they asked her if she was gonna sing.

Finally, late in the night Burkhart called her name and she walked up and said, "This is for my fighter over there in the back," and she took a deep breath and blew out a rich deep note that flowed into this bluesy folk song in a quiet *a cappella*.

Ten years ago, on a cold dark night
Someone was killed, 'neath the town hall light
There were few at the scene, but they all agreed
That the slayer who ran, looked a lot like me

Lauren looked at me, grinned, and touched the smooth glowing skin of her chest. Her voice expanded into the smoky room and suddenly my life was a movie.

She walks these hills in a long black veil
She visits my grave when the night winds wail
Nobody knows, nobody sees

Nobody knows but me

I gasped. I'd never heard a better voice in my whole life. Ever. I watched myself sitting in the chair listening to this exotic beauty singing her heart out to me, a song I hadn't ever heard before. Her voice fell back to her quiet almost whisper.

> The judge said son, what is your alibi
> If you were somewhere else, then you won't have to die
> I spoke not a word, though it meant my life
> For I'd been in the arms of my best friend's wife

Fucking cool story. The room fell silent with her, everyone listening to every little whisper. Burkhart crouched on the stairs next to me and hiked up his bushy white eyebrows, then snapped a few shots.

> Oh, the scaffold is high and eternity's near
> She stood in the crowd and shed not a tear
> But late at night, when the north wind blows
> In a long black veil, she cries over my bones

She looked at me, closed her eyes, slowly rocked her head back, and wailed. Her voice filled the dark basement and every being and object, even the bare floor joists hanging above running in lines straight from her to me, seemed to resonate with her sultry, strong voice.

> She walks these hills in a long black veil
> She visits my grave when the night winds wail

She opened her eyes; they locked onto mine like they'd been staring into me the whole time. The crowd roared as she hit her high note. Then she fell back to her sweet soft whisper.

> Nobody knows, nobody sees
> Nobody knows but me

She walked through the standing ovation, the people reaching for her and touching her as she passed them, walking to me. I stood and she planted a big kiss on my lips as our hands and fingers intertwined.

Later I followed her up a ladder to the big pitched-roof attic. A burnt orange street light poured in through the dormer window. She pushed me down onto the dirty carpet and crawled onto my chest; she pinned my shoulders to the carpet with her knees straddling my face, and lifted her skirt. Her shaven pussy glowed gorgeous and wet.

"Give me a kiss right here," she said, peering down at me.

She reached down with her long-nailed index finger and touched and rubbed her swollen clitoris. I leaned up and kissed it and she dragged her hand through my hair as I kissed it more. She moaned deeply and beautifully and I licked it and she ground it in my face. She reached back and grabbed my cock as it hardened. I unzipped and she flipped around and sixty-nine'd me. Her incredible mouth slowly swallowed me down to the base.

She got off, straddled my cock, and leaned back. Her brown skin glowed as she pulled her shirt off and her big heavy tits splayed out. Her brown pussy hovered dark and wet over my pale cock. She lined it up and she slid down it, slowly savoring the sensations. I strained so hard it almost burst, and her pussy contracted on my dick and she trembled terribly and cooed. She came as she sank all the way down on it. Her pussy trembled and gushed, and the fluids splashed all over my shirt and soaked it. She was hot and wet and she kept riding and came again and again and then we came simultaneously.

She'd soaked my shirt so badly that when we came back down the ladder, I took it off and draped it over my shoulder. Blood pumped through my muscles as we walked through the crowded room. She blew Burkhart a kiss as we slipped out the front door.

I took her down to Montrose Harbor, out by the point. We talked and watched the sunrise and fell asleep in each other's arms. I woke with two seagulls soaring around each other in loose circles and crying, their white feathers fluttering the golden dawn. Then they landed on the sidewalk and nuzzled each other. The white cock gull tried to mate the gray hen as Lauren woke.

"What the hell are they doing?"

"I think they're fucking."

"Kinky little birds doing it out here in public." She sighed and kissed me.

I drove her over to Standees on Granville. We sat in a booth by the big front windows and sipped coffee and nibbled on rare bacon and eggs over easy and crispy brown hash browns and she smoked a cigarette and she was so happy. I wanted to tell her about the old neighborhood but every time I tried it got all bottled up and finally she told me, "It's OK, baby, you can tell me about your old 'hood some other time."

"What's it like in New Orleans?"

"I'm from the Marigny, it's where all the musicians and artists live. Frenchmen curves out of Esplanade at the border of the Quarter and it cuts through the Faubourg Marigny. Frenchmen Street, that's the spot. That's the heart of New Orleans."

"You don't like the French Quarter?"

"The Quarter's pretty. It's where you go to make money, but it ain't a place for people to enjoy themselves during Mardi Gras. It's the place they wind up late at night, all sloppy drunk and hanging with the tourists and grabbing free drinks from their bartender friends. New Orleans's got soul like no other place in the world, but I like the soul up here in Edgewater, where my man is from. Ol' Standees is like a few diners down home..."

As she spoke I kept pinching myself under the table because it didn't feel real. How did I end up with this wild beautiful girl in my old neighborhood, talking about New Orleans?

"How'd you end up at Elmhurst College?"

"Me? I got the scholarship to come sing for their jazz ensemble. My granddaddy Punch Miller got me singin' since I was five. But I don't like it up here, Elmhurst is full of phonies. They want it all formal, by the book...no improvisation! Idiots wouldn't know jazz if it smacked 'em clean across the face! I wanted to go home so bad. Then I met you. Now, I don't know what I want to do no more. Why're you there, blue eyes?"

"I went to Elmhurst 'cause of this famous physicist named Erickson. He does experiments in the basement of the science building, he lets me help out sometimes. Erickson teaches at U of C, too, and he works at Fermilab on the accelerator. I'm gonna work there one day too. Well, I mean, it's like the dream of my whole life to work there."

"Then you will work there one day, Joe. I promise." She puffed and blew smoke softly in my face. "You're gonna be a damned physicist, aren't you?"

"Hopefully."

"You better not get all your brains knocked out boxing!"

I giggled.

"When's your next fight?"

"I'm going down to the state tourney next month in Danville, Illinois."

"You want to be a state champion?"

"Yeah, hopefully, we'll see who shows up."

"I hope you win, boy, ya heard me! I hope you become a STATE CHAMPION!" She squealed joyfully.

The waitress looked up, then went back to reading the funnies.

"Me too. Maybe I'll win it for you."

She looked at me startled, then smiled and shook her head crazily. Her hair blurred all over her face and shot about in all directions like a galactic fireball careening straight toward me.

Chapter 10: But There's Levels To It

LAUREN'S WHIRLWIND ENERGY SOMEHOW INFUSED MY TRAINING, MY FIGHTING. I stopped trying to annihilate everyone in sparring. Instead, I slipped into these cerebral chess matches—chess with thunder. Memories of sparring with Rico hung in my mind. How elusive he became in close quarters. I started to spar like Rico. Everything balance, everything defense, everything right there in the pocket. I calmed myself as their shots came. This wasn't kill or be killed. This was ideological, even spiritual: an exchange of human energy. Every time I made someone miss, a shot flew over my shoulder, a window opened, the boxer's arm extended and half of their body and head became defenseless for a split second. If I could balance myself in time, I could strike them cleanly, if I could sink my balance down as they missed and twist my shoulders to throw, I could tag them with a tremendous punch. I began to land three- and four-punch combinations after creating an opening with a slip or a roll. As the combination finished, I would roll and move out of range. This super-slick older black master boxer named Chet the Jet taught me that whatever hand you end your combination with, to roll out and away to that same side.

Sal encouraged my new work. After one six-round session where no bombs landed, he pulled me aside and told me, "Now that's how you work, Joe! You don't have nothing to prove with these guys. They respect you. You gotta work together like that and you both can get better. You keep boxing like that and you'll be a real threat at nationals."

◆

Brother pushed me hard and I poured everything into training. I started to break his punching bag. Knock it clean off the chain and it'd slam to the ground and Brother'd scream "Hit the wall!!!" while he inspected the damage.

My body morphed, fluid-like; it soared through water. My lungs sucked and expelled wind painlessly, no matter how hard we went. I glided like I was sailing on a tremendous gust in Da's sailboat off the shore near Montrose Harbor. I poured out six- and seven-punch combinations with effortless fluidity. I saw every shot coming; my head moved just as fast as my hands, slipping and rolling everything coming my way. At times I saw punches coming and slowed them down with my mind and slipped them by an inch—felt the slippery leather side of their glove glance my face and headgear as I gathered to deliver my counter combination.

Brother came up with a new torturous training idea. He brought me to the corner of the basement to a dark cement stairwell. I ran up and down those steps for three-minute rounds with thirty-second breaks. Brother kept time on his watch and counted reps. He convinced guys to come down and take turns trying to run with me and I fucking left them lying on the cold concrete floor gasping for breath, then did three or four more rounds before I collapsed.

A week out of the state tourney, I lay on my back listening to the wind sail through my lungs as sweat poured out of me. The cold cement floor cooled my back as my soaked shirt stuck to the dirty cracked surface. *I'm ready. More ready than ever. I'm gonna win it for her.*

Four guys entered the tournament. Antwone Thomas had recently earned a top-ten national ranking after placing fourth in the PAL National Tournament. He did it at superheavyweight and decided to drop down to 201—heavyweight. (In the amateurs they call cruiserweight "heavyweight" for some dumb reason.) He barely made weight. He looked sick at the weigh-ins, hollowed out but still big and mean with his shaved black scalp and black hoody. He came down to 201, thinking his power would come down with him. I weighed 193. I didn't care how big he was. I planned to beat him with speed. Everybody kept warning me: He has real power. He can bang, and if you trade with him, he'll stop you.

I went out and stopped my guy and Thomas stopped his and the next night we got in there. The roof of the convention hall was so low you could almost reach up and touch the dirty ceiling tiles from the elevated ring. I watched him scowling across the way. *I want to see how hard you can really hit.* Then I thought of Lauren, and having to come home and explain that I lost because I wanted to see if I could out bang the number nine guy in the nation at a higher weight class. *Fuck it, box.*

Even Brother repeated, "Box, Joe, box..." The bell rang and I started moving and slipping his hooks. I rattled back with five and six-punch snappy combinations that kept his hands at home. He'd try to trade with me and swing with me. I'd roll his hooks like they were in slow motion and glide away, with him following me with his plodding feet. Then I'd spring in with more combinations. I climbed way up on points after the second. Desperation only made it easier to pick Thomas off. He clinched me and I spun him. My hook split his guard and he staggered back, stunned. The referee started counting. It infuriated Thomas; he smashed his gloves together.

"I'm fine!" he sneered.

The ref finished the count, and Thomas ran across the ring and swung bombs. I slipped two and hit him with a snappy little straight right. I caught him squared up again and he dropped on his butt.

He shook his head in disbelief. He got up, took the count, and came at me more steadily. I just kept boxing him and he couldn't touch me and I coasted through the fourth and they announced me the Illinois Open Division Heavyweight State Champion.

◆

I went to Lauren with my trophy. She met me at the side exit of Stanger Hall. She looked amazing. Her makeup done and her big brown eyes glowing, her hair swirled up in a blonde-brown wave. I handed her the trophy.

"I did this for you."

"You won!"

She took it and leapt into my arms. I carried her in and took her to bed. And we made love over and over again, joy flowing through our intermingling moans. Then we lay as the sun rose and filtered through her window and cast her whole dorm room this hazy orange.

"I love you," I told her and she lay snug in my arms.

"I love you, too," she replied and twisted to smooch my lips with her luscious mouth.

◆

The Illinois USA Boxing officials told us that regionals would be in three weeks in Toledo, and that competition in the Great Lakes Region is some of the toughest in the country. A good chunk of every Olympic team hailed from the Great Lakes. Sal wanted me to step things up, so we planned to spar a lot in the lead-up.

This kid Erick Zuzisky—a six-foot-five half-Polish, half-Puerto Rican guy who for some reason thought he was black—won the 178-pound division open. Since we were teammates for regionals, he came to Windy

City for a couple weeks of sparring. He was a cocky ex-gangbanger from the Northwest Side with a pronounced brow, a sculpted face, an elaborate etched fade, and a neck tattoo of mother Mary praying. He was a Satan's Disciple but he got into it with the leader of the Royals one night; he dropped the guy a few times but the Royal got up and they started wrestling. Everybody thought the Royal was punching Erick as they wrestled around, but when it was over Erick stood up tall and pulled his sopping wet hoody up and had seven wounds all over his torso from a little buck knife. One punctured his lung and it collapsed. They threw him on a truck bed and floored it to the hospital and it was only because his boy had once been sentenced to boot camp and forced to learn CPR that Erick was alive today. It got him out of the life, or as much as you can when you get that deep. He'd committed to boxing and he was telling everybody he'd go to the Olympics, and he had a real chance. They called him "White Ali" 'cause he was flashy with his feet. But that inner gangbanger lurked behind his sweet skills, luring him into toe-to-toe banging, much to his detriment. His chin tended to fall apart on him and his scarred lung wasn't a hundred percent, but when he moved and boxed you couldn't find him and you couldn't beat him. He was a lot more like Hearns in that way. He had a jab. And when I say he had a jab I mean his jab could knock you out cold. He was built like a basketball player, with these enormous hands that made his snap like a brick smashing you in the mouth.

Our first day of sparring, Erick wore some long red shorts and a white Pippen jersey. When he geared up, his headgear, gloves, and cup all matched white. He smelled of Cool Water cologne and baby oil.

We climbed into the blue ring and he morphed into a shadow towering over me, backlit by the bright sun gleaming down from the skylight. *Fucking six five, might as well be seven foot!* Our first minute sparring he peppered me with jabs—up jabs, down jabs, double-jabs, triple-jabs—feinting and dancing around me like Ali giggling with his success. Rage exploded through my chest. *This is my gym, you lanky-ass motherfucker!* I loaded up and dug a deadly right to his body that he deflected partially with his elbow, but some of it put a dent in one of the red 3's on his jersey.

"Joe! Don't start that shit," Sal yelled disgustedly. "Just take his jab away."

I took a deep breath. *You're right.* I slipped Zuzisky's jab and looped an overhand over it that dinged him on the chin. He stumbled back blinking and jabbed again. That relaxed me. I slowed his jabs, slipping them as they glanced off my headgear, then jabbing him in the chest; it froze him into the ropes, where I rattled off a six-punch combination that put him in his shell. I spun to the side and dug a left hook to his gut and slipped a left uppercut through his guard. He danced off the ropes and threw six off the jab. And I slipped and rolled and he caught me with the last hook.

We moved and flowed back and forth like Frazier and Ali; he tried to pick me off from range with his jab as I slipped and inched closer, then I'd spring in with my combinations. He fired back using lateral movement. Sometimes it looked like Dempsey versus Willard. Other times like Hearns-Duran! Neither of us could take complete control, and that made the equation even more fascinating to me. We countered each other's counters, and countered again until our exchanges stretched—twelve punches...thirteen...

After four intense rounds Sal called us out. Guys watching around the gym actually applauded the work, which was a rare thing at Windy City. It meant something.

We sat together on the apron, cascades of sweat droplets falling from us, our faces, arms, and drenched shirts. A string of perspiration ran over his bulging Eastern European brow and down his tan face.

"Man, you're the tallest light-heavy I ever seen," I said.

"I tell you there's only one reason I always cut the weight to make seventy-eight." He yanked his white headgear off and a big spray of sweat whisked from his short black fade.

"What's that?" I rubbed a mound on the bridge of my nose that Zuzisky's jab'd sprouted.

"Aaron Williamson," Zuzisky said ominously. "I was sixteen, he was fifteen at regionals, Juniors Olympics, first round, he caught me, bam, scrambled my fucking eggs, Joe! I woke up on a stretcher board, they was carrying me out the fuckin' ring."

"Damn!"

"He a beast!"

People'd been giving me a good chance to win regionals and go to the USA Championships because I'd beaten and dropped Thomas, but nobody'd counted on a guy like Aaron Williamson showing up at the tournament. Williamson rode a fifty-six-fight winning streak as a junior. He'd even won gold at the AIBA Junior World Championships for fifteen- and sixteen-year-olds. I know what you're thinking: But he's only seventeen, he probably did it with speed and skill and can't swat a fly with his punches. Nope. He won the worlds by all stoppages; he stopped the Cuban, and he frickin' KO'd the Russian in the final.

Williamson's path to boxing was odd but not totally unusual. As a child he'd been in and out of foster care after his grandfather, who was a plumber, died unexpectedly and financially destabilized the family. He was a very tender-hearted boy, and the bullies preyed on him terribly. So DCFS moved him from Dearborn to a foster home in Detroit that just so happened to be down the street from the legendary Valentine's Boxing Club, which was run by Hall-of-Fame coach Emanuel Miller. At ten years old, Aaron's foster mother took him to the gym to teach him to defend himself and build up his self-esteem. His first time there, he accidentally bumped into an old pro nicknamed "The Alien." Then during his first lesson, he watched The Alien moving amongst the fighters shadowboxing and sparring, and his imagination made the Alien's skin turn green. Williamson quickly took to the sport; he saw it as a sort of role play, or even a video game. He took on personas when he stepped into the ring. This imaginative play meant he was no longer a bullied and abandoned child. It set him free from the traumas, and in that creative play, he became very creative in the sport. He'd won his first National Juniors title at age eleven, in only his seventh fight. By thirteen, he'd become the head coach's star beloved pupil; Coach Miller had even adopted him.

And now, at seventeen years old, he'd stopped everyone in Michigan in his first adult open tournament, including Michigan's reigning national champion, Oliver Stevens.

◆

At the registration for regionals Zuzisky pointed Aaron out as we sat in the bleachers. Williamson stood near the food booth with his team, all of them in burgundy Valentine's Boxing Gym track suits. Williamson didn't look like much of a puncher. He slunk around all lanky and awkward, about 6'3" with bad posture, plucking Cheetos out of a little bag; he was talking with another young boxer but I could barely hear him:

"I found a new cheat code for Super Mario World if you want to try it later." Williamson said in this wimpy kind of dopey voice.

"You still play that old shit?!" the kid whined.

"Super Mario World is the absolute pinnacle of the Nintendo gaming console..."

I winced.

To Zuzisky I said: "That's Aaron Williamson?! geeky high school kid?" I giggled. "He probably gets bullied in the lunchroom at school."

"Oh yeah, he a dork. He wants his fight moniker to be Luigi for when he turns pro. See that stupid mustache?"

Aaron continued to bicker with his teammate about Mario Brothers. His thick mustache hovered over his thick lips as he pleaded with his large hands.

Zuzisky went on: "He dress up like Luigi every Holloween. He says he hears the sound effects from Mario Brothers when he's fighting!" Zuzinsky guffawed.

"Un-fucking-believable."

"But wait till he gets in the ring though." Zuzinksy assured me.

The rhythm and the fluidity of Aaron William's punches astounded me during his first bout, against this guy from Ohio. He turned the guy's head around and damn near gave him whiplash. He stopped the guy in forty-five seconds after two eight counts and a knockdown.

I luckily matched up with Indiana. He boxed pretty sloppy and I pointed him easily.

Finals took place Sunday afternoon. It was weird to fight the most important fight of my life in a half-empty armory gymnasium. The afternoon sunlight flooded in through the windows high up above the sparsely filled bleachers. Emanuel Miller arrived to work Williamson's corner, which was something because the night before, Coach Miller had worked Lennox Lewis's corner on HBO. *That means he jumped a plane to Ohio after the fight, just to work Williamson's corner.* I won't lie, that shit got me nervous.

I headed in to the moldy locker room to get gloved up and wait.

"You can beat this kid, Joe. You gotta get him going backward. He's just a kid, Joe, you're older, you're stronger." Brother Alex paced around me as I sat on a wooden bench. "You're a grown man and he's a boy!" Brother said unconvincingly. Worry spread across his brow. *Jeez, Brother, you don't look so convinced!* "You're from Chicago, you gonna let this Dearborn dork beat you?" I giggled. *Yeah, he is from Dearborn, he ain't from Detroit, and that makes me realer than him, don't it?*

Brother pulled the hood of my black-and-gold Windy City Gym warm-up gear over my head. I bowed my head, put my blue gloves to my face, and entered a shadowy chamber. *I don't know if I can beat him. Brother's right, I can rough him up, maybe get him out of his game plan.* Then: *Well, this is your thirty-seventh fight, same experience Andy Velez had when you fought him. Aaron Williamson has over two hundred bouts and a Junior AIBA world title under his belt by all stoppages. But I guess you got a shot.* I sighed, letting the air out slowly.

I listened to the announcer in the other room. Zuzisky lost a close one to Ohio. "By majority decision…"

I shrugged. *It's OK, that guy's ranked second in the nation.*

"It's time!" Brother barked.

I got up, limbered my shoulders, and followed Brother out of the locker room. I watched Aaron approach the ring from across the big, dimly lit armory auditorium and its half-assed crowd of mostly just fighters and officials. *He's big and lanky but not a weak lanky, a long and elastic, heavy-boned lanky. Ah fuck it, he's just a kid.* I looked at his bushy mustache. *You really gonna let Luigi beat you?*

We climbed the ring steps across from each other in unison. *Well this is it, this's what you asked for, the finals of the Great Lakes Regional Tournament.* Williamson watched me from across the ring as he sucked on his white mouthpiece. His big nose stretched wide below his bashful eyes. His blue jersey read *MICHIGAN.* I glanced down at mine, *ILLINOIS* in orange letters. *Wish it said Chicago.* Coach Miller was a lighter-skinned small black man in his sixties; the image of him standing in the corner with his arm lounged on the top rope sent a jolt through me. *Damn, I seen his face so much on TV.* His thick eyebrows bopped around as he recognized people in the crowd. *Is he really standing here right now!* His letterman jacket read Valentine's Gym, in burgundy and gold. *Fucking coaching against me?!* We got a Valentine for you, mothafucka, I imagined Coach Miller thinking. All of this sent neutrons popping through my whole body. They kind of froze me up and made me drowsy. *Jesus, Joe, wake up!* I bounded around the ring to liven myself.

"Now be a sportsman, Aaron," Coach Miller said ominously. "Touch 'em up."

I bounced past them. Aaron made a point to touch up with me with both gloves.

"Good luck," he said through his mouthpiece with genuine sternness, his eyes wide and full of terror.

"Thanks! Good luck," I said to both of them as I passed, trying to stay warm and loose. Coach Miller bobbed his big chin up at me with a serene grin.

We went out there and he launched a long jab and his red glove pushed into my headgear and sent me in the air. I barely landed on my feet before stumbling backward. Williamson stepped in smoothly and hit me with a one-two. The whole room went black. *Why you turn the TV off?* I swung back with a hook as he gracefully lunged away and whipped another jab home that split my guard.

"Punch through the hole, Aaron." Coach Miller's soothing voice poured through the ring. "That's it." *What the hell is the hole?!* Williamson came in with a left hook off the jab. I slipped it and danced out into the center of the ring. He took these long slow steps that stretched like he was covering half the ring with them. He launched a jab. I slipped it, jabbed back, and mine came up short. *How the hell is he creating so much distance, and still hitting with power?!* The light slowly filled the room again as my head cleared. I stalled, moving laterally like one of those magic mushroom creatures in Mario Brothers. *How the hell can I score on him?* Thoughts blocked my output; hesitation made me feint jabs instead of letting them go. Williamson just slowly and smoothly stepped in and threw with effortless thunder that seemed to squash me flat. The punches shot me away like I'd smashed face-first into a red trampoline.

Then he dug an uppercut to the body that lifted me up off my feet again. He sank down on me. *Shit! I can't breathe!* I clinched desperately. The crowd oohed and aahed as each punch landed. *They're expecting you to drop!* These survival electrons sparked and coursed through me. *Hell no, I ain't dropping!* The electrons brightened the room and slowed the punches coming towards me in my mind. I slipped three consecutive punches, then clinched him. I bent at the knees and pushed into him. He gave in limply as I walked him across the ring. *I'm stronger than him, he's just a kid.*

The ref broke us. I came in with a jab to the body that he parried as I launched a big overhand right that clipped him high on the headgear. He spun away and caught me with an uppercut. An electric jolt shot through my ears. I wobbled, and I just pulled back his red jab shot at me. Dazed as I was, my instincts got my glove up to deflect it. *Shit! We been boxing for less than a minute! Feels like we been in a life-and-death struggle for a week! He looks relaxed enough to lie down and take a nap between rounds.*

Coach Miller's soft smooth voice flowed into the ring. "Now Aaron, put three together."

Aaron threw a one-two-three that I blocked, but each punch melded into the next and my head rumbled with the collisions. *How can this kid fucking punch this hard?! And how the fuck am I still standing up?!*

I relaxed a little. Then he stuck me in the sternum and a vacuum formed in my lungs again. I dove in and held breathlessly. The ref forcefully broke us and warned me for holding. I glared at the guy; he was portly and bald. *Fuck you, ref, you know how hard this motherfucker hits?!*

The bell rang and Brother climbed in.

"Well, you made it this far. Now let's try to win this thing."

I nodded.

And then it happened. Late in the second, he surprised me on the chin with a left hook from way out as I pulled straight back. My head whipped sideways. These Mario Brothers sound effects sparked up in my head *blupblupbling*! The room spun. I entered a green circular tube; it sucked into another dimension. Da's worried face appeared in it. *Am I dead?* Suddenly I popped out of the other end of the tube. The ref stood before me counting intensely with his fingers. I stumbled back into the ropes, blinking. The crowd went wild as I took the count.

The ref asked, "Are you OK?"

And I shook my head no, and he said, "Walk to me," and I did.

The ref turned and waved Aaron on for the slaughter. I took a deep breath; fear swirled positrons through me as Aaron swooped in for the kill behind the jab. I slipped under the jab and lofted a mighty uppercut. The positrons flowed up through my feet into my torso and up into my arm like it was a portal as my fist crashed into his chin suddenly a plant with teeth seemed to come out and bite into Aaron's head and it whipped back. *Bling! Shit, I caught him!* He stood up straight and rocked back on his heels. I stormed in and hit him with two body shots and pivoted and came upstairs with a left hook. He ate it and turned with me in his slick smooth way. I gathered and came with an overhand right and it landed, but he threw a left hook. A dozen golden Mario Brothers coins spilled through my vision and I was soaring through the green tube again. *Shit! He's got the cheat codes!* The bell rang and the referee got between us and grabbed me by my shoulders, looking me in the eyes. *My god, he stopped me.*

"Please don't stop it!" I begged, and the ref pointed Aaron to his corner. The ref didn't count. "I'm fine." He hesitated, then pointed to my corner.

The stool came down in my corner and Brother Alex grabbed me and slammed me onto the stool.

"What's going on with you, you OK?"

"No, I'm seeing Mario Brothers video game shit!"

"Mario Brothers? Are you alright?"

I laughed and shook my head, deliriously happy they hadn't stopped it.

"Maybe we should stop it. You're taking some big shots."

"Don't pause the game Brother, let me play till the end," I said.

"Okay, I don't know if we can get a decision. I don't know if we can get a stoppage. But you're gonna have to try."

"Try and stop Luigi?! How the fuck could I do that?" I seethed as these weird dots percolated in my vision like the screen of a video game getting wonky with static.

"You caught him with the uppercut! Be smart, don't sit there and take shots. Move and come back with the overhand and a left hook behind it. Dig to the BODY!" Brother seethed as the ten-second warning clicked and I stood.

The bell rang and I ran over and jabbed to the body and he countered with a check hook. I ate it, *bing*! A Mario Brothers coin flipped up out of my head. I came with my overhand as he leaned back. My blue glove just grazed his chin and he clinched me and spun me into the corner and the ref broke us. He fired a jab and I slipped under it and shot a straight right to the body and came up with a quick hook to the chin, spun him and hooked him to the body clean and hard. He came back and I tried to roll out but he caught me on the end of his hook. It froze me like they'd pressed pause on the video game. His straight right nailed me high on the forehead and sent neutrinos soaring through my ears and backed me across the ring. I went back to the feverish lateral movement like the magic mushroom guys in Mario Brothers. *I'm in great shape but his power and my fear, its draining me.* He stepped over for the finish and I clocked him with a left hook and he popped me with a right as I tried to move out of range again. *Maybe I should just shoe-shine him?* I dove under his jab then let my hands go to the body with a flurry *ding-ding-ding-bloom-bing*! I worked my way up with seven, eight punches and cracked the last to his nose, bouncing his head out of his shell. He shrugged and came back with a flurry of his own. I shelled up and took it and *ding-ding-ding-ding* the videogame coins flipped through my vision, then I slipped the last punch and rocketed back with my own combination. We exchanged a lot of fast punches with the Mario Brothers sound effects bopping and coins flipping all over the damn place. The bell rang and we stopped punching. The triumphant *deedala-deedala-dee, deedala-deedala-dee, deedala-deedala-dee-dee-dee-DEE* song played in my mind, the one where you passed through to the next level. The crowd resounded in a deep shocked *ohhhh*. I looked out into their faces; coaches and fighters stood, some of them gripping their heads, shocked and baffled that I was still standing. *Shit, I can't believe it either. How the fuck did I survive that?!*

I walked over to their corner to congratulate them. Coach Miller shot a line of cool water over my head.

"Man, he's good!" I said. "Congrats…"

"Joseph Walsh, uhuh… I'ma remember that name," Coach Miller said and winked. "That was a fine performance." He patted me on the back as I walked away. "Be prouda that."

Aaron won a shutout. Three to zero on all the cards. The ref raised his hand and pushed mine down. *Fuck it. Going the distance is a monstrous win.* First guy to take him the distance in seventeen straight fights.

We exited the ring together. Aaron sat on the middle rope and spread the top rope with his elbow for me to pass through. As I stepped down the stairs, he patted me on the back and said, "Good job."

"Good luck at nationals," I replied as I went down the steps. The black woman doctor called me to her as she stood ringside in her long white jacket. She took her time viewing my eyes with her little pen flashlight. As I looked at her finger, it seemed to be wavering slowly side-to-side.

"What day is it?"

"Sunday."

"Where are you?"

"Toledo, Ohio."

She turned to another official at the table beside us. "OK, I don't like his eyes but he's coherent. I'm on the fence here. He might need the month medical suspension."

"Well he wasn't stopped, he is coherent, I think we can let him go," the old white official said.

She handed Brother my little white USA Boxing record book. "He can continue competing, but I'd like to see him take a month off."

"I understand." Brother nodded and took my book.

We walked across the auditorium to the dressing rooms. Boxers and coaches from Ohio and Michigan came over and made like a tunnel; as I passed through them, they patted me on the back. Others just stared at me stupefied.

"Damn boy, you got a beard on you."

"Luigi stoppin' evera-body, man. How you do that?"

"Dat whiteboy got some balls on him, though."

I nodded acknowledgement to them, grateful for the praise. As I closed in on the locker room doors, the room began to sway. The adrenaline high faded as the electrons fell through my feet and a pulsing pain rose in my head. My chest squeezed. I hyperventilated and staggered into a side office in the back of the locker room. Brother kept asking what's wrong, what's wrong, what's wrong? Or maybe I was hearing his voice repeating in my mind. I looked at him and his body morphed into an echoing trail of his past actions, flowing behind him back out into the main room and into the ring. It cleared some, and I changed into my street clothes slowly, with my hands trembling. Then without warning it came back. It seemed like the light was penetrating my skull, and I lay down and crawled under a table to avoid the light. Sirens sounded in my mind. Some kind of a sharp metal hook stabbed high into my forehead above my temple, and the hook set. The pain worsened like the hook was digging deeper; blood squeaked in my skull as my brain twitched. *What the fuck is happening? Is this how I die? After some seventeen-year-old nerd beat my ass?! Having a fucking aneurysm?*

Brother gave me a bunch of ibuprofen and I barfed it up on the gray carpet. He half-carried me to a bathroom. I barfed for about fifteen minutes.

"Joe, we gotta take you to the hospital."

"I'm fine!" I moaned, lying on the bathroom stall.

The medics came in and took a look at me and started checking my eyes. They walked me to the ambulance. I trembled as I climbed in. They tried to get me to lie down on the white bed of the stretcher. I refused.

"We're just gonna take a look at you."

"I'm not laying down, 'cause that means you're taking me in."

"Look, kid," the black medic said. "It's just a precaution, we're gonna take you in and do some tests."

"Fuck all you motherfuckers!" I shouted and hopped back down to the street and walked back across the parking lot towards the Best Western where we were staying.

"Joe! Stop!" Brother yelled at me exhaustedly, then gave up and just sat on the rear bumper of the ambulance. "I'm sorry," he said to the medics.

I went into the crummy hotel bar and ordered a whiskey and drank myself through the worst headache of my life. It slowly faded. The guys from the tournament kept coming in and telling me how I did good and how Williamson would be the Olympian and it wasn't no shame losing like that to Williamson. I was grateful for that but I had other problems to worry about, like maybe serious fucking brain damage for the rest of my life.

Then Coach Miller came in. He sat down next to me at the bar and put his hand on my shoulder.

"Son, I hate to see you in here but I been here too. I can't help but say, watching the way you adjusted in there and never gave up, it made me proud. Look at him! Outgunned, first time at regionals, going all out against my boy! I'ma let you in on a little secret. Aaron, he gonna stop every boy in the country 'cept for one, and he may even stop him, too."

"You the only one he couldn't stop yet, now why?" His rich deep voice I'd heard so many times on HBO begged the question. "I don't know, but I want a front-row seat to find out." He stood up, laughing. "Joseph Walsh!" He clapped his light-brown hands three times. "You got something special. I'll be keeping an eye out, now. You see me around, come say hi. Don't be no stranger."

He reached his hand out and I shook it. It was warm and soft. I watched him walk away. Everyone greeted him and he greeted them back with simple kindness. *How the hell does a guy that famous, with that many world champions, keep track of something like it being my first time at regionals? He cares, I guess. What a nice guy.* I smirked. *Well, your boy almost killed me but I survived. I got that, I guess.*

I got real fucked up and went out on the loading dock of the hotel to smoke some weed with the Ohio middleweight, a mumbly black kid with a thick neck named Terrance that everybody called Ohio 'cause he was team captain. He'd won. He was going to the US Championships for the third time. They ranked him fourth in the country; he'd won two national titles already in the men's division and a few in the juniors. He'd already fought a bunch of international duels and matches; he was one of the most decorated guys at the tournament. He'd pulled me aside and asked if I wanted to smoke, his concerned eyes watching me like he knew something deep down inside me that he needed to explain to me.

Now we sat on the concrete ledge with our feet dangling off.

"How yo' head feel?" Ohio passed me the small blunt.

"Man, it feels like something's real fucked up inside." I took a hit.

"I had it befo', a bleed. It squeakin' in there, ain't it?"

"Yeah." *Damn, he does know!* I listened to the squeak that'd faded with the drink. I puffed and gave.

"The losses where they beat on me the worstest." He pulled and let the smoke climb his knotty brow. "Them's the ones, the mos' important fights, 'cause either you quit or you grow. And if you keep growing, you become a national champ, then an Olympic champ, then a pro world champ, then all that's left is getting up there to be a goat."

I giggled. "What the hell's a goat?"

"What's a goat? Come on whiteboy! Ali! Robinson! G.O.A.T...Greatest Of All Time!" Ohio mimicked Ali's singsongy speech.

I laughed. "Yeah, maybe one day, Ohio."

"You never know." He blew smoke; it flooded out like his mouth was the boiling goblet of some sorcerer.

I thanked him and went out and lay in the grass behind the hotel and Brother found me and yelled at me for not going to the hospital and then he brought me back to the room and gave me some Excedrin and it helped and I fell asleep.

I dream a gigantic version of Aaron Williamson stands across from me in a dark ring, in green trunks and a shirt with Luigi across the waist, a big bushy cartoon mustache wiggling over his lips. He steps toward me slowly, clinically, like an executioner. He hunts me and suddenly I look down and my body is the little tortoise guy from Mario Brothers. I slowly slink away around the ring as Coach Miller watches from the ropes calmly and soothingly tells him how to destroy my mind for good. Coach Miller holds a Nintendo controller in his hands and clicks on the little buttons; the black wire snakes into the ring and into the back of Aaron's head. "Jab through the hole, son, split his guard, now put the two behind it." Coach Miller clicks pause and we both freeze. He looks to the referee and says, "Come on now, stop this thing, this boy don't need to take no more abuse." The referee is suddenly a cartoon Mario in a referee uniform; he only giggles sadistically. Coach pleads: "Look at him! He running, he surviving, he ain't gonna win this fight. Put this boy out his misery, Mario!" Mario waves us on with his little white gloved hand. Coach Miller un-pauses. Aaron swings a punch up, and it comes down and smashes me and I float up out of the game. He takes my shell and starts running around the ring. "Let's get on to the Olympic Box Offs!" he says as the triumphant music rings in my mind.

I woke drenched in sweat. The headache had vanished but a fog filled my mind. Nausea swirled in my stomach. I staggered to the bathroom and puked all the booze up.

Lauren called.

"How'd it go?"

"I lost on points."

"Oh. It's OK, baby."

"Yeah, I feel pretty terrible. I love you, I gotta go. I'll be home tonight."

Brother drove us home. I slumped in my seat, nauseous and delirious. Brother kept talking about getting Williamson again, and how I could take him.

"You just got to go harder from the opening bell! And stay close and stay on him. Dig combinations to the body!"

"Brother, can we talk about something else?"

And he let up. And we talked about college, and the experiment I was working on with Erickson. And I couldn't form the words to explain it to him. All the terminology mixed in my head.

Then I sighed and said, "Man, I gotta work tomorrow." That deflated the conversation.

Brother dropped me off at my house. Lauren stood out front, waiting for me. She just held me all night. I'd wake from more nightmares about Williamson, talking delirious, and she'd be there hovering over me and holding me and crying and kissing me.

I couldn't get up the next day for work.

Dad yelled at me through the wooden door. "We're pouring today! Get ready!"

"I got a headache, Dad. I can't."

The headache was more than a headache. Depression, a deep, deep sadness, kept me in bed like a blanket of dark matter. *Maybe my brain's messed up for life.* Lauren held me, and Dad stomped off and left without me.

The fog started to clear around noon. Soreness awoke in my back, and stiffness ached in my neck from the way Williamson whipped it round with his punches.

I tried to stay positive. I told myself there were worse things than losing to a red-hot world junior champion. *He didn't stop me, but maybe that woulda been better.* Just like Coach Miller kept saying in my nightmares.

◆

The sadness didn't leave me for a whole month. Sadness and confusion slurred my speech. I mumbled and couldn't talk right. People kept saying, what? I tired of having to repeat myself. My inability to communicate enraged me, and Dad and I fell into shouting matches over the littlest things. But slowly my thoughts arranged themselves and I came out of the fog.

I came back to the gym and my sparring partners hit me easier. Little shots wobbled me. I furiously packed my gear after some novice rocked me in sparring. It disgusted me. *I might as well fucking hang 'em up!* I smashed my headgear into my gym bag as I sat on the long red bench lining the ring. Sal walked up, in a black track suit with white piping.

"What's the matter witchu?" Sal asked.

"I don't have no chin no more! I'm done!"

"Kid, you got a beard! You went the distance with Aaron Williamson! That guy stopped everybody, and got a silver at nationals." (After his fight with me, Williamson stopped everybody at Nationals in route to the finals, where he faced off against the number nine fighter in the world, Alvin Vargas. He was beating Vargas but they got in an awkward clinch and Vargas had clocked him in the back of the head, an illegal blow that the ref had missed.) "He only lost on a foul! I saw the tape, the ref missed it. Anyway, I was talking to Coach Miller about you. He's impressed. Said you gave them a great fight. Come on. Don't sell yourself short." Sal put his hand on my shoulder as the thunder of the gym swirled around us. "Look, I will always be very honest with you. You might not make it in this game, but it won't be because you can't take a punch."

I sighed. "OK."

"Now I'm pulling you off sparring for a month. I don't want you sparring nobody, ya hear me? Just stay away from boxing for a month. You need to rest your noggin." He patted the top of my head softly.

"Fine." I sighed.

"Ya promise?"

"Yeah, I promise." I took a breath and exhaled and looked up at him. A long trapezoid of light flooded in through the skylight and fell upon his bowed head; deep shadows formed on his wrinkled face.

"Good…" He reached out and squeezed my shoulder, grimacing back emotion.

The fighters shuffled their feet atop the wooden planks and whipped punches into the heavy bags. Jermaine thundered the speed bag across the gym from us.

Sal leaned into the shaft of sunlight and kissed the crown of my head with his dry lips. "My boy," he whispered.

Chapter 11: Regeneration

THE DARKNESS IS ALWAYS THERE, CALLING TO YOU, WANTING YOU TO COME AND LIE DOWN IN IT. You have to choose the light, and move towards it, or the darkness will keep you there in its arms forever.

The month passed and Sal called and I came back to the gym. I stood out front of the big red-brick factory with the little yellow-and-red sign that read *Windy City Gym*. The wires constricted in my mind. *Fuck, this place used to feel like home.* I sighed as the anguish of my past month set down on me. *Now it feels like some old house of mine some other crazy dreamer lives in now.* I took a deep breath and opened the door. *Might as well get it over with.* I climbed the dark twisting stairway. *Well, your head feels better now, who knows?* I stepped through the white door into the dank stench of sweat and Vaseline. The trapezoids of golden light poured down from the skylight and painted the blue ring golden as the thunderous and grueling symphony of agony rose to greet me.

"Aye, he's here!" Sal guffawed from the shadowy floor.

Several voices called out "Joey!" "Alright!" "He's back!" Carl Davies, Da Bomber, and Zuzisky sat on the ring apron; they looked at me with warm smiles and clapped. Zuzisky hopped up and came over and grabbed my shoulders with his big heavy hands. "Welcome back, Joey!" he said, then trotted back to the long bench.

"Gym ain't the same without you, kid!" Rocky called from a heavy bag and went back to digging shots.

Sal limped up, "You know, some of the guys, they said you wouldn't be back." He cupped my face in his hands. "I knew you would, kid. I'm proud of ya."

The wires evaporated. I grinned, looking Sal in the eyes. He put his arm around my shoulder and led me into the gym. "Now, we rebuild," Sal said as I followed him across the loud room. "It's an Olympic year. You got three shots left at the box-offs. No regrets, kid." Sal stopped me in front of the two gigantic mirrors. He spoke to my reflection as I dropped my gym bag at my feet.

"I've been thinking a lot about it. You're short for 201 but you're fast. Now being short is OK. Being short can be an advantage. Look at Montell Griffin. '92 Olympian, five-foot-seven at light-heavy and with short stubby arms. But he found a way to make these tall guys reach. With tall guys they say fight tall, don't give away that reach. Well, with short guys what's the point in fighting tall? Why not squat down, fight in a crouch, make it harder for the tall guy to reach you, way down there. Montell would crouch down..." (Sal painfully bent his knees because of the bullet shard still stuck in his spine.) "...'n rock way back, and these guys with four inches of reach on him, they'd stretch that long jab out, and Montell would lean just an inch out of range and *whap!* He countered them." I mimicked Sal's movements in the mirror. "Say what you want about the Jones fights. He made Jones DQ himself. He outboxed him through six rounds; he was the first guy to ever outbox Jones as a professional. How'd he do it? He made his odd height his advantage, Joey."

Sal led me past Willie's desk into the back office.

"Now you're more of an action guy, you're exciting, you like to throw a lot of combinations. Which is why I want you to study up on Mike Tyson. Now there's a lot of dummies out there. They think Tyson was a slugger, a bomber." He sat me down on a couch in front of a TV and VCR. "He kind of is now, he's kind of falling apart, loading up on one punch. But you watch him closely when he was young, when he was fifteen, sixteen, seventeen, before Cus died and a little bit after in his early twenties, Tyson was a downright masterful counterpuncher. I was out there at Cus's compound in the Catskills for about six months, one of his apprentices, Cus showed me the mechanism that made Tyson. Tyson was just fifteen and a work of art, Joey. I think Tyson could have been cruiserweight world champ at fifteen, as a pro! It was a great experience for me, but I had to come back, though. Chicago is home. But I've been looking for a guy who fits that form of Tyson. Tyson had enormous powerful thighs and buttocks, same as Frazier. The power came from the hips down. You'll never be a heavyweight, the bone structure is way too small, but you're a perfect cruiserweight." He pressed play on the VCR. Stock footage of Tyson shadowboxing as a kid lit the square plane. "My philosophy is, you can't have one philosophy. If I tried to make Zuzisky into a Cus D'Amato pressure fighter, it wouldn't work. Zuzisky, he's long, he's tall, he has smart feet, he can dance away like Ali, he can fire down the pipe like

Hearns, so I push him that direction, toward his strength. But you, kid, you could do a lot of the things Tyson did. You have the coordination, you got the explosive *pop!* from the legs, the left hook like Frazier. I'm not saying you'll ever rise to those heights, son; boxing is as much about luck and destiny as anything else. But I think you can build yourself into an elite national guy following Cus's school." Sal fast-forwarded, then pressed play. Young Tyson came into view in a black-and-white image—his head always swaying side-to-side, then rolling under shots and coming up firing ferociously. "Now, you'll see some of the shots that hurt and dropped guys; they weren't even thrown that hard, they just had good snappy technique. They surprised guys. Some people used to say Tyson slapped, and that's part of power, there's an element of finesse in power punching. Even Foreman had it when he was young, you gotta squash the bug, but the bug is flying, you gotta squash the bug in midair."

After about an hour watching tape, Sal took me back out to the gym. He set up the clothesline between two pillars near the entrance and walked me through drills.

"Let's slow it down," he said as he stood next to the clothesline.

"Slip the jab to your left." He threw a slow jab at me that glided over my right shoulder. He held his jab extended over my shoulder and continued. "Let that weight rock onto your front foot. Now you can counter with your left hook to the body or head. Now let the straight right go. Now roll to my right, roll right under the line. Good, now what can you do?"

"Straight right."

"Good, throw it. Left hook, now roll under the line. It never ends, kid, let your rolls and slips flow into your offense. See, take it slow. And we'll build up the speed later. Look, boxing is all about flowing from offense to defense at all times and every once in a while, when everything goes just right, your offense and defense can meld simultaneously. You don't have to hit hard all the time, you're learning that. Surprising someone with a quick shot with good technique on the button is twice as effective as hitting them with all your might with a punch they see coming. The only way to surprise good fighters is through defense, kid. You can stall too, you can move or clinch, but that is also defensive. Use it if you're trying to reestablish your rhythm.

"OK, a guy's got a good jab, well, take it away from him with head movement and counters. He jabs...slip, jab-jab. Now in his mind he's thinking, *I have a great jab and now this squat guy is outjabbing me? What the hell's going on?* He's got a great right cross? Slip it and dig a left hook into his liver. Then do it again and again, double it up to the jaw. You'll get in his head, punish him every time he throws it, and he'll stop throwing it. And while he's trying to figure out what you're doing to him you'll be busy winning the round and winning the fight. Defense first, Joey, defense is everything, without defense first, there is no offense. And if your defense is great, your offense will land easy. It's not just Tyson of course, I've got tapes: Dempsey, Patterson, LaMotta, even Vinny Paz does a lot of this stuff. There's a long lineage of intelligent pressure boxers, all of them underrated for their defensive boxing, Joe. Now let's get to work."

I spent a week on the rope. A lot of the stuff Sal had taught me already, but there was something about the way he talked, it put all the pieces together so I had a complete picture of everything that could come at me and how I should respond to it. My legs burned terribly but I began to find a rhythm copying and assimilating Frazier's, LaMotta's, and Dempsey's rhythms; my thick legs began to strengthen and find the elasticity they needed to slip and roll and come up punching with combinations. My balance settled in a squat and I realized just how much of boxing is balance.

At the end of that first week, Sal called me into the ring so he could hold mitts for me. Sal wasn't so great on his feet but his hands flowed quick and snappy. He slapped the shit out of everybody with those mitts. He never told you what to throw, just showed you the mitt at a certain posture. Then he potshot counters at you. He held for a jab and I shot it out and he cracked me with a counter right. He held jab again, I jabbed and I slipped his counter; he showed left hook to the body and I popped the mitt. He showed jab, I jabbed, slipped his right and dug the left hook. He swung wide with his left hook and I rolled and he showed right cross and I fired. I slipped, I fired, I rolled, I fired; he built combinations off of my slips; he pushed me, nudged me, forced me to balance myself. We flowed into an impromptu exchange of slips and counters; he just showed me what he wanted and I delivered the blow. Each exchange was done in a split-second opening: just punch, roll, punch, slip, punch, three-punch combo, roll, pivot, rip hook to the body, double up to the head, roll. Sal's grip on me strengthened until we were one mind; he pushed the buttons and I responded crisply, slowly. I forgot to think, forgot to get excited by the flow between us; when I knocked his mitt loose he just grimaced. "Hit the dot!" At times like those I realized that Sal was the artist and I was his canvas and paint.

Zuzisky started to school everybody in sparring, even the pros. He sparred seven, eight rounds; he slipped, shot straight punches, pulled back and saw frustrated left hooks miss by a mile as he danced off the ropes. Sal coached from the floor as I watched from the apron. "See what he's doing? He's using what he has, his height and speed, against them. He controls distance with his feet. They can't find him unless he lets them. He decides when to engage. What are you gonna do when you gotta spar him? How are you going to do what these good fighters here can't? Look at that jab...*pop-pop!* He's keeping them away, Joey."

"Slip and step in."

"Yeah, then what?"

"Shoot a counter right to the chest."

"Next, better not be a hook, he'll just drop step back, make it miss, and fire his straight right."

"OK, I fire a sharp jab. Smother him and move my hands in the clinch, then pivot right and double up the left hook, body-head."

"Now you got him shelled up maybe."

"Loop the right cross around his guard and pry him open. Uppercut to the chest, leave it in his chest, and dig it up between his guard in an uppercut. Overhand right over the top."

"That's what I'm talking about."

◆

The next week I sparred for the first time since Sal had sent me home after that novice rocked me. Fucking wires started up—constricting in my chest. I slipped through the blue ropes; nerves percolated in my belly like uneasy electrons.

Zuzisky laughed and said, "Welcome back, Joey! Now I'm gonna beatchyo ass, boy!"

I giggled as I bounded around the ring. *Wouldn't be the first time, you lanky bitch.*

The bell rang and I tensed up rigid. *Fuck, what if he knocks my ass out?* We touched up and Zuzisky lined me up with his jab. *Wap wap!* They're coming from his hip. I tried to move but they caught me in mid-motion. *Fucking hands are fast!*

"Move your damn head!" Sal called.

OK. I took a deep breath and let it out slow. I rocked my head side-to-side as Zuzisky picked me off. I lunged in with my jab. He check-hooked me and I staggered into the ropes.

"Settle down, Joe! Don't reach. Step to him."

I regrouped as Zuzisky laughed at me and danced around with his hands low. He shot a lead right hand. I kind of slipped; it glanced me in the ear. *Not bad.* I lunged out with the left hook and almost caught his stomach as he bounded backward like a gazelle.

"Watch! He ain't gonna hit me the whole round, boy," he said over his shoulder to Miguel, who giggled sitting on the apron. "Fifty bucks!"

"You on!" Miguel called through the ropes. "Let's roll, Joey-boy!"

I glanced at him and giggled. *You assholes.* I took a deep breath as my body began to knock the stiff rusty spots off and come alive, like a snake shedding its skin. My knees, hips, and shoulders found rhythmic sync. My head movement became more reactive. *Don't just move your head, evade the damn punches, you idiot.* His jab shot out and I slipped my head under it. Then his left hook crashed into my temple. A deep boom exploded in my mind. His right hand shot at me and I slipped it. His red glove shot past my face like a rocket. Zuzisky fell forward off-balance, surprised by me not being there. I pivoted and thudded a straight right to his chest and shot a nifty little jab to his nose. Zuzisky recoiled back, scowling like he got a whiff of something rotten. He threw the left hook and I rolled underneath it, the wind from his swing flowing over my back as the light poured in from the skylight above us. Our shadows melded on the blue canvas like one monstrous being at war with itself. I bounced out of range. *Alright motherfucker. I won that exchange.*

"Dat's it!" Sal shouted.

"He's back," Fearless said from the floor, where he'd been pounding a heavy bag.

"He just hit you twice, Zuzisky! You better have my fifty, bitch," Miguel called out.

"Fuck you, you owe me twenty anyway," Zuzisky shouted over his shoulder.

I rushed in, slipped his jab, and nailed him with a crisp snappy jab of my own.

Zuzisky fired three punches; the first two landed. I slipped his right cross, dug a left hook to the body, and doubled it up to the head as Zuzisky's left hook landed simultaneously. I took it with a grin and felt the world shift like someone reached in and cut the wires loose in my chest. *I can do this.*

I stepped out, and Zuzisky stayed in to continue sparring. The old joy coursed through my shoulders as Sal pulled my soggy headgear off. *That first round was special. He won the round but by our third, I probably edged him, and it's just my first day back sparring.*

"You can do this, kid." Sal patted my face softly and walked off.

Slowly as Zuzisky and I worked together the matches evened, and the guys crowded around to watch us in these volume-punching chess matches. It made me grateful to have Zuzisky because even though he fought different from Williamson, he had a lot of the same moves and was two inches taller. So if I could find Zuzisky, I could find Williamson, at least in theory.

◆

Golden Gloves came around. I was feeling good. I sparred with everybody, and they each gave me a new puzzle to figure out. My confidence grew round by round, until nothing could faze me again. In sparring I slowed down guys' shots and countered them easier. Then if they countered me, I slipped their counter and countered their counter. It got to the point where offense and defense flowed together; I could spend a whole round just rolling, slipping, and countering.

The beating from Williamson gave me a sense of compassion, something I'd lost touch with over the past few years. I didn't want to hurt guys in sparring. I threw punches softer and just snapped them through, and a few times when I snapped a shot on the button, guys' eyes rolled. But I stopped right away, gave them a chance to recover, and touched up with them. The beating had sent me into doom and despair; now it made me feel sorry for all the guys I'd put bad beatings on. I hoped I hadn't hurt them too bad.

But the hunger to win still raged in me.

Lauren dropped out of Elmhurst and moved into Burkhart's attic so she could live the artist's life. She turned me on to some philosophy about energy and Bruce Lee; soon I wanted to become a martial artist, not just a fighter. I wanted to master the art the way the greats mastered it. To develop a voice, distinct and original, and to find ways to apply it to every situation in a bout with anyone.

Meanwhile Sal pushed me deeper into Cus D'Amato's defensive system. His voice echoed in my mind all day:

"Make 'em miss, make 'em pay, build a combination off it. And complete it by rolling out and stepping around. Your combination is never complete until you are completely out and safe. Our goal is to make you a complete fighter, Joey."

Six open fighters had entered my bracket in the Chicago Golden Gloves that year. O'Sullivan had vanished, which eased my tensions, but I would have liked to have seen how my new skills matched up against him. (He hadn't won nationals the last year like I thought he would. A slick black kid from Los Angeles pointed him pretty easily. O'Sullivan did rock him late but couldn't pull off the stoppage. I'm guessing after that he figured he was too old to turn pro and just receded back into Cook County, breaking up riots and storming cells, soaring toward that pension—just another blue-collar legend.)

I cruised through the quarter- and semifinal bouts and matched up with a big guy in the final, a lanky guy a lot like Williamson. His name was Perkins; he was a real strong muscled-up black guy with face tattoos and he'd come out of nowhere, or I should say, Austin. A dark horse come to derail my Olympic bid. Perkins had stopped his guy in the semis real nasty. He'd battered him across the ring, and the guy had fallen through the ropes and onto the score table. The guy could not get back in the ring to beat the count. They'd kept him down and put him on the stretcher and taken him to the hospital to check him out.

Lauren had watched it with me. It'd scared her, but I could tell she didn't want to talk about it.

One night we were driving down Halsted on our way to Burkhart's, and I finally had to bring it up:

"Come on, baby, what's up?" I squeezed her trembling hand.

"That man is mean, Joe. I don't like it. I don't want you to end up like you were after regionals. It hurt me to see you like that. You could barely even talk some days, Joe!" She fought back tears. "I ain't coming to see the fight. I can't. I love you. I hope you win, but I can't watch no guy like that tryin' to hurt you, baby."

"Baby, come on!" I gripped the tan steering wheel. "I'm gonna whip him, you'll see."

"Well, Burkhart's jazz buddy got me a guest spot at the Mill."

"The Green Mill!?"

"Yeah, I can't believe it. But it's Saturday so I can't come to the fight anyway."

"Well, I'll come to the Mill with my belt, then."

"You just get your butt there in one piece." She ruffled her hand through my hair.

I went out and bought Lauren a beautiful gown for her performance at the Green Mill, a white gown with gold sequins that looked like feathers. It fit her flowing hips and just about every one of her luscious curves. She loved it.

◆

By then Saint Andrew's was like my damn living room, and it was a big family reunion in the crowd. A bunch of the knucklehead Walshes showed. A lot of the guys from the construction crews were there, too, and Jay and Rose even came. (They'd been living together for a year by then.)

They were sitting near the front row; Jay called me over to them after I gloved up. The bright lights played in Jay's dark eyes and sparkled in his diamond earring as he shook my hand and pulled me close.

"Joe, I know this nigga from County. He a GD," Jay confided. "He a bully. He ain't shit, though. You stand up to him, he gon' crack."

"If you say so, Jay," I said, straightening up.

"He looks scary but you're gonna kick his ass, Joseph!" Rose assured me in her loud wacky way, taking a sip of Bud Light from her big clear plastic cup.

Sal called me back near the glove table to warm up.

I boxed Perkins carefully; he loaded up and found air every time he swung. Then I'd pepper him with three, four shots and roll away. He didn't land a single punch in the first round.

In the second he pressed me into the ropes and landed a few good body shots on my ribs. I spun off the ropes and lit him up down the pipe with five unanswered punches. He cocked his fist and I slipped and he missed. He started taunting me, putting his hands down, bouncing before me. I laughed and feinted him and he kept them down and I feinted again and jabbed twice, and the second landed and he rocked back and launched a beauty of a short straight right that hit me dead center in the nose. *Shit!* Something imploded deep in my nose like the core of a nuclear bomb. Blood flowed down from the roof of my mouth and poured over my upper lip and I jumped back, blinking. The crowd awoke with a roar. I felt the room rise to their feet. The rowdy Garfield Park guys screamed, "You got his ass!" and "Stop dat whiteboy!"

Perkins glanced at them and grinned. My vision blurred and dots popped in the loud lights. *Shit, he fucking caught me.* The blood leaked down my throat. *Fuck, I can't breathe.* I stalled, moving laterally. His wicked tattooed face grinned out from under his black head gear. Alvarez, the Garfield head coach, stood up below his corner and waved him on. A whirling murmur rose in the big high-ceilinged room: "He's hurt!" Then: "Stand up to his ass Joe!" and "Stop this motherfucker!"

Suddenly a deep liquid voice shot above it all in a long slow note. *Lauren?* Her voice launched loud over the stirring room: no lyrics, just big long improvised notes of deep pain and joy and hope, like she was expelling every ounce of her self.

I dove under a shot and clinched Perkins, and I looked out into the crowd. She rocked slowly side-to-side in her white gown, out in the open in the path behind my corner, her eyes closed, singing.

I spit some blood out and took a deep breath as the ref broke us. Lauren's voice seemed to resonate in my chest and awaken the positrons and electrons. I feinted Perkins, pivoted, and caught him with a left hook; my blue glove smashed through his red gloves and into his black headgear. He stumbled and threw with me as I let an overhand go, and mine made it first. I spun his chin bad as I snapped it through. He wobbled as the ref pushed me away and started counting. I stepped toward the neutral corner as the crowd erupted, swallowing her voice. I looked back at her in her white gown with the shimmering golden sequins holding her hips snugly. As I got to the neutral corner, she opened her eyes and smiled. She threw her head back with joy and raised her arms triumphantly. I touched my heart with my gloves and she touched hers and the ref finished counting. I raised my right hand, turned toward Perkins, and jogged over as the ref said, "Box." Perkins threw wildly with wide desperate urgency. I slipped his left hook and hit him with an uppercut to the liver and doubled it up to his chin. He swung back with the right; I rolled underneath it and came in with a nice neat little left hook. He staggered again and fell into the ropes. I crouched low and put it all on him, every punch I had plus the kitchen sink. I lost count at six clean blows. The sink crumpled him into the ropes. His butt hung between the two lower ones as the referee tackled me into the ropes and waved his hand high over Perkins's head. The crowd rose in a triumphant explosion. I ran over and jumped up on the ropes in the corner near her and spit out my bloody mucus-slimed mouthpiece.

"I love you!" I shouted.

She laughed and mouthed "I loved you, too."

She climbed up on the apron in my corner, laughing in her sparkling white gown, and she put her arms out to me. I hesitated. *The blood!* And she just grabbed my arms and pulled me into her and hugged me, and I hugged her, and she kissed me on my mouth and blood smeared all over her lips and chin.

"The blood, baby!" I said.

"I don't fricken care!" She grinned wickedly.

My red smeared all over the chest of her white gown. It clung and beaded, somehow just right, like everything she ever seemed to do.

They gave me the nice blue belt with the golden center piece. Everybody came and took pictures with me. And it was a big party over by the back stairs. Jay came over with a big old plastic cup of Budweiser and handed it to me.

"You a mothafuckin' gangsta, Joe!" Jay said with his big wide smile.

I grabbed the cold beer and chugged the whole thing down. Blood and beer suds dripped all over my blue finals uniform as they cheered around me, grabbing me and hugging me.

Then I looked at her. *Night ain't over yet, baby. It's your night too.*

I drove her over to the Green Mill and we found a spot out front. Sparkling white lights spread above the wide front window with *Green Mill* written in green neon cursive. Burkhart burst out the door wide-eyed, his long white beard flowing in the wind under his black brimmed hat.

"Lou! Joe! Come on!" He waved us in, and this big Native American bouncer in a heavy black leather coat ushered us along. Burkhart guffawed at my blue Golden Gloves Championship belt draped over my shoulder. The long oak bar flowed back through the deep room. Big round booths lined the wall across from the bar and dotted the back room, all of them with big white tablecloths and little candles flickering inside small green glass cups. The full house bustled. The stage spread wide; it had an ornamental wooden backdrop with a red velvet curtain. A tiled pole cut the stage into halves—one half with the big black grand piano, the other with the mic. Jazz musicians tuned up in folding chairs behind it. A white marble sculpture loomed in a corner near a booth, a sculpture of a naked woman who was holding a bundle of fruit and watching the room like a ghost.

I ordered a whiskey neat from the bearded bartender. Above him, a wooden collage comic strip told the story of Al Capone's days when he frequented the joint back when it was a speakeasy, and how he'd escape the cops through the tunnels underground.

"This fucking place is legit," I told her.

She smiled and kissed my cheek.

A bald guy with a warm grin and circular wire-rimmed glasses walked up, and Burkhart introduced him as the owner, Jemilo.

"I heard so much about you, I can't wait to hear you sing," he told Lauren. We thanked him and they called her up to the stage, and I told her break both legs and an arm, and she laughed and winked at me.

Burkhart waved me closer to get a good view.

She got up there and she looked even better than ever; the white stood out against the red curtain behind her, and the dots of my blood popped in the light, rhyming with the deep red and brown hues like it was all meant to be. Improvised jazz filled the room; the drummer played a soft rhythm as the saxophonist launched into a long hard note. The stand-up bass player fingered a rumbling bass line on the long wooden stem. She touched her lips where some of my blood was, and she tasted it, smiling and looking out at me as she swayed to the music.

"Now as y'all can see, I got a little blood on my dress. Hope y'all don't mind. My lover over there, Joey Walsh, had himself a night at the Chicago Golden Gloves. Well, he got his nose busted, and he got a little cut under his pretty blue eye, and he knocked some big ol' scary fella through the ropes and got his hand raised tonight. So that boy's a Chicago Golden Gloves champion!"

The crowd looked over. I waved from the bar as they roared; people pointed at my swollen nose and the belt draped over my shoulder. Burkhart took a playful swing at my nose and pointed at it, hiking his white eyebrows as the band kicked up and Lauren sang her improvisations, and she was better and more beautiful than she'd ever been, and the crowd hushed and she poured herself into it with her eyes closed, and she passed into a state that was beyond words, and everything was perfect and everything was the greatest it'd ever be for us, and my whole life might have been downhill from that very moment on, and I could feel it shifting. But it was a peak of joy that only comes once in a lifetime.

They gave her a standing ovation at the break, and a longer one at the close. Jemilo invited us to stay after hours and sat with us at the booth. Burkhart snapped some photos.

"Lauren Dupré! Well, I'm convinced you're the new voice of the Mill. Can we sit down this week and look at a contract?"

Her eyes bugged out and she glanced at me. She tried but couldn't speak.

"Answer's yes," I chimed in.

We all giggled, and she nodded and reached her hand out and touched his.

"Yes, I would love to sit down this week and talk about the contract, Mr. Jemilo."

"Good." He grinned. "A toast to Lauren Dupré and the Green Mill."

Our glasses clinked; the candlelight flowing through the liquor made them glow like brown orbs of hope.

We went back to Burkhart's; we thanked him for everything and had a group hug in the living room in front of a tall painting of a white bird standing in a swampland.

"When you've got the magic inside like you two do, you become like a magnet, and the magic rushes to you from every direction," Burkhart said—joyful tears beading in his eyes.

And we headed up into her room and made love like we'd never done before, like we were crushing our souls together into one, then separating and crushing them again until we were one soul and one heart and one being, in the midst of some galactic cataclysm.

◆

A few weeks before the National Golden Gloves Sal kept me late watching tape after everyone left. Even Willie had gone to bed in his room on the other side of the gym. We sat in the big office separate from the gym. Sal broke out a bottle of Jack Daniels and filled two old cracked coffee cups neat and handed me mine.

"We'll drink now, because when it gets close we won't drink at all."

He walked back and forth behind me as I watched old black-and-white footage of Jake LaMotta against Sugar Ray Robinson. He made observations about LaMotta's work, how he closed the distance without taking too much punishment, and he refilled our cups until the bottle was nearly gone, just a small pool of brown liquid in the thick glass glowing in the street light. As the bout ended Sal clicked off the television with the remote and the room darkened and beneath the soft noise of the traffic on Ogden the silence rose up.

"Are you afraid of Aaron Williamson?"

"I am, I'm very afraid of him."

"Good, tell me. You can tell me everything. You can trust me."

"After the fight I thought I was dying."

"Why?"

"Because of the pain in my head and the noises."

"You may have had a minor bleed. The brain is very delicate, son. You have to protect it."

"I saw things when we were fighting."

"What did you see."

"They call him Luigi, and I saw everything like the video game Mario Brothers."

"Son, he pulled you into his game. He got inside your head. You have to strengthen your mind. What's the fight moniker you mentioned you wanted to use if you ever go pro? The science thing."

"The Annihilator."

"Yes... Son, it's simple. You have to annihilate the video game. Imagine the game. Close your eyes."

I did so.

Sal's disembodied voice floated in the blackness. "When you dream of him, is Coach Miller there?"

"Yes, how do you know I dream about him?"

"Son, I have been in this gym for longer than you've been alive."

Shivers ignited all over my shoulders and back.

He went on. "See the video game."

"I see him. Coach Miller is inside him pushing the controller buttons."

"How does the Annihilator work?"

"The particle accelerator?"

"Yes."

"You have to click on all the machines and then Erickson turns it on."

"How does he do it?"

"He pulls a long metal lever."

"See me pulling the lever." The sounds of the Accelerator began to hum in my mind. "What is happening in the video game?"

"He's chasing me and trying to squash me."

"Feel the accelerator come alive. Feel it."

I feel the accelerator, the positrons cycling through me, my whole body. The video game begins to disintegrate around me and fall through the ring. Coach Miller angrily clicks on the control buttons inside of Williamson's head.

"This machine isn't only about annihilation, Joe. It is an excellent marvel of science. Every aspect is seeking out scientific perfection. It is a perfect machine. This machine is inside you. It is your completely realized potential."

"Now see yourself in the ring, not in the game but inside the brightly lit ring at Nationals with the real Aaron Williamson. Now see yourself in perfection. See all those sneaky powerful punches coming at you trying to squash you. Slow them in your mind! See them slipping past your head. Are you there!?"

"Yes."

"Now strike!" My bare fist slips in between Aaron's punches and lands crisply, snapping his head backwards. "You are Joseph Walsh and he is Aaron Williamson. You are two young men. Nothing more and nothing less."

I stand before Aaron; he looks at me awkwardly. We are both naked except for old primitive brown leather protective cups; our hands are bound in old brown leather mitts tied with string.

"Open your eyes!"

I stood in the office. The TV was off. Beads of sweat covered my face and arms. My hard breath was the only sound. Then a car glided by below.

Sal stood at the window looking out onto Ogden. His silhouette glowed in the street lamp light seeping in through the dirty old glass. He sipped his coffee cup of whiskey.

"I was there in the corner at the USA Amateur Championships in Indianapolis the night that Chico Evans knocked out Mike Tyson. I was Griffin's assistant. Cus never spoke to me again til the day he died. You can imagine how close we were. I lived in the man's house for months, he was a hero of mine. I wasn't really the reason we caught him. Mike was too amped up that night, too aggressive, not making us miss. He ran into a shot, Joe. Mike defeated himself that night. But he learned. He grew. From then on, he took control with his defense. You understand me?" He turned his glare at me; a vicious sneer spread across his face.

He put his cup down on the window ledge. Then he approached me, his upturned hands out before him, fingers spread, gesturing emphatically as though he was sucking the truth out of the air around him. "You are always in control if you control your defense. You are always safe. Young Mike Tyson had great fear, Joey. And that fear may have been his greatest talent." He limped slowly towards me, his orange aura glowing in the street lamp. "His gift. Cus used that fear to shape him into a marvel." He stood within arm's reach of me peering up at me, his old broken nose barely visible in the dimness, his frizzy hair alight. Then he pointed directly into my heart. "Your fear will protect you, son." He tapped his fingertip into my chest, his dark eyes peering deep into mine. "It's our key to complete you."

◆

Nationals were in Memphis. They put the brackets up in the big convention hall; they were on several large white poster boards, with the fighter's names and their Golden Gloves franchises. I had to go through Aaron Williamson in the semifinals. I shrugged. *Hope I make it that far.*

Aaron started winning by decision in this tournament, and boxing much more carefully. Coach Miller came to town before the quarterfinals. He waved to me as he gave autographs to a bunch of kids in the convention hall, as he waited to enter the ring with Aaron.

Sal'd sent me to the dressing room to get Zuzisky's backup mouth guard. I ran in, grabbed it, and headed back out. My friend Ohio grinned at me in the hallway.

"Don't worry 'bout Williamson. Alvin took something outa him, he can't punch no more."

"Yeah?"

"He ain't no killa no mo' trus me."

I smiled as my hopes rose.

"You'll beat him the way you moving yo head so good now."

"Damn right." I grinned and walked back into the main room with hopeful electrons flying around my body.

I walked out into the convention center floor and looked into the black canvased ring as Williamson hit New York with one of those long jabs and New York bounced into the ropes and Coach Miller said, "Go on, Aaron," and New York came off the ropes and Williamson crumbled him with a tight little straight right. And New York tried to get up and fell flat on his face, and the ref waved it off as New York crawled around on his hands and knees looking for his mouthpiece. The whole convention center roared and oohed and aahed. Zuzinsky looked at me and just shrugged. My hands trembled as I handed Sal the mouthpiece case and walked back to the dressing rooms.

"Guess he can still crack," Ohio told me as I passed him.

Brother couldn't come because of school, and I missed his way of pumping me up before a fight. *Well, Joey, you can't dodge the Dearborn dork!* I heard Brother's voice in my mind and giggled.

I decisioned Philadelphia 2-1 and didn't take much punishment. The ref raised my hand. *Semifinals, huh? Aaron Williamson, here we go again.*

That night I dream the same old dream. Williamson is a giant, across from me in the ring with the video game mustache, wearing the big green overalls with the puffy green cap and green gloves with *Luigi* written across his waist. Coach Miller coaxes him through dismantling my thoughts, my spirit, and my will to win. The punches reach into me and steal memories from my mind and my heart. There is something smooth and clinical about what they are doing as I try to escape. Then I look and suddenly a miniature Coach Miller is inside Williamson's hollowed-out head; it's open to the world in the back like it is just a virtual reality head set. Miller is clicking on an elaborate black video game controller as he whispers nice and slow to Aaron.

I woke. Checked the clock, 4 a.m. Intricate wires wrapped around my mind and chest. *I don't want to sleep no more.* I lay wide awake on my back on the white hotel sheets. The wires dug into my mind. *I don't want to fucking go in there with Williamson again.* I willed myself to see me inside the ring with Williamson. *You got to, Joe.* The wires eased. *You just fuckin' got to.*

◆

In the dressing room before the semifinals, I sat on a turned-backwards folding chair across from Sal, my wrist and elbow resting on top of the cool metal backrests as Sal taped my left hand.

Coach Miller poked his head in the door.

"Hey, look who it is!" Sal said happily.

"Hey now, Sal, how are ya, now?" Miller said as he entered, his round chin pointed up.

"How are ya, Emanuel?" Sal grinned, letting a strand of tape drape down from my knuckle.

"Now, I just wanted to come and wish y'all good luck," he said, looking at me.

"Thanks, Mr. Miller," I said. "Good luck to you. It's a real honor competing with you."

"Now, look at that," he said with a warm grin, and put his hand on my shoulder. "It's an honor competing with you, Joe. You're a hell of a fighter. Now good luck, fellas, and see y'all in just a few minutes."

"And Mr. Miller," I said. "Please tell Luigi I said good luck."

Emanuel straightened and guffawed.

"How in god's name do you know about that silly thing? I will tell *Aaron*," he corrected me, "that you wish him luck." He continued towards the door. "I don't mess with that video game nonsense." He waved his hand dismissively and walked out muttering to himself. "I told that boy to stop telling people that nonsense!"

Sal and I chuckled.

"I told you he likes you," Sal said. "Are all the switches on, on the Annihilator?"

"Yeah," I grinned. It gave me a charge, a real positive charge. The positrons started cycling through me. *To have them come over to wish us luck? What a classy thing to do.* All the fear I had of them, all the thoughts that they could destroy me, left.

I climbed the steps into the ring in the center of the big brightly lit convention hall. I looked out at the whole national boxing community spread out across the floor seating and on the few portable bleachers. I watched curiously; some of them seemed to be arguing back and forth on who exactly I was. *I gotta show my best stuff. I'm so damn excited to get in this ring.* I slipped through the red ropes and jumped in; I circled the ring and bowed to all three judges. Williamson got in in his slow, careful, lanky, awkward way. He nodded to me as he kicked his long legs loose. Coach Miller winked at me.

"Now let's go. Show 'em what you got now, kid," Sal said, grinning proudly with his dark wrinkled face as he reached out both small fists and gave my blue gloves an energetic double fist bump.

I turned to face Luigi; his puffy black mustache curled slightly above his mouth. His black jersey read *METRO DETROIT* in gold letters above the thick golden waist of his trunks. My blue jersey had an orange *CHICAGO* written across the chest, with another Chicago patch on my shiny orange thigh.

"You belong here, Joe," Sal said behind me. "This is your time."

I flexed my thick pale muscular arms, then shook them loose. I bounced on my toes. *Look at us, Chicago versus Detroit, Windy City verse Valentine's, two of the best pro coaches in the world going head-to-head with their young protégés. Maybe one day our trunks will read Luigi and The Annihilator. Well shit, you still got a lot to prove. Now's your chance Joeyboy.*

The bell rang and Williamson came out with his slow steps and pawing jab-finding range. I used movement. He swung a loopy right and it glanced me as I slipped and I fired three straight punches. The third straight right popped his head. He hopped backward, planted, and check-hooked me. I blocked it and moved away. Aaron stepped forward, cutting off the ring, taking away my escape options. He jabbed to my chest and I jabbed back. He pulled back and it missed, and we fell into a real careful and cerebral boxing match. I made him miss, but I never relaxed, because his range was so long. When he caught me, I clinched and let my head clear. Then I would come back with five or six shots; I was finding little openings around his elbows and wrists. He tried to potshot me, but I was seeing them coming and he wasn't landing much. I felt good at the bell and Sal said, "That's your round!" as I approached the corner.

We came out the next round and Williamson was a little more fired up, trying to walk me down. He caught me with some nice combinations.

I fired back with mine and I wobbled him a little with an overhand. He hit me with a cross that made me freeze; *bumblunbonkbandadaa* resounded in my ears. *No, fuck that shit.* I blinked back video game graphics. I played it off that I was fine; the red-headed referee bought it. Then I started to fire counter shots off his jab. He'd jab, I'd get under it and *rata-tat-tat* him with straight punches, and the last punches had something on them. He blocked them, but he didn't like the last ones. I was finding holes in his guard.

The bell rang.

Sal doused my head with water.

"It's probably even now, but you finished strong, OK? Keep that up, head moving like a out-a-whack pendulum. Stay low, slip, and come up firing. He doesn't have an answer for that. Aye, look at me." He reached out before him and grabbed an imaginary lever and pulled it towards himself. "It's on. Hold nothing back. Scientific Perfection!"

I felt the particles cycling around me and did what Sal said, and soon I felt Aaron getting frustrated. He started throwing with lead again. I blocked one punch that stunned me through my guard. The bolt of energy resonated through into my brain. And suddenly I fell through the big green pipe into the Mario Brothers video game again. His shots came in and I was Mario, jumping, avoiding the *bling bop* sounds as I deflected more of the red gloves flinging in trying to squash me. I clinched him, blinking. *Fuck that video game shit, Luigi!* The particles accelerated through my back and shoulders, out into my hands and neck and feet. The video game slowly broke into pieces as I willed myself into the convention hall again. Aaron desperately wiggled out of the clinch, trying to keep me stuck in Mario World. The ref broke us and warned me for holding. I grimaced at Aaron. *No more of that Mario Brothers shit, this is the Annihilator's time!* The tremendous fear like positrons pulsed through my whole being. *Now move your damn head, Joe!* I saw the shots and evaded them; my head moved so fast and clean as the positrons rushed through me, close to the speed of light. His red gloves started to flow in slow motion and shoot past my head. I fired back, chopping little punches that scored as he missed. I accumulated points and he didn't land a single blow straight through to the bell.

The freckled ref stepped between us and Aaron dropped his head and walked sadly back to his corner. I followed him and Coach Miller gave me a big hug and whispered, "You won, Joe. You was great, kid."

Aaron draped his arms on the ropes exhausted, glanced at me and said, "Congratulations," through his mouth guard as I patted him on the back. I came back to my corner and Sal said, "It's close but I think we got it."

We waited with the ref in the center of the ring as they tallied the scorecards. Officials in their blue Golden Gloves button-up uniforms moved frantically back and forth at the long tables. The debates flooded through the big room. "Hell Naw! Whatchu fuckin' talkin' bout?" the chubby Puerto Rican coach from the Bronx whined, standing with his geared-up fighter near the red corner. "Chicago, fuckin got him! 2-1 easy, all day." He scolded a group of Texas fighters chattering near the front row in their black-and-white track suits; the lanky Mexican lightweight who got a gift the day before made a pained obnoxious face and shook his head no. I looked out and saw Ohio in his red warmup gear near the hall to the dressing rooms grinning wildly and nodding his head; he stared me deep in the eyes. "You Won!" he mouthed. *Really? Am I going to the fuckin' finals!?* I shrugged uneasy.

They announced the fight a majority decision; one judge had it for me 2-1 and the other two for Aaron 2-1.

Bickering voices shot back and forth through the stands. The young Irish ref raised Williamson's hand and kept mine down as a light simmering of boos swirled through the room, then came some laughter, then the boos caught on and got loud and long. The ref kind of tugged my wrist up a little. I glanced at him and he winked at me. *Really, even you think I won?! Did I? Fuck it, it don't matter what them scores read.* I sighed. *I won it in my heart. I faced down my demons and I found out they wasn't demons at all.* I glanced over at Coach Miller; he just shrugged in his Valentine's track suit and raised his palms up and gave an awkward grin. *They might even be my friends.* I congratulated Aaron as we walked towards his corner; he said "thanks" modestly. I grinned at Coach Miller; he hiked his eyebrows up and split the ropes with his knee and foot for us to climb out.

"We done caught a blessing, Joe," he whispered as I stepped through.

I headed back to the dressing room as Sal went over to work another Chicago corner. *Valentine's sent you home again.* I sighed. *It was a real close fight. What an honor to compete with such an incredible fighter like Williamson. He'll win the tournament, and that's that.*

As I was packing up my bag with my gear alone in the dressing room, a portly Italian guy in a black suitcoat walked in. His shiny black shoes had little golden tips.

"Joe Walsh, nice to meet you, my name is Angelo Dunkin."

"I heard that name before," I said.

He reached over and shook my hand.

"I wanted to tell you, I'm very impressed with your performance. Between you and I, I would have given the decision to you." He grinned genuinely—lines sprouted all over his pudgy face. "You're a really talented fighter. I manage professional boxers, and I think I'd like to work with you. I know it's an Olympic year, and I don't want to mess up your focus or anything like that, but maybe we can sit down and talk sometime. Here's my card. Give me a call next week when you get home and settled in." He handed me a glossy black card with golden writing.

Angelo Dunkin
Professional Boxing Manager
Manager of more than 50 World Champions

"Angelo?" Sal said, stepping into the doorway.

"Sal, how are ya?" They shook hands.

"I'm good. What, are you already trying to swoop in on the kid?"

"I think he won that fight, Sal."

"Maybe, it was close. What can you say? This is boxing. Matter of fact, this is amateur boxing in an Olympic year!"

"Anyway, I've got my eye on him and I think I want to sit down and talk, if you're interested, and see if we can do business together."

"He's his own man, Angelo, I don't get too involved with the business stuff anymore."

"Alright. Call me, kid!"

Angelo tapped his card in my hand with the tip of his pudgy index finger and walked off. *Did that shit really just happen?* I looked at the card like it came from outer space.

Sal hiked his eyebrows up. "He helped Manfredy turn his whole career around on the business end. He's one of the best. You get in with a guy like Angelo, good things are gonna happen for ya, kid."

I ran my finger along the golden letters. *That's a golden future.*

"If you want it. If you want to go pro. But the pros ain't for everybody. It's dangerous and it's a hard road. Look at Nate Bennett, Chicago guy, gets out a prison, makes the Olympics, he's already retired as a pro. But who knows, maybe it'll work out for you."

I could fight on ESPN, Showtime, HBO! Make a living fighting...

"But you still got a outside chance at the Olympics. The trials are coming up in a few months. Let's take it one step at a time."

I stood there in the dressing room listening to Sal. A vision of my future unfolded before me like a riffling deck of cards: fights, bright lights, card girls, Vegas, golden championship belts. *Fuck, I'm gonna be a pro...*

Chapter 12: Fairytales

SOMETIMES IN LIFE I FOUND THAT I WOULD ATTRACT TREMENDOUS ENERGIES, both positive and negative, and they always surprised me and made me wonder if I was in control of them somewhere deep inside of me. Or maybe it was like I was a neutrino, a neutrally charged particle; maybe that was my deepest nature. Set there to observe the positively and negatively charged universe with all its counter-intuitive profundity. And it seemed those negative and positive charges were aware of my neutrality and trying unsuccessfully to attract or repel me because they could see the inevitable collision of my fate that was careening in to annihilate me.

I walked into the kitchen one evening. Dad sat in his seat at the end of the old wooden table, pale and white-haired, drinking a green bottle of O'Doul's.

"We got that job at Fermi," Dad said with a laugh.

"What?!"

"Want to see it? I got the plans right here."

"Sure!"

Dad got up and flopped the heavy blueprint on the old table. He unrolled it; the elaborate blue drawing spread across the long curving grains of lacquered wood. We stood looking down at it.

"It's a drop shaft. We got to go down forty feet. We're building an elevator down there, and that's where the neutrino launcher is down there. Here." He pointed to a circular structure with his thick stubby finger.

"Wait, the launcher is already in?"

"Yeah, they already started working on it, doing tests. We're just building the access elevator. It's a three-year job, we're doing the closing phase of it."

"My professor is on that project! It's his fucking project."

"Well, you might run into him," he said, looking through his pocket notebook. "I just had a big meeting with all the physicists, they tried to get me to let them come down without building any safety path. There's all kinds of crap falling off the shaft. They're cowboys."

Huh, I haven't seen Erickson around campus lately. I went upstairs and emailed him and got an auto reply that he'd taken a sabbatical and wouldn't be responding. I closed my laptop. *Of course, he took sabbatical, his fucking project is about to start. I can't believe I'm going to be part of this thing.* I glanced at my bookshelf full of particle physics and astrophysics books. *It ain't my wildest dreams coming true but it's something. I can always say I was part of the Fermilab Neutrino Project. As a physicist? Naw, a grunt laborer. Haha, better than nothing.*

◆

The Feds made move-in miserable. They had us take classes and tested us on all the potential dangers of Fermilab, put us through federal background checks that a few of our guys didn't pass. So Dad hired Jay; he had some experience in construction, but I figured 'cause he was on probation he wouldn't pass either.

We finally cleared all the hurdles and pulled up in the box truck to the tall makeshift chain-link gate and little metal security booth in front of the site. A chubby blonde-haired guy wearing mirror sunglasses and pointy sideburns stepped briskly up to Rich's window, holding a clipboard in his hand .

"What do you want?" he said.

"I want to go to work," Rich replied.

"Well I don't know if you guys are going to work today. These plates aren't on my list, and the sticker is expired by two weeks."

"Are you serious?"

He leaned into Rich's face.

"Let me tell you something," he said, grimacing. "This is a federal laboratory, we don't cut corners here, and we don't put up with nonsense from construction crews that can't follow the rules."

We came back a couple hours later with the new sticker, and the security guard stomped up, even more pissed off than the first time.

"Open this thing up. Let me see what you got in here."

Rich got out and walked around back with him, undid the lock and latch, and pulled the sliding door open. The sunlight filled the big box as three of us sat on the benches that lined the walls.

"Wohoho… Were you gonna tell me about these three guys back here?"

"Uhh, yeah?"

"Are they cleared?!" he yelled. "How the hell do I know they aren't some terrorist motherfuckers come here to blow up the facility?"

"They're cleared, they have badges."

We all held up our lanyard badges.

"I'm sending you home for not notifying me about them."

"Are you serious, man?" Rich pleaded.

"I'm dead fucking serious," he roared in Rich's face, "about every single thing that comes in and out of this facility!"

Rich hoped back in and turned around and floored it, sending a spray of white pebbles at the security guard.

"This motherfucker's a Nazi!" Rich said, as we laughed in back. "He's the fucking Gate Nazi!"

From then on, he would always and only be referred to as Gate Nazi. We came back the next morning and there he was again, watching us with a bitter smirk. He strolled up with his clipboard.

"I talked with your boss," Gate Nazi told Rich. "He's got real a nice fuckin' vocabulary."

"Yeah, he's my dad, can you imagine how the motherfucker talks to me?"

"So the shitty mouth does run in the family…"

"OK, before we go any further, I got three terrorists in back."

"Badges, wise guy."

We all forked over our badges and he went through our names and passed them back through the window. Finally he walked over, unlatched the tall fence, and pulled the tall chain-link gate open.

"Thanks, Gate Nazi," Rich muttered as he eased into the facility.

The rest of us hooted. "Allahu Akbar!"

◆

Excavation went smooth; they used a big crane and pile driver to drive the brownish metal sheeting into the earth, then the big orange backhoe scooped out the dirt into the dump trucks. When the backhoe got deeper into the clay, us laborers climbed down there in the hole with our spades and filled the backhoe bucket.

A few days in I heard a voice up at the top of the hole shout out:

"Yo Joe!"

I looked up at the square rim of the hole. Jay's dark face smiled down at me; he had a new clean red hard hat on, and a security lanyard and badge dangling off his neck.

I guffawed. "Jay?! How in the hell did you, of all people, pass a goddamn background check?!"

His big white teeth gleamed. "I told you, Joe, I got acquitted everatime, brotha! The probation off a mistamenor."

"Get your ass down here, man! We need some help!"

Jay climbed nervously down the long wooden ladder.

"What? You scared a heights?!" I asked.

"Yeah," Jay said angrily, "but I'm cool though." He looked down. The ladder wobbled and gave him a fright as he trembled, gripping the rungs.

Jay was real fun to work with and loved to work hard. We were two peas in a pod. Rich didn't like it. Then this crazy little Mexican cat with a big goatee named Ziggy showed up. Ziggy just straight up started calling Jay "Nigger" like it was his name.

I thought Jay was going to kill him for a second, but then Jay just laughed and called him "Spic."

They started calling me "Honky," and I called Ziggy "Spic," but I wouldn't call Jay "Nigger."

Finally Jay got mad at me for that. He dug his spade into a big light brownish hunk of clay and gripped the handle near his neck with his blue work gloves. "Why won't you call me Nigger, you damn white-assed Honky!" he roared, playfully.

"'Cause you ain't no Nigger," I said.

That froze Jay, and he stared at me ominously. I dug my spade into the hard clay; my forearm muscle contorted as it sliced deep into a heavy glob.

"That shit dehumanizes black people." I went on.

"Nigger don't mean I ain't human." He spun around and looked at Ziggy. "Aye Spic, how you say black guy in Spanish?"

"Negro!" Ziggy said over his shoulder and flopped a chunk of wet clay into the mighty steel bucket.

"That's cause Spanish come from Latin. My grandaddy a preacher, I learnt latin. Nigger is latin for black. That's all it mean. Look at me mothafucker." He put his arm out towards me; it was especially dark with the summer sun he'd been getting. I put mine out beside it; mine was light brownish and a little red. An angular beam of light poured down on our arms from high above and made the hairs gleam with the oily sweat. "I ain't black and you ain't white but I'm a lot closer to black than you is, so calling me black make sense. Calling me black in Latin don't take away my humanity, Nigga! Only a weak mind would say that lame-ass bullshit." He dismissed the idea with a wave of his meaty arm. "You know what that Spic-ass 26 that shot me said before he pull the trigger?"

I shrugged.

"He whisper 'Aye friend.' Then *bam!* Shot me in the thigh. Don't be calling me friend, Nigga. Call me Nigger all day before you call me friend." He huffed and puffed angrily; his muscles swelled alive under his dirty gray shirt.

I watched his big frame, uneasy. *Shit, is Jay gonna hit me, or tear up?!*

"Joe, if you really my brotha you best call me Nigger. Now do it, you cracker-ass Honky!" Jay pleaded, gripping the handle and stem of his wooden spade and pointing the blade at me like it was a machine gun.

"Alright, Nigger, get back to work!" I faked a whip crack.

"Yessa, masta Honky!" he grinned delightedly.

We laughed and commenced to slicing into the hard clay with our spades.

"Aye Nigger." Ziggy looked around, mystified. "Where are you?!" He looked at me. "*No Momes Guey! He* fucking disappear again! *Santo Cristo de Dios!*" Ziggy crossed himself ominously.

"I'm right here, Spic!" Jay said, glaring at him.

"It's too dark down here." Ziggy kept looking around like he couldn't see Jay standing across from him. "I can't see you unless you smile!"

Jay smiled his big toothy grin.

"Ah, there he is!" He looked at me and explained. "I see his teeth, they white when he smile!"

"I don't have to see you, Spic," Jay said as he hefted a big boulder of clay up to his shoulder. "I can smell them refried black bean farts a mothafuckin' mile away." He gathered his legs beneath him and began to throw. "Spic-ass beaner!!!" He launched the boulder as if it was powered by his words and it shot up over our shoulders, spiraling, then clanged mightily in the backhoe bucket.

Our laughter rose up the curved sculpted clay walls. The clay ran in different hues, from a creamy white to a coffee brown to a deep dark burnt umber to a gray-black. The colors swirled together in the earth, telling the deepest of histories.

We howled and sweated and dug in the summer heat. It was cooler down in the shady hole, except near noon when there was no escape from the brutal sun. Clay ain't like dirt; it suction-cups your spade and your grip goes and you can't make a fist and your forearm cramps up, and you always got someone like Rich looking down at you, yelling every time you take a break to rub a damn cramp out of your forearms. We could see him damn near every time we looked up, his head peering down from that blue square of sky. But we still found a way to laugh through it just to spite him. Our arms were swelling up like balloons, and every once in a while, one of us would look up to the blue above and scream "I CAN'T TAKE IT ANYMORE!!!!!!" And we'd laugh 'cause this work ain't shit and we can take all kinds of hell 'cause being a grunt laborer is fun even when you're down at the bottom of the earth sweating and hurting all over with one boot on 'cause the other boot got stuck in the clay a half hour ago and it was too much to pry it out 'cause you were in a good rhythm.

Everybody thought it was funny that I only had one boot on. Jay said: "Look at this motherfucker with one boot, cutting clay like a madman!"

I laughed. "You know what, next time that fucking Gate Nazi tries some fucking shit, just take a big ol' chunk a' this"—I picked up a lopsided heavy lump of clay—"and smash it in his ugly ass face." I threw it in the backhoe bucket.

We finished excavation and shot all the grades and I was the only one who could shoot the grades and I lorded it over Rich 'cause he acted like he knew every fucking thing. And then Dad showed up and re-shot 'em and sure enough, everything was exactly perfect the first time. Fucker! And we started tying rebar for the foundation. And then Dave came down like a big hero to do the carpentry and level everything out just right while we shagged steel and lumber. We finally poured using the crane bucket; it was easy-peasy, dragging the vibrator through the mud, watching the oxygen bubbles slip up to the surface and pop. And that was just the start.

◆

Things had been progressing with Angelo Dunkin. We'd talked on the phone, and he'd talked with Dad and Mom. Part of me figured it was all talk, but he was actually being a man of his word. But having something that everyone wanted in boxing put a big ol' target on my head. Guys from all over wanted a piece of me and every time I sparred, guys were trying to knock me out. I had a few show fights against guys I already beat, and who knows if it was 'cause they knew I had a deal or because it was an Olympic year, but they fought their goddamned hearts out. I still won but razor-thin wins. Part of it was me too. For the first time in my career, I had something to lose. If I got knocked out cold, would Angelo still want to sign me? Sal wanted me to go down to the PAL Tournament in Florida but I just couldn't get it in gear.

Then I straight up lost to a kid I'd stopped before. But they announced me the winner, and it really dejected me, and the whole crowd booed. That kept me out of the gym for a while. I knew they'd only given me a gift decision 'cause I was ranked in the nation and was in contract talks with Angelo Dunkin. I felt like a big fat phony. And it didn't fire me up at all. I just wanted to hide under a rock until the deal was done with Angelo. I was stuck between an Olympic dream and a professional boxing dream. It was a weird fucking place to be.

◆

A few times back at the job I saw Erickson up at the top of the shaft looking down, puffy strands of his long white beard dangling over the dark metal shaft wall like Rapunzel's locks. *Man, I wonder if I could ever climb up to that level?*

Once I told Jay, "That's my professor." He gave a look like: talk to him, then.

A couple days later Erickson returned to the top of the hole. I shouted up, "That's him!" and Rich told Dr. Erickson that he had a student in the hole. Erickson came back and looked; his bushy white locks puffed out around his yellow hard hat. *Shit! Hide!* I bent back down inside my own shadow and took my little wooden-handled spinner hook and hooked it through the metal loops and snugged it around two green epoxied #7 bars and spun it tight. *What the hell would a Nobel Prize-winning physicist have to say to a grunt laborer like me?* Jay watched me disappointedly. *Come on, Erickson ain't like that.*

When we finished the elevator shaft a bunch of the physicists came down in the hole. We were working on the hallway to the collider room. Erickson walked in with two other guys; they were looking up at the ceiling, scared of falling clay and rock, and they all wore the same yellow hard hats and new clear safety glasses.

"Say what's up to him, Joe," Jay urged me. "Come on, Honky, whatchu scared of? Is you just another pussy-ass whiteboy?"

"Alright." I shrugged. "Nigger."

I walked up to Erickson. "Aye Doctor Erickson, remember me?"

He looked at me confused, so I took off my hard hat and my muck-covered safety glasses.

"Joe! What the heck are you doing here?"

"This is my family company. Remember you told me I might end up on this project one day? Here I am."

"Haha, you've got a good memory. Stevens, Perez, I want you to meet a bright young physics major of mine at Elmhurst College, Joseph Walsh."

"Nice to meet you guys." I took off my ragged gloves and shook their hands. Stevens was a tall, thin black man and Perez was short, fat, and hairy.

"Hey, we were just talking about getting a couple interns on this project," Erickson said, scratching his white beard.

"Ha, where do I sign up for that?!"

"You wouldn't be doing much but getting coffee and taking notes, but would you be interested?" Stevens asked, folding his long skinny arms over his chest.

I shook my head in disbelief. "Yeah, I'm interested. I just read your book on dark matter."

"You did?" He guffawed. "How'd you hear about it?"

"I have a suggested reading list for all my classes," Erickson piped in.

"What'd you think of it?" Stevens asked ominously.

"It's awesome, it gave me chills. You guys are so close to a big discovery."

He grinned and put his narrow hands on his hips.

I went on. "It blows my mind that one of the most mysterious phenomena in the universe might be drastically misunderstood on the particle level."

They giggled at my enthusiasm.

"You guys want me to get coffee for ya? Done. We're shutting down in a week, so I'm yours."

"I was talking to...I guess your Dad? We wanted to just leave it how it is, take the elevator down, and we'd just get hard hats on and kind of run across this little pathway. I can see now it's probably not the most safety-conscious idea."

"You're something else, Doctor Erickson. I love it."

"I just want to get started already. Do you know how long we've been waiting for this?" He looked at his project, so close to completion.

"Four years, I guess?"

"Much longer, my boy, much longer. A lot of us have been waiting our whole lives."

They took off. I grinned at Jay.

He shook his head. "Told you, you fuckin' honkyassed cracker!"

"When you're right you're right, Nigger!"

He grinned and patted me on the back, and we kept stacking lumber. Erickson gave me a call the next day.

"Joe, it's official. We're expanding our team, and since you already have your clearance and I enjoy working with you, and you impressed Stevens and Perez, we've decided to officially invite you on to the team."

"Holy crap!"

"Can you do it?"

"Yeah, when do we start?"

"Three weeks. Glad to have you on the team. We've looked into it, they'll be mailing you your new badge in the next few days."

◆

I cruised out to Batavia for my first day at Fermilab as an Assistant Physicist Intern. I pulled in to the grounds with the top off the Jeep and the warm summer air blowing through my hair. The clear sunny day lit the whole property. As I passed the buffalo, one young bull trotted out in the field by himself. His puffy brown coat glimmered in the sunlight as he tossed his curved horns in the air fiercely and joyfully.

It felt bizarre pulling up to the gate in anything other than a work truck. Gate Nazi looked at me, then took a double take.

"Oh no." He shook his head. "Uhuh, you guys been outta here two weeks, I don't have to ever deal with you knuckleheads no more." He walked up and put his elbows on my window sill. "What the hell do you want?"

"I'm here for work."

"You! What, do they need a ditch dug? The only workers left here are landscapers."

"I ain't here to build stuff, I'm here to destroy stuff. Fundamental particles and shit like that." I handed him my new badge.

"What is this, you get this printed up at Kinkos? Get outta here. Assistant Physicist Intern?" He held the badge up and looked at me. It was the same picture of me in my dirty work shirt with the sleeves cut off.

"Joseph Walsh." He glanced around my Jeep. "Alright, where's the camera? This is *Candid Camera*, right?" He looked out into the bushes.

"Call it in, Gate Nazi, you're about to be damned embarrassed."

"Call it in, call it in, he says," Gate Nazi muttered as he walked away to his little Nazi booth.

He got on the phone and read off the numbers, and Hitler must have told him something funny because he started laughing. He walked back to my Jeep.

"This is one of the damndest things I ever done, letting a knucklehead like you in this place."

"I'm a physicist, man, you didn't know dat?"

"You're a boxer and you ain't a good one. I don't care what they say. You're always walking around with a black eye." He looked at the badge and flicked it with his middle finger. "And now you're a flipping physicist?!" He signaled for the Nazi-in-training to open the gate. "How'd you do it?"

I shrugged as the gate swung open.

"Just got lucky, I guess."

"Lucky. Hmm, he's lucky..." He grinned and threw his hands up exasperatedly as I rolled through.

◆

I parked near the neutrino shooter. It was this white building with a red brick façade that read MINOS on it. I got out and went to the elevator and headed down.

I entered a big room. A technician in a white jacket was cranking on some bolts on a big contraption. *Is that the neutrino shooter?* I approached the elaborate machine; it had folded metal structures wrapped around the main barrel-like tube. Deep inside the barrel seemed to glow a light red, like the innards of being. The apparatus around the barrel was a thick circular refrigeration system. The tech turned to see me as I walked up behind him, and I saw a familiar set of bushy eyebrows around his clear-framed safety glasses: Dydecky!

His eyes bugged out.

"Joe?! What the hell are you doing here!" he asked, and dropped the wrench and reached out and squeezed my shoulder.

"I'm on the team, Dydecky, you didn't hear? I'm sweepin' floors and making coffee."

"Holy mackerel, Joe! Good on you." Dydecky grinned and picked the wrench back up. "Welcome aboard."

"You aren't leaving Gordon, are you?"

"Naw, never. High school physics is my calling. Erickson talked me into coming in for the summer. I'm free, so why the hell not?"

"How the heck did we end up back here again?"

"The world is circular, Joe," He twisted on the wrench in a big arc. "You seek hard enough, you end up right back where you started."

"Well, this place sure as hell ain't where I started!"

"Ha! Didn't you have a big boxing tournament or something recently?"

"Yeah."

"How'd it go?"

"I got obliterated."

"But not annihilated, I hope?"

"Almost, almost annihilated." I grinned and sat down in a roller chair near him. "But don't forget, I'm the Annihilator." I spun in a circle in the chair, feinted a hook at him as he chuckled.

◆

Early on we had to drive up to Minnesota, to the Soudan Mine where the target was. I offered to drive; Dydecky was my co-pilot. It was about a nine-hour trek north. I did it in eight, with the team laughing and dozing in the big white van.

The mine was in a state park at the base of Lake Vermillion. We got there after nightfall; we wound around a thick, dark, forest and parked near a big old mining operation with rusty structures that sprouted out of a hill, and a big bridge-looking thing that was an old conveyer belt for the mine. We grabbed the gear and walked down into the rocky old facility; it smelled like rust and mildew.

Down inside was a long, tall, rocky-walled room with stark lights rigged into the ceiling. A series of gigantic octagon-shaped metal structures towered over us.

"This is it!" Dydecky said. "This is the goal, my boy! The target!"

"So we're going to send neutrinos across the country through bedrock and hit this thing?" I asked. "What if we miss?"

"We won't." Dydecky winked at me.

As we stepped deeper into the tunnel, a huge mural came into view on the wall beside the target, a reddish-orange glob like a sun that faded to blue at its edges. It glowed alive and seemed to radiate energy. I peered into its yellowish-red eye. *The Annihilator's goal is a smoldering sun halfway across the country. Looks like a gold medal to me. Well, let's see if you can help 'em get gold, Joey.*

We bounced back and forth from Fermi to the Mine. I did all the driving. They loved it because most of them didn't even have licenses. I listened to their wild theoretical debates on the long rides. The Double Slit Experiment confounded me. It was an old experiment which sent light through two slits to a target on the other side. The experiment found that light changed its behavior depending on whether or not an intelligent observer was watching it. If no instrument was watching the photons, they acted as a wave and showed an interference pattern on the target. But if there was an instrument observing them, the photons behaved like particles when they hit the target. The idea was that somehow observation was interacting with the particles and making them conform to a different behavior. We put in long hours at Fermilab and the Soudan Mine. I stayed out of the way mostly and kept the coffee coming.

But I was slacking on my training.

After avoiding Sal for a week, I finally grew a pair and leveled with him. I gave him a call as I was leaving Fermilab after a long day making coffee and helping tinker around.

"Sal, I ain't focused, I ain't motivated, I ain't going down to Florida. I'm sorry. I know it's an Olympic box-off qualifier but I ain't going. I ain't going down there and getting my ass kicked 'cause I'm not a hundred percent focused. I just keep thinking about turning pro, and things with

Angelo are going good. And I got this project at Fermilab I'm working on..."

"Alright then, kid. Thank you for being honest. Take some time off and come back when you're focused."

"I just don't want to waste your time. I respect you too damn much."

"Damn straight, kid. Come home when you're ready."

◆

It was fun being around the Fermilab team. I was one of three assistants. The other two went to University of Chicago. They were really smart kids, and pretty easygoing too.

Problems disrupted the project early on. The neutrinos missed the target the whole first week. You ever seen a physicist have a meltdown? Erickson was literally pulling white hairs out of his head; his bald spot more than doubled in diameter that week. One of the UChicago kids was Korean; he kept bowing and asking if this meant he had to go home.

Dydecky told me to switch every pot to decaf. That slowed them down enough to figure out what was going on with the shooter.

The debate popped up over some coffee and donuts in the big board room.

"A hundredth of an inch off in aim is equal to a hundred yards when it gets there."

"That's not true," Dydecky said. "It's more than a kilometer! It's forty-five kilometers, to be exact."

"So you're telling me we're shooting neutrinos to Minneapolis?" I asked.

"No, we're shooting neutrinos into Lake Superior."

I laughed. "People drink that water."

"Purified Great Lakes water with neutrino flavor," Erickson said.

"Look, it's simple trigonometry." Dydecky started drawing triangles on the big whiteboard and arguing with Erickson, and finally they figured out they were shooting neutrinos near Green Bay, Wisconsin, which made us glad because Green Bay is full of dumbass, no-good cheeseheads. Even the Korean agreed about that.

Finally, they focused the target and the neutrinos fired through hundreds of miles of bedrock and managed to strike the target and disintegrate, splintering into tinier particles and sending data spewing out of the computers. But it was completely unreadable because they'd improperly installed the sensors.

It was another whole week before usable data finally began to flow through the system. The physicists ran around like little kids with their data; they called their parents and wives and old friends from school. Have you ever seen a sixty-year-old Nobel Prize–winning physicist jump up and give a fifty-three-year-old one from Belgium a high-five? I've seen things, my friends. The data staggered them, kept them there pulling all-nighters. I stuck around because it felt like at any moment, this evidence would alter the history of particle physics forever.

The evidence smashed a lot of hypotheses in the early going; at one point Perez from Argentina burst into tears looking at his screen. He'd spent six years on a paper that a major journal had published; he'd convinced himself that the evidence from this project would establish his whole career and get all his future projects green-lit, but the evidence proved him wrong and it was clear as day; his dream died on a computer screen.

Erickson walked up behind him, put his small hands on Perez's shoulders, and consoled him.

"I've put years on many theories, son, and they've flat-lined at this stage. Your idea was fantastic, that's why I picked you. Your ideas have great energy, and this mind of yours is sure to do wonderful things." He tapped him softly on the head with a rolled-up printout. "But this is science, and when the science knocks you down you have to accept that you've been knocked down, and get up, and start again. I didn't pick you for this idea. I picked you for this brilliant mind, which is capable of coming up with many more great ideas."

Erickson was a mixture of coach and guru. He didn't just lead the project; he worked to inspire the minds of the future. He constructed odd and diverse teams; he knew the basics of several languages enough to communicate ideas, and he always went to the math when the language barrier got in the way. He'd jump on the dry-erase board and argue with his marker and then hand it off to Zou, the Korean, who tried and often failed, and would then bow in submission to his maestro.

About the fourth week in it dawned on me that my duties consisted of more than just head coffee kid. (Though they did love the mean strong coffee I made.)

One day Dydecky got into a heated argument with Tompkins in the board room; by this time the white-topped tables were cluttered with paper, and the big white marker boards littered with equations in red, blue, and green ink. "Listen," Dydecky said. "This kid understands string theory better than you. Joe, come here, explain to him why dark matter is invisible." Dydecky's bushy black eyebrows popped up animatedly.

I walked up and carefully refilled their coffee mugs with the half-full glass pot. "Alright, so dark matter's an unobservable phenomenon which can only be found in mathematics and in the behaviors of massive gravitational objects. It's the invisible yin…" I gestured toward Dydecky with the coffee pot. "…to our observable yang." I swung the pot softly toward Tomkins, as he whisked his sandy blond hair off his forehead. "It's visible, as in gravity is visible when you throw a ball and it arcs to the ground. It appears invisible because it is made of something unobservable with our current tools, but it is visible like the blueprint of a building is visible. When you observe the structure, it's visible, like a man's ideas are visible in his eyes and in his language," I pontificated, raising the coffee pot towards the marker board; the bright white lamps shined through it and turned it a light-amber brown. "Dark matter is like a metaphor for everything we don't understand about all of existence."

"You get it now?" Dydecky urged.

"Ideas in his eyes?!" Tompkins smirked.

"Yes! Consciousness is quantum. Haven't you read Penlily's ideas on this?"

"Oh god, that's the one place where Penlily and I agree to disagree."

"Wait, consciousness is quantum?" I asked, as my mind reeled.

"Yes, there are microtubules in our neurons that create consciousness. It's been proven," Dydecky confirmed.

"If consciousness is quantum, then that solves the Double Slit Experiment. It's some sort of entanglement," I said.

"Joe!" Dydecky's eyes bugged out. "I've never heard it put so succinctly."

"Oh great, call up Penlily and have a big party!" Tomkins dismissed us with a sneer. "I won't be lectured about string theory by Erickson's little subaltern mascot. He's nothing but a laborer who gets hit in the head for fun! I hold a PhD in Physics from MIT!" Tompkins stomped off to field a call on his little cellular phone.

"Come on, Tompkins," Dydecky called after him. "Think outside the box, for Christ's sake!" Dydecky winked at me. "You're great at getting grants and doing talks, but you got a B in Particle Physics at U of C! I was there!"

◆

When school started up, they gave us assistants our walking papers. Gate Nazi X'd out our badges but let us keep them. I glanced at my badge, my stupid face; the day they took my picture I was just a construction worker excited to help build an elevator for the project. *I don't think I made any important contributions, but damn, this was one of the most thrilling times in my life. Well, there's always boxing...*

Erickson walked us to the gate and gave all of us eager handshakes. He looked me in the eyes and squeezed my hand energetically.

"I'm so happy we could work together, Joe. Thank you for your contributions," he said as his wild white locks spiraled around his face in the wind. He looked like a giant for a moment, not the short round old man that he was. We all seemed like tiny little children before him, sadly wishing we could stay and play pretend just a little longer.

"I wish you all the best of luck in your promising careers as physicists. Be in touch," he said, and I slinked off to the Jeep.

Well, you did it, Joe. I started the engine. You were a physicist at Fermilab. Probably the lowest rank humanly possible but you were part of it, anyway. It's all downhill from here, buddy...haha, well, maybe not.

I pulled up on Gate Nazi and paused as he smirked at me behind his mirrored sunglasses and leaned his elbows on the window of his little white Nazi booth.

"See ya around, Gate Nazi." I said with a grin.

"I don't ever want to see your knucklehead ass around here again," Gate Nazi told me, with a glimpse of sadness in his voice.

I cranked the radio and Tool spewed from the speakers. I floored it out of the lot with the top down and the doors off. *All because of Jay. I'ma have to do something special for that motherfucker.* I giggled as the wind whipped through my hair.

Chapter 13: Jay

SOON I WAS BACK AT SCHOOL AND PUTTING IN TWO DAYS A WEEK CONSTRUCTION.

I got a call from Dad sending me to DeCanio's to pick up parts and material and bring it to Rich's job way out west. I told him I'd meet him in a parking lot down the road from the job.

When I pulled up next to him and got out, he was twitching, all crazy amped up. His pudgy body trembled with energy under his gray T-shirt as he bounced around on the tips of his steel-toed boots.

"You hear Rose is pregnant?" he asked me.

"Really?" I asked. "Wow, no I didn't."

"Yeah, that nigger knocked her up."

"Wait, Jay and Rose are pregnant?" The idea of Rose and Jay starting a family first gave me fear, then joy.

I picked up a box of sixteen double-heads and carried them to Rich's truck. *They really love each other. I bet Jay'll be a great dad.*

"I just smashed his whole face open," Rich said.

"What are you talking bout?" I put the box of double-heads down in the back of his truck. "Stop calling him that shit! He's my friend."

Rich started talking fast and angrily. "That nigger is trying to pimp out our sister! You think he's your friend?!" He positioned himself like he wanted to sucker-punch me from the side.

Did he really hit Jay? Is this motherfucker gonna take a poke at me now? I plopped a box of tie wire in his truck.

"Whose side are you on?!" Rich roared, hovering over my shoulder.

The hair on the back of my neck stood up and pin prickles lit up along my neck and shoulders. I spun around on him. He grimaced, his bitch tits all swelled up, his fists clenched.

"What the fuck are you doing?!" I snapped. I tensed and squared up with him, clenching my fists as he recoiled and shrunk. "Don't ever fucking creep up on me like that!"

His face sobered and he started to help move the supplies from my truck to his.

"Look, I just, I want to protect Rose," he implored. "I can't let her get mixed up with this shit again."

"You think you're helping her? Punching the guy she's in love with? Are you fucking nuts!? Look if you really did that crap, you're a piece of shit. Jay loves her and she loves him. That guy is a good person, he's my friend."

I jumped in my truck and pulled off. *Did that shit really happen?*

◆

What really happened was Rose had woken sick again. She had a pregnancy test in her nightstand from a scare a few months before. She took the test into the bathroom and came out in shock. She yelled to Jay as he pulled his work boots on. They read the box together and they looked at the test. Rose started to cry. Jay took her in his arms and held her and kissed her and told her, "You're going to make a great momma." They held each other and they made love and they were incredibly happy.

Jay had gotten to work on time, and he walked up to Rich to tell him.

"Rosie pregnant. We having a baby!" Jay said with joy and pride.

Rich sneered and squirmed in his seat. And recoiled like he'd been stabbed.

"Well, you gonna marry her!?" Rich asked.

"Man, I ain't never gettin' married. I'm the daddy though, I'm the daddy of yo niece! We think it's gon' be a girl. We kin now, man!"

Rich rolled up the window in Jay's face.

"I'm gon' take care a my responsibilities!" Jay said, flustered.

While Jay got to work, Rich called Nancy and told her the news. He started to work himself up into an insane rage, taking what Jay said and twisting into some nasty nightmarish version of his deepest fears for his little sister.

A truck with a trailer full of lumber pulled up. Jay went over and started unloading it by hand. Rich got out and started following Jay as he worked, picking up stacks of two-by-fours off the trailer bed and carrying them to a cribbed-up stack on the site.

"You're fired," Rich said. "Get the fuck outa here."

Jay looked at him, confused. "I don't work for you, man. I work fo yo daddy." Jay walked back to the stack and grabbed another set of two-by-fours.

Rich followed him, looking ready to punch him. "If you ain't gonna marry my sister, then get the fuck outa here, you piece a' shit!"

As Jay bent down to place the lumber on the stack, Rich swung upward with all his might. His fist smacked into Jay's eye. The momentum of Jay crouching down and Rich punching up compounded the blow. The punch fractured Jay's eye socket and split open a nasty cut along his brow. The lumber tumbled all over the place. Jay stumbled backward, shocked by the sudden cheap shot while he was doing—of all things—his job.

Jay gripped his eye as blood burst from the cut and rippled down all over his neon green work vest. Rich hopped back and bounded up and down, a clownish version of a boxer—his fists clenched and up.

"I got you, now come on and get me, motherfucker!" Rich shouted in this weird high-pitched voice.

Jay looked at Rich, and looked behind him at the short concrete wall that lined the bridge. The heavy traffic from 88 was flowing down below, and he started for Rich, intent on picking him up and throwing him right off.

Then something came to him. He thought about Rose and that tiny little baby inside her growing. That baby was his and hers, and a creation of their deep love. He stopped and grabbed at his heart.

"We family…" Jay muttered.

He walked to his car, got in, and drove off. He got on the phone and called his best friend, who was down in Kansas City.

When the friend picked up, Jay just said, "I need you, nigga!" and hung up.

Then Jay called Rose and drove to the hospital, where they stitched him up and put a big patch over his eye.

◆

Rose was the one who told me what happened. She was so patient about it all. I just told her I loved her and was sorry it happened and congratulated her.

Over the weekend I finally got Jay on the phone. I was chilling out on my bed watching boxing, trying to get my head back into the game, when Jay picked up. I paused the TV on teenaged Tyson shooting a vicious hook in black-and-white footage with Cus looming in the shadows.

"How are ya, man?"

"I'm alright, Joe, I'm cool."

"Sorry about what Rich did. I tried to warn you about him. Man, he's a snake."

"Yeah, I remember you saying that, but I never thought he'd be a coward like that. Hitting me while I was workin'!"

"I'm sorry he did that. If I was there I wouldn't 'a let him sneak up on you like that."

"Yeah, I just can't believe he pulled that shit. I was gonna throw him off the fucking bridge!"

"Hahaha...I bet you were."

"I was sent off so bad I call my guy, my brotha. He drove up here from Kill City with guns loaded, ready to smoke somebody."

"Really?"

"He was gon' kill your brotha! But I told him naw. I still ain't tolt him what happened. It's cool though, I ain't seen him in a minute. We catching up."

I blinked, looking out my window into the bright sunlight bleeding through the tall pine tree that sat between our house and Rich's house. *Damn, what kinda guy would drop everything and drive eight hours to protect his friend? Fuck, what if Jay woulda told him what Rich'd done?* I sighed.

"Hey, look, but what I really wanted to say is: Welcome to our family."

"Thanks, Joe."

"Congratulations. I'm sure you're gonna be a good dad. I'm really happy for you guys."

"That mean a lot to me, Joe. Joe, man, want to tell you something, brotha."

"Go ahead, Jay."

"I love you."

It caught me off guard. I sat there with the phone against my ear, befuddled. An awkward pause bubbled up. *I don't want to say it if I don't mean it. Do I fucking love this dude? I never woulda started boxing if it wasn't for him. He got me to talk to Erickson that day, he's been good to Rose, he came to so many of my fights. All those days working in the hole with Ziggy. He's like a goddamned brother to me. Now he's the dad of my niece or nephew. Hell yeah, I love Jay.*

"I love you too, Jay."

"See, that's what I'm talking about. I told yo momma I loved her, and she wouldn't say it back. Hurt my feelins."

"Shit, get used to it. She hardly ever says it to me!"

He laughed.

"Seriously, though, Jay. Are you OK?"

"Everything else been cool! I came off probation now, I'm clear, and this mothafucker the other day he tried to steal fifty bucks from me! We was playing quarters and I stole on that fool, straight knocked him out."

"You're crazy, man! You have to cool that shit out!"

"Naw, man, fighting is what I love to do! That's why it was so hard not to throw your brother off that bridge the other day."

"I know it was, I can imagine. Thank you for not killing my brother."

He laughed.

"I might have to fuck him up over this, though. That shit was wrong. He tried to do the same shit to me a few times! I think he was trying to cheap shot me later that same day he hit you, but I just spun around on him and he got all scared and shit."

"He a coward."

"Yeah, he is. I tried to warn you, Jay."

"You did, Joe, you right."

"Maybe I'll fuck him up one of these days."

"Naw, don't do that shit fo' me, fool! Dat's yo brother! This shit ain't between y'all. It between me and him. Look, I got one thing I want to ask you for, something I really need you to do for me, Joe."

"Anything, Jay, anything, brother."

"OK."

"You know what I want. I want to get your brother down there with Brother Alex in the wrestling room. Just me and him with the gloves on, and you and Brother just close the door and leave us in there, 'til we through."

"Ohhhh man, that'd be beautiful!" I guffawed. "Yes, I'll do it! I'll get him down there. I'll fuck with him endlessly until he does it."

"Bet, that's a deal. Joe, thank you, brother. What's going on with you and boxing, what's next?"

"I don't know, there's the Olympic Trials coming up soon, the Midwest Trials, I can go out there and try. Then, if I win, I go to the box-offs. But I don't know, man, I might just turn pro or hang 'em up. I don't even know, it's all just too much for me right now. Too much pressure."

"Whatchu mean, 'you don't know'? People'd kill to be in your shoes right now! Man, sign me up for them Olympic Trials! But for real, Joe, you got to be crazy to pass this up, you never know! You could win that thing and go the Olympics, brah."

"Yeah..." I pressed Play on the video and young Tyson came alive on the screen. A symphony of punches erupted from his frame. *Even that kid wasn't the Olympian.*

"You got to go, man. Promise me you goin'."

"Alright, I'll go."

"Good, you could win it, man!"

"Thank you, Jay, I can't wait to see that baby."

"You know it's gonna be a girl, right?"

"How the hell do you guys know that already?! How far along is she?"

"Naw, it ain't like that, we just know, we got her name picked out and everything."

"Hahah, OK, great."

"It's Nolani."

"That's a real pretty name, man. But hey, Jay, I gotta go, I'll see you real soon."

"Aye remember, I loves ya."

"Love you too, Jay."

"Alright, peace."

"See ya."

◆

I went to the gym and trained that night and things went good for the first time since before nationals. I left feeling fine and crossed Ogden with my gym bag on my shoulder. *I'm glad I talked to Jay. All that frustration about what Rich did just disappeared. And Jay's right too. So many people'd kill to have a shot at the Olympics. I can't let this shit slip through my fingers. I gotta fucking go for it.*

I threw my gym bag in the back of the Jeep and jumped in. *Jay'll prove he's a good father, just watch. Fucking Rich the bitch.* Images of six-foot-one, 240-pound Jay whipping Rich around the old wrestling room until Brother Alex and I had to burst in and stop the fight. I saw Rich lying bloody on the mat screaming for help and laughed. I threw it in gear and whipped a U-turn. *I want to see that shit!*

As I passed over the shipping canal and accelerated into the ramp onto 55 some kind of galactic cloud swirled into the car. It sucked me into a deep dream. It was like someone else took the wheel and led me up the ramp onto the interstate.

In vivid living color, I watch as Jay and his friend pull up in front of Rich's house in broad daylight. Fresh bandages cover Jay's damaged eye. A neon-green hospital bracelet clings to his dark wrist. They exit the vehicle and dash up the porch steps to the front door. Rich sees them coming and turns and runs upstairs where he keeps his guns as they follow, scrambling up the steps as I float in behind them. I hear Rich chamber a round in a gun. A tussle as I float up the steps. Rich screams; a shot explodes through his voice, and they run through me down the steps and out the door. The car pulls away as I float into Rich's room. Rich lies dead, a bullet hole through his chest, his mouth open, face faded, gray. Nancy rushes in, kneels over him, screams. The gun lies beside Rich. I pick it up, run outside to the Jeep, floor it toward Maywood, pull up in front of Jay's house as they hop out of their car and run inside. Jump out, chase them. They see me. I shoot. They run up the steps. I follow inside the enclosed front porch. Jay lies on the floor, gripping the open trembling wound in his thigh.

I stand over him and put the pistol barrel to his temple. He breathes hard, stares into the dark wound in his thigh. I try to pull the trigger. I can't. *He's my friend. He's my brother.* I grip my head and scream. A force grips my chest. I look into my brother's eyes. They tremble with tears. "Naw, Joe, you got to. He's your brother. You have to," Jay says.

I point the gun to his temple and squeeze the trigger. I shoot awake cruising on the 1st Avenue exit ramp over the Des Plaines River with the highway lights gleaming over the waters. I burst out into laughter. *What the fuck was that?! I can't wait to tell Jay about that shit!* I giggled nervously. *That was the most vivid daydream of my entire life. How the fuck didn't I crash?!* I don't remember any of the ride—getting off at the exit ramp, nothing.

I pulled up in front of the house and all four of the cars'd vanished. *Am I still fucking dreaming? Naw, they just took the kids for ice cream at*

Tate's. Dad's working late, and Jan and Rose are out. Or maybe there's a birthday party or something…

I walked in the house. The lights, the TVs, all of them on. I walked around nervously. It was one of the few times in my whole damn life I came home to an empty house. *Maybe it's a joke? They're gonna surprise me…*

"Hello? HELLOOOO!"

I called Rose; she didn't answer. I called Dad; he didn't answer. I called Rich's house, and Nancy answered. I paced nervously in the TV room.

"OK… what's going on?" I said playfully.

"You didn't hear yet?

"Hear what?"

"OK, sit down, honey."

"Just fucking tell me!"

"OK, Jay got shot tonight."

"What? OK." I felt for my keys. "OK, what hospital is he at?"

"No, honey, Jay got shot tonight and Jay died."

"What?"

"He's dead."

A big old rusty hook stabbed me in the gut and ripped through my intestines. I fell to my knees gripping it. Then I reached down and gripped the rug in my hands and screamed with rage and agony and regret.

I must have dropped the phone. It was on the carpet next to me. I picked it up.

"…you OK? Do you want someone to come over there?"

"You're fucking lying to me, you fucking bitch! He's not dead!"

I hung up on her and called Dad again and he picked up.

"Is he really dead?"

"I, I can't believe it, Joe. He, he's gone. He's dead. We're at the coroner's office. He died right there in the street in Rosie's arms."

◆

Rosie came home last. I waited for her out on the curb. She got out of the car and I gave her a hug and I told her I was sorry and I loved her.

We sat down in the kitchen and talked about Jay. We talked late into the night. Her strength was overwhelming. I didn't ask her what happened; I figured she'd already had to tell the story a few times that night to the police and I didn't want her to feel like she had to tell me. We just talked like brother and sister about someone we both loved who passed away and was gone forever. I kept hoping that I'd blink and wake up and it'd be a bad dream and it'd be over and everybody would be fine.

Then she started talking about it.

"Jay got into a fight a week ago with this guy Sammy Evans, and he busted his whole eye open just like what Rich did to him."

"He told me about that yesterday."

"That's the guy, Sammy. That's the guy who shot him. Sammy killed Jay."

"Fuck, I tried to tell him not to be fighting out there."

We all heard the story eventually.

It started with Rose and Jay leaning against Rose's Tempo out front of Jay's house. Jay smoking a Newport and them hugging and kissing. Jay knew that Sammy was looking for him, but it wasn't the first time somebody had set out to kill Jay so he wasn't too concerned.

Rose had leaned her back against the Tempo, and Jay was kissing her neck. She noticed a guy come out of the alley walking right toward them. She pulled away from Jay and he looked at her and she looked at the guy walking toward them. Jay turned to look just as Sammy jogged up and raised a .44 and fired *Boom... boom... boom.*

As Sammy approached, Jay got in front of Rose and shouted "No!" then he nudged her behind a tree and sprinted the other way, taking the danger. He was thinking of the baby, I have to believe.

Jay was bleeding as he ran but Sammy followed him across the street, still firing. Rose jumped in the car and drove toward the gunshots as Jay ran through a cut, but Sammy had grown up with Jay and he knew all the cuts and there was no escaping. Jay sprinted toward Madison Avenue. Rose drove around and turned onto Madison. A squad car with its lights on responding to shots fired swerved around her as Jay exhaustedly dashed out into the street a half block down. Sammy followed him and squeezed a shot that struck Jay's arm and shattered the bone.

Jay collapsed into the middle of the street. Sammy ran out and stood over him.

"Sammy, man, stop! I got a baby, I got a baby on the way."

Driving fast toward them, the officers reached their guns out the windows and opened fire on Sammy, trying to save Jay's life.

Sammy shot Jay in the temple and ran.

The squad car swerved around Jay and chased Sammy into an empty lot, still firing on him.

Rose pulled up, threw it in park, and rushed up to Jay. He lay on the ground as blood pooled under him. So much blood it was a lake, with Jay as a ship in the center.

Rose held him as blood poured out in a pencil-thick line and spilled out and oozed onto the blacktop.

Jay's best friend ran up gripping his revolver and screamed, "Who dat is?!"

"It's Jay."

"Naw, dat ain't fucking Jay!" he screamed, and ran off.

The blood seemed to stop and she thought he died. People ran up, fought and screamed, and she stood and tried to call 911, and looked around for a street sign to tell them the intersection.

"Rose! Don't leave me, Rosie."

She looked back and he reached his arm out toward her and she ran back and kneeled and took his hand and held him in her arms.

Jay touched her belly and said, "I love you."

"I'm here, baby… I'm here… I wouldn't leave you. I love you, stay with me, the ambulance is coming. We love you. Stay."

Jay tried, but he took his last breaths and died right there on 15th and Madison.

Chapter 14: Neutrinos

WE LOST JAY AND I NEVER GOT OVER IT. Part of me was always hoping I would wake up and he'd be alive, just dip into some alternative universe where he escaped that night and never went back to Maywood. That last moment of his life touching Rose's belly, the baby, the last moments before he passed into the next world. It mystified me and would haunt me for all my days on this earth.

The thing Rich'd done made a bigger rift between us. Him and Blake had become these kind of fake good guys, villains who pretended to be heroes, and people bought it. They were like positrons, particles with false charge, so false that it created an existential threat. The weird part about it was they were family men. They were pillars of the community. It all made me resent society—resent the lie of it, the false human beings claiming to be pure and good and knowing that they were nothing close to that, that in fact they were bad and even monsters. It made me not want to be part of that society. Jay was like an electron, a being at peace in his nature. He lived a wild life, dealt drugs, and was in and out of jail but he was a good person, a generous friend. All of it confounded me—sucked me in and repelled me in equal parts. That someone could be summed up as bad or good, knowing that neither were true. Humanity was bigger than that; it was complex and confusing, and I grappled with that for a couple weeks. Trying to figure out where I fit in that good and bad structure and who I wanted to be in this world.

I tried to keep training, but Jay's death put me in a dark place. I didn't want to do anything. I just lay around and drank and talked with Lauren about it. I hit the gym and just couldn't break a sweat, couldn't muster up the hunger. As the Midwest Trials closed in, I just couldn't focus. I started second-guessing about even going at all.

My cell phone woke me up one Saturday afternoon. I lay on my back on the mattress on the floor of Lauren's room in Burkhart's attic with the blue sky in the window at my feet and the steady soar of traffic coasting past on Halsted. I answered.

"Joe? Emanuel Miller here. Sal give me your number, now what's this I'm hearing, you talking 'bout just up and turning pro and not fighting in the Olympic Trials?"

I sat up in bed.

"You're going to the Midwest Trials, aren't you?"

"I don't know, Mr. Miller."

"Joe, you will win the Midwest Trials. I've been calling around talking to the other coaches, we've been going through the list thinking of who could beat you, but we can't find nobody we're sure has a shot. There's a fella in Texas, and there's a guy in New York and one in California, and they are very good but when I try to put someone ahead of you in the Midwest here, there's no one I can think of. Aaron's already qualified, the boy from Toledo, they both qualified for the Olympic box-offs already, they won't be at the Midwest. I don't say these kind of things to young boxers, Joe, but it would be a crying shame if you didn't go to the Midwest Trials. It's every athlete's dream to have a shot at representing their country at the Olympic Games. Come on now, will you at least think about it, son?"

I closed my eyes. My head ached from last night's booze. Jay's face emerged in my mind; the wound gaped at his temple, dark liquid all around him. His eyes opened, watching me. I promised Jay.

"Joe?" Emanuel's voice snapped me out of it.

"Alright, alright, I'm going, Mr. Miller. Thank you."

"Good. Very good. OK now, the other reason I asked for your number is, we're putting a camp together next month and I need good sparring for my light-heavy Eddie Banks. He's going to the Midwest Trials and I've got a cruiserweight from Poland coming to town. He's getting ready for a big fight on HBO and a light-heavy contender needing work, and Aaron's here. It's two weeks of sparring, your food, housing, and evera-thang is taken care of and we give you an allowance too. But you gotta give us that good work."

"OK, I will." I rubbed my head, imagining sparring with Williamson every day for two weeks.

"Alright, so I'll be calling you in about three weeks and you can drive out. We'll pay your gas or we could even fly ya out, whatever you want."

"Alright, I'll probably drive."

"That sounds fine. Now come out here in shape or these men will put a whoopin on you."

"I will, I've been in the gym."

"That's what I figured. Talk with you real soon, son."

"Thanks for calling, Mr. Miller."

I lay on my back in bed staring at the ceiling. *Well, that was surreal. Emanuel Miller called you asking for sparring.* It wasn't so out of the ordinary; a lot of guys from Windy City went out there to Valentine's in Detroit and out to Big Bear in California. Sometimes they were the ones hiring sparring partners and bringing them into Chicago. There was a camp in Florida too and one in New York the guys had gone to. *Still, shit. This is my first time being asked. I must've impressed him.*

I headed to the gym and nervously asked all the guys at Windy City what sparring was like at Valentine's, and they said hard like a fight but even harder. That made me nervous and it lit a fire under me in the gym. I started getting ready for the Trials 'cause for all I knew these two weeks sparring at Valentine's might be harder than the damn Trials. I looked up the Polish guy, he was 23-0 with 18 knockouts. The interim WBC title was on the line and that got me even more nervous and excited, 'cause if I could hang with that guy, then that really meant something.

◆

Angelo Dunkin faxed over the contract to my dad's machine and we set up a meeting. Angelo planned to come to town in a few weeks to work on a deal with Golata and wanted to take Lauren and me out for a steak dinner, and talk about and potentially sign the contract. I talked with Dad about the contract and he said it looked fine and wasn't too binding, and that all it meant was that you intended to sign with him once you ended your amateur career.

Lauren and I headed down to Morton's Steakhouse and met Angelo and sat in a nice circular leather booth. The huge, blackened, and rare steak with the ground pepper and sea salt delighted us. We ordered a few drinks and relaxed and Angelo really made me feel like he cared about me and treated Lauren real nice and he laid it all out for me over a glass of aged Scotch.

Angelo undid his black tie and stuffed it in his suit coat. Perspiration dotted his wide balding forehead. His dark eyes focused on me steadily. A small jazz ensemble played lightly in the nearby bar section. Lauren watched them merrily, her head swaying slightly. Her gorgeous thick lips grinned in profile in the low light from the chandeliers.

"Now, if you win the Midwest Trials that will be very big for your career. It will put you in the Olympic box-offs. And if you are able to beat one or two of those kids at the box-offs and look OK when you lose, it's highly likely Top Rank, King, or Main Events will make an offer. If you lose twice right away, you might get an offer, you might not. If you are the Olympian, son, you'll be a wealthy man out of the gate. If you win a gold medal in Athens, I'll negotiate a million-dollar contract for you."

He winked at me as we both grinned and brought our thick short glasses of Scotch to our lips for a sip; the rich odor lit in my nostrils.

"But that's what we're looking at right now. If you don't win the Midwest Trials, don't go to the box-offs, not a problem, we turn you pro right away, fight you fourteen, fifteen times in the first eighteen months, easy fights but not all easy fights, we'll throw a couple tough cookies in there to get you rounds and develop you and then we get you a TV fight with stiff competition but the right competition, a guy tailor-made to make you look good. You win and one of the big three promoters will sign you. I have strong relationships with Bob Arum, Don King, and Gary Shaw, and it's all big TV fights from there on out, and we start looking to get you a world ranking and a title shot. It's about a five-year plan as long as you can avoid injuries and keep winning as we bring you up in competition. We're not going to step you up until you're ready, so if it takes an extra year or two that's OK, we need to think about your future and you need to start thinking about your exit plan, your way out of boxing. Buy a home, maybe some rental property, start a small business, make smart investments, and you two make babies and live happily ever after."

Lauren spliced her brown fingers through mine and nuzzled her wild hair into my face. I kissed her temple.

"And you can do all of this and never win a world title, Joe. You just got to listen to your team and trust us, and we'll get you where you need to go. We will make money and we will set you sailing into a sustainable retirement."

"And if you start to lose or it's not working out, we go our separate ways, kumbaya and all that stuff. I've taken gambles on kids and lost, but I have a very good eye for talent and more often than not when I see someone and I talk with them, you are a good person, I can see that, and you've got a nice girl here and your family is together, you work and you don't do drugs or none of that garbage. I'm careful, don't sign many fighters out of the amateurs. Eight of ten guys I sign out of the amateurs, we turn a profit and two or three out of ten become world champions and we make real money, career earnings of over a million, and one out of ten, they end up unified world champions, pound-for-pound contenders, multimillionaires."

"So, here's to you being that one out of ten, kid." He raised his glass; the liquid glowed in the low red light. I raised mine and our glasses clinked, and Lauren clinked her big wineglass into ours, and we sipped and put the glasses down on the table.

"I'm ready to sign, Angelo."

He grinned, patted me on the back, and pulled two copies of the contract out of his black leather briefcase. He plucked a fancy gold fitted pen out his inside pocket. I looked down at the little white papers folded open to the signature line atop the white cloth table with the little drops of steak juice sprinkled around them. I took the pen and rolled my signature on the contracts smoothly in the black ink. I looked at both signed contracts. *There it is, Joe. Almost too easy.* Angelo signed and Lauren signed as the witness. I shook Angelo's big thick hand; his golden WBC pinky ring glimmered.

"Welcome to my stable, Joe."

"You did it!" Lauren said excitedly and grabbed my head with both hands and gave me a firm smooch on the lips.

We wrapped up, and Lauren and I cruised 290 out of the city; the wind sailed through our hair as the buildings receded behind us. Our hands clamped together tightly as she sang in her clear and rich voice that was paying her rent now from her gigs at the Mill and a few other clubs. She popped the tape out and slid in one of her oldies tapes, and Sinatra hit the speakers. "Fairytales can come true, it could happen to you, if you're young at heart." She sang it to me. I sang it back but played with the lyrics: "If you're young and fart!"

"Stop it!" she squealed. "Real lyrics only!"

We barely kept our lane as we sailed out of the bright city into the darker suburbs. "And if you should survive to a hundred and five, think of all you'll derive out of bein' alive. And here is the best part, you have a head start, if you are among the very young at heart."

Hopeful tears welled in our eyes. Our hope felt more alive in that moment than it ever was before and ever would be ever again. I pulled her hand to my lips and kissed it. *All our dreams are coming true, just like in the movies.*

We parked in the lot beside my apartment on campus at Elmhurst. My spikey-haired friend Painter walked out with a big thirty-case of Busch Light on his shoulder and a couple friends behind him.

"Joe, you sign that boxing contract yet?"

"Just did!" I replied, waving it in the air.

His eyes bugged out as he reached his hand up and we high-fived.

"You a bad motherfucker. We're headed to a party at Stanger. Come on, let's celebrate!"

I looked at Lauren and she frowned at me.

"Maybe, let me talk with her."

"Cool..." He put his thirty-pack on his shoulder. "If you come it's Stanger, second floor," he said as they walked away.

"Come on..." I said to her.

"Joe, I don't want to," Lauren said.

"Why? Baby, this is my big night!" I smacked the contract in my lap.

"I don't feel right." She held her stomach.

"Are you sick?"

"No, I just got a bad feeling is all."

"Baby, don't worry, nothing can touch us tonight. Come on, just a few beers and we'll go back home. I want to celebrate this." I squeezed the contract in my hand.

She sighed, waved me on. I stuffed the contract in the box in the center console, hopped out, and started in the direction of the guys. I caught up with Painter, who was walking with this tubby black kid named Omar; Lauren lagged behind and took a phone call from Jemilo about some special event he wanted her for.

We crossed the big open field in the heart of campus with the tall full-leafed trees blotting out the black ornamental lamps as the branches trembled in the light breeze. As we climbed the little hill to the walkway on the other side, a group of preppy frat guys stood out front of Schick Hall.

"Kappa Kappa Alpha. I hate these bitches," Painter said as we approached them.

"Why?"

"We call em the KKK!" Omar piped in.

"They're always starting shit, bullying people." Painter explained. "They broke a bottle on some kid's head the other day for no fucking reason."

"What up, Painter?" A big stocky bearded kid in a plaid Abercrombie shirt nodded at Painter.

"What's up, Trent?" Painter replied without looking at him.

Trent stood with his fat chin upturned—a mischievous smirk on his face. He scratched his thick beard. The other guys sipped cans of Bud Light and snickered, muttering whispers to each other.

"That fucking guy is a piece of shit," Painter whispered to me. "He's the grand wizard."

Lauren finished her call and trailed behind us with her arms wrapped around her stomach. I glanced back and paused for her to catch up. Her elegant white gown flowed off of her wide hips. She passed this tall skinny blond-haired guy in a baby-blue polo shirt, and his eyes lit up. He nudged Trent with his elbow and stepped to Lauren.

"Ohh baby..." He reached out and grabbed a big handful of Lauren's ass. *What the fuck!?*

She spun around and slapped him across the face.

I started for them.

The tall skinny guy laughed, holding his reddened jaw. "Fucking nigger bitch," he said, as the drunk Kappa guys laughed.

I stomped up to the tall guy. He stood looking at me stupidly.

"What'd you just say?" I asked.

He put his hands out at his sides, surprised to see me, grinning with his bony angular face.

"Oh sorry, I meant to say half-nigger bitch," he corrected himself. Painter and his friends stepped up behind me.

"Watch your fucking mouth. That's my girlfriend," I shouted in his face. "You touch her?"

"Joe, stop it." Lauren squeezed between us and grabbed my arm.

"Yeah, I did, what are you gonna do about it?" He lunged at me and I smacked him with an open hand. His long chin twisted and he flopped over on the damp green grass in his baby-blue polo shirt and khaki shorts.

Painter and his guys burst out laughing.

"Damn! He knocked your ass out with a slap, Brad!" Painter said, standing over him with his hands on his hips. The Kappa guys swelled up as Brad got to his knees.

"Aye!" Trent squared up with me and grimaced, his torso heaving. "What the fuck? You want a problem?"

Lauren stepped between us and looked me in the eyes.

"Just walk away, baby. That's all you gotta do now. Just take me home."

I looked her in her big brown trembling eyes. Her face quivered, and the dozens of beauty marks bopped around like particles coming to life. I smiled as she took my hand. I nodded and we turned and walked back toward the apartment. The Kappa guys stayed there muttering. Painter guffawed and picked his case of beer back up; the cans thudded inside the cardboard as they flopped on his shoulder.

"Y'all a buncha bitches!" he said. He called to me as they continued toward Stanger. "Later, Joe."

We walked across the soft grassy field. She slung her smooth arm through mine and squeezed my wrist.

"I'm so damn proud of you, Joe." She kissed me on the cheek.

"Why?"

"You walked away."

"That was hard."

"I know it was, 'cause you a fighter. But you a lover and a fighter, aren't you..."

We cut through the buildings and I stopped under a little tree. The electric light flowed through the branches and speckled little wavering droplets of light onto us. I touched her face and kissed her lips softly as she melted into my arms.

"I'll love you for eternity," I said as she giggled.

"I know, but I will love you twice as long."

And that's when I saw them coming.

Three of them emerged over her shoulder, trotting down the concrete steps between the red brick buildings. Trent'd taken off his Abercrombie shirt, and his tits jostled in his white wife-beater. They swore and worked themselves up.

I pulled Lauren behind me as they rushed at us hard in a single-file line. *You better not hurt this girl. I'll kill all three of you.* Trent came first;

he tried to tackle me. I dodged him and hip-tossed him. He went tumbling away, trying to regain his balance, his legs kicking up wildly. Brad ran at me. He cocked back and threw a sissy punch, and I hit him with a choppy little right. His blond hair swooshed wildly with the collision, and he fell flat on his belly on the grass under the tree. The third one, a stubby kid with a reddish beard, rushed up but hesitated as he got close. I squared with him.

"Joe!" Lauren shouted just before Trent crashed into my back and tackled me to the sidewalk. *Shit!* I squirmed inside his bearlike grip. The stubby kid came up and swung his leg back to kick me in the head but hesitated. Trent tangled my arms.

"Kick him, Andy!" Trent shouted as I twisted to protect my head. Lauren reached out and clawed Andy's hairy red face. Andy's black Converse Chuck swung toward my head but only glanced it above my ear. Lauren psycho'd him, grabbed him by his hair, pulled his head down, and kicked him in the balls. I twisted around under Trent and jammed my index finger deep into his damp eye. My thumb slid into his lip like a fishhook and his mouth elasticated. I extended my arm and his neck stretched back.

"Get off me, motherfucker!" I screamed, and he rolled over, pawing at his eye and trying to push it back into place.

I jumped up. Andy tried to run from Lauren. Brad half got up. *Naw, naw, you stay down.* I stepped to him and kicked him in the face; my glossy dress shoe smacked square into his nose. The bridge of my foot burned as he melted back down to the grass. Trent got up, grimacing at me. His eye hung out of the socket a little, with a bloody tear dripping from it. Trent gathered and swung a heavy punch at me. I stepped back and his big hairy fist swooped past my face. He lost balance and fell at me. I gathered my weight, bending at the knees, and stuck a short left hook into his jaw. The collision made a bad sound, a hollow deadly *crack* that froze everybody. A vibration ran up my arm and resonated in my heart and seemed to set a hook deep inside it. Trent stood up tall and then his knees buckled and he fell sideways, real slow. *Fuck, catch him!* I reached out to catch him but he fell just out of my reach with his eyes closed. The side of his temple cracked into the concrete walkway and boomed like an asteroid impact. Trent's head bounced and his body went straight into convulsions. *Fuck!* I rolled him over. *Please, no.* Blood smeared down his face from a long vertical cut on his forehead near the temple. The whole side of his head swelled red like a balloon. His eyes twitched and rolled upwards in his eyelids like he was being electrocuted. The one eye a bloody mess, bulging out of the socket. His husky body trembled, sending shivers up and down his white dago tee like wind flickering through a white sail. *Jesus Christ, no!*

Andy rushed up.

"Get away from him!" He shoved me.

I fell on my ass on the sidewalk as everyone stopped and hovered over Trent. *Fuck. You hurt him bad.* I stood. *Please, no. Come on, stop trembling like that.*

"I'm sorry man, please be okay." I stood and hovered over him as foam started bubbling up in his open mouth near the crease of his lips. A long stream of dark blood poured out of his ear and dribbled on the light gray concrete.

"Get the fuck away from him!" Brad screamed at me. His long nose was folded sideways and spurting blood in purple streaks all over his baby-blue polo.

I gripped my head. *Did you just kill that kid? No! No way! That didn't just happen.* I walked in a little circle around them. Andy took off his white polo shirt and dabbed at the bloody cut on Trent's forehead. I pinched my wrist. *Wake up, motherfucker! This is a nightmare. This is not reality. Please, God this is a bad dream. Wake up!* I clutched at my chest, hoping to find my crucifix, then I remembered I'd thrown it away years ago. I heard Pat's sad voice in my head: *You're going to prison for this one, kid.* I folded over, gripping my heart. *No, I'm not.* The wires seemed to constrict every blood vessel. *No way in hell!*

Brad knelt at Trent's side and took his hand in both of his. "I'm here Trent, I'm here, you're gonna be okay." Then he turned and looked out urgently into the surrounding clean, brick dorms, the new blacktop parking lot, every corner brightly lit and clean. A group of girls stood looking worriedly near the library; a couple guys hung their heads out of one of the white-framed dorm windows watching us. Everyone seemed to be whispering.

"SOMEBODY CALL AN AMBULANCE!!!!" Brad screamed.

Andy pulled out his flip phone and dialed.

You gonna tell 'em what you did? No. What am I gonna tell the police? I'm a city kid. They won't believe me.

"Baby." Lauren took my hand in her cool long fingers. "We have to go, now."

◆

We grabbed a backpack and stuffed it with clothes out of my place and drove straight back into the city as if the suburbs had expelled us and launched us like an accelerator, like we were two neutrinos cycling with no safe haven. As we roared up Halsted my mind raced. *Is this shit really happening?* I opened the center console and looked at the contract. *Fucking ink ain't even dry on this thing! You already blew it, you fucking nut!*

I screeched to a stop in front of Burkhart's and we bustled in.

"What the hell's going on?" Burkhart asked as we burst in the porch door.

Lauren explained while I called Painter.

"Dude! The cops are all over campus looking for you. Trent's hurt."

"How bad?"

"I don't know. I'll call around."

"Thanks."

Painter called back an hour later.

"The cops got your name somehow. Don't come back to campus, man, they're already at your apartment."

We lay down on Lauren's mattress on the floor in Burkhart's attic. She lay her head on my chest. *This shit'll blow over. And either way, fuck 'em. They started it, they attacked us.* An image of Trent's twitching body flashed in my mind. *What if you killed that kid? Then what?* I took a deep breath and let it out slow. *He'll be fine.*

◆

Ma called early in the morning.

"The cops called looking for you."

"I know," I sighed.

Dad got on the phone.

"Joe, come home now. We'll go to the station together and figure it out."

So Lauren and I drove out there. It felt foolish to go back to the 'burbs; I never was meant for that place. Too full of rich phonies.

Dad coached me a little about what to say, then he followed us over to the Elmhurst police station. Officer Smith, an old black cop from the city, greeted us at the entrance and brought us down a white hall to a little room. He talked to me first, and then I waited in the hall while he talked to Lauren.

When it was done, Officer Smith combed his fingers through his trim white beard, looking over his notes.

"After talking to those boys I thought I was gonna have to charge you with a felony, Joe," he said. "I'm glad I got to hear your side. This sounds like a misdemeanor to me. I'll let the court decide on throwing it out or not." He got up from his chair. "I'm just gonna check in at the hospital and see how Trent is doing."

"See," Dad said. "Everything's fine. And like he said. You can press charges for the assault when Brad grabbed you."

I giggled. "Brad's gonna get charged with an ass sault." I told Lauren.

"Shut it," Lauren said and pinched my arm.

Officer Smith came back a few minutes later.

"Trent is responsive. He's still in pretty bad shape, but he's awake and talking now."

Officer Smith charged me with a misdemeanor battery. Lauren went to 7-Eleven to get some cash and paid a hundred-dollar bond, and Officer Smith walked us out of the station.

"I feel bad having to charge you at all," he said. "If this was the city, we wouldn't have charged you with nothing. Now Elmhurst campus security called, they want you to go over and make a statement." Officer Smith opened the door for us. "Between you and me. . ." Officer Smith reached his hand out. I shook it. "Good work." he winked at me.

Dad headed home. Lauren and I drove over to the campus security office.

A pointy-faced lady in a black pantsuit with a puffy-collared white shirt met us at the security office door.

"Joseph Walsh?" she said with a sneer.

"Yeah, that's me."

"My name is Samantha Blake. I'm head of security at Elmhurst. Come inside. I can't believe they released you at the police station."

"He didn't even want to charge him," Lauren said as we walked in. "It was self-defense."

"Self-defense!? Wait here," she said to Lauren, and opened the door to her office. I followed her in. It was shady inside—just one window, with the blinds only letting a little light in.

She slammed the door behind me and stepped behind her wide wooden desk. "You hurt three of our students! The baseball coach is fit to be tied! I've been fielding calls from parents. You're going to face the disciplinary board, and you'll be kicked right out of here!"

"Do you even want to hear our side?" I stepped towards her desk.

"Of course," She picked up her note pad. "So, is it true you kicked one of them in the face while he was down?"

"His friend'd just kicked me in the head a few seconds before!" I whined, and sat down in the purple cushioned chair in front of her desk.

She slammed her notepad down.

"Well, you don't look hurt!" She loomed over me, planting her hands on her desk.

"Wait, am I getting in trouble because I won?"

"So it was a fight and you feel like you won?" She sat down and started taking notes again.

"I defended myself! Three guys tried to attack me! They assaulted my girlfriend. I walked away and they came chasing after me. And they attacked me!"

"That's not true." She wagged her white pen in front of her face. "You were waiting for them to surprise attack them."

"Are you asking me what happened or are you telling me what happened?" I stood to leave.

"Oh, what, are you gonna hit me now?" she yelled, and stood up.

"I'm done! You're a crazy bitch!"

I got up, opened the door and walked out. Lauren stood up.

"Don't they want to hear my statement?" Lauren asked.

"Naw, they know the whole story already," I said. "We don't have to tell them shit."

"Consider yourself banned from campus!" Samantha Blake followed me out of the room.

"Good! I don't want to come back to this shithole anyways!"

The phone on the wall rang, and she answered it as we walked outside. We crossed the parking lot, and I opened the door of the Jeep for Lauren.

"Stop!" Samantha Blake screamed in a brittle tone from the security office door. "Something has happened at the hospital! The police want you to wait right here!"

I took a deep breath and looked at Lauren. She nodded for us to leave. Samantha Blake trotted down the steps to the parking lot in her clicky heels and rushed up to me as I walked around and opened my door.

She grabbed my arm and threw her head back and screamed, "Citizen's Arrest!"

"Get the fuck out of my face, lady!" I shouted, and shoved her off my arm. I slammed the door in her face and pulled away.

I took a shortcut through the neighborhood. We passed Erickson's white mansion with the big green bushes. *Could he help me? Do not drag him into this shit.* I just scooted past and onto 290 and floored it down the ramp toward the city.

I called Painter to get the goods.

"Fuck, Joe, Trent is in a coma."

I gasped as some old rusty hooks punctured my lungs and fucking set like a motherfucker. I hung up. This creepy voice leapt into my head: *Your fucking life is over*. I grasped at the wound.

"No, it isn't." I said.

"What?!" Lauren shouted, grabbing the wheel that I'd let go of. "What is it, Joe?"

"He's in a coma."

I squeezed the wheel and floored it east towards the tall buildings, feeling like I could hide behind them, but some circular force seemed to be accelerating everything in my life towards the speed of light.

Tears streamed down and dripped off her nose.

"Let's just get out of town for a while," she said.

"Where you wanna go?"

"You know where."

PART FOUR: PARTICLES

Chapter 15: Raceland

WE SHOT INTO THE CITY LIKE TWO NEUTRINOS.

"Don't speed, that's the last thing we need is to get pulled over."

"OK... OK... Let's go to Burkhart's, pack our stuff, and get out of town."

We pulled up in front of Burkhart's.

"Aye you two," Burkhart said from the porch railing, his long beard blowing in the breeze. "Well, if you're here, that means it couldn't be that bad."

"It's worse, Burkhart." Lauren rushed past him into the house as I followed.

"What the heck happened?"

"He's in a coma," I said. "The cops are looking for me."

"Joe, I'm...I'm sorry to hear that." He followed us in. "Is there anything I can do?"

I shrugged, and climbed the ladder up to Lauren's room.

She was already on the phone, scampering around and packing with her free hand. "Can I come there tonight? I'm in trouble. Thank you, Annabel." She looked at her watch. "We'll be there by morning."

She tossed some blue jeans and a skirt into her black duffel bag.

"Let's go," she said as I grabbed my bag and followed her. Fred waited for us at the base of the ladder.

"Lou, you gotta let me help."

"There's nothing you can do, Fred. Here's next month's rent." She stuffed a couple hundred dollars in disheveled bills into his hand.

"Keep it, Lauren. My god, you're like a daughter to me." He hugged her then reached out and squeezed my shoulder. "You, you're a good person. You'll make it out of this, you'll see."

We jumped in the Jeep and took off. Soon we were headed southwest on 55. As we passed Cicero Avenue, I thought of my family. My phone rang.

"Joe, where are you?"

"Dad? I'm going."

"No! That's not an option. You have to turn yourself in, Joe."

"Dad, he's in a coma! I ain't going to jail!"

"We'll bail you out!"

"No."

"You have to turn yourself in, goddamnit!"

"Well, I'm not fucking doing it!"

I hung up and my little gray phone rang again. I popped it open and took the battery out.

We closed in on the exit ramp to 1st Avenue. I saw my life in two paths, prison and the unknown. A seagull flew along the exit ramp and swooped up and sat atop a streetlight pole.

I accelerated and shot past the exit, headed across the country towards an unknown target. The old patches from the form-concrete repair job over the shipping canal coasted past below us.

"Don't take 55, take 57, it's a straight shot," Lauren urged. "It'll save us an hour."

We hit 294, took it to 57, and shot south. The sun set as we approached Kankakee. We zoomed past a refinery lit up like a monstrous medieval castle.

"Money? Fuck, we gotta get money out before we get too far south."

Lauren called up Jemilo.

"Hi Jemilo. Yeah, I'm on my way out of town. Something's happened." She struggled to control her voice. "I can't tell you much right now. I don't know when I'll be back." She started crying. "Thank you. Thank you so much for everything you've ever done." Big droplets rolled down her cheeks as she hung up.

"Maybe we should just go back."

"No... no... he said I'm welcome back whenever I come back."

"I'm sorry."

"Don't be sorry. There's nothing you could do different. You walked away... My god. It's just your destiny."

"No, it isn't! Look, I walked away, maybe I'll get off on self-defense."

"You think?"

"Yeah, maybe..."

"That isn't the city, Joe. It's the suburbs. They are gonna throw the book at you."

"OK... OK..." We zoomed past a big clunking semi. "We'll just get out of town for a few days, then we'll come back."

"Yeah, then we'll come back," she said, as if her soul was floating slowly out the window and seeping through the black web of tree branches flying past us and into the orange sky.

What the fuck, Joe? What the motherfuck? The wires slithered through my brain. *You really did it now. You fucking hurt somebody bad. They're gonna lock you up and throw away the fucking key.* I breathed hard. *Naw, fuck that. It's all gonna blow over. You're going out to Valentine's in a few weeks, and then the trials, and you're gonna win the fucking trials, watch. You'll be laughing your ass off about this shit in a few months, how scared you were. Trent's gonna be fine. He'll graduate and go off and be a rich prick the rest of his life, and make more rich pricks; there'll be a line of Trents going on for hundreds of years.* I saw Trent's body convulsing on the pavement. *Oh my fucking god, he's gonna die, isn't he?*

We approached a green exit sign that read *Olympian Drive.* I grimaced. *Pshh, maybe it's a sign.* I shook my head. *Are you going crazy? Olympian Drive in the middle of bum fuck Illinois, you don't think that's a sign?* Then: *Yeah, idiot, it's a sign. A road sign.*

"What's that sign say?" I asked her.

"Olympian Drive."

I zoomed towards the exit lane and careened down the ramp.

"What are you doing?"

"I don't know! Maybe I should get some money out."

I rolled into the gas station and stopped. I went in and walked up to the ATM. I checked my balance: $1,232.06. I tried to withdraw $1,200. *THIS MACHINE HAS INSUFFICIENT FUNDS TO COMPLETE THE TRANSACTION.* I tried $600. The machine froze. The clerk glared at me. Then came the sound of money flipping inside the machine.

"Please... Please..." The dispenser opened and the bills slid out.

I grabbed them, stuffed them in my pocket. I clicked another transaction. I punched in a $300 withdrawal. The machine froze again.

"Come on... come on!" I slapped the side of the box.

"Hey, whatduya think you're doing to my machine, boy?"

"Shut the fuck up." I glared at him.

YOUR BANK WILL NOT ALLOW YOU TO MAKE THE WITHDRAWAL AT THIS TIME. I punched cancel.

"Motherfucker." I stomped up to the register. "Twenty on pump five."

"You in a hurry, city slicker?"

"What the fuck's it to you?"

I went out and pumped. He watched us from his booth and got on the phone. *Are you giving us a problem, motherfucker? You calling the cops? Motherfucker, I will kill your ass!* I got $18.50 in, jumped in, and tore off.

"What's up?"

"I don't know, that motherfucker was giving me shit, and then he got on the phone like he was calling the cops."

"He's not calling the cops, baby. You're just being paranoid," she said, and drifted to sleep.

We shot back onto 57 and tore off into the night. I watched the rearview for cops. Fifteen minutes later we approached a cop car sitting in the dirt median. My heart shot into palpitations. Jail, court, prison, all of it flashed in my mind. *If he pulls me over, I'll fucking take his fucking gun and shoot him with it.* I caught a glimpse of the cop as I drove past and he sat hunched over sleeping. *Thank fuckin' god. I ain't going to prison.*

Lauren cried in her sleep. I asked her where to go and she mumbled, "Just take 57 all the way down across the state, to where it meets back up with 55, down in Missouri. 55 takes you right to my cousin's house." Then she was gone again. She'd wake and cry and sleep again.

We zoomed down I-57 and crossed the Mississippi at Cairo and we drove straight into the night. *Come on, Trent, you gotta pull through. Wake up! You motherfucker, why the fuck did you have to come after us?* Wires wrapped in my mind. *Everything's gonna be fine. It'll blow over. Fuck, what if he dies?* His pompous bearded smirk flashed in my mind. That dumb-fuck smug bully smile I'd seen a hundred times. Blake's face flashed for a moment. *Big fucking piece of shit got his motherfucking head smashed.* I giggled and then the joy dropped and the weight of it sank down on me like a cloud of dark matter. *Oh my god... If I killed him... if he dies...* I struggled to breath as the wires strained around my chest. *Please, please, don't you fucking die, you PIECE OF FUCKING SHIT!* Something poked my heart, I gasped for breath. *What did you do? Did you fucking kill somebody? Did you take somebody's life?* I flexed my whole body and mind. The wires strained and trembled then they snapped. *He fucking deserved it.*

I looked at my trembling hands. *What have I turned into? I'm a fucking monster. I'm not a monster. I'm not a bad person. I'm a good person. I just want to live my life. Please god let me live my life, like it was, like it was yesterday. Can I just wake up and have it all be a dream? I'd give you anything. I'd give anything.* I glanced at Lauren folded up in the passenger seat. *OK, I wouldn't give you her. With her I can make it through this. OK, I gotta make it through. I gotta find a way.* We flowed deeper into the South. *Fuckin' Olympic trials…yeah right! I got myself all inspired and fired up for nothing. It was all a big dream, a big stupid fantasy that a fuckup like me could never really live. 'Cause I'm a motherfuckin' low-life thug and that's all I'll ever be.*

I went five under the speed limit. *A speeding ticket, a flat tire, a broken tail light: anything could cross me with the cops. That'd end it all. I got a warrant probably, or I'll have one in a day or two. Who knows how fucking fast that shit works. I don't know. I don't know anything anymore, not where I'm going, not how we'll live, nothing. I'm totally and completely fucked.*

There was an ease to that realization, like something that always hung deep down in me, a darkness that lurked behind every hope and every success, like a shadow. A ball of dark matter inside me, always in me, and I knew deep down that sooner or later it would rear its ugly head and I'd become the monster that I always truly was in the end. I reveled in the darkness as Lauren slept.

A semi passed us and the wind almost blew us off the road. Lauren woke up screaming, "Noooooo!"

"Lauren, it's OK, it was a dream."

"Where am I? Where are we?"

"We're in the Jeep. We just passed Memphis."

"It wasn't a dream." She mourned her hope. "I had a nightmare." She broke into tears. "You killed somebody!" She paused and looked out the window as tears slid down her face. "What if he dies, Joe?"

"I don't know, Lauren." I sighed. "I go to prison."

"Joe, maybe we can just stay on the run. We can get new IDs down in 'Nawlins. Start a new life."

"Maybe, baby, let's just get down there and, and… I need some time. I need some time to think."

"We can find work and we can live quiet. You don't have to go to no prison."

"He ain't gonna die, OK? OK? I...I'm gonna call Painter in the morning, and he's gonna be fine, and it's gonna be over."

"You're right, you're right." But she didn't believe her own words.

Why the fuck did she dream that right now? Dreams come for a reason sometimes. They aren't just our fears. Sometimes they're messages.

"Tell me about your dream."

"No, I don't even remember it."

"Lauren, you keep a dream journal. You remember every damn detail of your dreams."

"Not this one, baby."

"Tell me, goddamnit!"

"No, please! No."

I glared at her and she took a deep breath.

"We were walking in New Orleans and we were happy and you picked a flower for me and I put it in my hair and people were smiling at us and waving to us and everyone was so happy in the sunny weather and then you got a phone call and you put it to your ear and you listened and you stopped walking and you dropped the phone and when the phone hit the ground it broke into a thousand pieces and it opened up a hole in the street and inside the hole, there was Trent on the ground twitching and then he stopped breathing and a voice said 'He's dead.'"

I didn't reply. *It's a fuckin' message. No, no, it ain't! Fuck all that hooky shit.* Lauren fell back to sleep. As the miles passed, weakness started to overtake me. I hadn't eaten. I hadn't slept much in two days. I started to veer, and fall into daydreams.

Emanuel Miller stands over a tool box and flips through levers. Aaron Williamson and some big muscular Polish guy sit before him. Their heads are open from the back. They look like puppets crumpled before him. He yanks parts out of the Polish guy's head. And then he puts a new gearbox inside. He looks at me and grins.

"You going to the Trials, ain'tchu, boy?"

I shot awake as the Jeep tires hit the cracked pavement of the shoulder. *I gotta sleep.* I pulled over at the next truck stop. I locked Lauren in and went in and ordered some bacon and eggs. I could hardly eat but I swallowed it down.

The sleepiness came and I paid and wearily made it to the Jeep, got in, cranked the seat back, and slept.

Dreams. I fall straight off the map. Falling descending into inky blackness. Nothing to catch me. The stars above. I stare into them. I flap my arms like wings. I look at my hands and they're white feathers falling off me in the wind. I scream and only hear a seagull's cry.

I woke. A state trooper tapped his nightstick against my window. I stared at him confused. Lauren woke.

"Roll down your window, son."

"No," I said, and I tried to put it in gear but it wasn't even on, we were parked. I patted my pockets for the keys. *I'm getting the fuck outa here.*

Lauren reached over me and cranked the window down.

"Yes, officer," she said sweetly.

"You two can't sleep here."

"Sorry, officer, we're leaving."

He pulled the brim on his trooper cap and walked into the truck-stop restaurant.

"Let's get the hell outta here," Lauren said.

I pulled out and we shot back onto 55.

"Jezus Christ."

"Fucking A."

"Damn that pig, I'm hungry!"

"We'll pull over at the next town."

We pulled into a little town in Mississippi and found a family diner. We ordered biscuits and gravy and eggs over easy.

"So we're going to New Orleans?"

"Yeah, but we're gonna stop and see my cousin on the way. She lives in the bayou." Lauren sipped her coffee. "I just gotta talk with somebody. Get a plan, figure out who's around. She knows everybody." She looked out the window into the smoldering morning sun; it was rising above a patch of woods. "She'll make us dinner. Maybe we can spend the night, maybe a few nights."

"Let me see your phone."

"Why?"

"I ain't using mine no more, the cops can get the records."

"You think they're gonna track you?" She snickered.

"I'm serious! They can see which cell phone towers I used. They might end up tracking yours too, but I gotta talk to Painter one more time."

I called.

"Who the fuck's this?"

"Painter, it's Joe."

"Fuck, Joe, I'm sorry, man. I got bad news."

"Is he dead?"

"No but he had an aneurysm, they had to do brain surgery 'cause there was pressure on his brain and they put him in a coma. A medically induced coma."

"Fuck."

"Man, it don't look good. Where are you?"

"I'm gone, man. Thank you."

I hung up.

"He had an aneurysm."

Lauren held in the tears as I moved to her side of the booth, hugged her and kissed her and reassured her.

"I been thinking, baby. No matter what it is. I can make it if I'm with you."

She nodded and squeezed her eyes shut as the sun broke above the tree branches and spilled golden strands of light on us.

◆

We shot down, and right when we were about to get to New Orleans we cut southwest and got on Highway 90. Just outside Raceland, we pulled off onto a dirt road.

"Good thing you got this Jeep."

We drove over rough surface and came to a bend with a deep pool of water in it. I threw it in four-wheel drive and motored in. We came to an old house up on stilts with a saggy screened-in front porch. Smoke poured out of the chimney. A chunky black lady sat on the porch in a blue house dress, smoking.

"Is dat my Louie-Baby?"

Lauren jumped out of the Jeep and ran up onto the porch. They hugged as I got out and walked up. A boggy river flowed around through the backyard of the house. A long motorboat bobbed next to a mossy dock.

"This is Annabel," Lauren said.

I walked onto the porch and said, "Hi."

"You the one got her in trouble?" Annabel's light brown pudgy face frowned at me.

"Yep."

"No, Ann, we both got in trouble. We're just trying to get out of it is all."

"You's a boxa?" She raised her round chin at me.

"Yeah."

"You box somebody in the street? You kill 'em?"

"He ain't dead yet," I replied and looked away.

"He ain't dead *yet* he say!" She guffawed and put her hands on her hips, real sassy. "Did he at least deserve the wallop?"

"Three guys attacked us, Ann! He was protecting me."

"You was just defending yo' self? Then what the hell you running for?"

"It's a fancy place, Ann! Fancy people. They're gonna string him up."

"They gonna string up this pretty whiteboy?" She waved at me dismissively. "I ain't never been to a place fancy enough to string up a whiteboy."

"Well, we ain't taking no chances, Annabel. I need your help, we're going to New Orleans."

"You ain't gonna stay here with me?" Annabel sat on the porch steps. We sat with her.

"How we gonna make money out here?"

"Shoot, you don't need no money!"

"Annie, we talking about starting a new life maybe. Now who's in town?"

"Most evera body except you, Louie-Baby."

"The Oven still runnin?"

"Yeah the Oven cooking evera day, all day."

"You think they'll put him to work?"

"Doing what?"

"Can't he do some security or something?"

"Naw, a whiteboy like him won't get no respect down in the Oven."

"He a boxer, he mean."

"Give me your mean face, whiteboy."

I stood, took my shirt off, grimaced, and flexed.

"Ohhh, you hiding some lumps under there! Damn, Lauren, this whiteboy got some lumps on him." She stood up and grabbed hold of my traps, then pulled me close and acted like she was trying to hump me.

We all cracked up.

"He'll do," she said. And to me: "But go see Dawkins with your shirt off or he'll laugh y'all right out the Oven."

"OK."

Then Ann looked me over real mean and suspicious.

"You know what you need? You needs help. You needs a prayer. You needs protection."

Lauren spoke up: "Can you, Annie? Can you protect him?"

"Hahahaha... I ain't made no magic like that in long time, Lou."

"Can you try, for me?"

"I ain't no high priestess, girl, I gave up on that path a long time ago."

"Anything will help Annabel, please! Pretty please! We need help."

"You do, don'tchu. Well, I ain't mess'n with no black magic. You want me to do somethin', it's gonna be white magic."

"That's fine. Anything you can do, Annabel."

"OK, you running from something in your recent past, well... Banishing spell?" Annabel muttered to herself.

"That's fine." Lauren nodded.

"What is it?" I asked.

"It take twenty-eight days for that though. The moon wrong, everathang wrong, Lou."

"Well, can we make a short version?" Lauren urged.

"OK, we can try, but the magic won't be as strong as it should."

I giggled and glanced at Lauren. "Is she fuckin' serious?"

"Joe." Lauren bugged her eyes at me. "It's real, it works. Stop it."

"You don't believe in voodoo?" Annabel huffed. "This is voodoo country, baby."

"Fuck it." I shrugged. "I need everything I can get, I guess."

"Getcho white-ass up outta here, boy." She shoved me away softly.

"No, I do!" I raised my hands. "Please! I do, I'm sorry. I believe."

"Alright, we'll try a shortened version. One day. You need to pray all day, you need to pray twenty-eight times before tonight."

She pulled a little yellow notepad and a purple pen out of her pocket and handed it to me.

"Write what you want to escape on this."

"The fight with Trent?"

"Hurting Trent is enough."

I wrote: *WHEN I HURT TRENT.*

Shivers ran all through me when I wrote it. The wires squeezed around my heart.

"Twenty-eight times today before midnight, I need you to read those words you just wrote. Then I need you to say 'I accept you as you are. Thank you for the lesson you gave me. From now on, you have no power over me. You are free and I am free, too. Goodbye, c'est la vie, don't come back now, ya heard?'"

I nodded. "OK."

"Don't OK me! Write that all down, whiteboy!"

I jotted anxiously.

"Just say goodbye is fine at the end," Lauren said as I scribbled.

"OK."

"You need to recite the whole thing twenty-eight times! It's gonna build up power as you go. Then tonight we do the ritual."

"So just sit here all day reciting this?"

"Yeah...well, naw. Go on out wit Jakyre and get us a snake."

"A snake?"

"Yeah, wrestle up a snake, I been in the mood for snake for a week. You gotsta pay me something, whiteboy! I ain't doing this fo' free now." We stood up. "And do yo prayers while you out dere."

"Jakyre," she called.

Jakyre appeared at the tattered screen door—a dark-black man, chubby, and shirtless, chewing a wad of tobacco.

"Take this fool out to check yo traps and get me a moccasin."

◆

We motored through the bayou in the long boat. The muggy heat baked us. Jakyre pulled up to a stump.

"Wait here." He came back with a small muddy cage and dumped it on the boat. A fat rat curled its tail and hissed at me.

"You ever wrassle a water moccasin?" he asked, scratching his thick mutton chops.

"Heh." I grinned, then realized he was serious. "No."

"Here." He handed me a plastic stick with a piece of wire running through it into a loop at the tip. The handle had a big trigger.

"Get the loop around his neck up by the head and pull the trigger." He pulled the trigger; the loop on the end shrank to almost nothing.

"OK." I shrugged.

"Now hold it tight or we gon' get bit." He glared at me. "Stick him in this sack." He nodded toward a big white sack at his feet with a drawstring on it.

"Water moccasins are poisonous, aren't they?"

"Is a water moccasin poisonous?" He laughed. "Is it poisonous..." He fired up the motor.

We motored deeper into the bayou. *We're in no-man's-land.* Every once in a while, we passed a rusty oil station. Strange birds exploded from trees as we motored through. A few small alligators slashed in the water.

It was a full hour before Jakyre pointed off by the black mangrove shoreline and cut the motor.

"See him?"

"No."

"Right there by that log."

A thick dark brown snake with black zigzag stripes lay along a submerged log, with his fat head sticking out of the water.

"Fuck, I see him, he's huge!"

"Yeah, he is. He gon' be good eatin'. Get your stick out front 'a you."

I knelt on the front bench and gripped the bow rim. Then I squeezed the handle and trigger and held the stick out as far as I could. Jakyre cut the engine and we coasted in slow.

He looked at us and his black tongue darted from his lips. He lay on the twisted knotty log. I reached the loop out near his head and he took off slithering across the black surface of the water.

Jakyre pulled the string on the motor and we gave chase. I lay out on the bow and reached as far as I could. He danced out of reach, about five foot long; the water splashed as his tail whipped.

Jakyre throttled and we chased the snake out into the middle of the channel. He slithered fast; his head hovered a few inches above the water. I reached out the loop and he shot hard right and Jakyre swung the boat after him and I almost rolled right over the rim and into the bayou. The moccasin soared out ahead of us. I shrugged and gave up, looking back at Jakyre. Then Jakyre's eyes lit up. I turned, and the snake seemed to tire, just out of reach. I stretched my arm as far out as I could and slid the loop over his head. He accelerated, urgently slipping through the loop. I pulled the trigger. It came tight about a foot down from his head. I lifted him up over the water; the dark droplets glistened as they cascaded down his length. Jakyre cut the motor and rushed up with the white sack. The snake's black pitted viper head swung around and launched at me as I flopped back.

"Don't let go a dat trigger, boy!" The snake bit the plastic stick, his slimy white cottony fangs flapped open. "Stick him in here!"

I shoved his head in the sack and Jakyre threw the rest of him in and cinched it with the stick still in.

Jakyre laughed and patted me on the back as we turned around and headed back home. The sun started to set. The cloudy sky struck orange above the tangled brush along the shores of the channel. The calm dark water reflected the sky with a reddish-brown tint as we cut slowly through it.

"You know what happen he woulda bit one a us?"

"No."

"We'd a died out here, boy."

"Pretty place to die, I guess."

"You right... Don't forget your prays now." Jakyre throttled the motor up.

I said my prayers on the ride home. Something deep inside me seemed to rumble with the words, a vibration deeper than the chugging motor.

◆

"Can I do the honors with the snake?" I asked as we climbed out.

"Sure." Jakyre giggled. "You must think it's gon' be easy kill that snake."

Jakyre dropped the rat cage in the bayou and waited till the bubbles stopped. He pulled the cage out with a dead drowned rat in it.

I got a club out of the boat.

"I can just beat the sack."

"Yeah but you gotta find the head or you'll ruin the meat."

"OK."

"And he can bite through dat sack."

I fumbled around with the sack as the length of him bobbed around. I found the head and smacked it with the club viciously until the snake stopped moving. I opened the cinch, picked up the bag, and poured the snake out in the dirt. Jakyre handed me a hatchet.

I grabbed the snake by the neck, swung the hatchet down, and severed the head. The snake sparked to life. His tail whipped and swung around at me. I shouted and waddled backward and fell in the dirt. Jakyre doubled over in laughter.

"You thought he was alive, didntchu?!" Jakyre laughed. "He dead, boy!" Jakyre lifted the snake up so I could see the blood pouring out his neck. His mouth opened and closed in the bloody dirt. "He just twitchin'! The dead be twitchin' sometime, an' wigglin'. You scareda a dead snake?"

"Yeah."

"We gon' cook him up. You won't be scared a him then, will you?"

"Maybe." I shrugged as he patted me on the back with his heavy hand.

◆

Jakyre fished the wet, dead rat out of the cage and tossed him at my feet.

"We gonna eat a swamp rat?"

"That a swamp rabbit, man, come on, that's a delicacy 'round here."

We skinned and cleaned the rat and the snake and started roasting them on the grill. Jakyre left the head on the rat, teeth and all.

◆

A beautiful thirteen-year-old girl stirred a pot in the kitchen while Lauren and Annabel sat at the table. The girl's creamy brown skin matched Lauren's. A big blonde streak ran down the center of her frizzy hair. Her knee-length dress swooped around as she stood barefoot on the dirty floor.

"See, she's like me," Lauren said.

"That's what you get when you mix a Creole with a Cajun," Annabel said.

"And some Houma Indian too," the girl piped in with a sweet little voice.

We ate the snake with the leftover gumbo and some homemade bread. I bit into the soft white snake meat and sipped the spicy gumbo off a wooden spoon. The rat was a little chewy but decent.

After dinner, Annabel and Lauren went out into the yard to prepare the ceremony. They called me out there. Annabel stood in a big circle of salt they'd poured on the grass. Charcoal disks and a big fat candle sat in the center of it.

"Step into the magic circle," Annabel said.

I stepped in with her.

"Where it is dark now it is light." She struck the lighter and lit the candle. Then she lit two sticks of incense.

"Relax," she told me.

I sat down with her cross-legged in the circle.

She gave me a long cord.

"What is it?"

"It's fishin' wire."

"For what kinda fish?"

"For gator! Now tie a knot in both sides near the ends."

I tied the knots in either end.

"The past is in your left." She placed the knot in my left hand. "The future is in your right." She placed the other knot in my right hand. "Now you have to cut the past from your future. Burn the cord in the middle in the candle flame."

I let the cord loop down and watched it smolder and slowly melt the line until it snapped. Something loosened in my chest. The fire sparked, and a flame spiked up and burned my right palm. I winced and looked up. Annabel shook her head slowly, her brow furrowed with worry.

"Now take the past knot and your paper you been reading from your prayer and burn 'em in here."

I tossed them into a little plate with the reddened coals. The cord curled and smoldered black as the knot melted.

"Now just meditate," she told me. "Thank God for his help."

I kneeled there and closed my eyes. *Thank you for helping me.* The fire slowly dwindled to ash as my thoughts floated out into the massive black abyss around me.

"Now take this to the river and let it take the ashes away."

I took the plate to the bank and kneeled down in the muddy grass next to the trickling waters. I reached the plate down and dipped it into the water. It sizzled as it sank down. The waters took the ashes slowly away in a gray-white cloud. *Please, let this be over.* I watched it dissipate to nothing. Something splashed faintly in the water a little ways out. Two eyes emerged and peered at me along the moonlit surface of the flowing waters that glimmered like a sea of shattered glass. *It's just the fucking beginning, ain't it?*

Chapter 16: The Queen

WHEN YOU'RE ON THE RUN, YOU EXPERIENCE LIFE DIFFERENTLY. Every second of freedom is some kind of gift, full of joy and terror, gratitude and sorrow. Your body is on alert always, always trying to get away, like some kind of soaring neutrino broken from the atomic structure of society. You are absolutely free, yet your life is utterly meaningless and directionless. Or maybe it has some deeper direction, some simpler purpose: survival, one breath to the next.

I could feel this tremendous force pulling at me in the morning when I awoke in the small house on the bayou with the bugs squeaking, and the roosters crowing sporadically in the yard. *Maybe he'll make it.* But right after that: *Even if he does, he won't be OK, Joe. And them people up there in the 'burbs, they'll make you pay for what you did.* Lauren gasped; her damp face heavy on my bare chest. Her big brown eyes opened slowly as she stared into mine.

We geared up into the Jeep and said our goodbyes.

"Take him to see the Queen, honey," Annabel told Lauren as they hugged through the window. "She'll do better than me."

We bumped and jolted down the muddy path, back out onto the highway, back to civilization. We came to a tall concrete bridge and a crossroads. One way headed north, 55 back to Chicago; the other headed east to New Orleans.

New Orleans might as well be another dimension. An alternate reality. Older than America. An unfathomable cocktail of cultures: African, Caribbean, French, Spanish, Indigenous, and still American, all blended uniquely, the most tender and violent amalgamation of humanity you will ever know. And magic—an unearthly magic, that when you believe in it, it takes you out of you out of reality and into the cosmos. New Orleans is a port city, but more than that New Orleans is a portal, and once you fall into that deep magical portal, part of you never leaves it. But I didn't know none of that yet. I just knew I needed someplace to hide for a while, and New Orleans was all I had.

We swooped toward the city. She guided me past the gigantic Superdome; it looked like a massive spaceship landed at the mouth of the city. *I'm like a damned alien refuge down here.* We looped around above an old walled cemetery with weather-worn crypts. *Trent, you motherfucker, you better not die.* Beyond the cemetery, a grid of dark brick housing projects spread out. We took the Orleans exit and curved around onto Canal Street, a six-lane street with a wide trolley lane running down the center. Big hotels and fast-food joints and tall palm trees scrolled past as we rolled in the slow traffic in the thick dank air.

"This is the face of the Quarter," she said. "It's just the front door."

An old-fashioned red streetcar with yellow doors and windows rolled past us in the wide streetcar lane that ran down the center of Canal Street. Deep metallic clangs resounded from it. *Damn, I never seen one of those before.*

We approached a big bustling avenue that cut into an older section.

"That's Bourbon Street." she pointed.

Hundreds of people milled in the street, beneath balconies that teemed with people. She directed me towards the Marigny. We cut down near the river to Decatur, past the line of horses and buggies sitting in front of the black metal fences around the big green gardens of Jackson Square and the tall dark-blue spires of the cathedral looming above. Then across the way we eased past Café Du Monde—people sitting at little circular tables between the cream colored columns. An elderly black man in a brimmed hat wailed on a shiny brass saxophone in a pointy little park full of bushes and benches. Ornamental balconies lined the colorful buildings along the lumpy cobblestoned streets; each intersection looked like a portal into the Old World. We followed Decatur as it curved onto Esplanade and then turned onto a diagonal street that cut behind a small fire house.

"This is Frenchmen, this the Marigny," she said.

We parked in front of a tall narrow joint called The Spotted Cat. It was closed. We walked around the corner to a little café. It was more like an artist's house than a business. We sat down on a little musty couch with some big mugs of coffee with cream.

"I'm gonna take you to a place. It's a secret place. It's dangerous, you gotta make an impression."

"The Oven?"

An old white man in a black top hat shot me a glare from the table across the room.

"Shh, don't say that name out loud." She took her knife out.

I whispered: "What is it?"

"It's an opium den and a brothel," she said in hushed tones, and slit the sleeve off my shirt.

"Well what the hell are we going there for?"

She slit the other one off and cleaned up the sleeves.

"'Cause dat's our ticket. We don't have enough money to live more than couple weeks." She sighed. "You're gonna do bouncing, and I'm gonna start singing at a jazz club if I can. We'll probably find something cheap for cash here in the Marigny. If we're lucky."

◆

Lauren took me walking into the Quarter on Bourbon, out near Esplanade. It wasn't much of a street out there: quiet and residential colorful old homes with ornamental balconies. Way down the narrow corridor people partied in the street with the high-rise buildings of the central business district hovering above. Lauren cut off of Bourbon and took me through a few other streets until I lost all concept of where I was.

She looked down a pretty normal street and said, "Yeah, uhuh."

She took me by the hand and led me up to a faded green door. It looked like any door in the Quarter. She knocked a little tune. The door rustled but didn't open. She crowed a pretty little high-pitched birdcall. The door opened.

It was a big heavyset black guy with a shaved head; he wore a brown suit coat.

"Lou?!" He bugged his eyes out. "When you get back to town? Get in here, baby."

We huddled in the dark hallway. He swiftly locked the door behind us.

"Who dis fella?" he said, and flopped into a leather padded chair near the door.

"This Joe, he a champion boxer."

"You box?"

I flexed my arms and grimaced.

"Oh yeah, this whiteboy bad. I can see it already."

"Y'all hire'n?"

"We can always use a little muscle. And if we can dress him up, even better."

"Thank you, Dawkins!" She sat down in his lap and hugged him.

"I ain't saying he hired, girlie. You gotta talk to the Queen."

"OK, she in?"

"Yeah, she in the back."

"Thanks, Dawkins. You a saint!" She hopped up and led me away down the hall.

"Tell my wife dat, baby, she don't agree."

I followed Lauren down the dark hall until it opened up into a wide low-ceilinged room. It smelled like creamy, sweet flowers and baked chicken. Tall hookahs sat in the center of little pillowed booths. A young black kid sat over an open-flamed brass lamp pulling at a glob of black tar as he ran it over the flame, stretching it and folding it. The tar glowed in the low red light like black lava.

"What's that smell? It's so good."

"You ain't neva smelt midnight oil?"

"Naw, what is it?"

Lauren giggled and looked back at me with her liquid eyes. "It's opium, baby. This an opium den. One of the last in the whole United States."

A waitress came out of the kitchen with a sizzling dish of some kind of Middle Eastern food I had never seen before. We walked past a booth with a white silk curtain pulled shut. I paused. In the crease I saw red lips sliding slowly down an erect dark cock.

"Damn!"

"Come on," she said, and took my hand again.

She led me down another long hallway that ended at a door. She knocked at the door.

"Come in." a voice came from inside with a hint of an accent.

She opened it and we walked into an office. An older thin black woman in a cream dress suit sat at a big slick wooden desk with a green lamp on it. Her face stretched long and narrow—fine-boned with pretty, purple lips. A fat cigar smoldered in her elegant fingers.

"Lou?!"

"My Queen!"

Lauren shimmied over and the Queen raised her hand and Lauren took it bowed her head and kissed her ringed fingers.

"Whatchu brung me? A fine whiteboy?"

"This my man, this Joe."

"Joe?" she said and scrunched her nose up at me.

"He a champion boxer," Lauren implored.

"A champion boxer from, Chicago?"

"Yesum."

I walked up beside Lauren. The Queen put her elegant hand out and I took it and kissed it right on a fat oval emerald.

"You tell him to do that?"

"Nope. He respectful."

Somehow, she towered over us even though she was small and seated and we were standing awkwardly before her. I looked into her dark eyes; they seemed to morph colors the deeper I fell into them until they were like the bluish-purple and yellowish-reds of the mural down inside Soudan Mine in Minnesota. Her gaze grabbed hold of me with a strange sort of gravity. As if I'd been careening across the country directly at her all along. Her knowing gaze seemed to say she'd been expecting me, and that I was only one in a long line of desperate and fragmented beings who'd come before and would come after. And even that she was only upholding a pillar of the underworld which was built and reinforced by a lineage of royal predecessors that she was indebted to. It was clear that this Queen understood her duty and purpose in this world, that she was to devote her services to all the desperation that flung through those doors to her like shattered beams of light.

"You in trouble, ain't you?" she said.

"Yeah." I nodded.

"Big, big trouble, boy." She kept gazing into my eyes with a hint of bemusement. "Why you bring me trouble, Louie-Beyb?"

"'Cause you the only one can help him."

"Ohheee... I can help him alright. I could do a lotta things with him." She reached out and squeezed my bicep with her firm fingers.

"A white man, I had me some vanilla men in my life but they never was very vanilla. Mmmmmm-mmmm, ya hear me, girl?" She looked at Lauren and laughed. Lauren giggled, blushed, and looked at me bashfully.

"Sit down, you two."

We sat in the fancy red cushioned chairs in front of the Queen's desk. She stared at us both, her face shifting from scrutiny to soft warm joy. We looked at each other awkwardly. She slapped her hands together and said, "Ou de renmen!" in a language I didn't recognize.

Lauren nodded. "Nau damou."

"What did you two do to end up sitting across from me?" She smiled at me adoringly.

"Some boys were trying to hurt us, and they got hurt, and one got hurt real bad," Lauren said.

The Queen interrupted her. "He in a coma. They had to screw the top of his head off 'cause his brain bleedin'."

I looked at Lauren. *How the fuck does she know that?*

Lauren shrugged.

The Queen glared at me. "I'm a fifth-generation high priestess, ya heard? I don't read palms. I read eyes, boy," she said, staring deeply into mine. My body stiffened, and I contorted slightly like I was caught in a galactic web. "His daddy real rich and if y'all woulda stayed, you woulda gone in the clink a long, long time." She leaned across the desk like she was climbing into me through my eyes. "Boy, you in trouble!"

"I know, your majesty," I said. "That's why we're here, we need your help."

"Yo majesty! Majesty! Mmmm, I like him, Lou." She looked at me. "I like you but it's on account 'a that, I got to tell you something, something that you need to know, more than you need a job or a place to hide, ya heard?" She eased back in her chair and pulled on the cigar. "Boy." She exhaled a tuft of smoke from her purple lips; it twisted into elegant vertical strands. "You got bigger problems than that kid up in Chicago and them police up there looking for you. You know about voodoo?"

"No, not really."

"In this world there's black magic and white magic. And they are in everything. And they are at war. But sometimes there's truces in the war, and sometimes they help each other out. And there's black magic and white magic insidea every soul too. And they play by the same rules. If you happy and you want everything to stay the same, you want a truce, if you suffren', if you desirin' something, you want the magic to work together to help you get what you want. Boy, if you dyin', if your life fallin' apart, then the magic at war inside you and you betta choose one side and fight on that side. But you gotta choose, that's your only chance. Choose the white magic or choose the black. But only one can save you..."

"How do I choose?"

"You need to do something. To let the magic know you ready to make your choice." She extinguished the cigar in the black-and-white marble ashtray. "Catch a white animal. Hold on to the animal. Keep 'em safe. That animal is your magic. You have to think long and hard about what to do with that creature. You are either going to bring him to me to sacrifice him, in which case the black magic will swirl up in your world and protect you. Or you gotta set em free. If you set the critter free the white magic will flood in to protect you. But it's a different contract. Both come with they benefit and they own special price. But you have to make the choice, boy. It's one or the other. Ain't no middle ground here in this time in your life. I hardly ever seen a man more at war with himself, especially not no white man. You need to choose sides and fight, ya heard me?" She emphasized the last bit as if she was expelling the last of her energies.

She motioned dismissively with her elegant hand, her rings sending colorful shards of light across our faces as we stood.

"Thank you, Momma Queen."

"Thank you, your majesty."

"If Dawkins want him, he on. Just figure out the schedule. He probably gon' be on nights to the morning, mopping up puke and helping carry fools out."

"Thank you," I said, surprised.

"Don't thank me, thank her." She glared at me. "Evera-day of your life."

I kissed Lauren's temple and we started towards the door.

"Lou." The Queen opened a drawer, fished something out and tossed a small black ball to Lauren. "Go ahead, y'all need it."

We went to the room and found an open booth. They brought out some whiskey and the boy came over and crawled up to Lauren and gave her a hug and she kissed him on the cheek.

"Love you, Boo," she told him.

"Love you, Louie-Babey" he said with a smile.

Boo took the ball and lit the lamp and started to play with the ball over the flame. He rubbed and pulled on it, and stretched it until it became viscous and pliable. We sipped the bitter and rich whiskey. The boy placed the ball on a metal stand, then pulled a long brass straw out of his pocket and held it up to the smoldering tar. Lauren leaned in; her thick lips enveloped the brass tip. She pulled hard on it and pursed her lips and let out a little plume of smoke and blew it toward me and I inhaled it as she grinned. Boo held the brass straw to me with the smoke twirling around the ball and his small hands. I leaned in and the smoke oozed out of the tar and flowed into the straw as I inhaled. It struck smoother than I expected; the warm smoke seemed to crawl into the little branches of my lungs. Then I let the smoke out and all my anxieties seemed to flow out through my mouth in the light cloud that hung briefly in my face then dissipated into the room. A warm blanket settled down on me and pressed me into the pillows. Lauren seemed at peace as well, looking at me from across the way.

A waiter brought out a big tray of Middle Eastern food and a little basket of spongy pancake-like bread, and Lauren ripped the bread and dug it into the exotic food and ate. Lauren smiled and dug her bread into this glob of tan paste with a pool of oil and red spices on top of it.

"What the hell is that!?"

"It's hummus."

"What about them?" I pointed to some small roasted chicken–looking things. "Chicken?"

"It's quail, beef kafta, lamb shawarma, chickpea rice, butter nan..." She pointed through the meats, bread, rice and sauces.

We feasted and toked on the midnight oil, and I felt all the incredibly tense wires that strung through my life release and flow away until I floated in a warm golden paradise with Lauren in my arms atop the little pillows in the curtained booth. I dozed and fell into a deep sleep.

I enter an operating room. Trent is on the table with a big bright light above him. His head is open and the entire top of his skull has been removed and his bloody swollen pinkish brain sticks out of it lopsidedly. Surgeons gouge and saw at his brain. The doctor's hands are bloody and covered in green goo. Da suddenly is the surgeon. He works feverishly trying to mend the protruding brain, then stops and shrugs. Da looks at me and shakes his head No. Another surgeon steps up, it is Emanuel Miller. He holds a black video game control box. He looks into the cavernous hole in Trent's open skull. He tries to place the box inside the gooey tissue but he can't connect the wires. He looks up at me.

"Sorry, son. You done run yourself right outa luck."

I look down at Trent's face and suddenly it morphs into my own as they slowly pull the white blanket over my face. Then I'm flying. I fly with a great fleet of bright white seagulls, but their heads are black like the seagulls of New Orleans. We cry and flutter and soar up over the Gulf of Mexico. I can see New Orleans surrounded by a web of waters, and then we turn and swoop into a great lake and soar low on its waters to a big huge plantation on the far shore, full of medical patients. They wear blue gowns, and the white-clad staff wheel them around the fields. An older patient sits in a wheelchair with a gray blanket over his knees. He is black and thin, and he holds an elaborate shiny brass cornet in his lap. I land on the railing before him and he sees me and begins to laugh, a wild joyful laugh like a giddy child.

"You a sick birdie... You a sick, sick, little birdie and you gon' die. Just like me but worse. Worser than me."

Then he picks up his bright cornet and blows out loud and big notes that float into my mind and suddenly I see a great and monstrous contraption. It moves to the music but it has so many intricate moving parts inside. Its shape resembles a pyramid. The structure slowly decays and unravels at the foundation. The pyramid falls apart and I know the pyramid is my mind and I see its foundation crumbling down into a river at the base of the pyramid. It floods down into the river with all of my ideas, all the ideas I ever had and ever knew and my memories go with it. I see little precious moments from my childhood at the Hollywood Avenue block party melting and flowing away. Da with his black cocker spaniel Sheba walking up to the porch with a smile as I eat a red Popsicle on the steps. Jan and Rose squealing as they exchange water-gun fire at close range out in the street. I see Rose as a child and wonder if that's how Jay and Rose's baby girl will look one day. Her silly playful squeal, all that joy bundled in a little brown smiling ball. I see Dad watching them from the screen door with his big jagged jaw, his heart convulsing with love. I know that everything will be OK with Rose. She'll be a good and happy momma and I cry out with joy.

I awoke in the red booth, lounging undressed atop the elaborately stitched silk pillowed couches, with Lauren's face hovering over me and the red crushed-velour curtains drawn. She kissed me; the yellow lamps glowed in the smoky haze, highlighting her wild tendrils of hair. Suddenly the Queen was there beside me. She rubbed my belly, and I realized she was rubbing my hard dick in her palm against my stomach. She gripped it, and it strained in her small, fine, ringed hand. She aimed the pale thing upwards towards Lauren, and Lauren bowed her head down and kissed it and took it in her wet lips and the Queen leaned down and kissed my mouth; hers was firm and strong. I kissed her back and she seemed to suck the breath out of me and I descended again into sleep, and now I float out into the stars and the stars emit a cacophonous electromagnetic music and I am in a colorful nebula, a haze of purple swirling into pink and the stars birthing warm and bright, time stretching and shrinking, endless rebirths of stars in a rhythm older than time, in a rhythm that is time circling back on itself infinitely, and I am awake again. The Queen was on top of me now, settling her dark glowing mahogany-toned pussy onto my pale dick like I was her throne. All ten of her long burgundy nails dug into my bare pectorals. As she slid down, a swirl of red veins swelled in me, lit in the yellow light, and slowly disappeared inside her. Her wet pussy contracted on me as she looked down at me; her eyes burrowed deep into mine, owning me to my core, delicately opening my soul, peering into my mind, my memories, my potential paths, and there was absolutely nothing between us, just a building rumble as I seeped up into her. Lauren kissed my neck, touching herself watching, her creamy brown skin tone exactly midway between the Queen's and mine. We peered up at the Queen as her small breasts heaved and her mighty breath built, and the Queen came, contorting atop me peering into me, speaking that language I never heard before.

"Ou se min... Mwen pral pwoteje ou."

◆

I woke alone.
A deep voice came from across the dark room. "Come on."
I looked and saw Dawkins sitting on a pillowed bench watching me.
"Can you walk?"
I tried to get up.
"I tolt them, I ain't carry'n yo ass."
I got up wobbly—still high.
"Good man."
I followed him out the front door into the midday sun of the Quarter.
"You fixin' to stay in my shotgun. I gots a double, you'll be beside us."
A shotgun? What the fuck is that?

I followed Dawkins out of the Quarter into the Marigny. He lived in a long narrow peach-colored house with flowers all along the balcony of the shared front porch.

"This a shotgun, double barrel. That's me." He pointed to the white door on the left. "And dat's you." He pointed to the busted-up door on the right. He tossed me the keys.

I opened the door and peered in. One room gave way to the next, with no hallway. There was a kitchen in back.

"We renovate'n so it's a little raggedy."

"Thanks Dawkins," I said and walked up and flopped onto a dusty mattress on the floor next to a stack of laminate flooring.

"You on tonight midnight to 7 a.m. Lou gon' be around in a little bit." Dawkins said, and closed the door.

Lauren came home with groceries.

"I got a job!"

"Yeah?!"

"Bartending on Bourbon," she muttered. "But they want me to sing on Saturday."

"That's great, baby!"

We put the groceries away and went for a walk. We strolled through Frenchmen's nice and easygoing vibe. We went around to the quarter and drank coffee at Café Dumont. The pigeons landed on our table and tried to eat our beignets.

We headed down to the Mississippi riverbank. The sun sparkled on the dark, slow-moving waters. We climbed on the big white rocks that she used to play on as a little girl that sloped down to the water. Seagulls with black heads soared above us and floated in the dark water beside huge iron barges and the old-time paddle steamboat with the big red paddle wheel. The warm buzz began to lift from the night before and the wires of anxiety strained at my throat and little hooks stabbed at my chest as I thought of Trent and all I was running from back home in Chicago.

We climbed around, playing on the rocks. My foot slipped into a deep hole. I looked down into the hole and something flopped around in the darkness. It took a second for my eyes to adjust, but wings flapped inside. *It's a bird?* It cried softly and exhaustedly. I cupped my eyes from the sun and the image cleared. A creature with a long, thin, curved red beak blinked at me. A ripped net entangled its dark muck-covered body. It twisted and tried to stand, but just flopped back down in the grime.

"Lauren, it's a bird!"

"What?"

She climbed over to look. There was just enough room between the rocks that I could reach inside. I stretched my arm down to it and it weakly tried to peck at my hand with its long curved red beak. I got a hold of the gooey netting and pulled him up. He came alive, flapping and crying, sending flecks of muck onto us. The net wrapped around his neck and the hooks in the net clung to his feathers. Lauren gave me her little Swiss Army knife from her purse and we sawed the mossy green lines off of him. He flopped away, leaving black slime on the white rocks, but his wing fumbled underneath him and he fell into another crevasse.

"He's hurt."

"Remember what Momma Queen said?"

He sat with his wing folded up under him crying—a muddy small crane-looking thing with red legs and feet and red circles around his eyes.

"Let's take him home," I said.

Lauren wrapped a blue satin scarf around his head and I held his slimy muck-covered body tight to me under my arm. He calmed down some as we walked back to the shotgun house.

We hosed him down in the backyard; he flopped around trying to escape but he couldn't fly. We scrubbed him up good with a wooden brush, and as his feathers began to dry in the sun they shone bold white. The feathers running up his neck and onto his head spiked up—all rowdy like a mohawk.

Dawkins poked his head out of the back window of his side of the double.

"What de hell you doin wit dat ibis, baby?"

"We found him, Dawkins," Lauren said. "He's hurt."

"What kinda bird is it?" I asked.

"It's a ibis."

"What the heck is dat?"

"You don't know about no ibis?! Let me learn you something, the sacred ibis from ancient Egypt was a god. Djehuty, or they call him Thoth too. He was a god of wisdom, knowledge, and mathematics."

"How the hell you know all this?" I asked.

"I'm an Oungan, mothafucka, you didn't know dat?!" Dawkins looked at Lauren. "Lou, you need to learn dis boy somethin bout were he at!" Dawkins said. He shut his window, disappearing inside.

Lauren laughed, "Joe, Dawkins is a Oungon. He's a voodoo priest."

"Even the doorman at the Oven is a priest?"

"Head of security, yes. You're the only one who's ever worked there who wasn't a priest or priestess or in study, or at minimum a devoted believer."

"Maybe I'm turning into a believer too." I looked at the bird as he walked around picking at the long grass in the backyard. "She said catch a white creature huh?" The bird eyed me. "You sure as fuck are white."

"This how New Orleans is, honey-child," Lauren spliced her cool fingers with mine. "You done got yourself in deep in the Big Easy."

I popped my eyebrows at her and crouched down, inspecting the bird as he stepped delicately with his long red legs and webbed feet, his little red eye darting around like a crazy person.

"So, you're a god of wisdom, knowledge, and mathematics," I said to him. "Well, howdy dodido, little fucker. What's two plus two?"

He squawked at me angrily and stepped away. Then he dug his long beak into the dirt and extracted a small black worm. He shook the dirt off of it as it writhed in the hard lips of his beak, then he flipped it up into his mouth and swallowed it down his long white neck. He flapped his wings triumphantly and squawked at me.

"Well, I guess two plus two is 'I'ma eat worm, fuck you!'" I said, as Lauren giggled.

We fed him some seeds from the corner store and a few hunks of bread. His anger subsided. He hopped up on my leg and cried out. I tried to pet his feathers. He pecked my hand and hopped off me.

"You little fucker!" A small red bead bubbled up on my palm. "Don't forget I saved your ass!"

He cried angrily and raised his beak defiantly from the floor.

"Better be careful or I'll bring you to see Momma Queen, you won't like dat."

"You name him yet?" Lauren walked in from the kitchen.

"I don't know, I just keep calling him Little Fucker."

"Ohh... Little Fucker, that's so cute."

Little Fucker liked Lauren, and they actually cuddled when she took her nap. When I came back in the house after my shift at the Oven, he squawked at me and stood on her back.

I took him and pushed him right off the bed and got in, and she came alive against me and pressed herself into me and gasped, and I slid my cock in her warm wet pussy from behind and she sighed and said, "Morning, baby..."

Little Fucker watched angrily from the floor, his eyes wide as saucers.

Chapter 17: White Magic

NO MATTER HOW MUCH YOU FIGHT IT, how you twist and squirm and beg and hide and flee, your time eventually runs out.

It seemed Lauren had taken me adrift in this great river of Louisiana magic. I was captive in the waters and simultaneously protected by them, yet there seemed to be a daunting kind of inevitable dread floating there, an inescapable nature to that world that was at once graceful and merciless. Music poured out of every corner. People paraded for everything: birthdays, weddings, funerals. Black men wearing colorful Indian headdresses popped up sporadically, sometimes leading the second-line parades with the loud brass bands. Dawkins was an Indian too, and he schooled me how the runaway slaves were taken in by the Choctaw and Houma tribes and how the bloodlines of the blacks with deep ties to New Orleans were full of native blood.

Violence was sudden and brutal; machinegun fire burst out nightly in the nearby 7th Ward. Elegant old wealth stretched up Saint Charles Street into Uptown. Bourbon was full of panhandlers, drug dealers, religious freaks, bad old drunks, and rowdy young ones looking for fistfights and fast women. Frenchmen was loud, fun, and weird. I spent most of my time working at The Oven, watching the operation. A high-end clientele—local politicians, and sometimes celebrities, actors, and musicians. I had to carry Nicholas Cage out one morning and stuff him into a cab. It wasn't just the opium or the sex or the food. A lot of them came to see the Queen for guidance and spells. She was deep in the magic, regarded as the highest of high priestesses. Many of the priestesses and oungans came to her for guidance.

I began to study the magic. Dawkins gave me books from his massive library, and we'd discuss them out on the back porch smoking local hand-rolled cigars over our coffee before we headed into work. His wife Miss May and him would brew up big cauldrons of chicken gumbo and Creole-style jambalaya and red beans and rice. I'd go to see Lauren sing on my nights off, and sometimes on my way in. She performed under the stage name "Louie Baby," and people came to see her; even the musicians would cram in and invite her to sit in, and she'd be so graceful trying to fit them into her schedule and she always kept her promises and she'd take me to jams sometimes in backyards amongst the factories in the 9th Ward and they'd go deep into the night and end glowing in the hazy purples and blues of the sunrise with everyone loving each other, swaying home drunk in dirty streets with the roosters crowing and the traffic of normal society building, and the money was good and the living was easy and I wanted to stay forever.

We got fake temporary plates from one of Dawkins's friends and kept the Jeep in the driveway next to the shotgun house. I sanded down the paint and sprayed a coat of flat gray primer on it. Little Fucker followed me around squawking and got high on the paint. He danced around, flapping his healthy wing and waving the other one, which we'd mended with some duct tape. Then he just lay on his side looking up at the whitish clouds, his eyes darting around horrified like he was about to die. But he didn't; he rolled over and wobbled around some more and squawked even bitchier than before 'cause now he was a hungover Little Fucker.

I loved living in New Orleans. Every street surprised me. It felt like walking through some exotic dream. The colorful homes with their high-porched entrances pushed right up onto the avenue—the balconies hovered above with purple-flowered vines hanging from them. Strange and entertaining characters milled past at all hours.

After a couple weeks we drove to Mississippi and called Painter. They said Trent was showing signs of brain function. He'd woken up and talked a little but then fallen back into the coma. I was sure any day now he'd wake up and be fine. We started getting sloppy. Lauren got a new burner phone. I called home with it and told everybody I was fine. Dad tried to get me to turn myself in, but I wouldn't.

Another couple weeks passed. The only thing that was bothering me is this tall skinny bum-looking guy named Ace. He was a drummer and Lauren and him had some kind of history. Every time they played together they'd both get the sniffles. At first, I thought it was coke but it wasn't. She was snorting heroin again. She'd played around with it before, but she assured me it was under control.

◆

When it finally did come, it was like I fell deep into the most peculiar and terrible of dreams.

I was strolling through the Quarter with Lauren in the warm afternoon sunlight. I picked a velvet flower from a vine hanging down the side of an old red-brick building. I swung around a black pole of a balcony and handed it to her like in an old-time movie. She laughed and put it in her hair. And we walked onto Canal Street and the sun came through the clouds. We looked up into the sky.

"Whatchu thinkin 'bout?" she asked sweetly.

"Trent. He's gonna be fine. I just know it." My heart swelled free of the wires. I looked into the faces of the people we passed, and they all smiled at us. *They know he'll be fine too.* A dark-skinned guy in a suit and a light-brown Cajun-looking woman in a flower-pattern dress walked past holding hands with a little girl in a cute white dress. She squealed as they swung her up, her light-brown skin a perfect mixture of theirs. *Is that what our baby's going to look like? I want to have a baby with you.* I looked at Lauren and she grinned and squeezed my hand. *I still got time to get out to Valentine's and train for the Trials. The Olympic team...* My torso swelled alive. I felt free, like a damn bird soaring through the air.

Lauren stopped walking and let go of my hand. She rifled through her purple purse and found her burner phone. She handed it to me. I grabbed it and pressed the green button. Dad sniffled and tried to speak but he couldn't.

"He woke up, didn't he?" I said.

"What? No, son. The kid, Trent, he died... It's in today's *Tribune*... You're wanted for murder... You have to come home."

I dropped the phone to the sidewalk. It broke into a dozen pieces. I fell to my knees in the midst of all those joyful faces swirling around me. I clutched my chest with my left hand as a large sharp hook came out of my fingertip and sank into my heart. I couldn't hear anything. *Your life is over.* A big colorful commotion swirled all around me. *It's all over.* I looked at my hand. Dark gooey blood oozed down from my fingertips. I stared at the darkness.

Inside my blood Trent lies facedown on the pavement. He rolls over, trembling terribly. He opens his eyes and stares at me angrily.

"No, please don't call him an ambulance." Lauren pulled my arm. Two police officers were jogging up to us as I kneeled bewildered. I looked at them. *This is it. This is the end.* I reached out my wrists to them. They stopped, looked at my wrists, and grinned.

"Had a little too much to drink, buddy?" the white one said, scratching his gray beard as they both laughed.

"Are you alright?" the black officer asked, the sunlight gleaming off his shaved head.

"Take some deep breaths. You look pale, buddy."

"I'm OK, officers, it's OK, go ahead." I raised my wrists to them again and they looked at Lauren.

"Is he on drugs?"

"No, he's not, he just upset, he just got some bad news."

"He died," I said.

"Oh... I'm sorry to hear that," the white officer said.

"You don't want any medical assistance?" the black officer asked Lauren, gripping his radio on his chest.

"No, we're fine, officer," Lauren said. "Thank you."

◆

She picked up the pieces of her phone and got me into a cab and we headed toward Frenchmen Street. Everything faded to grayscale. The dusk lit the cab up in stark light. Tears slid down her beautiful face. We stopped at a newsstand that had the *Chicago Tribune*. Lauren grabbed one and we headed out to Frenchmen.

"I need a drink."

"I know. Me too."

We sat at the long bar in The Spotted Cat and drank. A stinky bum slumped at the end of the bar.

"We can never go back, that's all," she said. "We can stay here and we can live, and we can live good lives. We don't ever have to go back." Her body slouched deeply in her dark green gown.

College Student Dies After Campus Brawl

Trenton Wacker of Elmhurst died early Tuesday morning at Elmhurst Community Hospital, four weeks after a brawl on the campus of Elmhurst College. Wacker was left with a brain hemorrhage

after a fight which involved Olympic
boxing hopeful Joe Walsh. Doctors
performed surgery to remove the
hemorrhage and placed Wacker into a
medically induced coma, to no avail.

Wacker was a star baseball player
at Elmhurst College and studying
business. Walsh is a Chicago Golden
Gloves Boxing Champion and was
preparing for the Midwest Olympic
Trials later this month. Police say they
have upgraded the warrant against Walsh
based on Wacker's death. His
whereabouts are currently unknown.

I rested my chin on the dark wood bar as the bassist strummed his stand-up. The faded sunlight came through the wide windows and painted the dusty wood floor.

"You think they'll look for me here?"

"They might, if they know you're with me."

"Do people know you're here?"

"My friends know."

"From here though. But people back in Chicago, any of them know where you are?"

"No."

I gave her a suspicious look.

"Just Burkhart."

"Call him."

She pulled out the burner. "Burkhart, hi, it's me... Well, the police might come looking for me there... Just please don't tell them where I am... Thanks, Fred, you're a great friend... OK."

Lauren handed me the phone.

"Joe, how are you?"

"Not so good, Burkhart."

"Ahh, things happen. It's the magic of the world, things, they come and they swoop us away and we have to find our way back. It's never easy, Joe, but you are strong, you'll survive."

"Thanks, Fred."

"I'm praying for you, Joe. Always and always."

"Thanks, I appreciate it."

"You be good to that girl of yours. She's your angel."

"I know."

"You just hold on to each other tight and you'll fly right through this like a couple of birds flying through a storm."

I fought back tears.

"Be cool, Joe, and just fly…"

"Thanks, Fred."

I hung up and looked at Lauren.

"I need to smoke."

"Yeah, me too."

♦

We went to see the Queen. We walked in with Lauren holding my hand and hiding her face in my shoulder. We stood before her in the dark office. She sat in her throne wearing an old maroon Choctaw dress with orange and blue flower leaves around the neck and white lace over the chest with elaborate orange, blue, and green stars at the waist of the long white skirt. A tail came out from the back and there were eagle feathers at the ends, and she fanned herself with the feathers looking at me deep in the eyes knowing what I'd come to tell. It was there in the room, in the current of my movements, in Lauren's wet and ruined face.

"He's gone, isn't he?" she said.

"Yeah, your majesty, he died."

"Well, son, it's time, time for you to choose. Bring me the bird or let him loose."

Lauren and I went into one of the booths and ordered the China White. Boo warmed it for us and pulled the claylike ball until the smoke lifted from it like some terrible comet approaching the earth. The smoke flowed into my lungs smooth and creamy, and the warmth ballooned up before me and pressed me into the red lace pillows until the light faded.

I fly free and through the warm clouds—rising, rising triumphantly in the bright white clouds. Suddenly Trent is beside me, flying turbulently but smiling. He shoots away. In the distance he turns in a wide U and when he faces me, he morphs into Little Fucker, but a huge Little Fucker. He shoots at me. His sharp red beak jabs at me. I grab hold of his long white neck as he screams in my face. He opens his mouth and his beak encircles my head.

I woke. Lauren lay beside me watching.

"I gotta kill Little Fucker."

"Alright, let's go get him."

We walked home high but still clear in the mind. I pushed open the door and the streetlight swept through the room. Little Fucker stood on my pillow on the little mattress on the floor. A droplet of white crap fell from his ass and splattered on my pillow.

"You did that for the last time, Little Fucker!"

I stomped up as he scurried away; he tried to hide behind a stack of lumber but I snatched him up. He cried out as Lauren cooed to him and kissed his head. I softened my grip and he nuzzled his beak into my chest.

As I carried him toward The Oven, his body felt warm. It throbbed against my side. *Am I really gonna kill him?*

Lauren petted his head as he batted his eyes at her.

"I'm gonna miss you my sweet, sweet, Little Fucker," she told him with tears in her eyes. An image flooded my mind, an image of her dancing with him at the jam session in the side yard with the Christmas lights strung all through the bushes and the horizon aglow in a blue haze. The Queen's voice flowed through my head: *white magic or black magic, but you gotta choose.*

Little Fucker squawked—a long curious call that sounded like a W and shot up towards an I.

I stopped walking. "Did he say, 'Why?'"

"He said something…"

I put him down and he stood in front of us blinking, the feathers on his head and neck spiking up.

"Say that again, Little Fucker."

He looked up at us, befuddled.

"We gotta go, babe. Momma Queen is setting up the altar."

"I ain't going nowhere with him until he says what he's gotta say."

"Babe, you is crazy!"

"I know I am!" I screamed. "I know I am."

She backed off. "Baby, I'm going, then. I gotta sing tonight."

"Should I free him? Should I kill him?"

"Baby, I don't know what you should do with him. But I know you got to decide on your own."

She bent down and tenderly combed her fingertips through his shiny head feathers and down his long white neck. Then she stood, turned, pecked me on the cheek, and walked away.

"Thanks a lot, Lauren. That was very helpful, as always."

She looked back over her shoulder, smiled, and flicked me off.

◆

I squatted down in the center of the street while Little Fucker looked around and pecked at a flattened wax paper cup. Beyond Little Fucker the blurry chaos of Bourbon Street simmered; above that, the huge downtown buildings loomed in cold judgment.

"You're gonna help me decide, Little Fucker. If you can fly, you'll live. If you can't fly, you gonna die."

"Yeah," Little Fucker said and flapped his bound wing at me.

Pigeons flew above us and Little Fucker tilted his head and peered up as they glided past.

"Yeah, you're gonna fly with them, Little Fucker, or the Queen's gonna kill you."

I undid the gray duct tape holding Little Fucker's wing closed. He squawked miserably at me as some of his feathers came away with the tape. He pecked me one last time on the palm of my hand; a miniature bead of blood rose up along my life line.

"Now get the fuck outa here!" I told him, standing up.

He stood in front of me, his silky head and neck feathers all sticking up in a mohawk again; his eyes rolled around wackily in their sockets.

"I said get the fuck out of here, Little Fucker!"

I brushed him back with my shin. He stumbled and flapped his wings. The memory of his bad wing came to him. He considered it—his red beak muttering angrily. He stretched both wings wide and showed me his bright beautiful white chest. He cried at me bitterly but with pride. A wind stirred his feathers. He tilted his head as a fleet of pigeons swooped from one rooftop across the street to the next.

Little Fucker kept his eye on them. He flapped and trotted away down the street. He gave a few great flaps and flew up, but he twisted in the air and flopped on the hood of a rusty Ford Escort. I stomped up to him angrily as he flapped, his bad wing folded up behind him. *He can't fly.*

"You're dead, buddy."

I picked him up. His wing slid back in place and folded beside him. I walked with him under my arm as tears welled in my eyes. The birds flew again. Little Fucker looked up at them and tried to wrestle himself free. He looked at me. I looked at him and something whispered to me: *Let go.* I did. He started to fall, but his wings went out and flapped. He skinned his belly against the crown of the street and swooped up and flew straightaway from me down Bourbon. Then he swooped up high, turned, and came back toward me. He stopped in midair before me. He spread his wings. His tail feathers came down and he hovered there in front of me for a moment. *You saying goodbye, little buddy?* His long red beak squawked as his white wings flapped awkwardly. Then he twisted and flew away into the bright chaos of Bourbon Street and disappeared into its haze. *Goodbye, my friend.* I followed him, somehow knowing everything would be OK.

I bought a chubby of Jack Daniels and stumbled into the chaos. *OK? Nothings gonna ever be OK again. You're gonna see hell on earth soon, Joe.* Walking down shadowed streets of empty white cups, water, garbage, liquor flowing to the drains running fast accelerating faces, faces, nameless intoxications unknown, new masks broken out, these are days of undoing these are nights of catastrophes moving, flowing missing collisions. *You might as well kill yourself.* Dark water sharks circled unseen. I seeped through the street, watching the plastic beads of all shapes and colors infect minds with lust chaos creating galactic madness, brown Colombian ass hanging over a balcony glowing in the streetlamps, *damn she pulled them jeans down slow. Just get a gun and blow your brains out already.* This roar: we travel amongst it, within it, somehow maintaining order of the mind. The sparkling current of bodies swept me up and dragged me along, trying to make me forget the depths of the city shadows.

Her voice suddenly shot through the madness.

I followed it to a bar near Canal Street. I walked in and she stood on stage with a four-piece band, her wild blonde-brown hair twisted up like an elaborate crown glowing in the loud lights as she sang Thelonious Monk's "Round Midnight." She saw me. I raised my arms at my side and flapped my wings like Little Fucker had. She smiled and kept singing.

Let our love take wing some midnight
'Round midnight
Let the angels sing
For your returning
Let our love be safe and sound
When old midnight comes around…

I checked my watch. Just shy of midnight. She grinned and shook her head. At the break she disappeared with Ace into the bathroom. She came out sniffling and walked up to me.

"What the fuck is this shit?" I asked her.

"Babe, I just needed something to settle me down."

Ace had walked over to the bar; I glared at him as he wiped his nose with his dirty-blue coat sleeve.

"I'm gonna slap the shit outta that motherfucker."

"What, why?"

"What if you OD, huh? I'd really have nothing to live for then."

"I barely did a bump, baby." She squeezed my traps.

"Stop that stupid shit!" I shrugged her off and went outside to buy a pack of smokes.

As I walked down Canal Street a white bird emerged soaring above the trolley lane. Little Fucker? He flapped an angry circle as I walked under him, squawking at me with his long red beak. Then he tore off, flapping down the trolley lane in a wobbly flight. *Where you going, buddy?*

A ruckus kicked up a block away in the direction he'd flown. I walked toward it, down the empty trolley lane.

"Hey!" an old black man's voice screamed. "Leave them alone!"

What the fuck? The ruckus pulled at me with an urgent gravity, as if I was caught deep inside of it and there was no escaping. I saw a mob of about a dozen roughnecks in their late teens shouting and rejoicing, their big shirts hung above their saggy pants and colorful sneakers. A homeless-looking black man in a wheelchair followed after them. *What the fuck are they doing?* They walked with that hitchy, gangsta stroll that reminded me of me, back when I was fourteen and still gangbanging, back in the old neighborhood. Their body language full of those same traumas and wounds that they were set on expressing and righting, just playing in the mercilessness the world had shown them, so unaware that they were stuck in terrible cycle that would lead to nothing but destruction of others and themselves, so oblivious that they were just a dark manifestation of their environment. I jogged towards them, and in essence I jogged towards the old me I would have still been had my father not saved me all those years ago. As I drew parallel with the mob, I finally saw they were following a preppy white teenage couple. *No way.* The boy's short blond hair hovered above his baby-blue polo. The girl's long reddish-brown curly hair dangled down over the jersey. It was the boy's big green Newman High School football jersey with the white letters *FONTENOT* above the number 9. *They need help.* I paused. *Do not go over there. You are not Jean-Claude Van Damme, motherfucker.*

"Police! Where the police at when you need em!" The old black homeless man wore a backwards Saints baseball cap; he rolled swiftly behind the mob. A cardboard sign on his wheelchair arm read *Disabled Veteran.*

One black teen in the front of the mob screamed an indecipherable slur and spit a loogie that arced up and smacked onto the center of the boy's back. The mob rejoiced.

I started to go towards them. *No! You're gonna get pinched for sure, you idiot!* I paused. *I can't, I couldn't live with myself. Maybe they deserve it, maybe it's their fucking magic.* I stepped into the traffic on Canal, then stepped back. *They got people who love them.* Another wad of spit flew and landed in the girl's long hair. Rage ignited in my heart. I sprinted out, cutting into the traffic on Canal. A yellow cab swerved and blared its horn at me. *You're the only one who can do anything.* I looked at the mob. *Them guys are strapped for sure. Maybe they'll kill you.* I took a deep breath and sprinted towards them. *Maybe it's better that way.*

"Leave them damn kids alone!" the homeless man begged with deep emotion. His one pant leg flopped around empty as he angrily wheeled himself towards the mob.

"Shut yo ass up, One-Leg Chuck!" one of them responded.

Several white wads of spit covered both of the teenagers from their heads to their legs. As I finished jogging through the traffic on Canal Street and closed in on them, the teenaged boy finally gathered the courage to stop. He turned around, trembling. *Fucking brave kid. Okay, I'll risk it all for you, buddy.*

"Leave us the hell alone!" he screamed, tears dribbling off his chin as the group halted and partially encircled them in a C shape.

"Let's just go, Logan!" the girl begged, mascara dripping down her face as she tugged on his arm.

Jesus Fucking Christ!

The mob laughed and jostled each other. "Whatchu gone do, Logan?" A fat one in a white wifebeater asked in a whiney voice as I jogged up.

I slowed to walk and stepped up adjacent to the kids and finally got a real look at the little mob. A tall older white guy with bleached spikey hair stood dead-center in the C-shaped pack. He held a camcorder, filming their assault; his wicked angular face giggled like some kind of maniacal director as he watched the little flipped-open screen on the camcorder. A big silver nameplate hung on a rope-chain around his neck; it read *WHITE MONEY*. He tried to keep the camcorder still as the others jostled him.

"Knock his ass out!" the white guy demanded.

"Still on his ass, Ronnie!" another echoed.

"Come on, make sure you get this shit, White Money!" the one that must've been Ronnie said to the white guy with the camcorder. Ronnie limbered and wound his right fist in circles.

I stepped up in between Ronnie and Logan as Logan stood trembling with rage and humiliation with the girl still tugging at his arm. Logan had pissed in his pants. The large wet spot at his crotch spread down his inner thigh. I looked Logan in his eyes.

"It's gonna be OK," I whispered.

Then I turned and looked into all the twelve goonish faces with the evil-looking White Money in the center holding the camcorder at his chest with the little red light on it glowing.

"What the fuck?" Ronnie stood tall and skinny, with gold teeth and a long mop of dreads. I squared in front of him as he looked me over nervously with his surprised eyes. Then he leaned back and looked at his eleven guys behind him. They guffawed, high and drunk, gripping each other.

"Who the fuck is dat?!" White Money said joyfully, glaring at me wide-eyed.

"For the love of god, stop this nonsense!" One-Leg Chuck pleaded as he wheeled himself up to us.

Ronnie started to say, "What the fuck you gon' do?" But as he spoke I crouched down low and when he said "gon'" I sprang out and up with a furious right cross. Ronnie saw it coming. He recoiled and threw his upper body all the way back, lunging his head straight away from my fist. I followed through completely. His lunge backward halted and my fist burst into his chin. He flew back, perfectly parallel to the sidewalk. His knees jerked up violently, then kicked out, and both soles of his sneakers almost hit me in the stomach as I rocked back. He floated into the mob of dudes behind him. They split out of the way and didn't even try to catch his fall. He smashed flat on the sidewalk, bounced, and lay still. His guys' faces shifted from predator to prey. *Didn't expect that shit, did you, bitches?*

I turned to Logan and the girl.

"Run! Get in that cab and get her the fuck out of here!" I shouted.

Logan nodded.

"Come on Camille!" He took her by the hand and they darted across the street and hopped into a white cab with *AMERICAN* in red letters across the door. I bounced away from the kids and pulled the mob towards me, keeping an eye on the kids. The mob tried to fight their fear of me and started to surround me. I cocked my fist to hit them. They lunged away so wildly they fell all over each other to get away. I stood in the middle of them as they hesitated, too scared to move on me. I watched the cab with the kids in it as it pulled away out of sight down Canal.

A big fat one with a puffy fro was trying to hold his ground.

"Getcho Bruce Lee-ass up outta here, nigga!" He tried to kick at me with some clean white Nikes. I lunged at him and he stumbled backward, gripping his jeans; they sank down to his thighs, revealing fuzzy red plaid boxers.

"Fuck this! Blast dat mothafucka, Thumper!" White Money demanded like some kind of wicked puppetmaster, still filming as Ronnie's body started to flop around.

"Yeah, shoot me motherfuckers! Come on, bitches! I got nothing to live for!"

A little guy seemed to step out of White Money's shadow in a gray Adidas track suit with the hood up. He pulled a black snub-nosed revolver out of his waist pocket and pointed it at me. I rushed at him, peering into the black hole of the barrel. His hand flexed as he squeezed. A shot burst from the barrel. The bullet whooshed past my ear. I reached my hand out to grab the gun. He shot again and blew a hole through my palm. The bullet soared through and hit my chest like a red-hot sledgehammer and knocked me flat on my ass. Burning, burning, a white-hot flame burrowing through me, until a great blackness swallowed everything.

I opened my eyes. Sirens swirled around me. White Money and the rest of them'd all disappeared. One-Leg Chuck'd wheeled himself up to me and was yelling for help as tears rolled down his stubbly face. Blood pooled under me and saturated the back of my shirt, jeans, and shoes. The terrible noise of my blood trickling out of me like a garden hose cut through the blaring sirens. *You did it now, didn't you?* A heavy weight and numbness pinned me to the sidewalk. I held my bloody hand up before my face. *Dead center through my lifeline.* The wound poured blood that ran down and flowed off my elbow in a steady line. I spread my fingers. A ray of the streetlight pierced through my hand and painted my flesh a glowing light red. *Was this your destiny?* A shadow flashed through the light in my palm. A small white bird seemed to fly out of my hand over Canal Street. *Little Fucker?*

"You're a goddamned hero," Chuck said, and waved down a squad car. *Buddy, that's a real funny way to help a fugitive.* The squad pulled up and a fat white cop hopped out.

"What the hell happened?" the Officer asked.

"He saved them kids and they shot him!" Chuck cried.

I closed my eyes. Fuck it, maybe it's time. The ambulance showed up. The medics cut my shirt off inspecting the wound. One Leg Chuck talked with the officers with tears still dribbling down his dark brown face.

"That White Money, he the problem! He been running around with that little crew 'a nappy-headed niggas. He leading them boys down the wrong path! He turnin em into something wretched."

They stuffed the wound in my chest with a long white string of gauze, then used a big long brown wrap to hold it in place around my torso.

"It's all on that camcorder White Money got. They stickin' tourists up, they knockin out drunk fools, grabbin on woman's asses all up and down Canal Street! It's been going on fer weeks now!"

The medics pushed a ball of gauze into the hole in my hand then wrapped it. My whole body numb, I felt I was floating in a big cold river.

"Then this man come outa nowhere try and save them kids and they shot him! It make me sick."

They pushed a hard thin board under my body. Then transferred me to the stretcher.

"White Money made 'em do it, ya heard me? White Money, he, he, he caused this darkness."

And as he said it I looked up into the street lamps above Canal Street and this white light expanded out of it. It enveloped me and I slept for a very long time.

I woke in a cold room naked under my blue hospital gown with a handcuff around my good wrist cuffing me to the hospital bed. I was alone but I could hear a cop talking near my open door.

"Some bum was crying and gabbing away to the TV that this guy saved some kids. My ass! There's no kids to be found. So, I say let me take a look at this big hero. Illinois ID. I make a call, sure enough he's wanted for murder up in Chicago. That's my first murder arrest! Cracked that baby right open! Fuck, Broussard, I'm getting that promotion, you watch…"

Look what trying to be Jean-Claude Van Damme got you. Dumb motherfucker.

A nurse came in and wheeled me off into the surgery room full of contraptions. The young female anesthesiologist came in and made me sit up and lean forward and she poked me high in the base of my neck with a little needle thing. A warm numbness slowly worked through my shoulder and flowed down my arm to my fingertips.

I lay back down and they undid the wrapping on my hand. A diamond-shaped wound the size of a quarter sat in the heart of my life line. The blood oozed slowly from it as the dark red tissue fibers glowed. At the center was a small hole of light, like the pupil of an eye. Nausea rose in my stomach as they put my hand down and strapped my arm to a board.

They set up a little blue tent on my chest to block my view. They worked for an hour on my shoulder and then my hand. The Middle-Eastern surgeon wrapped up and came around to my other side. He pulled his blue mask down and grinned at me.

"You're very lucky. The chest wound didn't hit the lung, artery, or nerve. The hand is a bit more complicated. Tendon damage. But you're young, you do the proper rehabilitation and you can recover most of the strength and mobility in the fingers."

"How long will it take?"

"Six months for the shoulder. A year or more for the hand."

"Fuck." I closed my eyes.

"Joe, you have to look at the bright side. An inch over and that bullet pierces your lung. Also there's an artery that runs through the shoulder down the arm. The bullet brushed it. The bullet severs that artery and you might have bled to death. Your hand, my god, a millimeter one way or the other and you never make a fist again." He pulled his blue gloves off. "You're very lucky."

"Lucky? I'm lucky…" I sighed. "I guess I am."

They wheeled me into a recovery room. I sat for an hour waiting to head to my room. Sleeping elderly bodies surrounded me, their old spirits creeping toward death. *Do you really want to get old? Die old in a place like this? Fuck that.*

◆

A nurse came in and wheeled me out. A uniformed officer waited at the door.

"Who the hell do you know?"

"Huh?"

He shook his head in disgust. "This shit is totally against protocol."

The nurse wheeled me into my hospital room. Lauren got up from the cushioned couch and smiled bashfully.

"How are ya?"

"I'm alright, I guess. How'd you get in here?"

"The Queen's got the chief of police in her pocket."

Lauren positioned the pillows for me and the nurse pushed a shot of morphine into my IV. Lauren crawled up on the bed with me and laid her head on the good side of my chest. She pulled out her little red Swiss Army knife and unfolded the little blade.

"What are you doing?"

She nodded at the keyhole on my cuffs. "I think I can pick it."

"Stop, baby," I said. "I been thinking about it. I don't want to run no more. I want to go get it over with. They're gonna lock me up for a few years maybe. They say with good behavior you only do part of it. I might only do six months, eight months, who knows. Then we can be together and we don't have to hide and run. We can start a real life together."

She batted her big brown eyes.

"And…I don't know, maybe I do owe something for killing Trent. Maybe I owe…"

"OK."

"You'll be waiting for me when I get out, won't you?"

She smiled. "I guess."

◆

On the TV in my hospital room there was a lot of coverage of the shooting. Then a WGNO reporter named Wild Bill Wood called my room and interviewed me. A lot of it was still blurry and I couldn't remember the names of the kids. Later that day there was a big full segment with pictures and everything.

"Just one month ago, twenty-year-old Chicago native Joe Walsh was a nationally ranked champion boxer headed for the Olympic Trials." Images of me boxing in the Golden Gloves flashed, and me at Windy City. "Everything changed the night he got into an altercation on his college campus." A picture of the articles about the fight projected across the screen. "Walsh claims he tried to walk away, but a fight ensued which left one young man in a coma clinging to life." Wild Bill Wood, a thin man with bright eyes, flashed on the screen talking from the grassy neutral ground on Esplanade. "Walsh went on the run and ended up in the Marigny where he apparently rented a shotgun house and worked for cash as a bouncer. Then tragically, the man he fought with in the suburbs of Chicago died." The *Chicago Tribune* article flashed on the screen. "Walsh was now wanted for murder. Just hours after he learned he was wanted for murder, he claims he was walking down Canal Street when he noticed a commotion. Walsh says he ran to the aid of two high-school kids who were being followed and spit on by a group of hoodlums. Walsh says he did what he does best: fight." Wild Bill was suddenly on Canal Street.

The shot switched to Chuck in his wheelchair. "He knocked one of em flat. Then the kids run off. Them thugs were scared of him. They were trying to fight him but they kept falling down trying to duck his punches," Chuck said.

"That's when one of the hoodlums allegedly pulled out a gun." Wild Bill pointed his finger.

The image switched back to Chuck. "The one started shooting at Joe and Joe just ran at him but then the second or third shot hit him and he fell down. He saved them kids. If it wasn't for Joe them fools might killed them innocent kids."

Footage of me unconscious on the gurney being pushed into the ambulance danced across the screen. The camera switched to Wild Bill, who was now in front of the hospital. "Walsh was rushed here to Memorial Hospital with two bullet wounds. While being processed, police found the warrant for his arrest. WGNO has been unable to find the two high school students who were allegedly at the center of the incident." The shot switched to a phone number for the detective working the case. "Anyone with more information about the incident is encouraged to contact the New Orleans Police." It switched to a live shot in the studio; the anchor looked up as Wild Bill finished. "Walsh will remain at University Medical Center New Orleans until he is stable enough for transport back to Illinois to face the charges against him."

The anchor nodded. "What an incredible story."

"It'll be interesting to see if those kids do come forward."

"If they exist. In other news…"

Lauren angrily clicked off the TV.

"Why won't those damn kids come forward?!"

"Who knows? Maybe they snuck out of the house. It was pretty late."

"They could help you! They should fucking help you!"

"Look, that kid'd pissed his pants. He's probably pretty traumatized about the whole thing. Maybe the parents don't want to get 'em involved in that. Those fucking guys are dangerous, you don't want to stand witness against people like that."

"Fuck them little Newman brats!"

"All that matters is they got outta there safe."

"You got shot! You nearly got killed!"

"I coulda ran. I think I wanted them to shoot me."

"What?! Why?"

"I don't know." I sighed. "I think part of me wants to die."

"After everything we been through, you were gonna leave me like that?"

I tried a shrug and winced in pain. I started wiggling my wrist in the jagged cuff.

"You're giving up on me?" she asked.

"No. No, I ain't never giving up." I put my bandaged hand on hers. "I realize that now."

◆

Other stories came out in the *Chicago Tribune* and *Sun-Times*. They were even more skeptical. Ma called and read them to me. WGN Chicago used the footage of Chuck's interview in their segment and the phone calls started pouring in. Lauren answered the calls and held the phone up to my ear.

Brother Alex called.

"Joe, thank God you're alive!"

"Brother?!"

"I've been worried sick about you!" Brother Alex said. "Why didn't you call me!"

"I didn't know what you'd think of me."

"What I'd think of you?" he said, incredulous. "Joe. I'm religious. People tell me stuff. Maybe not as much as a priest, but you'd be surprised."

"Well I guess I didn't want to drag you into it."

"Drag me into it! You jerk! I love you. There's no dragging me into anything! I'm with you in all of it, whatever, I'll be visiting you when you get up here. They better not let me in with you or I'll smash you in the gut."

"OK, OK! Thanks, jeez."

"Joe, you're a jerk, don't ever forget to call me if you're in trouble!"

"OK, Brother, I'm sorry."

Sal called from the pay phone inside Windy City.

"Aye killer, how are ya?"

"Sal..." I sighed.

"Too soon? What? Come on, have a sense 'a humor. We're all real proud 'a ya at the gym. You saved them kids, boy, you're a damn hero! Hey, all the guys wanta talk so I'm just gonna let the phone hang... Aye, guys, he's on!" he shouted into the bustling gym symphony. All the guys took turns and got on and started telling me wacky shit and wishing me well.

"Joey! Look, kid, if you go to the pen let me know! My guys will protect you!"

"Thanks, Fearless."

"You're a fuckin' real American hero! GI Joe!" he said, and passed the phone to Zuzinksy.

"Joe, I'm gonna win the Midwest Trials for you, boy!" Zuzinsky said.

"I knew you had power, but damn!" Jermaine told me. It went on like this for a while, so long I got uncomfortable.

A couple hours later Coach Emanuel called.

"Joe, I was downright heartbroken when I heard, but I'm proud 'a you. I hope them kids do come forward."

"Thanks, Coach."

"Hold on, somebody want to talk to you."

"Joe?" Aaron's childish voice came over the phone.

"Hey, Aaron."

"Joe, how are you?"

"I'm OK. They say I'll heal up."

"Good, are you coming to the trials?"

"I don't think so, Aaron, but good luck at the box-offs."

"I wanted to know because I didn't want to have to fight you again! You good, you tricky!"

"Hahaha naw, Aaron, I hope we never have to fight again. You took me into Super Mario Brothers that first fight."

"Was you really seeing everything like in the video game?" Aaron said, thrilled.

"Yeah your punches were turning into the green pipe!"

"Did you hear like *bling bling bling* when I hit you?"

"Yeah! I still have nightmares about Super Mario Brothers!"

"I hear it too, but in the second fight I couldn't hear it. And your head kept disappearing. Then it would reappear again somewhere else."

"Really?"

"Yes, that's why I kept missing," he said curiously. "How yo do dat?"

"I don't know."

"Well anyways it's real hard to hit you, when you disappear like that. I just wanted you to know."

"Thanks." I told him. "Well you be sure to put all those motherfuckers in Super Mario Brothers at the Olympic Box Off's. OK, Luigi?"

"I'ma try to real hard, Joe." Aaron said like a little boy. "Get well soon, Joe!"

He handed back to Emanuel.

"Alright, well, everybody out here in Detroit around Valentine's wish you well, and when you get through all that mess, you welcome to come on out for some work anytime."

"Thanks, Emanuel."

Angelo called and told me, "Whatever happens, kid, you go away for a little bit, it's OK, when you come out, the deal is on!"

Burkhart called. "Joe, you have to see this as a sign. You might have taken one life but you saved two. Always remember that."

As I hung up, the Queen materialized at the door to my hospital room in a puffy purple business suit coat with a short skirt, black nylons, high heels, and a purple velour hat with a little black veil.

The cop at the door arched his eyebrows at her.

"What?" she said. "You betta watch your stare. You want me to call Sargent Robideaux?"

The cop lowered his eyes.

"That's what I thought."

She stuck her nose up, walked in, and sat beside me in the chair. She leaned in and took my hand in her cool, soft fingers.

"So the white magic won after all. I wasn't sure about you, boy. You got some black magic in you, baby."

She bowed her head down and kissed my cuffed hand.

"Well, are you happy with your choice?" She sat on the edge of the bed near my hip.

"I think so, your majesty."

"Good. It's turn'n out OK. You famous now, boy!"

"I don't know about that..."

"One thing I do need to hear direct from you..."

"Shoot, your majesty."

"The bird, did he really lead you to the kids?"

"I never woulda saw 'em if it wasn't for Little Fucker."

She stared deep into my eyes peering through my thoughts and memories. She sighed and grinned.

"This one for the history books." She slapped her thigh. "Do you know who White Money is?"

"No. You know him?!"

"That boy family been messin' with the darkness a long time. Black magic, old as New Orleans. Kinda darkness come from way deep inside and don't never go away, passed from one generation to the next. You talk about an inheritance, ya heard me?! But I'ma tell you about it some other time, I'm gonna let you rest, son. You got a long journey ahead of you. Both 'a you."

She got up and hugged Lauren.

"Thank you for everything, your majesty."

She leaned down over me.

"The honor was all mine, Joe," she whispered. She kissed my temple softly and glided out.

◆

The story of White Money slowly materialized over the next few weeks and years. The Queen knew about him and she knew several of his relatives. A few were even regulars at The Oven over the years, and there were ties between White Money's and the Queen's lineage that intertwined all the way back to the formation of New Orleans. White Money's real name was Clarence Jean-Baptiste Beauregard III; he was a descendent of P. G. T. Beauregard, a Confederate general whose family owned Chalmette Plantation. Later White Money's ancestors got into oil in the region and White Money's grandfather had set up a large trust fund for him which paid out two thousand five hundred dollars a week. White Money'd grown up in a luxurious Saint Charles Street mansion with big white pillars. But White Money was troubled and rebellious. Some older neighbor kids had bullied and abused him. He'd fallen into addiction and eventually started buying heroin from a crew in nearby Central City. He dropped out of Tulane shortly after his eighteenth birthday, when access to his trust fund kicked in. He bonded with a group from Central City called G Blocc, first through drugs and music, then later through the violence White Money wanted to inflict on the world. He fell into the street life and funneled money from his trust into the G Blocc's drug operations, which is how he got his nickname, because G Blocc loved the white money he poured into the crew. All of this made White Money a high-ranking shot caller for G Blocc. He began to form his own sub crew in the organization. The operation escalated to armed robberies, which hit their peak the night they shot me.

In the aftermath of the incident the police caught images of White Money's face in several surveillance videos from the storefronts. His parents saw White Money's face on the WGNO News and went straight to the authorities. They caught White Money a few days later. Being that he was not from the life, he gave up Thumper and several other important players in the G Blocc organization, and they were promptly arrested. White Money's parents sent in a team of elite lawyers and called in various favors to various councilmen, and White Money avoided any charges against himself by turning witness and giving up the video tapes.

But in the end that didn't save him. He tried to return to Tulane and the elite life. But a year later he was dead, gunned down in retaliation by Thumper's cousin.

I'm getting ahead of myself, though.

◆

Dydecky called.

"Joe, how are you?"

"I'm OK, Mister Dydecky! Thanks for calling."

"Joe, I'm so sorry about what happened. You keep your spirits up. I'm here with Erickson. He wants to talk with you."

"My god, Joe, I heard about the mess on campus and read about what happened in New Orleans. I can't believe it. Are you OK?"

"Yeah I'm alright, Doctor Erickson, thanks for calling. What's going on at Fermi?"

"The experiment is going fantastic, Joe! I wish you were here with us, you wouldn't believe it!"

"I'm glad."

"Joe, you're a great guy. Don't let this mess defeat you."

"I won't, Doctor Erickson. Thank you."

Lauren hung up the phone and nuzzled her head into my neck. *Jesus, there's so much damn love coming my way.*

◆

One-Leg Chuck showed up to see me on my last night in New Orleans.

He'd cleaned up and shaved and was wearing a dress shirt. He rolled in with his chin high, smiling. He stopped at the foot of my bed and saluted me. "Joe Walsh," he said, with pride glowing in his eyes.

"Hey, Chuck! I thought I'd never see you again."

"I was gon' find a way to see you, Joe Walsh. I want you to know that what you did for them kids, it was real brave. I gotta go all the way back to 'Nam to remember young men willing to risk their lives to save their fellow man. It brought back a lot of memories for me, a lot of things I been hiding from in the bottle. I ain't drank in two weeks now, Joe. You might think that's not a lot a time for an old-timer like me but it is. It's the longest I been sober in more than a decade. And it's on account of you. I reconnected with my family and I been staying with my sister. And my life is a lot different now. And I want to keep it that way. You inspired that, Joe. I want to thank you. My grand niece and I, we made you something." He pulled out a shirt from a bag on his lap. It read: *You Got A Big Ole Heart!* There was a big red heart in the middle.

He rolled over and handed it to me. "I told the police they should give you a valor award for what you done. They don't want to listen. Say they can't find the kids. Well, they got me, I tells em! They just laugh. I got a Purple Heart in Vietnam, I tell 'em. They just say yeah, yeah, where is it? There were other medals too, but my platoon leader, he died on Hamburger Hill, same artillery round that got me, took my leg. I don't care about the medals, but maybe it woulda helped convince them you deserved one."

"It's OK. I don't mind, Chuck. A medal ain't gonna help me much now."

"That's what I figured you'd say. Medals don't do much for me neither. I sent my Purple Heart to my lieutenant's wife for their son and daughters to have. Told them…" Chuck choked a little and started to cry; I reached out and held his coarse hand. "…I called 'em and told 'em, 'Your husband and father was a great man and a noble soldier, and I wanted you to have this because he saved my life and many soldiers' lives in battle. I owe my life to Lieutenant Gowen.'"

"That's beautiful, Chuck."

"I didn't mean to come in here and cry like this, like some damn fool." He wiped at his tears angrily. "I just want you to know I will sing your praises to anyone who will listen. Joe Walsh, the Hero of Canal Street. And I wrote you this and got it notarized." He handed me an envelope. I opened it; it was a letter with his statement about the incident. "Maybe it'll help you in court up in Chicago."

"Thank you, Chuck."

The Queen and Dawkins stepped through the door and smiled at me. They were in formalwear; Dawkins held his black, brimmed hat in his hands.

After everybody left, I lay awake, while Lauren slept with her head on my chest. Nurses came and went. The traffic outside trickled past. My mind raced with thoughts of violence inside the cells and out on the yard—some daring escape, climbing the razor-wire fence. An ambulance siren sprang up as the lights swirled up on the buildings across from my window and across the walls of my room. Suddenly a voice sprang out of the siren and spoke to me. *You think because you saved those kids everything'll be all good, with a happy ending? This ain't no motherfuckin' Disney film! You think that cute little T-shirt you got on gonna protect you from a shank?* Of course not. *You're going to prison, motherfucker. They're gonna rape you before they kill you. Maybe during and afterwards, too.* No, they ain't doing that shit to me, come on. *What? Cause you can fight? If you fight they're gonna put you in the hole for weeks, they're gonna put you in darkness. You're going into the darkness now fool.* The ambulance siren clicked off and the room faded to blackness. *You're gonna die in there. Or worse, the darkness is gonna get inside you and stay with you forever.* The air constricted in my lungs as the wires squeezed them. *You should have never saved those dopey-ass kids.* Sharp painful hooks stabbed and planted through my shoulder and my palm. I love those kids and I love what I did. Our father who art in heaven, hallowed be thy name. *You are the stupidest motherfucker in the whole damn universe.* Thy kingdom come, thy will be done, on earth as it is in heaven. Give us this day our daily bread, and forgive us our trespasses as we forgive those who trespass against us. *You will never be forgiven for what you did! You will burn in the pits of hell for eternity!* And lead us not into temptation, but deliver us from evil. *You think that stupid shit is really gonna protect you from the darkness?* Our father who art in heaven...

◆

I woke in the morning with Lauren next to me; I breathed in the sweet creamy scent of her. The rising sun bled reddish-orange through the buildings and filled the room in a hazy glow.

"How are you?" she asked. "You scared?"

"It might be hard in there, baby. Might be real hard. I keep thinking about if they try me in there, what I'll do."

She looked at me with her thick lips pouting. Her brown hair fell in messy strands over her face.

"Just survive, baby." Her big light-brown eyes peered into me. "Don't be no tough guy. Just do what you got to do to survive."

PART FIVE: PANOPTICON

Chapter 18: Broken Glass

AS YOU CAN IMAGINE, I COULD FEEL SOMETHING BAD COMING, but back then I could have never of comprehended the profundity of what incarceration actual is.

When an individual enters the corrections system, their life shatters into an elaborate series of conflicts. They are in conflict with the judicial system, the judge presiding over their case, and the various attorneys and the laws themselves, and the victims of their crimes. Simultaneously they are at war with the corrections system—their cage, the officers who yield incredible and often unchecked power. They are in struggle with their fellow prisoners and the jail culture, gangs, and rules. And they are in strife with the broader society: their family and the fear that they will always be seen as a dangerous criminal. They are also in battle with their past—the actions that led them to incarceration, the earlier traumas that often caused them to break those laws. And most gravely of all, they are at war with their own soul.

This environment will crush a normal person. They will be faced with many impossible decisions, places where the system presents them with a choice: survival, or their humanity. They will have to fight to keep themselves intact, and if they are unable to win that most precious battle, their future will be darkened beyond measure.

◆

The US Marshals shackled me and took me in a plane to O'Hare, then in a jail van out west to DuPage County Corrections. As we soared along 88, I remembered Ma taking me to Oak Brook mall for the first time: the fancy walkways with greenery and the ponds, a place I'd only seen in the movies. The Walshes' great escape. *You're back in the 'burbs, Joeyboy. Welcome. Well, you're a killer, now. Guess you always knew you didn't belong out here. It'd always end up like this.*

We approached the huge complex with three massive buildings with blue-tinted glass and little ponds between them. The van pulled into a razor-wire-fenced loading dock in back and they led me inside into a glass-walled bullpen with six other prisoners sitting along a few concrete benches. Piss filled the metal toilet to the brim, and a cloudy white strand of toilet paper swirled to the surface of the piss like a trail of smoke.

An old skinny black bum with a big gray afro sat across from me in the bullpen. I recognized his jovial raspy voice from the night I lost to O'Sullivan; I'd seen him around Maxwell Street Polish too. He went by Bird-Man 'cause he always fed the birds; the birds loved him—all kinds, pigeons, seagulls, even the sparrows. They said he had a friend falcon he fed chicken hearts to. He sold porno tapes and DVDs out of a big black garbage bag down on Maxwell. We did a job down the street from Maxwell and Halsted and we'd go to Jim's Original Polish every day for lunch.

"Bird-Man..." I said with a grin.

"Oh yeah, I know you! Joe the fighter."

I shushed him, not wanting anybody to know I was a boxer.

He nodded and grinned. "We had us a drink and a talk one night, and you used to always be around Maxwell."

"And you was always tryin' to sell me tapes!"

"You bought some though, didn't you?"

"Yeah."

"You see that R. Kelly sex tape?" a fat mean-looking black dude in a gray hoody asked from down the concrete bench.

"Is it real?" I asked.

"Yeah, it's real," Bird-Man said. "I had it for a while." He shifted uncomfortably in his seat. "I sold that thing for months and then I finally sat down and watched it. Ah..." He hung his head in shame. "That man, he peed in that little girl' mouth! That just, it jus' wadn't right." He grimaced. "I took 'em all and I throw'd 'em away. I don't want none 'a that magic on my hands."

"I'd watch dat shit!" the mean black dude said. He flipped his gray hood over his round black head as the bullpen rippled with laughter.

A skinny little Mexican dude in a dusty Carhartt jacket slept on the bench all curled up like a baby. Little gang tattoos covered his hands and face. He giggled about the R. Kelly tape and drifted back to sleep.

An older white guy came in the bullpen in a white dress shirt and black slacks. He nervously paced the bullpen. The hooded black guy started fucking with him. Telling him nasty shit.

"You finna' get raped in there, boy!"

The white guy trembled on the concrete bench.

"Man, shut the fuck up," I sneered at the hooded black guy.

"Fuck you, you hoe-ass whiteboy!" He sneered at me and jumped up off the bench.

Brittle rage pulsed through me as I shot up and reached my hand into the dark cave of his hoodie and clasped my hand around his cool flabby throat. His throat seemed to fold shut as he grabbed my forearm with both of his hands, and I drove my legs and his head smashed into the glass window with a deep thud like the beginning of some colossal evil. I cocked my right back, but I couldn't make a fist.

The door slid open and three guards rushed in and wrestled us apart. They cuffed us and put us in separate little glass phone booths. He paced and glared at me, throwing up the pitchforks. After a few minutes, they came and got me and led me down a white corridor. As I passed him, he flipped his hood off and I saw a big spattering of scars traced over his ear like someone'd thrown acid on his head.

"On the SIX I'ma kill yo ass," he told me, and smiled through a deep grimace that quivered all over his face.

I stepped over the long orange-clothed leg of a light-skinned black guy sitting on the floor half-in and half-out of a cell with his back against the doorjamb. A white paste covered his entire face. His insane light-brown eyes lit up as I walked past. He smiled dimly. Huge bandages covered both wrists. A guard sat across the narrow hall reading the *Daily Herald*. They opened the cell next door to his. A bloody blue rag lay in the middle of the floor of the gray solitary room. A concrete bed sat on one side with a black bedroll folded up on it. I lay down on the cold hard bed as the guard slowly closed the windowless door. The light squeezed down to a big fierce blackness, then just a faded glow around the rectangular door. *You been in here twenty minutes and you're already in solitary. Welcome home, Joeyboy! You really started some shit now, didn't you.* Something moved in the dark. It was a subtle shift in the room: a lean to the left, and the voice shot up out of it, grumbling. *They're doing it. To a lot of people, all over the corrections system. And they're going to do it to you, trust me. Ain't no escaping. Welcome to the darkness. Every time you try to do good in here, you will be punished a thousand-fold. That demented ass GD you just choked will never stop coming after you until he gets you, and he has an army of soldiers in here. You are here to burn in a hell of your own making.* Fuck you too motherfucker, get the fuck outta here.

A new guard came and relieved the other one in the hall outside my door.

"What the hell'd you do to yourself?" the guard asked.

"OK, well," the guy with the white paste on his face started. "I took my shaving cream and painted a big pentagram on the floor, then when they came with the razor I broke it real quick then laid down in the pentagram and cut both my wrists! The guards came to try and help me but I told them, 'Stay back, I gots AIDS!' They went and checked my chart and it wasn't true, then they came back, and now I got me a big ol' puddle of blood, and I tell 'em 'Let me die with the devil, motherfuckers!' And they come in and I try fighting 'em and they hit me over the head with the nightstick and I go into a deep sleep, best sleep I had since I been up in here," he said as the guard giggled and folded the newspaper. "So I'm sleeping and dreaming I'm there beside the dark one, Satan. And he points up and said 'is dat yo bitch?' I look up and this light goes on above me and it's warm and glowing. All the sudden this beautiful face appears in the light and I look into her eyes and I fall in love right that second and she falls in love and all the sudden I'm in a room full of nurses and doctors. She's a nurse, looking down at me, and she put her hand through my hair and I tell her I love her. She didn't say it back, but I know she do too. Well, the only way I can see her again is if I cut my wrists again, so I'm thinking 'bout doing it again tonight!"

The guard laughed and turned the pages in his paper. A couple hours later a new guard came in and he told the story all over again.

Finally after about twelve hours, a big mean gray-haired guard came in my cell grimacing at me.

"You gonna be a problem?"

I shrugged and said, "No."

They processed me; they took my clothes, and my underwear too because it was gray and not white. I geared up in an orange button-up jumpsuit. They gave us bedrolls and led me and another guy down a series of long white hallways with blue lines painted down the center. As we went, wind slipped through the jumpsuit button holes and breezed against my genitals. We arrived at a black-tinted-glass control room.

Three pods branched out from the corner. A door slid open to a two-floor pod with all-glass windows and twenty single-person cells.

Door 13 buzzed and slowly slid open on the second floor. *Lucky 13.* I climbed the metal steps, walked the railed balcony and into the cell with my sheets and pillow. They shouted "Close 13" and the glass doors slid slowly into place and slammed shut with a loud long *boom. Locked in a cage like a fuckin' animal again.* I sat down on the concrete bed. *Maybe I shoulda let those motherfuckers fuck those kids up on Canal Street.* The lights clicked off in the whole POD. *Look what being a fucking hero got me.* I sighed and lay down on the bedroll atop the concrete. *Naw, fuck that.* I closed my eyes. *You did the right thing.*

When they let us out in the morning I headed to the pay phone and called home.

"Dad?"

"Joe?"

"Yeah, I'm here in DuPage. What's going on with the lawyer?"

"He thinks you have a very good chance of getting off on self-defense. But if you're convicted of involuntary manslaughter, the most you can get is about five years. With good behavior, you might be out in ten months."

A huge black guy got up from the metal tables and started walking toward me. He stood over six feet tall and had a wide muscular neck. As he approached, I looked him in the eyes. He looked back dismissively. He grinned as I ignored him and kept talking with Dad.

I glanced up at him and he walked right up on me, grinning down at me. I jumped up and crouched, cocked my fist back. He halted.

"Woh-woh-man!" He raised his palms to me. "I'm just trying to use the other phone." He picked up the other phone and dialed.

"Sorry," I said and sat back down on the floor as he took the other phone off the hook.

"I gotta go, Dad. Ten months is a long time."

"Joe, it could have been ten years! Or more! This is good news."

I hung up and walked over by the blaring TV. *Fuck this fuckin place.* I sat down at one of the metal tables. *If they let me go I could still get out in time for the trials.* I looked at my hand all contorted in a weird fist. *What the fuck are you gonna do? Make the Olympic team with one hand?*

◆

Jail life is mechanical, and boring as fuck. You wake, you eat, you sit, you play dominoes, you eat, the doors slide open, the doors slide closed.

My time in the pod felt tame. Mostly guys were in on silly crap. I got along with a couple old Vice Lords and the one big guy that I almost swung on. They taught me to play dominoes, and told crazy stories about riots and gangster shit in Garfield Park and Englewood.

Court felt weird. A little brown room with long fuzzy benches. The judge looked like a cold motherfucker: tall, with white hair, an old mean face, and golden wire-rim glasses. All these strange motions, court jargon, They set the next court date for a month away. It infuriated me. Belmonte, my lawyer, pulled me aside.

"A month!?"

"A month is good, kid!" Belmonte said. "The place you're in now is like a hotel compared to the penitentiary. You just keep your head down and don't get in any trouble."

After the jail authorities found out I was staying a while, they came in and got me and told me I'd made trustee. They scooped up two of us and brought us down to the old section of the jail. The doors opened. Crazy dudes in green smocks and pants filled the musty room. They greeted me as I walked in. Bird-Man sat on the blue foam couch in front of a TV; he gave me a wave as I passed. Old rusty metal bars formed the cell doors. The guard led me to my cell.

"You're commissary, but you're helping out at the laundry tomorrow. 5 a.m."

Bird-Man came to my door.

"Welcome to the trustee row house, Joe."

"What the hell's going on?"

"You made trustee 'cause you caught a manslaughter. That's a long case. You on the commissary crew."

"What the hell's commissary?"

"It's for groceries, soap, shavers, food, all that. You know, you buy it with the money on your books. You pack the orders and then you go all around the jail, deliver 'em."

"All these guys are commissary?"

"Half 'a us commissary, half laundry. I'm laundry. You come down and help us once a week. Any mo questions? I'm finna crash, we gotta be up and out at 5 a.m."

◆

They rounded us up in the morning dark. We lined up, went down the long wide hall to fall into line with the laundry crew.

They'd lined the bulk of the crew up in front of their huge dorm room full of bunk beds they shared with the kitchen crew. Two weird-looking corrections officers in black uniforms patted down the inmates in their brown trustee uniforms. The taller one looked Latino; he wore his hair in a close-cropped fade, with shaped eyebrows. A pencil-thin mustache sat over his thick lips. The other officer was a goofy white guy with short spiky hair and small feminine facial features and big clunky black boots. They held us up and lined us up, with the laundry crew facing the wall. The two weird officers walked through the line inspecting us. The Latino guard kept stopping, leaning into prisoners' faces and whispering in their ears as the white guard with his immaculate short blond hair trembled behind him with his head bowed and his hands clasped together over his crotch.

The Latino guard stopped in front of me and spun slowly to face me. He raised his chin and peered at me with a perverse smirk. He glanced back at his partner and pointed at me. The white guard walked up with an embarrassed grin and knelt at my feet, while the Latino officer stepped around behind me whispering.

"You're a bad one, aren't you? Bad-bad-bad. You don't want us to take away your good time, do you?"

The scent of baby oil and lime wafted off of him. The white one sat on his own boots and patted his thigh and looked at me strangely.

"Put your foot up!" he said urgently.

I placed my foot on his knee. He slowly removed my white Velcro shoe, put it delicately beside him, and started fondling my foot through my white sock. His hands trembled as his breath quickened. *What the fuck is this?*

"You gonna give us a problem?" the Latino guard whispered in my ear as he slid his hands over my sides and up to my chest. He slid his hand over my crotch; his hand lingered longer than it should have as his fingertips tingled over my balls and held them snugly. His smooth jaw touched my neck as his hot breath swirled in my ear. "He's a good boy. Gonna give us a good time."

The blond officer at my feet jammed my shoe back on and switched to the other one. He took the shoe off, stuck his fingers all inside it, and brought it to his nose. He sniffed it while looking up. His eyes sparkled, and I realized he was looking the other officer in the eyes. The blond officer smiled up at him like a naughty school girl.

"Mothafuckas," Bird-Man muttered next to me.

The Latino officer swung around and jumped in his face.

"You like your good time?"

Bird-Man looked down in silence.

The Latino guard snapped his fingers.

"On the line! Let's go."

The white officer at my feet shoved my shoe on. There seemed to be a little tent at the crotch of his black pants. The prisoners turned and stood on the long black line. They started moving down the hall following a red line on the floor. I walked with my white Velcro shoe half-on.

"That didn't take long," Bird-Man said over his shoulder to me.

"What the fuck was that?"

"You got introduced to the Nut-Hugger and Dr. Soles. They like you. You lucky you ain't on laundry every day. Disgusting motherfuckas."

"What the hell's he talking about, good time?"

"We get one day a good time off our sentence for every day we don't get in trouble. But the guards, they could take it away from us. These faggots, they be threatenin' us, to take away our good time if we complain about the nasty shit they do to us. I got sent six months, that mean' they could take three months 'a my life from me."

"That's some evil shit right there."

"Sho' you righ'."

They led us down to the loading docks. This part of DuPage County Jail is maximum-security. We had gyms but no yard, no windows, nothing, no fresh air, no sunlight. I didn't realize how much that sensory deprivation affected me over those few weeks. But when we got to the loading dock and they pushed a button and the gray metal sliding garage door rolled slowly up, a swirl of free air spilled in. The scent of trees and grass, the chirps of birds singing, all washed over me.

As the garage door slid open an enormous tree came into view out past the tall razor-wire fence, across the train tracks. The reddish-gold sunrise lit it up from the side. The wind rustled through the browning leaves in a rhythmic undulating wave. A fleet of brown sparrows ascended from the tracks and fluttered up into the branches. I ain't never appreciated a motherfucking tree so much in my damn life. The free air particles energized me. A sudden cloud of antimatter crashed into my chest. My heart pumped full of explosive life. The laundry truck turned around in the lot and slowly backed up to our dock as the razor-wire gate slid shut. Visions flashed through me. *Kick Officer Nut-Hugger in the nuts. Jump down off the dock and rip open the truck door, drag the fucking truck driver out, jump in and floor it through the fence over the tracks. Run. Carjack the first car you come across, drive away free and never look back.* I took a deep breath and closed my eyes to the magnificent tree. *You have a debt to pay.*

They wheeled twelve huge blue carts off the truck. All the clothes were wrapped in biohazard bags. We wheeled them into the big freight elevators and went up to the laundry room. A series of a dozen long folding tables led to a big metal row of industrial dryers and washers. Square cloth laundry carts sat everywhere.

Laundry was fuckin' shitty work. Two trustees geared up with black rubber aprons, elbow-length rubber gloves, and face masks and plastic goggles. They took box cutters and sliced open the biohazard bags. Then they pulled out the soiled linens, gowns, and what the guys call diapers.

"What the fuck's a diaper?" I asked Bird-Man.

"So all this biohazard shit is from the county old people's home across the way," Bird-Man told me. "The old people, they can't hold it no more, they about to die. They shit and piss in bed. So the nurses come in and they undress 'em and wipe 'em, but the shit still on the sheets, so they put down a diaper on the sheet. Then they tell 'em go back to sleep." A few of the younger guys giggled and nudged each other, eyeing the diapers. "Fucked-up thing is when they wash the diapers and sheets, the crap, it detach from the cloth, and when it get into the dryer, somehow it harden and compact into these little walnut-sized rock-hard lint balls made of shit."

I puked in my mouth a little.

Bird-man went on. "The guys call them Tootsie Rolls. They gon' try to get you to eat it at lunch, don't fucking do it," Bird-Man urged. "It ain't no candy, it's shit."

"Thanks, Bird-Man."

"My name Fanzo, nigga."

"Thanks, Fanzo."

We folded some leftover orange jumpsuits and smocks as we waited. Then new stuff came hot from the dryer. The diapers were pink satin on one side and a hard thick white cloth on the other. We folded diapers and sheets for hours. We ate lunch in the laundry room, and on the break, the big pockmarked Native American they called Injun who ran the dryer sat down next to me.

"You try the chocolates?!" Injun asked giddily.

"Fuck you," I replied. "I know what it is."

All the trustees in the laundry room cracked up.

◆

Commissary was a whole lot better. Hundreds of boxes of products, including every fucking type of ramen noodles you could imagine, filled the big stock room from floor to ceiling. There were so many different kinds of ramen you'd think you couldn't ever outrun the disgusting plastic salty nastiness.

We ate whatever the fuck we wanted as we packed the orders in the commissary into big paper sacks. Us trustees threw packaged food at each other and clowned around until the big fat gray-haired commissary chief opened his office door and screamed, "SHUT THE FUCK UP!"

One day we filled sacks, the next we delivered. We just went back and forth Monday through Thursday. We wheeled the bags in carts to every wing of the jail and all four floors, to maybe a thousand inmates. If we fucked up an order we bartered our mistake with sodas. The creepy ass sex-offender pod was the worst.

They broke the jail up by gangs. The inmates came from all over; some were from the 'burbs but others had come out from the city for whatever crazy reason. They held the high-profile murder cases in the basement in segregation. They only allowed them one hour out of the cell, one at a time. Them motherfuckers were crazy as shit. One old, bald, light-skinned black guy had been down for over eight years fighting seven counts of murder on a serial killer charge. Every week or so he lost it and started saving up his feces in his toilet, then he smeared his own shit from out his asshole all over his cell, screaming in tongues. Eventually, he smeared it all over himself. He did it so often the guards just waited till he calmed down and sent in a bucket and a mop and he cleaned the whole mess up himself.

I liked our row house: free movement, TV at all hours, a couch. It made me grateful I wasn't in the basement. The guards only came in on a thirty-minute cycle; they walked back to the far wall in the room and held a little wand to a sensor in the wall, and it beeped and then they left. The old cells stank. A nasty paste covered the walls. Getting locked up at night brought some safety with it, but it really depended on where in the jail you were. The knuckleheads on the commissary crew with me seemed pretty harmless. The laundry and kitchen dorm sounded like hell. Every day Nut-Hugger and Dr. Soles fondled those guys. It took a toll on them. They fought constantly. We listened through the vents as they screamed and attacked each other. Some laughed, others cheered, then the guards'd rush in. I remember a man's desperate voice screaming, "I'm a human being! I'm a motherfucking human being!"

I started to get to know the commissary guys. They were a bunch of fuckups. The more we talked, the more I learned about the drug trade: heroin, cocaine, and meth. They all had their hands in it. You could make real money and real fast. One religious muscular black guy became a heroin addict after he narrowly survived a car wreck that crushed his pelvis. A little Puerto Rican with a dragon tattoo on his neck—Ambrose from Aurora—ran from the cops and then got on 88 going the wrong direction trying to make them call off the chase, but he crashed. One goofy white guy worked downtown in an office; his cocaine problem sunk him for possession when he got pulled over in the 'burbs. The guys really fucked with him, told him he needed to learn to fight to survive in prison. Everyone agreed prison held serious danger; you fought every day just to survive. There was no minding your own business and keeping a low profile.

When they found out what'd happened with me, they gave me plenty of space. I didn't want them to know I was a boxer, didn't want them to see me as a challenge. I didn't want to lose the sense of surprise when they did try me. But this loudmouth Mo from Maywood got me talking about boxing. They called him Gaddafi 'cause his big nose looked Middle Eastern and he wore an orange towel on his head; he ripped the edges into a string and tied it in back like a do-rag. And when he found out I was a boxer he tried fucking with me.

"What? You wanta step to us?"

I was like, "What the fuck you talkin' about, Gaddafi? Who the fuck is 'us'? You got a mouse in your pocket?"

The rest of the crew burst out laughing as Gaddafi sulked off to his cell to cry about his girlfriend, who'd gotten him locked up for beating her ass.

◆

My lawyer Belmonte was a fast talker from Midway with gray slicked-back hair and a fake-bake orange face. He seemed to be trying real hard, but I didn't trust him though. Something in his demeanor screamed "con man."

They gave me a few minutes with him in a side room before court.

"OK, Joe, the state is pursuing involuntary manslaughter and that holds a five-year max sentence."

I tensed. The thought of getting hit with five years flashed through my mind. *Coming out at twenty-five with a murder on my record.*

"But cheer up, kid! We got a great case for self-defense."

"OK." My mind raced. *Could I still box after that? My hand ain't right and my shoulder ain't right.*

"I'm going to request a bench trial."

"Why?"

"Because you don't want a jury. They'll see pictures of the kid and want to throw the book at you."

We went in and Judge Peterson snarled at me from up on his podium. He had this real jagged jaw like the Silver Surfer, and was pale white with white hair. Peterson raised his chin and straightened up tall and peered down at me like he was looking down from the clouds, like he was the Saint Peter of the 'burbs. *So this is the motherfucker gonna decide my future? All by himself, huh? I'm fucked.* The jargon started flying and I didn't understand anything until Judge Peterson picked up his gavel. He set the bench trial for a month away. The judge glared at me angrily and banged his gavel home and they led me out.

Lauren came out every week to visit me. She encouraged me and showed me these exercises she'd learned from a physical therapist friend. She kept telling me, "Our life is waiting for you." I worked through a series of rehab exercises, hoping to get my hand healthy and strong again. The nerve damage caused severe pain and reduced range of motion in my fingers.

They didn't give me any medical support in DuPage. I was laying in bed one night after lights-out doing the exercises when my hand seized up in an ugly claw. I looked at it in the low light as it twitched. *Who am I kidding?* I glared at it angrily. *I can't even make a fucking fist.*

Hope drained from my heart as my days fell into the dreary machine.

◆

I got another letter.

Dear Joe,

I heard about what happened and I'm real sorry, kid. Hope your hand and your shoulder are ok and you can still box and everything. I know those guys were in the wrong and there's nothing to do about it now. But if they lock you up, I'm gonna see to it you're protected. That fight we got in man, it is what it is. I probably had it coming. I got strung out and shit happens. I'm sorry. I love you, you're my kid brother. I didn't realize you'd grown up so quick or I wouldn't a tried fighting your little ass. Boy, you're quick! I fought it out with some of the baddest mofos in the prison system and I ain't never been hit like dat, kid. Anyway I hope you can forgive me. I'm sorry about it all. I wish it could have gone better. I wish I could have made it on the outside. Best of luck with the trial and hope they don't convict ya. But if they do, I'm here.

Love, your Brother,

Pat

◆

I entered court for the bench trial. Lauren and Painter showed up, and Trent's friends and family showed too.

I knew I was in trouble when Lauren said, "He called me a 'nigger bitch.'"

Trent's Kappa Kappa Alpha friends giggled and tried to twist it into coughs. I watched Peterson's face for a response and he hiked his eyebrows up, then gave her a dismissive grimace.

The muscular state's attorney dragged his fingers through his slicked-back hair and picked away at all of Lauren's recollections of the fight.

Trent's friend Brad lied his ass off.

"We were just going to our car to go home, and it was like Joe was waiting for us near the parking lot. He just ran at us and attacked us all. It was really scary."

Belmonte did a pretty good job cross-examining them and they faltered a lot, but Peterson seemed uninterested in Belmonte's cross-examination. It seemed like he'd already made up his mind on the whole case.

Belmonte chose to have me not testify on my behalf, which might have been good because all of it stirred up so much rage and anguish. I don't know if I could have gotten through it without screaming or crying. I just got up in the booth and said, "I plead the Fifth" while the state's attorney glared at me.

As Belmonte finished his closing statement, Peterson held the gavel.

Peterson asked Belmonte, "Are you done?"

Belmonte shook his head yes.

Peterson glared at me.

"I find you guilty," he said and banged the gavel.

Trent's tall, wrinkled mom cheered from the front row and raised her veiny fists above her thin white hair. Peterson looked at her and winked. Weakness shot through me. I glared at Peterson. *I want to fucking kill your ass.* He set sentencing a month away.

Judge Peterson was known for giving out foul sentences for minor crimes and traffic violations. Half the people sentenced in DuPage County were Peterson's cases. The jail received funding for each bed full, so anytime there was an empty bed in DuPage, Peterson started dropping the hammer on guys, mercilessly receiving kickbacks and helping his friends who ran the jail. It was a racket, and the cops in DuPage were in on it too, and anytime a roughneck from the city passed through DuPage County he had to spend some time in the Hotel. (Which is what they called the jail, because it was so much nicer than Cook County.)

◆

The black dude I choked in the bullpen my first day became a Trustee and made cook. He was a GD and the whole kitchen crew were GDs. He saw me headed to the laundry and eyeballed me. That nasty scar along his head was from a childhood injury; he'd fallen out of a project window five stories up and was caught in a thorny bush. A few of the laundry guys were GDs too, and tension started to build.

Injun kept asking me to help him hand out dinner trays, and finally I got bored enough to go with him. They paid with an extra tray. I agreed. The work made the time pass fast. I just wanted to keep my mind off my sentencing coming up in a couple weeks.

I sat down in a little side room with Injun after handing out two floors of trays. I had my two brown plastic trays with their little sections full: a cold bun, iceberg lettuce with ranch dressing, red Jell-O, and the biggest section full of meaty red chili. I eagerly dug my plastic spoon into chili and gobbled it. I always eat fast, just like Dad—it comes from working construction; when the pour's on, you gotta eat quick. I lapped it up loud like a dog; the chili was gross but it was better than that nasty chicken. I finished the first tray, shoved it away and pulled my second tray over. Something burned in my throat and slid down my stomach. *Man, the chili ain't that hot, and it ain't that spicy.* I scooped several more spoonfuls into my mouth and swallowed them down. I felt someone's eyes on me. I glanced up as the rest of the kitchen crew; these two dark-skinned black guys in the green trustee shirts eyed me through the glass. Then one of them threw up the pitchforks. *Do I look like a motherfucking gangbanger to you, you piece of shit?* I placed the spoonful of chili in my mouth and bit down on a jagged shard of glass. It cut my lip. *What the fuck?!* I spit it out on the table and picked it up in my fingertips. A jagged little pebble sized piece of clear glass. I inspected the rest of chili; little shards of glass speckled the red goo. This sandy dust texture slathered around in my mouth and tingled all through my teeth and down my throat and burst in my stomach. *These motherfuckers poisoned me.* I glared back at the window. The two kitchen crew guys burst out laughing, pointing at me. I spooned through the rest of the tray and tiny pieces of glass sparkled everywhere. I grabbed the first tray and all that was left of the chili sparkled. I dipped my finger in the red sauce and rubbed it in my fingertips; the sandy coarseness of the glass tingled.

"There's fucking glass in my chili!" I yelled.

Injun laughed, "Who you kidding?"

"It's real." I showed him the glass hunk. "Don't eat another bite of it."

He stood up, shocked. "Is it in mine?"

The trustees pointed at Injun, laughing. I spooned through his chilli: no glass, nothing.

"No, it's not in yours."

"Joe, I didn't know. They told me to get you to go, but I never thought they was setting you up."

I looked him in his eyes. They trembled with fear. *He's telling the truth.*

"Try to throw up, man! Jam your fucking finger down your throat."

I tried. The guard buzzed opened the door.

"What the fuck's going on?"

"Them motherfuckers poisoned me!"

I leapt up and barreled towards the door to get out in the hall at them. The guard blocked the door and grabbed me in a bear hug. His partner rushed in and they pinned me to the wall. The GDs' laughter resounded in the big hallway as the other guards poured in from guard station. They urged me to force myself to vomit. I dug my fingers into my throat and puked up a long string of yellow bile with little spots of blood.

They brought me to the medical ward. The doctors ordered a scan, but the glass particles were too small to make a surgery worth it. They gave me some medicine and assured me the glass would work through my system.

The jail did an investigation. Nothing came of it.

◆

My stomach was fucked up. I could feel the glass oozing deeper inside of me, working its way through my innards. The glass dust sparked alive in me like millions of tiny particles of dark matter. They emitted a heavy, dark energy that permeated my entire being. I shit blood off and on. Little blotches of pink formed throughout my torso, like it was working its way to the surface of my skin. Spikes of pain jolted me awake at night. I stopped eating from the trays and just ate prepackaged food from the commissary. Sometimes I ran out of food. I lost weight. I wanted to eat but the glass stabbed at my stomach. I couldn't risk glass (or worse) in my tray.

I couldn't sleep at night. I heard things through the vents. Then one night I was lying there wide awake when that demonic voice sparked up through the vents like on my last night at the hospital in New Orleans. *I told you. You know they poisoned you. The darkness is inside you now, Joeyboy. This is your new life, get used to it. They all want you dead. Stab one of those motherfuckers when they're lined up getting fondled by those faggots. Shank 'em right in their fucking throat while they ain't looking.* No. I got up and went to my sink. If I kill somebody in here they'll keep me here forever. This ain't no place for a human being. *I don't want to be a good person no more.* I stared into my thin face in my scratched-up mirror. *I'm gonna fucking kill those motherfucking GDs.* I gripped my sink and tried to rip it off the wall. It cracked near the spout. *You're gonna die in here if you kill somebody. You gotta get out of here.*

I picked up a postcard Lauren'd sent me that sat on my table, a picture of a bold white lotus flower in full bloom standing tall above its circular green leaves, spread across the surface of a pond. It was from some Buddhist organization called SGI. Lauren'd moved back in with Burkhart; she was singing again at the Mill, and a drummer in her band had turned her on to Buddhism. She was studying this Buddhist text called *Lotus Sutra*. I hadn't read her postcard yet; I was saving it for a dark moment. Her words were often the only thing that got me through the day. I lay down on my thin mattress and put the postcard to my nose and breathed in her creamy perfume scent. *Well, that motherfucker said what he said, now whatchu gotta say?* I flipped the card over.

BabyBoy,

I was studying today and I came across this line that made me think of you: we must turn poison into medicine. I know, I know how hard that thought

must be for you right now where you are
and how you're feeling. But the white
lotus when it is planted in the darkest
mud in the most unfriendly conditions
it grows the most powerful flower. My
love, you have to fight for the white
magic and grow into the most powerful
spirit with the mightiest of hearts! You
have to become the white lotus.

With all my love,

-Lauren

I lay the card on my chest. I imagined the glass circulating through my digestive system as roots reached down into me. I imagined my heart was a mighty lotus flower bulb beginning to grow. My heart began to pound with a great power. *I will not let this defeat me.*

◆

A new guy started up on the Laundry crew—tall, lanky, and stupid. Mikey. Hundreds of terrible little jail tattoos lined his arms and neck. A big BGD marked his forearm. BGD means Black Gangster Disciple but Mikey was motherfuckin' white. A crackhead, he'd gone into a gas station and bought a pack of gum, and when the cashier opened the register he'd lunged over the counter and grabbed the stack of twenties and ran. He told the story repetitively the first day.

"The cops came from all directions! I ran into the forest preserves and the police helicopter came out there and I found a pond and swam into the middle where there was a sandbar. I just hung out there for hours while the cops surrounded it and the helicopter flew overhead and then the news helicopter showed up and I flicked them all off, just chilling out there in the pond until they got a little boat and came and got me."

The story rolled on and on in a constant loop for the next three hours we worked. Everybody wanted Mikey to shut the fuck up.

Finally lunch came and we all knew what time it was: it was time to get Mikey to eat the Tootsie Roll.

The dryer guy, Injun, sat next to Mikey and asked, "So how'd you get locked up, Mikey?" like he hadn't heard him loudly recounting the story all morning. Mikey started talking joyfully, and Injun put a Tootsie Roll on Mikey's tray and another one on his own as Mikey gabbed on obliviously. About a minute in Injun asked, "Ain't you gonna eat that chocolate?"

Then Injun picked up the Tootsie Roll from his own tray and faked taking a bite out it. And Mikey picked his Tootsie Roll up, and everyone turned and leaned, on the edge of their seat. The glass in my stomach poked and dug around in me.

Mikey grinned proudly, thinking he'd gotten all our attention with his story again. He gestured with the Tootsie Roll, and in his whiny, stupid storytelling voice said, "And I looked up at that helicopter and I flicked him off!" And Mikey took a bite of the Tootsie Roll.

Our laughter filled the big laundry room. The pain in my stomach twisted to a warm joy. Mikey laughed, thinking we were laughing with him. He chewed on his Tootsie Roll a few times, then spit it out.

"It must have gone bad."

We nodded and agreed.

And Mikey went on with his story. We laughed at him the rest of the day. It felt good to laugh at Mikey. It satiated my hunger to hurt somebody. It seemed to take the pokes and stabs of pain away from my stomach.

◆

Soon after that these two gay GDs started preying on Mikey. They always folded near him, and they'd say nasty shit to him. Mikey'd recoil, grossed out, and he'd move to another table, and they'd follow him, giggling sadistically.

The next week, Mikey pulled me aside.

"Joe, you're a boxer, right?"

"Yeah, I was. Why?"

"I'm in trouble. Them two sickos, they're on me."

"What do ya mean?"

"Last night I was laying in my bunk and someone grabbed my ass. I looked one way and saw nobody, then I looked the other and there's the big one with the afro smiling at me."

The glass stabbed me in my spleen.

"Why you telling me this?"

"I'm scared they're gonna try an' rape me, man!"

"Fucking defend yourself! Whatduya want me to do?" I stomped away from him, back to the table to fold.

I called Lauren that night. She had been at the Buddhist center downtown and chanted with hundreds of other Buddhists, and she was so thrilled. She explained to me that Nicheren Buddhism, which was Japanese, was a Buddhism of the normal average person. It was a doctrine that claimed that anyone could reach enlightenment. That we all could be Bodhisattvas of the earth. All we had to do was chant *Nam-Myoho-Renge-Kyo* and pray to attain our earthly desires and help others. It sounded a little culty and crazy, but I needed something to get me through, so I figured I'd try it. She explained the Japanese words: *Nam* means I devote; *Myoho* means mystic law. (The mystic law essentially means that everyone is able to attain enlightenment, even the most unenlightened.) *Renge* means lotus blossom, which grows in the muddy waters and as it blossoms the fruit of the lotus is revealed, which is symbolic of the law of cause and effect. *Kyo* means the *Lotus Sutra*, and so all of it together is basically a devotion to this Buddhism.

I was at the pay phone in the dark shower room with the curtain drawn; the guys were just on the other side, watching *The Tonight Show*.

She started chanting slowly and smoothly, and I began to follow her. A few seconds in I closed my eyes and suddenly the glass came alive in me. The particles hurt, all through my esophagus and down through my stomach and intestines, and even in my asshole. "Nam-Myoho-Renge-Kyo. Nam-Myoho-Renge-Kyo. Nam-Myoho-Renge-Kyo. Nam-Myoho-Renge-Kyo." Then suddenly as I chanted the glass began to sparkle alive in me, and as I chanted more the particles began to hum and send these wonderful cool shivers all throughout me, and some pressure began to build in my chest.

"Nam-Myoho-Renge-Kyo. Nam-Myoho-Renge-Kyo. Nam-Myoho-Renge-Kyo."

"Do you feel it, baby?"

"Yes. I feel something."

"Nam-Myoho-Renge-Kyo. Nam-Myoho-Renge-Kyo. Nam-Myoho-Renge-Kyo."

We chanted for a good fifteen minutes and stopped.

"Now you are officially a practicing Buddhist," she told me.

When I hung up I realized the TV was off. I thought it was weird, because they usually watched it all night. I went out from the curtain and the guys were all in Buddhist poses with their eyes closed—even Fonzo on the crummy little couch sitting Indian-style with his arms out and his fingertips pinched together.

What the fuck?!

"Babobubababo Babobubababo Babobubababo!" Gaddafi chanted as he materialized in front of me, his head bouncing with the brown rag flailing around as he stomped out a little rain dance.

"Fuck you motherfuckers," I told them, grinning as they broke character and burst out laughing.

"You know that bitch is fine as hell if she got a nigga saying dat shit!" Gaddafi said over the roars.

Later, I lay down in bed and tussled with the voice. *You really think that saying some stupid Japanese cult chant is gonna help you!? First it was white magic! Now this bullshit!* Fuck you, man. Get out of my fucking head.

Sounds woke me in the middle of the night. A commotion funneled through the vents from far away, followed by Mikey's trembling voice. "No... no, no, please no!"

They wrestled. I heard Mikey screaming. One of them growled, "Shut the fuck up!" Then I could hear the rhythmic motion.

My body tensed as the glass seemed to come alive inside me. A sick joy bubbled up in my stomach. *They're raping Mikey. Fuck that annoying piece of shit. Maybe you'll rape a motherfucker one day.* An image of a tiny jailhouse tranny in a short pink skirt flashed in my mind. My cock stirred in my underwear. Suddenly Mikey cried out like a child. The dark particles sparkled in my stomach and singed my esophagus. I sat up in my bed. *No, no, I'm not like them. I'm not fucking like them!* I jumped up and ran to the glass window that looked out onto the hall. I banged on the glass; a young guard ran up and the door buzzed open.

"They're raping Mikey in the laundry dorm!"

"Yeah, right." The young guard winced. "How the fuck do you know that?!"

"I can hear it in the vents! Just go help him, please!"

The guard buzzed the door shut and ran off. A big commotion exploded in the vents. Mikey sobbed as they led him off to the medical ward.

Fanzo woke up and walked to my cell door.

"Das a good thing you did right there, Joe." He gripped the bars of my open cell. "You might be a convicted killer, but you gots a good heart..."

"I just got tired of hearing that motherfucker cry, Fanzo."

"OK... OK." He giggled and walked off.

I chanted *Nam-Myoho-Renge-Kyo* in my mind for Mikey until I drifted back to sleep.

◆

It wasn't all bad in there. We had fun too. The night after them GDs raped Mikey, we were hanging around the day room watching TV. There was some kinda weird energy in the room after what'd happened to Mikey; they were trying to make jokes about it but that shit wasn't funny. Then Fonzo decided to show us how to build a Fifi. He got up with his crooked back and puffy gray fro and went to the bathroom and came out with a new roll of toilet paper.

"I'm a show y'all somethin. Now sometimes mothafuckas get lonely in the pen. But you don't gotsta go off in a man's asshole. All you gotsta do is build you a Fifi." He sat back down on the couch. "First thing, you get you a roll 'a shit paper. If you got you a King Kong Dong, maybe you needs you two rolls 'a paper." He motioned like he had another roll on his lap as we giggled. "All you need is a roll 'a paper, a rubber glove, and a tooth brush." He laid the objects out on the floor between his feet. "First thing is: takes the glove and the tooth brush and tie the middle finger and ring finger on the brush." He took them and tied the two middle fingers of the glove around the brush. "Double knot the bitch, 'cause if it come loose, good Lord you gonna be a sorry mothafucka." He doubled the knot. "Den you take the shit paper." He picked it up. "And you pull the glove through the tube." He feathered the wrist of the glove into the tube and dug his finger in and pulled the wrist through. "Den you stretch it around the roll." He pulled the rubber and fitted the elastic wrist around the outer edge of the paper. "It ain't as good as no pussy, but it a whole lot better than some nigga asshole!" He flipped the Fifi in the air and caught it. "I used to have me all my porno magazine spread out all over my cell. Put some baby oil in the Fifi...sometimes I had like three Fifi's! I be having me an orgy up in there!" He stood up, his eyes glowing in the flickering TV light. He started humping the Fifi, holding it still in front of himself, looking out into the distance with a kind of tunnel vision. We burst out laughing. "And when you about to bust a nut, you can squeeze dat bitch!" He threw his head back in ecstasy and squeezed his hand around the toilet paper roll. "Good Lord!" Fonzo yelled as we roared. Then he fell back onto the crummy red couch. "Clean up easy as long as you don't let it spill out. You just pull dat wrist off and tie it in a knot." He tossed the Fifi towards Ambrose who caught it, giggling, his eyes bugging out at us. "Das why I made my life in the pornography business, cause I love pornography. It help me not ever go off in no man ass in my seven years in the penitentiary."

"What up though, girl?" Ambrose's eyes lit up as he inspected the hole in the Fifi. He licked his finger and dipped it inside. "Damn, dat shit tight!" He finger-banged the Fifi, smiling at us with his buck teeth; we all broke up. "I'm about to go hit dis!" He tore off jogging towards his cell as we laughed and hooted.

"This nigga about to lose his virginity!" Gaddafi yelled, and we roared.

Abrose stopped at his cell door, cocked the Fifi back like a quarterback, and threw it at Gaddafi. The Fifi spiraled across the room as Gaddafi balled up, flinching against the cinderblock wall near the big wide window that led to the glowing hallway. It bounced off the orange rag wrapped around Gaddafi's head and toppled to the greasy cement floor.

That started some silly bullshit. We chased each other around with the Fifi for a half hour like a buncha dipshit ten-year-olds, laughing maniacally.

◆

Dr. Soles and the Nut-Hugger continued to molest the kitchen and laundry crew every morning. The two gay GDs liked it. They'd laugh, and almost volunteer to be touched, but the rest hated it. Their rage built day after day of abuse. As sentencing closed in, I walked past them knowing I'd be in their line the next morning. My mind raced with possibilities. *Hit Nut-Hugger right in the throat, knee Dr. Soles in the face.* I felt Nut-Hugger's eyes on me watching me like prey. The glass dug into my gut and released a cloud of neutrinos. *I'm gonna kill you, you sick motherfucker. You take our humanity, I'll take your life. You're using a position of authority to impose your sexual fetishes on innocent people. Or maybe you think we deserve it, because we're in here? Is that what you're trying to say? That we're in the wrong, that we're bad people and deserve this? Fuck this shit. This ends tomorrow.*

I got a hold of a pen with a white plastic grip and borrowed Ambrose's lighter to melt the plastic tube, and I sharpened it against the dirty gray floor in my cell until it formed a hard dagger. *If those motherfuckers try and touch me again, I'm killing both of 'em.* I held the white jagged blade, peering at myself in the mirror. *Now that's what I'm talking about! That's a piece 'a real white magic!* I ran my finger along the strong white tip. *Shut the fuck up.* I slipped it under my bed roll and slept.

In the morning we lined up with the laundry crew in the long hallway facing the wall. I'd rolled the shank into the elastic waistband of my pants. I happened to be next to the new guy, Larry, a little black plumber in his early forties with gray spots in his gnarly hair. Judge Peterson had just dropped the hammer on him for driving without insurance. He had a record from way back for some driving stuff in his early twenties, so it was a repeat offense. Now, twenty years later, he had a wife, two kids, and a home, and he was losing it all over forgetting to update his payment method at Allstate. The day before, I'd heard him telling Fonzo all of that, and it'd made me tremble—because if Peterson hit him with that, what would he fucking hit me with?

Officer Nut-Hugger approached us from way down the line. His dark Latin skin was damp with lotion. There was something menacing in his close-crop fade and pencil-thin mustache. His sliver correction officer badge gleamed in the stale white light like some shield from the Dark Ages. A perverse smirk sat on his angular face, as though he was in some rehearsed act. Dr. Soles followed him with his head bowed submissively.

As they approached me, the glass sparkled alive in my stomach. *Kill both these sick motherfuckers.* I touched the hard shank in my elastic waistband.

Officer Nut-Hugger stopped before me and slipped between me and Larry. The scent of cocoa butter and cool water cologne wafted past. Officer Nut-Hugger positioned himself behind Larry. *Thank god it's not me.* The joy of it not being me faded as Larry started to tremble beside me. Officer Nut-Hugger pointed to the ground in front of Larry, and Dr. Soles fell to his knees. Dr. Soles patted the black thigh of his uniform, motioning for Larry to put his foot on it. Larry did, and Dr. Soles started to undo his white Velcro shoe. I unraveled the shank from my elastic waistband in my fingertips. *They do this shit to one of us, they do it to all of us.*

Officer Nut-Hugger leaned in behind Larry so his thick lips were nearly touching Larry's ear.

"You got some good time don't you?" Officer Nut-Hugger whispered. "Six months for driving without insurance. That's three whole months of good time."

Larry winced and nodded.

"Don't want to lose that good time, do you?" Officer Nut-Hugger reached his hands out and began to drag his fingertips along Larry's stomach.

"We're gonna have to take your good time, unless you give us a good time," he whispered, then started to dip his hands down over Larry's crotch as Dr. Soles picked up Larry's foot and sniffed his toes. "If you don't give us a good time, we're gonna have to give you a bad time."

The shards of glass in my intestines caught on something and exploded my belly. A cloud of dark energy swirled up into my torso. I squeezed the shank in my palm. *I'll rot in here for life, happy as hell. Fucking evil deviant motherfuckers.* I twisted my head and looked at Nut-Hugger; his thick lips were almost touching Larry's ear. I cocked the shank as Officer Nut-Hugger turned to look at me, real sassy-like.

"I can't take this shit no more!" Larry whispered; in a flash he bowed his head forward and then propelled it backward with all his might.

The back of his bald head cracked into Officer Nut-Hugger's teeth. Nut-Hugger staggered back screaming, and hit his head on the clear glass window that looked into the dorm.

"Faggot-ass mothafuckas!" Larry yelled. Then he reached out and grabbed Dr. Soles by the sides of his blond head and kneed him in his pale nose. Dr. Soles's head recoiled backwards and he fell to the shiny white floor on all fours, a geyser of blood pouring out of his nose.

"Dat's what I'm talkin bout!" Fonzo yelled from down the line.

Officer Nut-Hugger cupped his mouth as blood oozed through his teeth. He pinched his radio at his shoulder.

"Oh my god!" he squealed. "We need backup! All officers get to two! A trustee just attacked us!" He pushed between us and picked up Dr. Soles, and the two of them ran down the line while all of us laughed. I slid the knife back into the elastic in my pants and rolled it. The hilarity of it finally hit me, and I started to giggle.

"Oh yeah, it's a good mothafuckin day!"

"Dat's what I'm talkin bout!"

"Run, faggots!"

A few seconds later officers poured in and sprinted up to Larry. They cuffed him and led him away to the hole.

"Man, I hope they don't charge him wit gay bashing!" Gaddafi yelled out.

Everybody started clapping for Larry as the guards looked at us uneasily. Larry definitely lost his good time, but he didn't have much else left to lose.

A few of the new guards led us to the laundry, and I never had a better day in the clink. We laughed all day folding sheets and gowns and diapers. We retold the story, and what Dr. Soles and Nut-Hugger said, and how they screamed like little girls. The two gay GDs didn't like it; it was like it'd ruined their fun. They sulked off to the side. The louder we talked the more they recoiled. Finally, the big old head guard opened his door and screamed, "SHUT!!! THE FUCK!!! UP!!!!!!"

And we all quieted down and giggled and tried to hold it in but the joy was too much.

"Watch, that shit'll cool off now." Fanzo snickered.

"Fanzo, I was gonna kill those motherfuckers this morning."

"What?" Fanzo guffawed, folding a diaper. "That's what you wanted the shank fo?"

"Yeah, I was gonna stab 'em both in the throat."

"Joe, my man, you can't let those motherfuckers keep you in here. You gotta get your ass up outa here."

"Yeah, I don't give a fuck no more, Fanzo." I slammed the diaper I'd just folded into the big rolling bin.

"You should, motherfucka!" Fanzo said painfully, "You got something out there for you. None of us got shit."

"What the fuck I got? Look at my motherfuckin' hand! I can't barely make a fist." I raised my mangled palm.

"You just gotta keep tryin', man. Don't be no mothafuckin' crybaby. You let this shit get to you in here"—he touched his temple—"then you ain't neva getting out. Even if they *let* you out. You gon' be a prisoner yo' whole goddamned life."

◆

At sentencing, I stood in my brown trustee uniform on the brown carpeted floor of the small courtroom with Belmonte on one side of me and my father on the other, both in ill-fitted suits. The young guard hadn't cuffed me for some reason. Lauren sat in the third row in a blue dress. Trent's mom was in the front row with a black dress on. Peterson loomed atop the big wooden structure with the witness booths below him and the pudgy court reporter typing away. An American flag hung limply on a pole behind Peterson as he glowered down at us with his pale stern face. I figured after more than two months in jail, maybe they'd just let me out. But Peterson just glared at me with a slight grin on his thin gray lips. *Naw, I bet this motherfucker hits me with the full five like the piece of shit he is.* The tiny glass particles came alive in my innards and swirled up into my stomach as Belmonte presented Peterson the letter from One-Leg Chuck saying how I saved the kids. As Belmonte spoke, Peterson plucked up his glossy dark wooden gavel and scratched his temple with it.

"I would like the court to reflect on the fact that while the defendant was on the run, he risked his own life to come to the aid of two teenagers. He was shot and nearly killed in the process."

"Do you rest?" Judge Peterson asked with a wicked grin.

"The defense rests, Your Honor..."

Peterson squeezed the gavel and brought it up high over his head. "Five years!" he shouted, and banged it down hard so it crackled through the room like a rifle shot.

It was like it blew the top of my skull off.

The dark energy rushed up my throat and erupted up out of me like a geyser. *Them animals are gonna rape you in there!*

"Five! It should have been fifty!" Trent's mom's shrill bitter voice screamed out.

Dad's mouth gaped open. He reached up his thick hand to cover it. Peterson grinned at us pompously and hiked up his eyebrows.

"Fuck you, motherfucker!" I screamed, and grabbed the wooden ledge before me. I dug my white Velcro shoe atop the ledge and leapt up at Peterson, and slammed my hands onto his altar and lunged up, reaching my hand out at his face. His eyes widened as he fell backwards in his rolling chair. As he fell, he threw the gavel at me; it whizzed past my head, flipping end over end. As Peterson fell, he reached out and grabbed the flagpole. The red and white stripes fluttered as it toppled to the carpet. Peterson's gown flipped up, revealing a gray suit and brown penny loafers beneath it. I lifted my knee onto his altar and reached down for Peterson and nearly snagged his leg when a mighty hand grasped my ankle. I looked back as Dad squeezed my ankle with both hands, he was half up on the podium.

"Help! Guards! Help!!!" Peterson screamed, terrified. He crawled frantically over the red and white and blue of the flag toward his chambers as the corrections officers poured in and wrestled me off the podium.

"You ain't laughing now motherfucker!" I screamed as they wrestled me down. They got me down onto the floor as I twisted, writhed, and kicked. "Go hide in your motherfucking quarters, you old bitch!"

The officers got one wrist cuffed, I squeezed my fist to my chest on the ground. Dad begged me to stop as Lauren chanted Nam-Myoho-Renge-Kyo slowly and steadily from the benches. Her voice slowly eased the tension in me and took the fight out of me. They finally clanked the cold metal cuff down on my other wrist.

"Just look at that animal!" Trent's mom screamed. "Lock that monster up and throw away the key!"

I laughed wickedly as they pulled me to my feet; I glared at Trent's Mom.

"Fuck you too, bitch! Your son was a racist bully and a sack of shit!" I screamed.

The pudgy black officer who pulled me to my feet tried not to laugh as they yanked me toward the doorway.

"Baby, you have to escape this!" Lauren was standing on one of the benches. "You have to escape this animality!"

My heart exploded. "I love you," I told her.

They shoved me through the door and back into the bullpen, and the sergeant screamed at the young guard for letting me in the court un-cuffed.

Once everything settled down, Belmonte came to the little booth to explain everything. They processed all new state inmates in Statesville for one month. Afterward they'd send me to Menard for the remainder of my sentence.

"It wasn't gonna be too bad. Due to the overcrowding in the prison system, you were gonna serve two months on a year, and they've given you time served for your two months in DuPage. So with good behavior you would have only had eight months' prison time to serve. But I doubt this counts as good behavior…"

They put me back in solitary. I lay down on the concrete bed. The buzz of nearly getting Peterson faded. *Eight months...but now maybe more. The Olympic team'll be decided before I get out. I'll turn twenty-one in prison.* The light glowed around the edges of the doorway. *Pretty good, Joeyboy. You had old Peterson pissing in his judge dress. A little quicker and you mighta got him.* Shut your bitch-ass up too, motherfucker.

I grinned, seeing the fear in Peterson's face, the wicked joy of that moment. *I hope they don't add no more time to my sentence.* You stupid motherfucker. *What the fuck is she, a buddhivistsa of the earth, or a voodoo princess?* Come on man, it's just life.

I heard her voice as she told me on the phone a few days back: *Nam-Myoho-Renge-Kyo and the Lotus Sutra are instruments of the white magic.* I closed my eyes in the massive darkness, and the room suddenly spun. *White magic? What the fuck? If white magic is real, then why did all these white motherfuckers put you in prison? White magic, my ass. You and Moma Queen shoulda killed Little Fucker. You shoulda plucked those dumbass feathers, fried him up in some grease, and eaten him like a piece of motherfuckin' chicken.* I burst into laughter in the cool darkness. *You chose this, this is what you fucking get! White fuckin' magic, my ass.* I forced my eyes open, and slowly the white haze flowed around the edges of the closed cell door. Momma Queen's voice flowed through to my mind: *You have to choose one side, and fight!* I sat up and clasped my hands in prayer: "Our father, who art in heaven..." *That motherfucker ain't gonna save you!* "Nam-Myoho-Renge-Kyo. Nam-Myoho-Renge-Kyo. Nam-Myoho-Renge-Kyo. Nam-Myoho-Renge-Kyo..."

Trent, I'm sorry. I'm sorry about what I said to your mother. She didn't deserve that, and you didn't deserve to die. I lay back on the concrete bed and sighed out a long breath. *Five years, two months on the year? Fuck... I guess I can pay that.*

Chapter 19: Panopticon

AS BIZARRE AND TORTUROUS AS MY TIME AT DUPAGE COUNTY WAS, it really was just an annoying hotel stay in comparison to the Illinois prison system.

Prison is an elaborate and ever-changing structure of gangs and racial affiliations, a massively powerful set of unwritten rules built on decades-long legacies and vendettas. It would have taken years of study to comprehend it all. Part of me wondered how Pat navigated it when he first entered the system all alone. And I marveled at how he was able to pick up the pieces afterward and make any semblance of a normal life on the outside. It made me respect him and his struggle.

When normal people find out you were in prison, their fears almost always drift to the most horrific thing they can imagine: dropping the soap, prison rape. Sorry to disappoint you, but it ain't really like that. Now prison rapes do happen in a variety of situations. Sometimes the prisoners are just rapists preying on the weak, like what happened with Mikey. Other times, they are trying to enforce power or enact revenge. But for the most part, sex between inmates in prison is consensual. Men away from women can be pretty miserable. We all need touch, and sometimes random acts of violence aren't enough. Luckily, my time was relatively short, and Fanzo had taught me how to make the Fifi. So I never took part, but many prisoners were what you called gay for the stay. Some were submissive, others just closed their eyes and imagined they were kissing their wives or girlfriends. Sometimes the sex was a negotiation of protection or transaction: money on the books, packs of smokes. (A funny note: wearing your pants sagging actually came from prison and was a signal that you were open and willing to take it up the ass.) Some prisoners were gay on the outside as well, and had long-term loving relationships behind bars. Others got around a lot, and spread STDs. All I can really say is, it isn't like it is in the movies, and the ones having sex weren't outliers. Some were fierce soldiers, and even shot-callers in the most powerful gangs.

All this is to say that later on, when normal people brought up dropping the soap with me, I'd swallow down my rage as I looked them in their eyes trying to read if they were asking me if one of those animals raped me. The whole time my mind would be racing through the real danger: the stabbings, the killings. Something I did become very intimate with.

◆

They led a string of us in through the frigid winter air to a squat brick building in Statesville for processing. It took a while; there were a lot of real bitchy officers screaming in our faces. Then they finally led us into the gigantic circular brick building; they called it F House.

I walked in the long line holding my bed roll to my stomach. *F for us fucking failures, I guess.* A bright light at the end of the tunnel opened into a monstrous circular auditorium-like room. A three-story guard tower stood in the center of the circle. The octagon-shaped observation deck was covered with big tinted windows. Two bright blinding lights shot out of the hood of the tower like menacing eyeballs. The steel girders of the roof came to a point seven stories up. Four floors of cells encircled us as we walked out into the cacophonous noise of the room. My shoes squeaked on the glossy concrete floor. A hundred whispers bounced and ricocheted off the walls and disintegrated into murmurs.

A tall guard with a pointy cap stood near the center of the room. His resting bitch face scowled at us as we lined up before him.

"Welcome to the Panopticon. Since I know all you maggots paid plenty of attention in school, I'll give you a little history lesson." He strolled before us in his shiny black boots. "English philosopher Jeremy Bentham designed this facility. In essence, in the panopticon, we can see you…"—he pointed up to the watchtower deck—"…but you can't see us. You are under twenty-four-hour supervision. You cannot take a crap without us seeing it. You try something stupid in the panopticon and we'll march right up to your cell and straighten you out." He stopped, put his hands behind his back, and puffed his big chest out. "Welcome to the Illinois Department of Corrections. The eye is always watching." He grimaced at us with his pointy face. The watchtower seemed to grow out of his cap and peer down at us. "Don't make me come up there."

I ended up on the third floor. Three of us in a cell. One hour to roam the floor a day. Twenty-three-hour lockdown. We even ate in the cell.

There's something about being watched. I spent a lot of time staring into the eye, into those two beams of light. *It's like the Double Slit experiment, we behave differently under the eye of an intelligent observer.* My head began to ache. My mind raced. Everybody went crazy after the first week. Screams and sounds flowed around like phantoms, bouncing back and forth between the curved walls.

After nineteen days, the second deck finally went up during their dayroom time. From my third-deck cell it was like watching a Shakespearian tragicomedy on a balcony in the Globe Theatre. They refused to line up. We watched as the tension built in the guards' voices and lifted up through the balconies. Then a few dozen prisoners finally lined up, but then a few grinned and broke line again and started walking around the room. One fat black guy with a 'fro started doing the moonwalk in his white Adidas sneakers. The decks erupted in laughter and cheers.

The guards called for backup. Several of them stormed in, batons out. One skinny little dark-skinned black dude with knotty hair darted around like Barry Sanders as the guards gave chase. Three had him trapped near the wall. He juked left and cut right, his black sneakers squeaking loud on the shiny floor. One linebacker-looking guard made a diving tackle, and Barry leapt up and hurdled him as the guard flopped hard and slid on the smooth cement floor. The roars twisted through the balconies like a tornado as Barry ran a big circle through the room, celebrating like he'd scored a damn touchdown. Then he spiked an imaginary football and did a little chicken dance, his knees flipping up joyfully. His wide eyes looked up into the hundreds of roaring prisoners encircling him on the balconies. Every cell in the panopticon rejoiced. *Motherfucker could play in the NFL!* This powerful joy swirled through my chest. Comradery in that simple joy of escape united the room.

When the guards finally grabbed him, they bounced his head off the cement a few times. As the blood pooled under him, a dark rage descended on the balconies. Fires lit on every floor in protest. Guys tossed burning crumpled-up pages of the Bible out of their cells and they streaked down like meteorites. Armored guards with big metal shields stormed the cells and dragged those prisoners out and down to the hole. Meanwhile other fires ignited.

"We can't see you!" my cellie screamed from the door. "But we can see *us*, mothafuckas!" The mountain range of saggy fat rolls on his back heaved as he yelled. *We're just a bunch of pathetic little conformed photons expressing our altered consciousness.*

The fires finally stopped after three days. Voices still rose and fell. I tried to sleep. They never ceased. They crept into my mind until I didn't know if I was listening to some sick motherfucker whispering shit, or some other dark being inside me softly telling me the most horrible of things. *This is it Joeyboy! One of the darkest structures humanity ever built. Sure there were gas chambers, dungeons, the iron maiden. But this one is especially wicked, because this is where the darkness seeps inside you and stays forever.*

I dream the panopticon is the center of a terrible universe. The eye morphs into a being—the lights his eyes, the tinted glass his mouth, the stem of the tower his neck. "I know everything..."—the voice like a mechanical god, the entire panopticon resonates with it—"...your thoughts, your hopes, your desires, your secrets, even your fucking future. You're going to die in here where you belong..."

I woke as the mail deliverer slipped some letters through our cell door. I took one. It was open. *Yep, they do know fucking everything.*

Dear Joey,

Good news little brother you're coming down here to Menard with me, where I can keep an eye on ya and protect ya. I've got seniority here. I run the show for the TJOs, so you'll be safe. Ryan's here too, he's excited to see you again after all these years, even though you never visited him, ya asshole. Naw he's happy to know you're coming. He misses ya and I miss ya and we're gonna have a good few months together.

Your brother,

Pat

Ryan. After all that time, after what he did to Rose... Ryan.

◆

Being locked in that small room is no good. The tension built and hardened my face and my body. A lot of rage flowed through those balconies. They went up often—guys fighting each other in their cells. The guards would stomp down the hall, beat the fuck out of them, and drag them out by their ankles down to solitary.

It was hell on earth, to be honest. Bad people all around you, bad thoughts in your head, bad energies in your body. My hand got worse, rather than better. I lay in bed one afternoon doing my hand exercises when once again it cramped and twisted into an ugly shape. I just closed my eyes. *You'll never box again. You can't even work construction like this. And fuck physics...they'll never let a convicted murderer into Fermilab. Your fucking life is over. It was all just a stupid fucking fantasy. All of it, a wild crazy dream.* Reality just finally caught up. *You're just a piece of shit from the hood like the rest of these fucks. Like Pat, like Ryan, all of them.*

A prisoner began to hoot and yell like a gorilla, it filled F House. *I was headed here sooner or later, no matter what. Well, I'm here now, better get used to it.* I smashed my contorted hand into the cinder-block wall beside me.

I pulled Lauren's unread letter from under my mattress. It sparked the hope and love inside me. She was back singing at the Mill, and she got signed to do a tour, and she was gonna go all over the East Coast and play the clubs and sing her heart out for me. She'd sent pictures. Her letter smelled like oils and her perfume. I kissed the letter. *She's still very much in love with me.* I saw her body above me, straddling me. My dick sprang hard. The fatass in the bunk above me rolled, and the squeaky springs sagged. *Motherfucker. I can't even yank one out 'cause I'm trapped in here with this disgusting motherfucker.* Then: *just beat him to fucking death!* Good idea, you got one fucking hand. *Maybe you can just fucking kick his head in.* I did the exercises again and the hand started to loosen up after that. *I gotta survive in Menard with one hand? Fuck that,* I pounded my hand against my pillow until it opened.

I looked at Pat's letter again. *I ain't writing him back. We'll say it when we see each other.* Then I figured it was nice to know where he stands on it all. *I don't want to go over there and try to survive on my own 'cause there's fucking demons everywhere. They'll fucking eat me alive if they get the chance.*

I felt my heart hardening for what was to come—it was a terrible ride until the demonic voice in my head melded into my own voice. My mind flew through options, potential threats—my mind never rested, I barely slept. Nightmares visited constantly. My hair started falling out. I had them buzz my head completely, and the guys looked at me differently when my hair was buzzed short. My muscular head showed. I liked the way they looked at me 'cause they didn't look like they wanted to try me. They looked like they wanted to give me plenty of fucking space.

◆

Finally after thirty-one days in that disgusting little cell, they came in and shipped a group of us out. We rode five hours south on the snowy roads to Menard Prison in the full long white school bus as the guys nervously chattered. I tried to relax. My shackles clinked as I rolled my shoulders. *I'm ready for whatever.* I could make a complete fist now but it couldn't hold up to much of a blow. But it was enough to keep a guy honest if he tried me. Enough to set up a big left hook.

We drove along the Mississippi River. A tall icy bridge sat just south of us like the crown of a queen. *Bust outta here and float south to N'awlins. The Queen'll protect me.* I glanced at the ice shelves along the shores. *Maybe in spring. Naw, that's the first place they'll look.* We passed a sculpture of a lion above the welcome sign. Then we pulled up to a tall old stone building with big Greek pillars surrounded by a tall chain-link fence with razor wire at the top. A new watchtower with tinted glass stood before the entrance. *The whole world is a fucking panopticon.*

A large group of prisoners lined the fence when we got off the bus; they wore beige hoodies and brown Carhartt-looking coats. They threw up gang signs, their breath lifting off of them in heavy clouds. Some of us new inmates laughed and waved from our shackles. I didn't look. Then someone yelled, "Aye, Joey!" and I saw Pat there wearing a black skull cap, all big and muscley—gripping the fence with black gloves with the fingers cut out. Tears beaded in his eyes. He clutched the fence like he wanted to tear it down and come hug me. I gave him a sad grin. He nodded and shot his bearded chin toward where a stout red-bearded guy stood with his beige hoodie hanging over his freckled face. He looked a little like Mickey

Reid except not as ugly. The guy scowled at me, and my eyes locked with his fierce green eyes, deep in the shadows of his hood. He pulled his hoodie off and showed his peach-blond mangle of hair. Thick acne covered his cheeks and faded into his gnarly red beard. He patted his chest angrily.

"It's me, motherfucker!" he shouted. "It's Ryan!"

The glass in my stomach seemed to explode into something else.

"Ryan?!"

He burst into a chuckle, showing those old crooked teeth.

The guards yelled at us to line up and walked us into the prison. They gave us new uniforms and some winter gear.

I got out on the yard the next morning. Big squares of concrete, some fields of dead grass with little patches of snow melting on them. Some basketball courts where everybody was layered up, looking big and strange in skullys and hoodies. Pat stood near the weight benches in a black hoodie with the hood up. He saw me and his eyes bugged out.

"There he is!" he shouted. "My kid brotha!"

He walked over tall and heavy with open arms, his big paws out with the fingers spread. I opened my arms and hugged him.

"Kid, I've been so worried about you." He ruffled my hair; he smelled of Marlboros and Old Spice. "I'm so glad you're here with me now. I'm sure you'll be outta here soon."

He let go.

"How's your hand?" He peered at me with his concerned blue eyes.

I showed my palm. The scar had shrunk down to about the size of a nickel. All the lines of my palm morphed around it irreparably. I turned it over. The exit wound was more like a quarter.

"How's the recovery going, you been doing your rehab?"

"Yeah, I just started making progress on it."

"I been looking it up, we got you a bunch of ideas on how to rehab it. We got a racquetball you can squeeze. And there's these little weights, and you can roll 'em out to your fingertips and then roll 'em back. And we got these rubber strap things too; we could hold 'em for you and you can spread your fingers and squeeze 'em."

"Thanks, Pat."

He brought me over to the weight racks: a series of bench presses with barbells, dumbells, dip racks and pullup bars. He introduced me to a bunch of crazy-looking white guys.

"These are the fellas."

"Where's Ryan?"

"Ryan the Red? He's in the hole. He fucked up this SD, shot-caller named named Biggie Bomb. Caught him without his enforcers, it was beautiful. He's in there for a couple days, maybe less."

I winced.

"Don't sweat it," Pat said. "It ain't his first rodeo. He's my enforcer!"

"*He's* your enforcer?" I shook my head with disgust. "After what happened to Rose?"

Pat glanced away. "Look, it's not like that with us."

"What is it like, then?"

"It's all right. He's all right."

I deeply breathed the sharp cold air. *Nam-Myoho-Renge-Kyo.*

He gestured around at his guys.

"Look, I was thinking," he said sheepishly. "Maybe you could show some of these guys some boxing. Ya know, they need to sharpen up."

"Boxing?"

"Yeah. We're outnumbered here but we got steel, so if you need something to protect yourself with, we all got it, alright?"

"OK. Fuck it. Sure, why not."

His eyes brightened back up. "Aye knuckleheadz! Look, my brother's a boxing champion, almost won the nationals, OK? He's gonna teach you fools some shit, alright? Learn it, it's gonna help protect us all, OK?"

The guys shrugged. I started teaching them a basic stance and a jab. It was nice to move around and keep warm in the winter air.

◆

I was sitting on my bunk reading a letter from Lauren when someone walked up and stopped at my open cell door. I looked up and it was Ryan the Red, slouching dizzily in his beige jumpsuit. His forehead gleamed clammy and pale beneath the spattering of freckles; his short peach-blond hair was all miffed and twisty. A big wide red beard seemed to sprout from the dark-red acne that scorched his face; it fanned out to cover his square jaw. The light on the big windows across from my tier cast him in a cool shadow.

Something warmed in my stomach as I stood up.

"Joe. Never thought I'd see you in here." Ryan said, and something big unfurled in my chest.

"Ryan, man, how you been?" I struggled to talk with the thing swelling in me; it squeezed my esophagus down to nothing.

"I'm alright, Joe. They put me in the hole, man. Motherfuckers! No light, no sleep, all that bullshit. I'm feelin' better though." He grinned. "Heard you's a boxing champion now."

I nodded.

"Well, I been working on my hands in here too." He put up his fist; nicks and scars littered his knuckles.

A fogginess enveloped his green bloodshot eyes. The old warmth grew between us; it reminded me of running around the street together in our childhood. The thing in my chest grew; it had soft contours to it, and its roots seemed to dip down from my stomach into my thighs and all the way down to my toes.

"We went through a lotta shit together, Joe, remember?"

"Yeah, Ryan, I remember."

"Why you never visited me?" He looked down and started hyperventilating.

"I don't know, man." But I did know.

"It's alright. You was living your life 'n shit. That's the best thing you coulda done was go become a champion boxer and go to college." He looked away down the tier far, far away. "I had dreams about you, man. So many conversations in my head. What the fuck are you doing here, though!?"

"Don't worry about it. I'm here now, man." I reached out and grabbed him by his thick traps and hugged him.

"Yeah, you are. And you ain't supposed to be." He went rigid and there was something hollow and cold in him as he pulled away from me.

"Whatdaya mean?"

"Pat told me the story. That shit was self-defense. And then the kids you saved in New Orleans, man, that was real sweet of you, you was always a sweetheart." He grinned and wagged his finger in my face. "With the girls especially. You gotta girl, man?"

"Yeah man, I'll show you some pictures. She's beautiful, she's real special. She's a jazz singer." I pulled a shot of Lauren on stage at the Green

Mill, the light all sparkling in her eyes as she leaned into the big chrome microphone, her thick lips slightly parted.

"A jazz singer?" He took the photo; his red eyebrows hiked up. "You motherfucker!"

"I'm a lucky dog, man," I said as Ryan handed it back to me. "If she waits for me."

"Shit, you're only in here for a minute! If she can't wait for you a few months, she ain't worth shit." This pointed hardness punctuated Ryan's voice. He tensed as his eyes darted around. "She's a fucking bitch!"

"Yeah? I mean, she'll be there. I hope." I sighed.

Under his flexed brow his green eyes glowed with rage. His voice sounded like that demonic voice that spoke to me sometimes. He'd go from being this foggy happy dude to this savage motherfucker ready to explode on something. Then back to foggy nice guy. It scared me. It was sad as fuck. It was like he was way deep in the darkness, so deep he could never get out even if he had a million years. But there was something in me that mourned the kid I knew way back in the old neighborhood. And I could still see that child in him. I wanted to help him. But still I had to talk to him about Rose. I couldn't just let that go.

We headed out to the yard together. All the Kings and Vice Lords and Black Stones greeted Ryan with grave looks and respectful nods. "The Red… The Red…" they murmured as we walked the yard talking.

"Ryan man, I wanted to ask you something about that night back in the old neighborhood."

"Yeah? Shoot."

"You know you shot Rose, right?"

He froze. "What? Who told you that? Your brother said the same shit. That shit's coming from you? What, are you a fucking sleuth now?"

"They said it was a .25."

"How could they know that?"

"Because it bounced around inside of her."

He reddened and his back swelled under his ragged Carhartt jacket. "Coulda been another one 'a them. Bobby Doo-wop had a little .22!"

"There weren't no fucking .22 casings on the ground."

Ryan breathed hard. He twisted at me, then stopped himself. He glared at me with his deep green eyes trembling. Then he looked out at the yard. He spit on the gravel. Then he paused and muttered to himself.

Tufts of steam billowed up from his mouth, and I knew the truth was somewhere in that faint little cloud.

"Maybe it was a revolver, huh!" He twisted back at me, voice loud again. I flinched. "You ever consider that!? And what the fuck was she doing over there anyways!? Before you know it, you'll be flipping and running over there to the Folks side! Be one 'a their turnt out little bitches..."

The Kings watched us, and somebody pointed, and three of them jogged towards us.

"Yeah, look at this. You want me to tell these three how your sister was a Lady GD?! See how they take that? You aint gonna be welcome over this side 'a the yard no more."

"Ryan, man? It's me, man." I pleaded, looking him in the eyes. "Look, man, fine. It wasn't you, okay?"

The Kings trotted up glaring at me.

"We good." Ryan dismissed them with a wave of his pale hand.

"You want us to fuck him up, Red?" a little one asked with wicked eyes.

"We'd all go to the hole for the Red," the chubby one confirmed. "We don't give a fuck!"

"Naw, naw, this is my brother from up north. We're just arguing about some old neighborhood shit." He grinned, showing his crooked teeth.

They nodded, and turned and walked back towards their pocket of the yard.

We continued our walk. "Look, Joe. I'm sorry your sister got hit, but she lived, OK?"

I didn't say anything to that. What could I say?

"Now I don't ever want to hear shit about that shit again! Understand? I did juvenile life for that! You were out there footloose and fancy free." He walked up to the fence, clutched the links, and stared out into the woods beyond. "Now we're in here, we got different laws."

He stepped on and I followed. A big cloud of steam enveloped us as he guided me in a loopy circle over the field of cold-hardened mud and half-frozen grass. We never got too close to the Folks' side, but still they watched him and stood and bunched up every time we approached their half of the yard, and sometimes one would sprint off across the yard to fetch something.

There weren't any seagulls in Menard's yard—just sparrows, blackbirds, and big old nasty crows. A few times we saw hawks, and every now and then a vulture soaring around over a dead beast in the big wooded hills that surrounded the prison. I thought I could hear seagulls crying sometimes out on the Mississippi on the other side of the prison, but I never saw them. Their cries floated above the prisoners and guards, the concrete and manicured lawns and razor wire, like they were phantoms from some other dimension.

◆

In the chow hall, I ate lunch with the guys as a soft cold rain thrummed on the roof; we sat at long tables on metal benches, and everything was bolted to the floor. The stale concrete room bustled with the trays and the utensils and the gossip.

An old fella with a narrow bald head sitting across from me looked at me with a mischievous grin.

"When you gonna get your ink, Lil' Walsh?" he asked.

"He don't need no fucking ink," Pat snapped at him.

"Everybody gotta get some ink if they with us, Pistol."

"Let me think about it, Lemmy."

"Another special pass for the special boy..."

"Whaddaya mean? If it goes up, you're gonna be glad he's fucking here, all right?"

"All I'm saying is everybody's supposed to earn their keep and earn their way in. That's straight outta the Lit."

"I ain't sending him on no mission. Just shut the fuck up about it, would you please?"

"Joey, you didn't get a mission yet?" Ryan said, nudging me. "Oh, they're fun. Missions is what I get up for in the morning."

Everybody at the table laughed. *I don't like the way this shit's going. I hope I can just keep my nose clean, get through this.* A ruckus broke out across the chow hall. *Fuck it, Menard ain't a place you can just get by quietly. You hafta fight.*

A bulky black guy walked past with two thin pieces of string in his hand tied to two skinny effete guys' necks; one was black and the other white. They followed him, grinning gaily, walking and swaying their hips, blowing kisses to their friends and saying sassy things to them. The bulky guy sat down at a table and the other guys stood behind him, heads bowed submissively as he ate their trays.

The TJOs watched them, giggling and elbowing each other.

"Take a good look. That's what happens to whiteboys that don't fight, Joey," Lemmy said. "If you're soft even for one day, you end up like him."

Ryan nudged Lemmy and hiked his red eyebrow at me.

Pat sighed.

"We've carved out our own little square," Pat said and grimaced toward them. "Our own little place at the table. And it's war just to keep that."

◆

We lived in a constant state of tension in the big house. Training gave us our only release. Violence sparked up in the blink of an eye. The gangs split the prison in two: Folks and Peoples. Other factions existed, but they had to make strange truces or pick a side. The TJOs fell under Peoples, but also under the Dirty Whiteboys, a white pride organization which spanned the whole United States prison system.

I started work on my right hand. My middle two fingers presented the biggest challenge—pain, stiffness, and weakness. The scar from the hole darkened and shrank. Range of motion was a bitch, but Pat and the guys pushed me. I didn't have time to lay around and feel sorry for myself. We needed to prepare to fight, prepare for war.

Pat built me up to the guys as a great boxer. I started giving them more serious lessons, two or three at a time. We built a pair of mitts out of bedroll cushions, and I ran them through basic techniques. Taught them to bend at the knees and get their legs into the punch, to snap and turn over their shots. Where to hit guys—the chin, jaw, the temple, the throat, the liver, the kidneys—and how to snap through the target. Some of them had pretty good talent. Others didn't want to learn shit; they thought they knew better than me. The GDs watched us from the other side of the yard, laughing and nudging each other.

Finally, after a couple of days, three black GDs crossed over to our side of the yard and approached us. Two older ones—one huge and light-skinned and the other one fat, with a hitchy gate—and a younger guy about my size with crazy hazel eyes. As they murmured between each other, trails of steam twisted off of their mouths.

"Who is it?" Lemmy asked.

"It's Big Lowe and Smokey, and some crazy-looking motherfucker." Pat said, and stomped over to meet them.

"What the fuck you want, Smokey?" Pat sneered, puffing on a cigarette.

"Now Pistol, my nephew J Rock here got a challenge for ya," Smokey said as he limped up to us.

"What, this mothafucka over here think he a boxin' guru or something?" J Rock said, his crazy eyes darting around back and forth between Pat, Ryan, and I.

"Yeah, maybe he is a fucking guru!" Pat replied, as Ryan stepped up beside him. "What's it to you?"

"You a boxa?" Big Lowe asked in a deep booming voice.

I sighed and shook my head no.

"What the fuck you come over here for?" Pat asked.

"I came 'cause I know I can whoop him," J Rock said.

I tensed as a jagged shard of glass stabbed me in my spleen.

"You callin us out?" Pat replied.

"I'm callin him out." J Rock pointed at me. "Let's knuckle up. I'll whoop you, bitch," he said as I glared at him.

"Aight, bet. It's on, motherfucker," Pat said. "When?"

"Right now," Smokey said. "Stevens on duty, he'll let 'em go."

Pat looked at me. "You good?"

I shrugged. *You know I ain't good, I got one hand and a bunch of glass in my fucking stomach.* I breathed hard. *You scared, Joeyboy? Shut the fuck up. He ain't bad as Luigi.*

The three of us and the three of them headed across the yard to a little guard booth. A tall middle-aged officer in sunglasses opened the door and looked out at us.

"Officer Stevens, can we settle something?" Pat asked.

"You fellas got a beef?" Stevens asked, peering at us over his sunglasses.

"Yeah, they want a try my little brother," Pat sighed.

"I'm finna get in his ass," J Rock said.

"Interracial! Oh, I love me some interracial violence," Stevens said.

He turned to mutter something to his partner inside the booth. Then he came out of the little guard booth wearing a long blue guard trench coat. He opened the fence and led us through it to a grassy hill behind some buildings. The prisoners on the yard watched us, hooting and hollering. We got to a secluded little slope of dead grass that flowed down to a ten-foot-wide strip of gravel that ran along the tall fences with the razor wire hanging twenty feet above. Then another patch of gravel with an even taller fence. Stevens stood higher on the hill as we gathered a little below him.

"You all know the rules," Stevens said, peering down at us with his stern angular face. "Any one of you motherfuckers jump in and I'll bounce you down the stairs to the hole. And you really fuck up, guards in tower three." He pointed up to the tower, a tinted glass guard both hovered above the razor wire. A guard stepped out on a metal observation deck with a long gun in his hands. "They gonna shoot your dumb asses." He folded his arms over his chest. "Fight ends when either one can't fight no more or quits. You shake hands, it's over."

We took our coats off, and our shirts too. The cold air burned on my already warmed-up body. Steam lifted off of J Rock's muscular shoulders; a big dark-blue six-point star sat on one pectoral, and some faded memorial tattoo on the other one. *His upper body's about as strong as mine but he don't know I got some tree trunks under these pant legs.* I squatted down and bounced a little on my hams. I raised up and shook my arms out.

"Aye, be careful but fuck his ass up." Pat told me as he gripped the back of my neck and kissed my forehead.

"Joey, I been praying to see you fight one day." Ryan said, stroking his long red beard and grinning with his crooked teeth.

Well, I got ten pounds on him, but he's gonna be quicker. It only takes one punch and I only got one hand. And the other voice: *Now's your big chance to get the GDs back. Whatchu gonna do, bitch?* The tiny particles of glass suddenly burned all through my stomach and up into my throat.

"Get his ass, J Rock," one of the GDs said.

J Rock threw his hands up. I just turned and walked away from him, down the hill toward the fence where it flattened out and turned to gravel.

"Where you going?" He jogged after me.

"I ain't fighting you on this stupid hill."

Crazy eyed J Rock came trotting down, steam lifting off his nostrils. I feinted a jab at him and he sprung back with his chin high. He lunged in quick and threw some fast slapping punches that missed. I stalled and moved until he rushed in, with his fists high in a low wide crouch. His body moved oddly, but extremely reflexive and agile.

He pinned me to the fence and threw quick punches. I slipped them but he glanced me with a left on my temple and I went wobbly. I shelled up as he dug about six punches into my stomach and ribs and the glass clinked in my innards with each shot. Then he came up to the side of my head as I leaned against the chain-link fence. It felt like the blows to my body opened up the wounds from the glass as a lump rose above my ear.

I spun off the fence and danced to the side. The GDs laughed.

"He runnin'!" The Big Lowe said.

"He a bitch!" Smokey confirmed.

"He scared, J Rock!" The Big Lowe said, grinning proudly.

"Hahaha... He said he was a boxa!" J Rock followed me with swooping steps; his muscles swelled alive. "He ain't shit!"

Fear surged through me. *Fuck, they're right. I am scared. Is he really gonna knock me out?!* Hot blood filled my stomach as the tiny glass particles emitted a dark energy. *Hell no, he ain't.*

I looked at Pat, who watched me with eyes hopeful. Ryan stood beside him holding my hoodie and shirt disappointedly, like when Tank beat the shit out of me all those years ago in the old neighborhood when I hardly fought back.

"Come on Joey," Pat said ominously, squatting down on his hams. "You better do something kid..."

He's right, don't let him get going on you. Then: *Savage this motherfucker already!* The particles exploded and sent energized dark particles through all my limbs. *Don't hit him in the head. If you hurt your good hand, you'll be defenseless.* My lungs constricted; the cold air burned in them.

J Rock rushed in and threw a haymaker overhand right; as he missed, his foot kicked up, tossing a spray of stones. I rolled under his punch, gathered my power in my legs, and sprang up with a tremendous left uppercut to the liver. It planted in his extended body, pushed in deep to the tender warm flesh. Then I snapped it. Something cracked and seemed to crumple against my knuckles. His feet rose a few inches above the gravel as the darkness flowed up into him. J Rock's whole body tensed, and a shockwave ran through it. He screamed and melted to the gravel, gripping his liver; his left leg flapped around under him like a broken wing. *Haha! GDK Mothafucka!*

"Uh? Whats wrong, J Rock?" The Smokey limped over to him. "Get up!"

J Rock lay in a snowy patch of gravel with the bright sunlight pouring down on his face. He gripped his liver with his eyes closed, yelling out furiously.

"J Rock!?" The Big Lowe stooped over him.

"He is a boxa." The Smokey guffawed, looking at me in awe.

"He shank me!" J Rock pleaded, as Big Lowe inspected him for a wound.

"It's just a liver shot, man" I opened my palm to the Officer Stevens, who nodded and grinned.

"Yeah." Pat walked over to me and grabbed my wrist. "And show him your other hand." He held my mangled hand up to the rest of the GDs. "He only got one hand!"

"Knocked his ass out wit one hand, an' to the body?" Smokey said, and kneeled over J Rock. "Why you messin' with this boy? He a champion boxa!"

"He knock J Rock out wit one hand, damn!" Big Lowe said mystified.

"Let the motherfucker's hand heal up he'll knock any 'a you bitches out." Pat confirmed.

"It ain't fair calling him out." Ryan whined as he walked up to me with my shirt neatly folded over my folded hoody. "It ain't right 'til he heal up."

"Aight. When it heal, I want some," Big Lowe said, puffing up at us.

"Cool." I shrugged, pulling my shirt on.

"An' if you want me, you can have me now," Pat said, swelling up at him.

"One's enough for today, I got shit to do." Officer Stevens looked at me. "Now shake his hand."

I pulled my hoodie on and stepped to J Rock and reached down as he writhed on the gravel. Finally he peeled his hand off his liver and I shook it softly.

"Feel like he broke a bottle up in my stomach!" J Rock said as we walked away.

As we approached the fence back into the yard, everyone could tell by the big smiles on Pat and Ryan's face what'd happened. The Peoples roared, and the Folks kicked snow and spat. Big Lowe and Smokey almost had to carry J Rock, who kept yelling out sporadically. As we passed through the fence, Ryan threw up the J as he stomped towards the Peoples side triumphantly.

"The Champ is here!" Pat yelled to King Kong, squeezing my shoulder.

King Kong grinned sadistically and threw up the crown; a thick golden chain glimmered around his neck. All the other Kings rejoiced and high-fived each other all around him. G Herbo and the Stones were laughing their asses off near the pullup bars. Willie Lord shouted out to us, "My Niggas!"

After that, everybody wanted to learn, and they listened to all the stuff I taught 'em.

◆

J Rock ended up in the infirmary for a week. A rib had broken and lacerated his liver; he had to get surgery and everything. When word got out about that, Lord Gino and King Kong sent over some Kings to learn, and G Herbo even had his Stones come over too. Willie Lord sent over some Unknowns, and this one swole up Insane Vice Lord was always there to learn as well. After that I didn't have to fight no more, 'cause the Peoples were grateful for the lessons. So when Folks called me out, dudes jumped up: "Naw-naw-naw, his hand hurt! Why you calling out my man, he only got one hand! You's a bitch!" Once you called somebody a "bitch" it was on, they had to fight, it was an unbreakable rule in the joint. So I'd go over to the hill with them, coaching them up on how to whip their guy and advising 'em while they fought, too. They said the fights used to be about 50-50, but since I started teaching, we won almost three outta four. And that's how I made it through my stretch in the pen with only ever throwing one uppercut to the body. But fighting was one thing. The hits were another.

My hand wasn't really ready to fight with anyway. I had good days here and there where I could make a fist and the guys would hold the mitts for me, but then I'd wake the next morning with it curled up in a ball and I'd barely be able to open it. Either way, Pat was real proud of me, and even Lemmy let up about the ink. I just became one of the guys, and a valuable one too.

Everything went smooth for a while as I counted down the days, I almost started to believe I'd slip through the cracks. But there weren't no cracks in Menard. Nobody got out unscathed.

◆

A couple months into my sentence, we were in line walking to chow hall when we turned a corner and the smell of shit and piss and fear struck my nostrils.

Murmurs rose up ahead as guys tried to step around something. A body lay on the concrete floor. Blood pooled out underneath it. I recognized him as an older high-ranking Vice Lord. He lay on his belly with his mouth and eyes open, completely still. Bloody handprints smeared the wall. We tried to avoid the blood but stepped in it. A trail of hundreds of bloody footprints led to the chow hall.

Loud conversation clamored in the hall. The GDs and SDs laughed across the way. Some Vice Lords finally got up and ran up on them. We all hopped up, but the guards poured in with pepper spray spraying and nightsticks waving. We all lay on our bellies looking at each other under the chow hall tables.

Ryan giggled under his table, his green eyes glowing bright.

"It's war, Joey!" he said, just like a little kid at Christmas.

We waited on our bellies until they cleared the chow hall. They locked us down.

◆

When movement opened again, Lemmy showed up at the bars of my cell and told me to go up a stairwell in our cell block 'cause Pat wanted to talk with me.

I headed up the stairwell. Pat stood at a bend in the stairs, gripping the metal meshing on a window. The golden morning sun poured in through the mesh.

"What's up, Pat?"

"I just wanted to see you."

I sat down on the top steps, just below the small landing he stood on.

"I spent so much of my life in here, kid, I hate this fucking place. I hate that I let all my chances slip through my hands. I wanted better for you. But you comin' in here, the way you changed this place for me...you inspire me, kid. I wanna get out… I want to be there when you fight for the world title."

"I don't know if I'll ever fight again, Pat."

"You will! It's getting better, Joe. Don't lose hope. Don't be like me and lose hope and end up back in here."

"I ain't never coming back here."

"That's what I'm talkin' about. Never come back." He looked back out, past the fences and towers. "I get so worried about you. These guys in here, they're gonna try an' get you 'cause you're my brother. That's why I'm always working with everybody, inviting them over for you to train them. I want everybody to protect you, but maybe I'm drawing too much attention to you. But they're just like you…" He took a deep breath and winced. Crow's feet crinkled the corners of his eyes. *Fuck, he's getting old in here.*

"I don't know, kid, but I want you to know I'm proud of you. You're making these months fly by, and I'm gonna miss you, but I'm gonna be so happy once you're gone. But then I wonder about how it's gonna be, if it'll go back to the way it was…" He turned and looked me in the eyes; tears welled in his. "I just… I…" He didn't say the words. Tears trembled in his eyes, and he looked out the mesh window like he was looking deep into eternity.

I looked down at the shadows the mesh window made on the steps.

At last he spoke again. "Things are gonna get real bad for a few weeks. Just do everything I say and you'll be alright."

Chapter 20: Dark Energy

SOMETHING DARK HOVERED OVER THE CHOW HALL AT BREAKFAST. Everyone whispered. The Folks and Peoples looked over at each other—dark anticipation flickered in their eyes.

Pat pulled me to the side as they started to clear the hall.

"Do not come out to the yard today. I don't care who tells you you gotta come out. I don't care what they say, or what you heard. If you come out there to the yard, as soon as I see ya, it's you and me heads-up, and I ain't gonna lose this one." He towered over me.

"Alright..." I turned and walked out, then hesitated at the doorway and looked back. Pat grimaced and jabbed his index finger toward the hallway, back toward my row house.

I went to my cell and lay down trying to sleep—listening.

An old Vice Lord in his sixties walked up to my cell and stopped. "Whatchu doing here, soldier? Relaxin'?"

I didn't answer.

"Somethin brewin', boy, can you feel it?"

"Yeah."

"Whole yard finna go up, you watch."

"I should be the fuck out there."

"Not me," he said and limped away.

The glass particles sizzled in my stomach. *Please God, don't let nothing happen to Pat or Ryan. You're acting like a little bitch hiding in here! You should be out there, you fucking coward! People are going to kill and die out there on the yard today!* Then: "Nam-Myoho-Renge-Kyo. Nam-Myoho-Renge-Kyo. Nam-Myoho-Renge-Kyo."

A roar swirled up in the distance like a barbarian war cry. The roar swelled, then faded. The long swaying sirens pierced through it. *Just let them get through this please.* Big *pops* sounded in the distance as the guards fired beanbags and tear gas into the riot. *Just don't take them from me, not now.* Corrections officers ran down the hallways. Commotions erupted all around me, like some kinda bombing raid.

"Fucking whole yard just went up!" some of the guys shouted on the balcony.

I got off the bed and walked over. I looked out across the balcony, out the windows at a section of the yard. Tear gas wafted up from canisters on the grassy field. Several pockets of inmates cowered, covering their heads. Others ran. Several SDs and GDs had a few Blackstones and some Kings on the run. They chased them down, shanked them, and jumped on their heads. A muscular GD with his shirt off stooped over one King, shanking him in the chest and stomach as his arms flailed. A beanbag hit the GD in the face; it almost tore his head off. He fell unconscious on top of the King he was shanking. The King wrestled the knife out of his hand, then started cutting him in very bad places.

◆

A half hour later the doors opened, and some of the guys flooded in all busted up and covered in blood, pawing at their eyes.

"What the fuck!"

"You get Bobo?"

"Yeah, I got him."

"They fucking killed Vinny!"

"Naw, naw, Vinny cool. He breathin'."

"Pistol don't look so good."

I jolted up. I ran down, found Lemmy. "Where's Pat?"

"He in the infirmary. They gonna come down and grab you in a minute." Veins'd surfaced blue all over his pale shaved head.

◆

A few minutes later a trustee came to the door. They buzzed it open.

"Joey, come wit' me, kid. Your brother need ya."

I followed him to the infirmary.

Pat lay on a table. His shirt was off and there was a big tan wrap around his torso that covered a big lump of bandages on his side, and an IV plugged into his arm that looped up to a bag hanging above him. Pat's face flushed very pale. So damn pale it tore a gaping wound in my heart. He trembled there on the steel table.

I rushed to him.

"Joey!"

"Pat, what happened?" I took his big cool hand in both of mine.

"They shanked me bad, kid."

"Where?"

"They got me in the liver."

"Fucking motherfuckers!"

Pat's eyes faded as he stared up at the light hanging above him.

"Now I… I don't want you to try and get no vengeance. He'll die. He'll die in here. I know it. You're out of here in two months, kid. You get out of here as far away as you can, and you don't never come back."

"Pat."

"Ohhh…" He gripped the bandages covering his liver.

"Y'all better hurry up with that ambulance!" I yelled.

Pat passed out, and I held his big hairy hand. He squeezed my hand every once in a while like he was just checking if I was still there and he wasn't alone.

A nurse came in and checked on him. She frowned and left.

After a few minutes, he came to, real serene and quiet.

"I ever tell ya, I always wanted to have a family of my own?"

"No, Pat. Tell me about it."

"A home and a little boy. I wanted to be a dad…" He trailed off and got that bad, far-off look in his eyes again.

"You will be, Pat. You're gonna get out a here, far far away from here. You're gonna meet a nice woman, and you're gonna buy a house and get married, and she's gonna give you a beautiful baby boy with a big old head like I had, except his hair, his hair's gonna be red like Blakey's kids. You're gonna get big and fat and have a big ol' blue pickup truck and live out in the suburbs, and you're gonna be happy."

"You think so, kid? That'd be nice."

"I know it, Pat. You just keep thinking about that."

He smiled, but his breath strained into a wheeze.

"I'm cold… I'm ha…having trouble breathing, Joey."

"It's OK. Just hang on, the nurses are coming. You just keep thinking about that house you're gonna live in, and your wife, and that baby boy of yours. OK? You gotta stay with us, Pat, you gotta stay… we need you…"

"I love you, Joey."

"I love you too."

"Tell Ma and Dad for me."

"I will, you're gonna make it, Pat. Just hold on…"

The medics came in and wheeled him away to the ambulance. I whispered "Nam-Myoho-Renge-Kyo, Nam-Myoho-Renge-Kyo, Nam-Myoho-Renge-Kyo," as he slowly disappeared down the hall.

He never made it to the hospital.

As they drove him through those wooded hills that surrounded the prison he left this world. He was gone, flying, soaring into the sky where he could finally be free.

◆

I didn't go to the funeral. Couldn't imagine having to go in shackles. Ma and Dad chose to cremate him anyway.

We made a little ceremony out on the yard. The Kings, Vice Lords, and Stones all showed their respect. Lord Gino, King Kong, and Willie said some real beautiful words of love and brotherhood. And that was it. Pistol Pat, gone but not forgotten.

Things cooled down. Ryan sat in solitary for a month; they had him on tape shanking two SDs. When he came out he wasn't right, wasn't talking, was drooling on himself. Then he'd just burst into laughter every once in a while.

It turned out the guy who killed Pat was this GD named Benny from the Jungle. Pat and him'd had a twenty-year-long beef, and Benny finally got him. They couldn't ID Benny on the yard tape, so they released him back to Gen Pop around the time Ryan got out.

As you can imagine, I wanted to kill Benny real bad. I didn't know how I could get to him, though. I'd see him in the yard—a pudgy light-skinned black guy just under six foot with a blue rag hanging out of his back pocket. A few times I caught him staring at me real sad, like almost remorseful.

Benny was a nickname; they'd named him after Benny the Bull, the Chicago Bulls mascot. Benny was in on a murder, but he'd caught a lot of bodies over the years and he wasn't ever going home. Benny was famous for chasing guys to the stairs when the POD went up. He'd run them to the stairs, and as they ran up the steps, he'd jump from the side of the metal staircase, grab the railing with his free hand, pull and swing himself up twelve feet in the air, and stab them in the back as they retreated. It was Benny's trademark, like the Bulls' mascot running across the court jumping on a trampoline and flying through the air for a dunk. Benny couldn't really fistfight; he got tired quickly and punched sloppily. But when he had that steel in his hand, he became superhuman, like the blade possessed him and guided him through its bidding. Benny was a fuckin' blade artist.

He'd stabbed Pat before in the ribs, back in the early 90s, but Pat'd caught him with a loopy hook and dropped him. Pat had always laughed and taunted Benny that Benny couldn't fight. But in the midst of the riot on the Menard yard, four GDs'd rushed Pat. Pat'd gotten lost in the tear gas and stood his ground. He dropped one and staggered another but they just kept coming, grabbing at his legs and feet until they got him down. They rolled Pat on his back on the grass near the courts. Benny stabbed him deep in the liver. He stood over Pat knowing he'd killed him, knowing it was just a matter of time. Benny laughed wickedly and ran off to shank up some Kings.

Something about a GD being the one that killed my brother brought the pain from the glass inside me back, and I started shitting blood again.

◆

I sat out on the yard with Ryan reading a manuscript Dydecky'd sent me on Erickson's recommendation. It was all about their discoveries with dark matter. Ryan just grinned, his face turned up to the sky as he sat on the concrete picnic table cross-legged, like a Buddhist monk meditating. I folded the manuscript and laid it down on the table and looked up at the blue sky.

"Ever imagine what life woulda been like if we grew up someplace different?"

"Naw... I love who I am," Ryan said, without opening his eyes.

"But like, maybe Pat coulda been something different. Like a political leader or something."

"Naw, Joe. We're all who we're supposed to be."

I sneered as a shard of glass stabbed into my gut. No way. All he was supposed to be was some gang leader who got killed in prison? He was more than that. Coulda been way more than that.

"It all happened for a reason, Joe."

I got up and put the manuscript in my waistband.

"Where you going, Joe?"

"Going to H Wing to mop some floors."

"Why you didn't tell me about that? You know the rules."

"I'm just doing it for smokes. That trustee Tre's givin' me two packs for it."

Ryan opened his eyes, grinning into the sky, his face bright red and burning in the light.

"Thank you," he whispered. His thick red beard glistened like it was oily.

"Ryan, man, get out the sun. It's burning your fuckin' face."

He didn't reply, glaring peacefully into the sun as I walked off.

◆

I was finishing up mopping the last hallway in the quiet H Wing. This white guy named Tre walked up, his skinny frame bouncing eagerly. He grinned and handed me two packs of Marlboros.

"Thanks." He scratched his temple, where a string of tiny little gang tattoos encircled his face.

"No problem," I said as he walked off quickly.

Tre'd befriended me after the riot. He was a Black Soul. He always said his skin was white but his soul was black. I know what you're thinking, whiteboys can't be Black Souls. But he'd grown up in Garfield Park, and he'd killed a Black Mafia who'd just murdered Jack Bobo's beloved nephew. He ran the Mafia over in a minivan, then threw it in reverse and made sure to roll right over the guy's skull. Jack Bobo was the originator of the Black Souls, and when you kill a man for him without him even asking you to, you're made for life with the Black Souls, even if you are white.

Tre'd come to the memorial and said some nice things about Pat. And I thought the Souls were with us. So I thought I was OK helping him out; I thought I was OK being there. But the Souls flowed back and forth between nations. Pat woulda known better. He would have warned me.

I finished mopping the gray concrete floor, put the mop and bucket up in the closet, and let the wooden door start to close. I turned to walk out.

Benny stood a few feet away at the bend in the hall, with his big beige inmate shirt hanging off him like a drape. He stood with his chin tucked into his flabby throat, looking at the floor as he waited for me. Without looking up he pulled his long silver blade out of the elastic waist of his light-brown cloth pants.

The door to the closet shut and clicked locked behind me. *Nowhere to go.* The galaxy of glass particles sparkled in my insides. *It's you or him, Joeyboy.*

Benny's pudgy face trembled. Tears dripped down his ugly face, real tears, washing over the three black teardrops tattooed under his right eye—one of them fresh ink.

"I kilt yo brotha..." he said, suppressing emotion. "Wanna know why? My sista was in that building he burnt down all them years ago up by the North Pole."

I squeezed and released my right hand as it painfully loosened.

He finally looked up at me with his insane brown eyes. "They burned my little sister alive in there. I thought killing him would take all the pain away that I been feeling all these years." He bowed his head and closed his eyes. "It didn't though. It didn't do nothing." He opened his eyes again and glared at me. "But maybe I kill his little brotha... Maybe then..."

My heart ached for her. I saw her burning, saw her skin melting in the crack house fire. That thing unfurled in my chest. *You shouldn'ta done that, Pat.*

"I'm sorry for what Pat did to your sister... I got sisters too. Somebody take them from me, and I'd kill 'em too... What was her name?"

"You don't give a fuck about some black girl, nigga!"

"I do! My sisters are black. They're Dominican, they're adopted."

"What?!" He winced at the thought. "You lyin'! You tryin' to trick me to save yo ass aintchu?"

"No, I swear! Swear on my life!"

He leaned back for a sec like he was contemplating. Then he said: "Well shit. We got different laws in here."

He bounced on the toes of his white sneakers and raised the blade at his waist, slicing the air artfully. He stepped toward me. I tensed. *Nowhere to go.*

Ryan materialized behind him, grabbed his wrist, and slammed him into the wall.

"Help!" Ryan yelled, as I dove in and smashed my elbow into Benny's chest and pinned him against the wall. Benny struggled as Ryan turned Benny's own blade so it pointed up under Benny's sternum. Benny gasped for air. Ryan started to push it in. Benny tried with all his might to keep it out.

"No, Ryan," I gasped.

"Joe." Ryan looked me in the eyes, frightened like a little boy. "Help me."

The roots twisted through my thighs and dipped down into my toes. *Help you what? Help you kill him or not kill him?* Benny reached up with his other hand and clawed his index finger into Ryan's green eye. *You know exactly what he's fucking asking for!*

The glass particles awakened and sent dark energy rushing through me, and I grabbed the hands that gripped the blade. I pushed up and in with all my might.

The jagged blade tip broke the brown cloth of his shirt as Benny shook his head 'no,' his mouth open and drooling. Then it pushed into the skin. His fatty stomach resisted until his flesh snapped like a rubber band; blood spilled down the blade onto all of our hands as the blade slid home. Benny's face contorted, his mouth hanging in a big low O. His hand slid down Ryan's face and grabbed a fistful of his long thick red beard. We pushed the knife deeper, and both Benny's hands let go and fell limply as his blade sunk all the way in, all the way to the duct-tape grip.

Benny's heart convulsed above the steel. I let go and stepped back. Ryan savagely yanked the blade back and forth, sawing his insides. The hole opened larger as the blood cascaded down to the shiny white floor. Benny tensed, his mouth open, eyes peering out at me, and I swear to you I watched his dark, shadowy soul vacate his body, fall and morph into the blood pouring out of him and onto the floor. He slid down the wall and lay twitching and gurgling.

Ryan smiled at me.

"I love ya, Joe." Ryan grinned. His eye bled a bloody tear down his scorched red face, and it disappeared into the red forest of his beard. "Now get the fuck out of here. I'm gonna have some fun with him for you and for Pat."

Benny contorted on the floor; he kept sticking his fingers into the hole and pulling out globs of blood. His mouth hung open—peering up at Ryan with shocked eyes like he was looking into the face of a wrathful God.

Ryan dug the knife deep into Benny's neck below the ear. He ripped the blade slowly across his brown throat and crouched over him scowling, determinedly sawing on the flesh. I walked away and looked back one last time and saw Ryan covered in blood to the elbows hunched over Benny's body, decapitating him in the center of a big red lake. The manuscript'd fallen from my waistband; it lay crumpled at the edge of the red pool— the blood just starting to swallow it.

I walked away, reached into my pants and wiped the blood off on my underwear, and went back out onto the yard.

◆

It might be hard for you to imagine that I wiggled my way out of it all and dodged everything, but you know me by now, I'm one lucky motherfucker.

Ryan of course testified he acted alone. I coasted through my last weeks in a daze.

On my release day a dark-skinned black guard in his mid-thirties with a shaved head came to get me. He was lean and tall and looked like an athlete in his white officer shirt with a golden badge on his chest. I'd seen him around; he was one of the good guards, straight-laced and fair. As he escorted me out, we turned the corner into a long hallway, with the light flooding in through the tall windows and splaying out on the concrete floor in a pattern of golden rectangles.

The guard heard something he didn't like. He grabbed my arm and rushed me toward the door as Big Lowe and two other GDs entered the hall behind us. Their eyes lit up when they saw me; they sprinted toward us with shanks out in their hands, their beige jumpsuits whipping through the bold light.

The guard pushed me through the door. Then he entered, turned, and slid the door behind us, and it clicked locked.

He pinched his radio at his chest.

"A few of the animals got out they cages on three."

They slammed into the bars and yanked on them with their mighty dark hands. They pointed through the bars at me, their big torsos heaving.

"You a lucky mothafucka!" Big Lowe shouted.

I glared at them. *Yeah, lucky me, motherfucker.* Guards came running behind them as my guard led me away.

"These guys, they think we don't know when these hits are coming. We know. It's easy to add up, especially when they know a guy is going home. A lotta guys get shanked when they're on their way out. Mosta the time we don't care if they get got."

I shook my head.

He went on. "But you... I was a boxer too. Won the Silver Gloves and JOs a few times. Always lost at Regionals."

"Michigan?"

"Yeah, sometimes Ohio too."

"What's your name?"

"James, but they call me Jay."

A wave of shivers swirled through me so powerful I couldn't breathe as something big in my chest seemed to blossom. I gasped, grabbing at my heart. I closed my eyes to keep the tears in.

"Thank you, Jay," I said with whatever air I had left.

"Now go do something with this chance," he said as we stepped down the hall.

I closed my eyes and saw Jay, big and strong with his close-faded head gleaming in the afternoon light as we shoveled clay deep in the shaft at Fermilab. Jay laughing at me, then just grinning, with his tongue sticking out between his big teeth. *Thank you, my brother.*

They gave me my belongings. The colorful T-shirt One-Leg Chuck had made me was a little moldy-smelling and crinkly; the red heart looked like a big crusty scab. *You Got A Big Ole Heart.* I slipped it on; the scab of the heart scratched at my chest as the blossom still sat there inside me.

As we were boarding the white prison bus to drive to the Greyhound station, Jay drove up in his new blue Toyota Corolla, still wearing his white CO shirt. He popped his close-cropped fade out the window, smiling.

"Joe, I'ma take ya," he said.

I got off the bus, blinking in the sunlight, and climbed in with Jay. Just sitting there in the passenger seat, his car felt as strange as a UFO.

We pulled through the facility, following the white van.

Jay spoke as he drove. "I got something to tell you before you step up outta here. I was a GD growing up. All my cousins and uncles too, East Garfield Park."

I glanced at him, wide-eyed.

"Yeah, GD Love. GDs got love in 'em, too. Don't take that hatred out into the world and end up back in here. What happened between your brother and Benny, that was between two men before it was between Folks and Peoples. You know that right?"

"Yeah." I let out a long sigh, thinking about Benny's little sister burning to death in that fire all those years ago.

"You know you owe me, don'tchu? So I want you to promise me I'll never see your face again, unless it's to visit one of these knuckleheads. Like your friend Ryan. You owe him too, don'tchu, yeah, you owe him everathang just like you owe me. Your whole motherfuckin' life." He paused as the prison gates slowly slid open with the razor wire trembling and shimmering atop them. The white bus pulled out ahead of us.

"I promise," I told him.

He pulled us through the gates and onto a slowly curving wooded road.

"Look at that, now you a free man! But you gotta work to free yourself in here," he said, and reached out and patted the big red heart on my chest. "I was incarcerated as a juvenile. Took a long time to free myself. Had to get away. Down here I got a family, a home, a new car. I got a pension to look forward to, watch my grandbabies grow up. You get away from this prison, you make good, make a baby. I tell you, son, when you look into your child's eyes for the first time, everythang gonna change. And you get that hand right you can even go turn pro with Angelo Dunkin. Make a run at a title." He glanced at me and hiked up his eyebrows.

How the fuck does he know about that?

"Come on," he nudged my shoulder. "You still don't know what this is? I just got off the phone with Sal. I fought Fearless seven times. We was three an' three, then we met in the finals of the '91 Golden Gloves. I whooped him, but they gave him the decision. It is what it is."

"I'ma ask him about that. What's your full name?"

"Jay White, but they call me Speedy."

We cruised through open corn fields. *My guys will protect you.* I heard Fearless's voice in my head and smiled. I saw Sal grinning in the musty old gym: "Welcome home, kid."

We pulled up to the little station as the white prison bus was slowly emptying. The long blue Greyhound grumbled, waiting for us with the door open.

"Promise me, I ain't never gonna see your face down here again." Speedy reached his hand out to me.

I took his cool heavy hand in mine. It was gaining strength every day, little by little, just like Pat said it would.

"Jay, I promise you, you are going to see me again down here. I'm gonna bring a big golden championship belt down here to show you and Ryan."

"Alright then."

I opened the door and stepped out of the car.

"And don't forget," he said. "Tell Sal and them I said what up, though."

I boarded the Greyhound into the city. I didn't want to tell my family I was out just yet, but Lauren knew. I'd written her a letter and told her to meet me in the meadow near the harbor with the birds at sunrise.

I dream on the bus as we shoot up 55. I stand out in the middle of a dark still lake. I am alone and I look down at my reflection in the pool. I see my face: older, harder, meaner. Then I peer into my eye and Benny's face is there in the center.

"I'm coming fo' you, Joe. I be waiting here for you," he says.

I sparked awake. *There ain't gonna be no peace in death.* Outside my window the hazy monstrosity of the city surged into the sky in the distance like a glowing being with eyes, ears, and terrible hands. Chicago… *You have to escape this animality.* Lauren's voice in the courtroom echoed through me. I began to whisper: "Nam-Myoho-Renge-Kyo. Nam-Myoho-Renge-Kyo. Nam-Myoho-Renge-Kyo." I prayed for Benny and his little sister, that they could find peace in the next life. These wonderful cool shivers came alive in my back and shoulders, swirling around, like the glass particles were releasing and rising up out of me.

I took the Red Line up north and got out there early in the morning dark. The spring chill floated in the air, I fell asleep in the grassy meadow and woke with the cool dew wet on my back and fingertips. The sun slowly rose out of the dark lake. A group of white seagulls bedded down in the lumpy grass all around me, forty or fifty of them snuggled in the green like me. I thought about Pat. Tears gushed down my face for the first time since I held his hand in the medical ward. I looked up to the fiery orange bubble pushing the darkness from the sky. The thing swelled in my chest like a white lotus blossom; it unfurled and spread wide. *Is that where you are, Pat? Maybe all your energy is scattered into all of oblivion. Or maybe you're up there looking down at me… I'm free, Pat. I'm alive. I made it out of there…*

A motion caught my eyes near the harbor. I turned as the seagulls erupted into flight; a thick wall of fluttering white and gray feathers lifted before me. Lauren's smiling brown face emerged through the feathers, her hair twisted up like a blonde-brown smoldering neutrino shooting at me from a far-off nebula. Tears dripped down her chin onto her peach-colored satin dress. She glided toward me over the dark-green grass as the seagulls lifted into the turning sky.

ACKNOWLEDGMENTS

I want to say that I've been very fortunate to have many wonderful teachers, gurus, and friends who have helped me get to this beautiful place in my life. Brother Peter Hannon came into my life at Saint Joseph High School and forever altered it for the better, not only through his boxing coaching but in the classroom as well. Brother Peter confronted me about my belief that I wasn't smart, and instilled a ferocious work ethic in me that continues to drive me to this day. David McGrath opened the door to literature for me at College of DuPage. Ron Wiginton at Elmhurst College blew wind into my sails as a young writer. Fred Burkhart sucked me into the underground arts world in the city. Marc Smith intoxicated me with the poetic magic of the Green Mill. Thom Jones, your friendship, boxing stories and guidance has deeply inspired me. Don De Grazia took me under his wing, gave me permission to write and welcomed me into Columbia College where my writing flourished under John Schultz Story Workshop Method. Irvine Welsh has been one of the great gurus of my life and continues to inspire me as I walk this path as a writer. Jordan McClements, you are a hell of a friend, confidant, student, and advisor; I look forward to the day your first book arrives, buddy. Ted Van Alst, you made me feel I belong in academia, and I can't wait to see the heights your new book reaches. Sam Colonna's era of the Windy City Gym was a revelation and a second home to me. The Chicago boxing community is a special place full of unforgettable characters whose spirits litter this book and bring bright human resonance to it. I will always be a grateful, friend, fan and devoted member of the Chicago lineage of boxers, especially to JoJo Awinongya who is a true prodigy and a joy to observe in and out of the ring. It should be said that I didn't achieve the things Joe Walsh did in boxing but I was around many who did, and I came close to doing them but I was a typical dreamer, gym-rat, under-achiever and I'm at peace with that. Boxing was very good to me. I want to thank my New Orleans friends who helped me understand that fascinating city more deeply: Chuck Perkins, Ryan Rogers, Lugine Gray, and Wild Bill Wood. Jerry Brennan, thank you for believing in this trilogy in progress, you are an excellent editor and I am proud to be part of Tortoise Books. Thank you, Soren Chang; I never met you, but Jerry says you helped a lot. And to my family, I love you all, any negativity in the book does not present my true feelings about you; this book is a fictional and nightmarish monster version of what we are in reality, and I hope that's obvious. Paula Andion Zabalza, you have blown the sweetest, most delicate yet powerful love into my soul, everything I do is for you and us and for our future babies, I love you.

ABOUT THE AUTHOR

Dr. Bill Hillmann is a full-time professor of English and Communications at East-West University in Chicago. He is the author of three books—the novel *The Old Neighborhood*, and the memoirs *Mozos* and *The Pueblos*—and is turning *The Old Neighborhood* into a Trilogy. His writing has appeared at CNN, NPR, and VICE, and in the *Chicago Tribune*, the *Daily Mail*, the *Toronto Star*, and various others. He created the National College Story Slam competition, where students from across the country compete telling five-minute personal stories. Hillmann is a former Chicago Golden Gloves boxing champion and union construction laborer, and is married to Paula Andion Zabalza.

ABOUT TORTOISE BOOKS

Slow and steady wins in the end, even in publishing. Tortoise Books is dedicated to finding and promoting quality authors who haven't yet found a niche in the marketplace—writers producing memorable and engaging works that will stand the test of time.

Learn more at www.tortoisebooks.com or follow us on Bluesky @tortoisebooks.bsky.social.

www.ingramcontent.com/pod-product-compliance
Lightning Source LLC
Chambersburg PA
CBHW020413030726
47495CB00006B/1490